A WOMAN OF PROPERTY

KT-432-646

By the same author

The Breadmakers
A Baby Might be Crying
A Sort of Peace
The Prisoner
The Prince and the Tobacco Lords
Roots of Bondage
Scorpion in the Fire
Dark Side of Pleasure
The Making of a Novelist
A Very Civilized Man
Light and Dark
Rag Woman, Rich Woman
Daughters and Mothers
Wounds of War

A WOMAN OF PROPERTY

Margaret Thomson Davis

ARROW

Published by Arrow Books Limited
20 Vauxhall Bridge Road, London SW1V 2SA

A division of Random House UK Ltd

London Melbourne Sydney Auckland Johannesburg
and agencies throughout the world

First published in Great Britain by Century in 1991

Arrow edition 1992

5 7 9 10 8 6 4

© Margaret Thomson Davis, 1992

The right of Margaret Thomson Davis to be identified
as the author of this work has been asserted by her in
accordance with the Copyright, Designs and Patents
Act, 1988

This book is sold subject to the condition that it shall
not, by way of trade or otherwise, be lent, resold, hired
out, or otherwise circulated without the publisher's
prior consent in any form of binding or cover other
than that in which it is published and without a similar
condition including this condition being imposed on
the subsequent purchaser

Printed and bound in Great Britain by
Cox & Wyman Ltd, Reading, Berkshire

ISBN 0 09 974380 9

This book is dedicated to
Campbell McLaren

I would like to thank everyone who was kind enough to help me out with my research but I feel special mention should be made of the following who gave most generously of their time: Madge and Isaac Kerr of Gorbals, Marie Coffey and Etta Boyle of Inches, Mr and Mrs Mathieson, Sir Robin MacLellan, the chairman, directors and tradesmen of McLaren Property Group Ltd and director Adam Birch in particular.

Chapter One

Christina tried to convince herself that this dank, bleak 4th of January 1915 was the happiest day of her life. She was about to marry Adam Monkton, the son of a prosperous Glasgow businessman. She was about to escape from the inhibiting atmosphere of the gloomy manse hunched in the shadows of the Martyrs Church. She was about to be free of the duties that being the Minister's daughter entailed and the image she felt obliged to live up to.

She couldn't be sure of her mother's feelings either. Ada Gillespie always wore a little black dress and a pained sympathetic face as if she were at perpetual attendance at a funeral, and this occasion was no exception. At the moment she was fussing around Christina along with her larger dressmaker friend, Mrs Bella Duffy. At least her black dress had been relieved for the occasion with a fawn lace collar and cuffs.

Standing helplessly in front of the wardrobe mirror, Christina began to feel sick. Perhaps it was the stale sweat from the bouncingly obese Mrs Duffy that was turning her stomach, or the stench of camphor overflowing from the wardrobe. But it could have been the fact that she was pregnant. Not that her mother knew anything about that.

The wardrobe door had been opened so that Christina's reflection could pick up the most light. It would have been better if the gas mantle had been lit because the room was so shadowy, but a minister's stipend meant strict economies had to be adhered to wherever and whenever possible, regardless of the occasion.

A blustery wind worried the branches of the trees that surrounded the manse, making wooden fingers scrabble forlornly against the dripping panes.

Her brother Simon would be with Adam Monkton now. Simon was to be Adam's best man. They would be waiting

1

in the church or perhaps they had not yet left Monkton House which was only a few yards further along Queen's Drive. Simon had been delighted about her proposed marriage to Monkton. The two men had been friends since childhood.

She had seen Simon earlier that morning and had thought he looked exceptionally handsome in his army officer's uniform. She and her parents had been very upset when Simon had announced he was joining the army. He had not been long settled in a local medical partnership and seemed to have been doing well. Certainly he was a very popular doctor. There was no need for him to join up, especially as everyone knew the war wasn't going to last any time. Admittedly there was a great deal of pressure from outside sources for men like Simon to answer his country's call. Adam had tried to join up too, but had been turned down because of an old eye injury.

Simon had always been lucky in being able to do whatever he wanted. He seemed to have some sort of guardian angel looking after him. He had invariably escaped retribution for all the various misdeeds he had perpetrated at school. He had got up to all sorts of pranks at university and without seeming to study at all had passed every exam.

She had not been sent to private school like Simon, but the headmaster at her local secondary school had tried to persuade her mother and father to allow her to stay on there and prepare for a place at university. This, however, had been out of the question – simply, Christina gathered, because she was a girl. It was a waste of time, they said, for a girl to go to university. Not that she'd minded being denied this opportunity. What she had longed for was to go to the Scottish Academy of Music. Her mother and father were both musical although their taste was mostly in sacred music. Her father played the violin and her mother often accompanied him at the piano after dinner.

Her mother had taken pleasure at first in giving Christina piano lessons, but soon she was confessing to her husband 'Chrissie's quite beyond me now. I don't know what to make of the child,' and apology crept into her voice. 'She can play Beethoven's C Major *Concerto*. Surely that's not natural for a child of eleven?'

One of her father's congregation, a retired concert pianist, had discovered her talent and offered to give her free tuition. Her weekly visits to Max Hamlyn's villa in Pollokshields had made her life worth living. They had lasted for several wonderful years. Her joy had been complete when he told her that one day she too could be a concert pianist, but first he would arrange for her to have tuition from his old friend, the great Marceau in Paris. She was technically brilliant, he said, but her performance lacked warmth. She was too clammed up, frozen inside. He felt it imperative for her to break away from her present ambience.

Her parents had been horrified at the idea of a teenage girl travelling so far on her own. Living on her own in Paris was absolutely unthinkable. They had looked at her in reproach and disappointment. It was as if they were saying: How could she be not only so stupid as to harbour such shocking and impractical ideas but also how could she be so disloyal? They had been very conscientious in teaching her where her duty lay. The Reverend Gillespie and his wife had looked at one another and in that look Christina saw the end of her dreams of being a concert pianist and the end of her association with Max Hamlyn.

Yet for a long time she couldn't believe it. Refused to accept the fact. The extreme bitterness of her teenage years hardened in time to the cold ice of resentment. She felt guilty about harbouring unchristian emotions towards her parents and so she kept them buried deep down where they bitterly simmered.

Now her mother's voice broke through Christina's thoughts. She was addressing Bella Duffy in a heartbroken tone.

'She is lovely, Bella.'

Mrs Duffy stood back for a few seconds to admire her handiwork.

'As sure as my name's Bella Duffy that girl's the most beautiful bride I've ever clapped eyes on.'

This could not possibly be true. Christina looked as thin

and timid as the proverbial church mouse. Her hair was mousy brown, straight and smooth around her small colourless face. It was parted in the centre and hung in a swathe over each ear before being looped up and secured at the back of her head.

Mrs Gillespie said, 'Thanks of course to your clever fingers, Bella. You excelled yourself with that dress, dear. And it was so thoughtful and generous of you to offer your labour as a wedding gift.'

The dress was a work of art with its fitted bodice and wide shawl collar embroidered with french knots. The shawl lay over an underbodice of pleated ivory muslin set in a V-shaped neckline with an inner yoke and high, boned collar. It was so high that Christina could feel the trimming of narrow satin ruching brush against her ears every time she turned her head.

Proudly Mrs Duffy smoothed down the long sleeves, then tugged at the straight skirt before arranging the free-hanging train from the back of Christina's waist. The end of the train, like the front panel of the skirt, was embroidered in french knots, but the train was also covered with pink and ivory flowers. As Christina stared in the mirror – at the dress, her pale anxious face, her mother, Mrs Duffy, the room reflected behind them with its giant darkly polished furniture, its sepia photographs of solemn-faced Gillespie ancestors, its big brass bed covered in the patchwork quilt that she had spent many a long winter evening sewing – the whole situation distanced itself into unreality.

Christina had experienced this odd feeling before. She'd be dutifully pouring out tea or handing round salmon sandwiches at one of her mother's church women's meetings, or she'd be standing in the shadowy drawing room repeating the Lord's Prayer after her father or in the church singing hymns at choir practice when suddenly she'd feel as if she'd separated from her body and was viewing the scene from outside. It was as if she were dreaming. This day wasn't a dream, was it? She felt frightened and confused. Marriage to Adam Monkton was her only hope of escape.

Her mother and father would be horrified and saddened

if they knew what she had done. Not only was her father an impassioned preacher but he worked tirelessly visiting and ministering in every way he could to his respectable working-class and middle-class Queen's Park parishioners. His angular bewhiskered figure was also well known plodding through the meaner streets and wynds of Glasgow where he struggled to bring God's word and saving grace to the poor, especially to fallen women. He wrote and personally distributed religious pamphlets explaining to the poor their place in the divine order of things. He always maintained that although the bible said 'exhort servants to be obedient unto their masters and to please them in all things' the masters also had responsibilities in looking after their servants and being compassionate to the destitute. He was an ardent campaigner against strong drink, blaming it for the plight of most of the poor.

Her mother, with an expression of earnest pursuit, busied herself continuously with charities as well as with church social occasions and other Christian duties. She was at her best in visiting the bereaved. No one could be more patient, respectful and sympathetic. Indeed, her mother's soft voice and deferential manner admirably suited her for most of the situations she found herself in.

In all her twenty-one years Christina had never felt that she'd been able to live up to her parents' high standards or their equally high expectations of her. They never punished her. They only showed disappointment and sadness. Often Christina felt they subtly withdrew their love. Her father always shook his head with a sorrowful indrawing of breath. Her mother eyed her with gentle reproach before silently turning away. There had been occasions when a reprimand had been deemed necessary, and it had always been delivered by her mother with gentleness and by her father with prayer.

What Christina found most distressing was how hurt her parents could seem as the result of even the smallest wrongdoing on her part. Once when very young she had been caught reading a comic paper instead of the picture book of Jesus they had given her. The comic had actually

5

belonged to Simon but it had never occurred to her to point the finger at him. Later there had been other books belonging to Simon that she had actively helped to conceal. These books would really have horrified their parents. They referred to intimate relations between the sexes and one of them even had drawings.

Despite the differences in their ages – he was six years older – she and Simon had always been good friends. Often he would delight her as well as shock her with stories of how mischievous he had been. She had never felt jealous of him, her bitterness had always been directed at her parents. It was them she blamed for raising no objection to Simon playing tennis, cricket, football and rugby when at the same time she was never allowed to take part in any sports.

She was told that she was not strong enough to swim or play tennis or do any of the leisure or sporting activities of her contemporaries. She'd never even been allowed in the Brownies or Girl Guides. The Brownies were banned after her mother discovered that as part of the meetings they sat on the floor of the church hall. Christina got chilled so easily, her mother had explained to those concerned. Even at such a young age, however, Christina had known that the real reason was because she had been tumbling about the floor and laughing and having fun with the other children.

Her parents belonged to the Scottish Calvinistic tradition that saw anything enjoyable as wicked. Camping, such a feature of the Girl Guides and much longed for by Christina, was also out of the question, her mother insisted, because of Christina's chest. The tales of the other girls when they returned from these camps, tales of happy times, of hikes, of community singing round camp fires, of fun and fellowship and laughter, became too painful to listen to. She shied away from them, shrinking into the lonely centre of herself in brokenhearted despair.

Her mother was often heard to say to members of the congregation, 'Christina has always been a delicate child, I have to be so careful with her.'

As a result of such conscientious care, Christina had had very little opportunity to make friends. When she had tried to break away from her mother's influence and make friends, especially when she neared her teenage years, she was made to feel cruel and selfish.

'Well of course, dear,' her mother would say with the pain of disappointment in her eyes, 'if you don't want to help me with the sale of work I'd never dream of forcing you. I have been doing my best to raise money for the deserving poor but if you don't know where your duty as the daughter of the manse lies, that is between you and your maker. I'll struggle along somehow on my own and I'll ask God in my prayers not to be too harsh on you. And of course I'll ask your father to include you in his prayers at church.'

All her life Christina had been under this veiled threat, the dreadful humiliation of her father praying in public for God to forgive her regrettable weakness in character and behaviour. As a very young child the threat had been more specific. Daddy would tell the congregation what a naughty, selfish little girl she was. Daddy would ask everyone to pray that she would say sorry to her mummy and promise never to talk back to her mummy again. Or skip in the street or talk loudly or play with boys or get her pinafore dirty or forget to say thank you or do any of the thousand and one things that would be natural behaviour for any other child. Especially she was never to succumb to the Devil in the form of love of material things. This was rigidly guarded against. If she revealed by any careless look or touch that she was fond of a hair ribbon, a clothes-peg doll, a seashell, any little piece of property she had somehow managed to acquire, it was immediately taken from her.

Sometimes her heart raged against this loss but she never dared show her anger for fear of being publicly shamed in front of God's and her father's congregation. Sometimes looking back she thought she would have gone mad had it not been for her music. Her hours at the piano had brought comfort as well as joy, although she had tried, alas in the end unsuccessfully, to hide the joy. It was her life. But her parents had taken away even that. Apart from the fact that it was wicked of her to enjoy her music so much, or so they inferred, they did not want her to make it a career. They did not want her to have any career at all.

They did not want her to get married. It went without saying that her duty lay in staying at home to be a help, a comfort and a companion to her mother, then eventually to take care of both parents in their old age as a million Scottish daughters had dutifully done before her. Only she couldn't bear it. Night after night she had lain in the brass bed and thought about the barren life ahead of her, the repression, the frustration. She knew she couldn't face it.

Mrs Duffy was lifting the veil from where it lay like a ghost on a chair.

'Now for the final touch.' She held the veil reverently high as she swept towards Christina. A circle of orange blossom was placed like a crown of thorns on Christina's head. Mrs Gillespie began to sniffle into her hankie.

'She's far too good for him, Bella.'

Mrs Gillespie had never thought there was much wrong with Adam before she'd heard that he was going to marry her daughter. On the contrary Christina had often heard her mother remark in the past on how hard-working Adam was and what a credit to his mother and father.

A shadow darkened the pale face in the wardrobe mirror only for a second before the eyes lowered and it was gone.

Chapter Two

Christina believed that it was deep-seated resentment which she and Adam Monkton had in common. Not that she'd known much about him when they were both young, he had been Simon's friend, but even they only got together during school holidays. Monkton attended an exclusive boarding school in Edinburgh called The Royal. It was a castle of a place where the sons of both titled and wealthy men were educated.

She remembered Adam losing much of his Scottish accent and acquiring a polish that seemed very strange and anglified. Not that he had spoken to her apart from a passing 'hello', but she had been flattered even by this. Sometimes he simply gave her a cursory nod of recognition. She was six years younger than him, a mere child not worthy of his attention. She'd paid attention to him, however. For years she had watched him with interest and secret admiration.

She had overheard her parents speak openly about him over the years.

'Moses Monkton has worked like a trojan all his life,' the Reverend Gillespie once pronounced. 'This Edinburgh notion is yet another of his wife's foolish and extravagant ideas. She'll fritter away the savings he has struggled to accumulate.'

'It'll cause nothing but trouble,' Mrs Gillespie agreed. 'I'm afraid Beatrice's ideas for the boy are too grand. I tried to warn her quietly and tactfully, of course. 'My dear Beatrice,' I said, 'don't you think a nice select private school in Glasgow, like the one our Simon attends, would be better than packing young Adam away to Edinburgh?' Mrs Gillespie sighed. 'She wouldn't listen, of course. I'm afraid it's as you say, William, Beatrice is a foolish woman.'

'I'm surprised Moses allowed to her have her way in this.'

It wasn't until Adam was sixteen that the bombshell

exploded and his father suddenly intervened. Adam was informed that he must leave The Royal and start right away as a joiner's apprentice with Landsdowne's building firm. Landsdowne's was owned by a friend of his father. Adam was to remain at the firm for five years until he'd finished serving his time.

Adam had argued and protested all to no avail. His mother had taken to her bed in hysterics after trying everything else and failing to change her husband's mind. Later Adam told Simon he'd never forget the day the headmaster spoke to him and his father. He could still see the headmaster resting his elbows on his big mahogany desk and placing his fingers together as if in prayer.

'Mr Monkton,' he said gravely, 'I appeal to you to allow your son to complete his education.' Then he had gone on to explain why, his lean, intelligent face hovering between an expression of desperation and exasperation. Opposite, Moses Monkton's iron-hard body and brown weatherbeaten face had an aggressive determination that the headmaster found impossible to break through. Eventually Monkton leaned forward and stared the headmaster straight in the eye.

'You will never understand my reasoning. I was brought up the hard way and that's the way it's going to be for him. He's had too much of the good life here. This is all very well but I am now going to show him the other side of the coin. He's going to start as a joiner's apprentice on thirteenth September and he'll serve his time for five years the same as I did.'

Christina remembered that winter. Sometimes if she wakened early in the morning and happened to look out of her bedroom window she would see Adam, shoulders hunched, battling through the rain and snow dressed in his workman's clothes and carrying his swollen bag of joiner's tools. Even as a youth he was tall and well built, with a jutting barrel chest. He had acquired an aggressive swagger and an 'I don't care a damn about anything or anybody' attitude. Christina guessed it did nothing to improve his popularity on a Landsdowne building site.

She used to sit for a long time afterwards, elbows propped on the window sill, chin cupped in hands, day dreaming about her brother's friend. She thought of all sorts of daring things. She imagined them running away together, holding on to each other, even kissing and caressing each other. Her cheeks would burn at the wickedness of her thoughts.

Mrs Gillespie was full of compassion for both mother and son.

'Poor Beatrice is in such a state,' she'd confided in the Reverend Gillespie. 'You're a friend of Moses. Can't you do something, William?'

'It would be wrong of me, Ada. Very wrong of me,' the Reverend Gillespie informed her, 'to interfere in a family matter between father and son. Moses is doing what he believes is best for the boy.'

'Bless my soul, William. How can it be best for him? The Women's Guild is buzzing with stories about how he's being tormented by the workmen. They're jealous of him and causing him every difficulty and trouble they can. God forgive them, they even mock the way he talks. That young man is getting into so many fights it'll be the death of him yet.'

It was common knowledge that some of the men at Landsdowne's had been fired from Monkton's and they had old grievances against him. Unable to settle them with Moses, they were grabbing their chance to avenge themselves on his son. Even in the tough hire-and-fire building trade, and especially in the maintenance side in which Monkton's specialized, Moses Monkton was notorious for his harsh and uncompromising methods. If a man was caught having a quick puff at a Woodbine on the job, loitering over a brazier to heat his hands or apparently slacking in any way whatsoever, Moses fired him on the spot. It would be to no avail to plead that he had a sick wife and ten children to support. No use showing anger, either. More than one man had felt the hammer blow of Monkton's fist.

The Reverend Gillespie always insisted, however, 'Moses Monkton is a fair man. A generous man. A generous man.'

The minister had a habit of repeating words for emphasis when the occasion warranted.

'At all times he's a good and upright Christian. A good and upright Christian, Ada. I have known of men injured in an accident at work who have been visited by him and given money. Money to tide them over their bad time and sustain them and their families. Say not a word to me, not a word, against Moses Monkton.'

It was not long after Adam left school that he sustained his eye injury. It left a scar that slightly pulled down one brow and gave him a narrow-eyed and rather wicked look. Adam refused to be drawn on the subject and no one ever found out who was responsible for the injury. Christina did find out about Adam's bitterness, however. She knew what not staying at school had meant to him. His ambition was to be a doctor. He and Simon had often spoken about going on to university together and studying medicine. One of Adam's Royal school friends had told Simon that although Adam hadn't been academically brilliant he had a determination to succeed. As a result he had worked hard and got a decent pass in all his exams. It was probably because he rose well to any challenge that he excelled in sports. He'd been captain of the shooting and rugby teams to mention but two of the fields in which he'd shown himself a superb sportsman.

Beatrice had been more proud of his sporting accomplishments than his ambition to be a doctor. As she never tired of telling everyone, 'Adam takes after Pater, you know. We were landed gentry in my native Ireland. How well I remember Pater striding around our estate with his gun slung on the crook of his arm.'

She had often confided to Ada. 'It was a terrible shock I received when I came over here a young innocent bride, only to discover that my new husband was little more than a common jobbing slater. Oh what a deceiver, Ada. Him leading me to believe that he was a successful businessman.'

'Poor soul,' Ada sympathized. 'But my dear, large trees from little acorns grow and Moses' business did grow after all.'

'A wicked deceiver,' Beatrice repeated, fluttering the fan she always used if she felt hot or faint. 'The only good thing that has come from my marriage is my son. He shall not become coarse like his father. He will get an education and a polish that will enable him to take his rightful place among the highest in the land.'

'God help her,' Ada mournfully reported to the Reverend Gillespie at the time. 'She had such high hopes for Adam marrying the daughter of one of the Highland clan chiefs. Her son being employed as a common workman is a terrible blow to her pride. She was only the daughter of a country squire, you know, for all her fine talk.'

Some of the wealthiest clan chiefs had town houses in Edinburgh and Glasgow. The daughter of one, the young Lady Glencannon, was a special favourite around whom Beatrice spun many dreams.

'We must remember Beatrice in our prayers, William. She's losing her way,' Mrs Gillespie said. 'There seems no deviousness to which she'll not stoop, no expense to which she'll not stretch in order to move in the social swing of those Highlanders. But,' she added, not knowing then how prophetic her remark was, 'pride goes before a fall.'

'Yes indeed. Yes indeed,' The Reverend Gillespie tugged at the lapels of his jacket in the same way he always grasped his clerical gown when wishing to ram home a particular truth in his sermons. 'Moses Monkton has a heavy cross to bear. A heavy cross.'

'She believes it's for her son's sake, of course.' Ada's voice bent in sympathetic compassion. 'The poor woman.'

The Reverend Gillespie shook his head.

'Beatrice would be the ruination of her son if she had her way. The ruination, Ada. It's a blessing the boy had such a good Christian father.'

Any time Adam heard his father referred to in these terms, and specially by the minister, his lip would curl and his eyes harden, but he kept silent except on one occasion when he'd remarked sarcastically to Simon, 'He thinks by keeping in with the minister it'll secure him a place in heaven.'

13

Christina got to know Adam gradually over the years. Or thought she knew him. She believed that because she had suffered in her life and been denied her chance she could understand his bitterness and resentment.

They had talked often as she'd grown older and she was more than willing to listen sympathetically to his occasional outbursts of frustration and resentment. As they had gradually over the years become friends of a sort, so her dreams about him had increased in intensity. In bed at night she would imagine him touching her most private places. His broad hands would fondle her breasts, her abdomen, her buttocks, the secret throbbing places in between her legs. Time and time again in her dreams his big body came down on top of her and she felt the hard penetration of him. She would feel the resulting moisture between her legs and would burn with shame and terror in case by some God-like magic her mother and father would find out. She lived with the constant horror, the dreadful nightmare of every sin, every secret thought being revealed in front of her father's congregation.

She realized that by trapping Adam Monkton into marriage she was probably lighting a fuse to an explosive situation. The knowledge both terrified and excited her. She also felt guilty. She wanted to beg his forgiveness, but a natural caution held her back from doing so. After his wedding ring was safely on her finger would be soon enough.

Her parents' opposition to the marriage had been so unyielding at first, Christina wondered if they'd heard any of the gossip about Adam, of the type that she herself had overheard from the servants. The story went that Adam had got one of the young maids in Monkton House into trouble. For the master or son of any house to have his way with one of the servants was not an unusual occurrence. The situation had come to a head when Adam had been up north for a few months on a job. The girl had fainted while on duty and the truth had come out. She was immediately dismissed and that should have been that. What was different and shocking about what had happened to the Monkton establishment was the fact that this servant had fought back. The idea of fighting back in this, or indeed any situation, had thrilled Christina. She was filled with secret admiration for the girl. The expression of her own fighting spirit had long since been quelled by threats of God's wrath, or even worse, God's disappointment in her.

Right away she'd guessed which of the servant girls the gossip concerned. Many a time she'd gazed in awe at her beauty when visiting Monkton House with her mother. Annalie Gordon was one of the parlour maids who often served them afternoon tea. She had raven hair, a smooth creamy skin and the most compelling eyes Christina had ever seen. They were dark with a hint of violet about them. What made them so remarkable, however, was the personality they revealed with such unashamed openness. There was a zest for life, a love of life in those eyes. A fiery passion and pride in abundance.

Doris, the other parlour maid, admittedly much older, moved in comparison with quiet discretion and was barely noticeable in the room. It was impossible not to be aware of Annalie Gordon. Her vibrant presence, her every movement a celebration of sensual awareness, stopped all attempts at conversation. Beatrice and her guests – all that is except Christina – automatically stiffened in disapproval and waited until the servant had left the room.

It was a well-known fact that old Mrs Monkton, Beatrice's mother-in-law, had engaged Annalie Gordon while she had been in charge of the household when Beatrice was on a visit to Ireland. It was more than Beatrice was capable of to risk the old woman's wrath by dismissing the servant. Beatrice was plagued by a delicate nervous system and recurring states of anxiety.

Gladys, the Gillespie parlour maid, was friendly with Doris, and Christina overheard Gladys telling Mrs Kelvin, the cook, about the scandal.

'It's obvious which girl,' Mrs Kelvin sniffed. It was that dark-eyed gypsy-looking one, wasn't it? Annalie Gordon. I always knew no good would come of that girl being there.'

'She really is a gypsy,' Gladys breathlessly informed the

older woman. 'Or at least her mother is. A dreadful woman, apparently. There was a terrible scene in Monkton House, Doris said. Doris said you couldn't believe the way that girl carried on. The mistress was good enough to give her some extra money in her wages when she dismissed her, and do you know what that girl did? She flung the money in the mistress's face.'

'No!' Cook gasped.

From where she'd been standing on the shadowy stairs that led down to the kitchen, Christina's hand clapped her hand to her mouth to contain her own exclamation of surprise. But her shock was mixed with wicked pleasure. Good for her, she couldn't help thinking. She'd often had an urge to throw something at Beatrice Monkton herself.

'It's true. Doris was in the very room serving afternoon tea. She flung the money in the mistress's face and told her it was marriage she wanted, not money.'

'No.'

'To Master Adam! And him such a gentleman and her little more than a tramp and there's such bad blood in her veins. The mistress took hysterics. She's a very highly strung woman. Doris had to drag the girl away. Mr McKendrick, the butler, was going to send for the police. That soon got rid of her. She was still cursing though, right to the last.'

'What would worry me,' the cook confided darkly, 'is has she put a gypsy curse on the family, especially on Master Adam?'

It was this overheard conversation that made Christina start dreaming of the exciting idea, her plan of escape. Obviously for Adam Monkton to marry a servant girl was out of the question, but if the daughter of his father's best friend, if the respected minister's daughter became pregnant, that would be a very different matter. Her fantasies about making love with Adam intensified and became all the more exciting because they were now laced with the heady danger of possibility. With breathless daring she worked everything out. She felt certain Moses Monkton would not be able to bear any responsibility for his family bringing disgrace to any member of the manse. She became so feverish with the idea of a real-life love affair between Adam Monkton and herself that she could think of nothing else. She couldn't sleep, she couldn't eat, she violently trembled and felt butterflies in her stomach every time she saw him.

Adam must have noticed. At least Simon did. He began tormenting her.

'You've taken a shine to my friend. Come on now, admit it.'

She had hastily to hush Simon in case her parents might hear. His tormenting was such a constant agony to her that she began shrinking from his company too.

Simon, of course, had always been in the habit of saying and indeed doing most outrageous things and getting away with them. In her mother's and father's eyes it seemed he could do no wrong. If by some mischance he was discovered, which rarely happened, he could charm his parents, tease them, make them laugh until they forgave him. Despite the fact that Christina knew only too well how easy it was to forgive Simon she always felt a certain amount of bitterness against her parents for the difference in their attitude to Simon and herself.

To Christina's extreme embarrassment she realized that Simon must have disclosed to Adam the secret of her seemingly sudden romantic feelings towards him. Adam began to treat her with an unusual amount of gentleness, even affection, but it was the kind of attitude of a man to a favourite child.

Eventually she was overcome by such a sense of urgency and desperation she was continually on the verge of proving to him that she was not a child, of actually doing something about her dreams. Instead, when Adam came to the house she did everything possible to avoid him. Then one day he arrived, having heard that Simon had joined up, and wanting to hear all the details. Simon was not at home, neither were her mother and father. Christina knew this was her opportunity, one that might never happen again because if Simon was sent away by the army Adam would no longer visit the manse.

Christina was crossing the hall when Adam came to the door, and she unthinkingly opened it before the parlour maid arrived from the kitchen. She asked him in, and as he followed her up the gloomy stairway to the drawing room, the beating of her heart was drowning out the tick-tock of the grandfather clock in the hall. Instead of sitting in a chair opposite she joined him on the settee.

'Simon's out,' she said.

'Oh?' There was a slight lift of surprise in his voice as well as disappointment.

'Mother and father are out too.'

She was going cold with horror and had an almost over-whelming impulse to run from the room, yet at the same time she knew she loved him. Indeed it was then that she realized for the first time that she had always loved him. She also experienced the absolute conviction that if she walked away from him now, she would be condemning herself to lifelong spinsterhood and repression in the manse. Now was her only chance of love and fulfilment.

Her hand, like a delicately fluttering leaf, descended on his knee. He fixed her with one of his penetrating stares. It seemed to be trying to dig into the deepest corners of her mind. He had a rugged face, too broad-boned to be conventionally handsome, too aggressively masculine. She moved her hand slightly up his thigh and was surprised and frightened by the rock-hard feel of his muscle.

'Christina,' he said. 'What the hell do you think you're doing?'

Having gone so far there was no turning back. She was in a nightmare from which she couldn't wake up. She wondered if what her mother said about male sexuality was true. Ada always maintained that men were completely at the mercy of their carnal impulses. *He* seemed in perfect control of himself. The humiliation of his not responding to her was worse than if he had. She kept trying to calm herself by remembering that here was someone she'd known all her life. Her mind, her body however, would not be calmed. He was a man, a stranger, and she was afraid.

18

She began unbuttoning her dress, illogically resenting him almost as if this dreadful situation were all his fault.

'Christina,' he repeated. 'My dear child.'

She rose, allowing her dress to slither to the floor.

'I'm not a child. I don't want you to treat me like a child any more.'

She was suddenly wretchedly conscious of her unglamorous camisole and knickers. All at once she saw herself in sharp comparison to Annalie Gordon and could have died at Adam's feet. She imagined the gypsy girl standing before him, black hair tumbling wildly about her shoulders, her voluptuous body sensually undulating.

Christina's embarrassment at her dowdy underwear overcame for the moment her horror at her own wickedness. When she was fully clothed her equally unflattering outer garments made her look excessively thin and flat chested. Standing naked before him, she prayed that with the shapeliness of her legs, her narrow waist, the rosy-tipped nipples of her breasts, she would prove more appealing.

'Don't you like me at all?' Her voice quivered near to tears.

Suddenly he drew her down onto the couch beside him.

'Of course I do. I've always liked you. Not just as a child.' His eyes wandered down over her body. 'You're beautiful.'

He began touching her and she could hear his breathing become laboured. Her mind flew to Annalie Gordon again in her desperation to please Adam, but she did not know how to be like her. All she could do was to be as submissive as possible, to allow him to do whatever he wanted with her.

The wickedness of what he was doing and making her do shocked and excited her. She felt it pulled them closer together in a veil of secrecy and guilt. All the time, despite her mounting ecstasy she felt terrified that someone would come in, discover them. She knew she would die of shame.

Her mother had not told her how a woman could be aroused. Christina was astonished and confused by exquisite sensation. She closed her eyes, her body shivering with

19

pleasure under his touch, her moans and cries filling the room.

Afterwards she was exhausted and painfully vulnerable in her nakedness. Hastily she gathered her clothes and went behind a screen to dress. A glance in the mirror above the fireplace revealed her flushed face and normally neat hair which had escaped from the restriction of its many hairpins. She was once more in confusion, but it was of a different kind. She felt shy and embarrassed but happy too. Surely she had pleased him. She felt a little proud now of her daring. She emerged timidly from behind the screen and went over to sit opposite him. She was taken aback by the anger in his eyes when he looked at her. He had been smoking a cigarette and he stubbed it out and ground it into the ashtray for a few seconds before speaking.

'You've known me for years, Christina. Why this sudden irresistible impulse for sex?'

The vulnerability of nakedness frightened her again. She lowered her eyes.

'I don't know.'

After a few moments of silence he said, 'Look, you're a very attractive woman but I'm not in love with you. I hope you realize that.'

Head miserably lowered, she made no reply. He rose.

'Oh God. I'm sorry this has happened, Christina. Words can't convey to you how deeply I regret it.'

She rose too, avoiding his eyes, trying not to reveal how much his words had wounded her.

'Tell Simon I'll be at Monkton House,' Adam continued. 'I'd like to see him before he goes.'

She followed his burly figure towards the door.

'If you come back in a couple of hours,' she ventured, 'he'll be home by then.'

He turned at the door and looked at her.

'No, Christina. I won't be back. Just tell Simon to come along to Monkton House.'

Her legs couldn't carry her downstairs. She stood helplessly listening to the front door bang shut. She hardly knew how she passed the rest of the day.

That night lying in bed, she could only pray that she would become pregnant. That had been her motivation, her original idea. But now it had taken on a different urgency. She wanted Adam Monkton very much, not just as a means of escape. She wanted him desperately. Her mind seesawed between a pit of doubt and heights of resolve. She compared herself hopelessly with the colourful charms of the gypsy girl, and cringed at the idea of herself, such a timid and mousy offering for Adam. What must he have thought of her?

Time and time again she anguished over the scene. Just as often, however, she would pray fervently that God would give her another chance to make him love her. She would do everything in her power to make him love her. She would do everything she could to please him and make him happy. Please God, please, please God, she kept praying, let me be pregnant. It never occurred to her that Adam Monkton might refuse to marry her. She believed what Doris had said. He was a gentleman. Even though he obviously regretted what had happened he would accept his responsibilities and do the right thing by her.

At the back of her mind she was still aware of the original safety net she'd thought of in the form of Adam's father. She had no pang of conscience or guilty thought about making Moses Monkton think it had been Adam who had seduced her. Such was her desperation. It was a case of any means to an end. She would make him a good wife. This belief justified everything else in her mind.

She was overjoyed when very soon after that evening her monthly bleeding did not appear when it should have. She was as regular as clockwork and had never missed a day before. This convinced her that God had answered her prayers. She had not seen Adam since the day of their lovemaking, and wondered if she should go along to Monkton House. That way, however, she would be taking the risk of Adam not being there. Although she could be certain of a welcome from Mr Monkton she knew from past experience that Beatrice, like her friend Ada, would treat her more like an unpaid companion than anything else. She

21

would keep her busy plumping up her cushions, passing chocolates, reading to her, playing the piano for her entertainment. Christina was too distracted by her problems to have any patience to pander to Beatrice Monkton. She took instead to watching from the manse windows for Adam passing along Queen's Drive. She knew he spent part of his time in the Monkton offices in Pollokshaws Road when he was not travelling around inspecting maintenance work or a contract in the process of being completed. She often used to see his tall figure striding past the manse. Now she watched anxiously for him. Fortunately, on the day she spotted him she was on her way into the church to help her mother with a sale of work. Christina had come through the opening in the bushes between the church and manse and was cutting across towards the front porch as Adam was passing the pillared entrance of the drive. She called to him and ran down the drive. He stopped and waited, his manner cold but polite.

'Yes?' he asked when she reached him.

'I must talk to you,' she said breathlessly.

'About what?'

'You . . . You know,' she stammered timidly, avoiding his stony stare.

'No. I don't know,' he said.

'I'm pregnant,' she blurted out.

There was silence for a minute then he said, 'You can't be. How can you possibly know so soon?'

She raised a flushed, joyous face to him.

'Oh I know, I know. There's no doubt about it.'

He stared at her long and hard. She added recklessly, 'We'll have to get married.'

He raised a brow. 'Oh?'

'Think of the scandal if we don't.'

'I've no intention of marrying you, Christina,' he said.

Chapter Three

If there was one thing Adam Monkton valued more than anything else in the world it was his independence. He'd long since got over his father forcing him from The Royal and away from his chosen career into the building trade. Or at least he thought he had.

As a lad in his teens, despite an ingrained sense of duty, he'd hated his father and made no secret of the fact. There were times indeed when they'd come to blows and these occasions would have been more frequent had it not been for the intervention of his mother. Her fluttering into the scene in distress or fainting or taking hysterics soon put a stop to that kind of behaviour. Anyway, having read something about medicine and the workings of the human body and mind he realized that hatred and bitterness would harm himself more than anyone else.

After the worst of his rage had simmered down he could see the old man's point of view. He'd spent his life building up the business from nothing and it was vitally important to him that it should be continued. The only way to continue it was obviously through Adam. He'd eventually accepted the whole thing, not only as a duty but as a challenge, and just battled his way through the initial years as best he could. Now, looking back, he wouldn't have been without them.

He'd never been able to admit to the old man that he'd probably been right. He was more suited to be a builder than a doctor. From quite early on he had enjoyed the open-air work and the sense of freedom it gave him. Serving his time proved invaluable to him. He understood the work. He knew immediately if anything was wrong with a job and how to put it right. There was no deceiving him.

He maintained his enjoyment of sport and made a habit of going to the gym and keeping fit by doing a bit of boxing.

He'd also acquired an interest in jujitsu. He recognized it as a great art. He'd seen Raku Tani give music-hall exhibitions and was amazed by the simple manner in which a powerful man could be overcome in a question of seconds by the quick-moving little Jap.

When Tani visited Glasgow he did his training at the same club as Monkton and on one memorable occasion he'd had a contest with his hero. First they wrestled and the Jap had been fair and made no attempt to use his jujitsu locks. But soon the smaller man had tripped him as he had applied the hold to his jacket. Monkton had hit the mat and before he could spring to his feet the Jap's two feet were at his neck, choking him. The feet were naked and all Monkton's strength failed to pull them apart. There was not only strength in that hold, but some peculiar knack. Monkton kept trying but as he seized Tani's canvas jacket he fell backwards. A foot was applied to Monkton's abdomen and he sailed through the air as the Jap hit the mat with his back. Again those sinewy feet held him by the neck. He could still remember that grip, stronger than any man's hands. He was too busy to train to the sufficient standard to take part in contests himself now, but he was backing and encouraging one of his navvies to do so. Big Geordie Cameron had the use of the gym in Pollokshaws Road just a few blocks along from the office, and Monkton often went there to supervise his training and to enjoy bouts with him in the ring. He was glad of the concentrated skill as well as the rough and tumble of this sport now. It helped him to forget his frustrations and anger against Christina Gillespie.

Sometimes, if Geordie was working on a job, Monkton would just go into the gym and do some bagwork, stabbing at the bag with his bandaged fists until they bled and, despite the bandages, red spotted the leather bag. His anger was directed as much at himself as Christina. He was so furious at being caught as he had, especially by Christina of all people. After all, he'd known her most of his life. Even as a boy he had seen how repressed and unhappy she was. He'd never thought much about her then, but when he did he felt sorry for her. As the years passed he'd seen her grow into quite an attractive woman, but at the same time become obviously more repressed, more introverted, more unhappy. Occasionally he'd remarked on this to Simon.

Simon had said, 'Yes. Poor Chrissie. I suppose it's with her being there all the time. At least I was away at school and escaped most of the awful atmosphere of the manse. I don't know how she stood it, to be honest. It would have driven me mad. It's impossible to stand up to them in a serious way. That's the devilish thing. They just bring God into it. There's always the spectre of religion behind everything. I just laugh and make fun of them, but then it's easier for me, as I say. It's no joke for poor Chrissie. She's there all the time.'

There had been occasions when he and Christina had talked together, actually shared confidences. He told her of the bitter, resentful feelings that he had towards his father and she confided how broken-hearted she'd been when her dreams of a musical career had been shattered. Again he felt sorry for her, deeply sorry for her this time. He understood so well how she must be feeling. Because of that understanding he had developed quite an affection for her. To him she had become as much his sister as Simon's. Knowing her as he did he should have realized that, unable to stand up to her mother and father, she would find some means of escape. It should have occurred to him that marriage, and marriage to him in particular, would be the only route open to her. Particularly him, because shy and timid and repressed as she was, he could not imagine her having the nerve to try to seduce any man who was more of a stranger to her. She knew, or thought she knew, that she could trust him.

The fury and the feeling of being trapped returned to give him a blinding headache. To think that for years he'd managed to prevent Fiona, the Lady Glencannon, from pinning him to the mast. She was an attractive girl and he liked her, but she had been too keen on getting married. She had made no secret of the fact and he'd been equally frank with her that he wasn't interested. He had expected her to give him up then, or at least go into a sulk, but not the bold Fiona.

'One day you'll change your mind,' she said. 'You can't tell me you're not the marrying kind.'

In truth, any thought of losing his independence appalled him. It flung him back in time to the constrictions of his youth when his father had forced him to comply with his will. He had felt trapped then. He had been like a trapped animal battering at the bars of his cage to the point of self-injury. If only Christina had spoken to him, had confided in him, he would have done his best to help her. Now part of him thought of her as a devious, scheming little bitch and hated her with all his being. Another part of his mind told him that her way of getting what she wanted was as old as Eve in the garden of Eden. She'd probably not thought anything out as a plan of action at all and had merely acted on instinct. This knowledge, however, did nothing to soften or alleviate his resentment against her.

When the Lady Glencannon had learned of his impending marriage she had been furious and he didn't blame her.

'You rotten cad,' she'd accused, and added spitefully, 'I always knew of course, as the son of a common builder you couldn't really be a gentleman.'

He'd felt like taking her over his knee and spanking her, but what was the use? The affair was over and that was that.

Sometimes he couldn't believe that his life had changed so much and all because of one timid little mouse of a woman who looked as if butter wouldn't melt in her mouth. The trouble she'd caused didn't stop at trapping him into marriage. She'd set him at loggerheads with his father again and now he had to struggle with the guilt of having been the cause of his father's near fatal stroke. And it wasn't just the guilt he had to confront. With the bitterness against Christina, all the frustration, hatred and resentment against his father had somehow become stirred up. All these emotions were churning about inside him so strongly and so constantly now he couldn't control them.

Most days, when feeling like this, he would work out

26

his emotions and frustrations in the gym, pound, pound, pounding at the bag, or he'd get into the ring with Geordie and they'd have a really tough slog. Sometimes, if the slogging didn't work, he went straight from the gym to the nearest bar and sat drinking steadily for hours.

As the wedding date drew near his every emotion intensified and jumbled together into a kind of madness. The pity, the guilt, the sense of duty, the frustration, the anger towards both his father and Christina. Most of all, though, towards Christina there was the hatred. He kept thinking: Damn it, I won't marry her, I can't marry her. There was absolutely no doubt in his mind about this. There was no way he could possibly face the prospect of tying himself for life to the wretched girl.

Chapter Four

'Chrissie.' Mrs Gillespie's tone was intimate. 'Is anything wrong dear?'

Christina gazed uncertainly at her mother who was leaning towards her wearing her most pained, compassionate face. She was also wearing a black velour hat with a spotted veil attached to the brim and stretching down under her chin.

'Oh Mother,' Christina said. 'I feel so upset.'

If she had not felt conscience-stricken and guilty about appealing for Moses Monkton's help before, she certainly did now. Her mother squeezed her arm.

'Prenuptial nerves, dear. Your father and I have had to deal with so many faint-hearted girls at a time like this.'

Christina shook her head. 'If only it was as simple as that.'

'I know, dear,' her mother sympathized. 'It's all been so terribly difficult with poor Moses taking his stroke and insisting that he wanted to see you married before he died. Although I believe that if we all remember him in our prayers, God will surely spare him. People do recover from strokes.'

Mrs Duffy settled the coronet of blossom further down on Christina's brow.

'They say he's completely paralysed down one side.' Mrs Gillespie's voice dropped until she was barely mouthing the words.

Near to tears now, Christina said, 'It's not fair to get married like this, but what can I do?'

'I know, I know, dear,' her mother soothed. 'All this rush, rush at the last minute. It really is a miracle, Bella,' she said, turning to the other woman, 'how you got that dress made in time.'

'What else could I do?' Christina repeated.

28

There had been something else of course. Adam had wanted her to get rid of the baby. It wasn't a baby at such an early stage, he'd insisted. He would get her something to take. Instead she'd confided in Moses Monkton who'd been shocked and furious at Adam for taking advantage of the child of a man of the cloth. There had been a violent argument between father and son. An argument of such violence that shortly afterwards Moses had taken his stroke.

'You did the right thing, dear,' her mother soothed. 'The only Christian thing to do. You'll get a home of your own soon enough. You've always put your Christian duty first and that's how it should be.' She turned to Bella again. 'Between you and me, Bella, Beatrice Monkton is just no use in a crisis. She always goes to bits and this time has been no exception. Our Chrissie will have her work cut out there between the pair of them.' Switching back to her daughter again she gazed pityingly at her. 'But don't worry, dear. You'll manage with God's help.'

'It's not myself I'm worried about. It's Adam.'

Her mother's mouth tightened and her head gave the little wobble on her neck that always indicated she was annoyed or offended.

'Well, you know what your father and I think of Adam Monkton. But then, he's your choice, dear. And while we're on the subject, I know perfectly well that it would be him that would be the cause of all the secrecy.'

Christina eyed her mother warily. 'Secrecy?'

Ada Gillespie's head gave another wiggle.

'Adam Monkton has been coming here man and boy for years on the pretext of seeing Simon and all the time it's been you he's been after. Even his mother never suspected. You'll have to try and be patient with her, Chrissie. She hardly knows where she is just now, what with the shock of the illness and then the wedding.' Mrs Gillespie gave Mrs Duffy a knowing look. 'She was so convinced, you see, that her son would marry into the landed gentry.'

She gave Christina's arm another reassuring squeeze. 'Never you mind, dear. You'll make a better wife than any of them. Just you remember always to say your prayers and ask God for strength and you'll be all right.'

Mrs Gillespie's long black coat was lying across the bed. She went over and put it on, buttoning it neatly up to her throat.

Mrs Duffy, who was wearing a bottle green skirt and cream lingerie blouse with an enormous jabot that accentuated her already generous bosom, donned a three-quarter-length jacket. After adding a huge-brimmed hat, she recrossed the room like a ship in full sail to put the finishing touches to Christina's appearance. She spread out the veil across Christina's shoulders then delicately lifted part of the featherlike material over Christina's face.

The images in the mirror misted and became even more remote. She looked like a ghost between the two dark-clad and more solid figures of the other women.

'Here are the flowers, dear,' her mother said reverently as she arranged the long-stemmed lilies into her daughter's arms. The waxy flowers brought a chill. Christina was reminded that when her maternal grandmother died there had been lilies on her coffin.

'Come, dear,' Mrs Gillespie urged. 'Your father will be waiting.'

Christina slowly descended the stairs, taking care not to catch the toe of her ivory slipper in one of the frayed patches of carpet. The banister was like all the woodwork, dark as treacle toffee. It clung to her moist palm. The shadows on the stairway were like a smokescreen through which the gaslight flickered feebly. The grandfather clock deep in the funeral gloom slowly clanged the hour. The noise almost drowned out the gasps of admiration issuing from the knot of servants in the doorway that led to the nether regions of the house.

Mrs Kelvin called out, 'Good luck, Miss Chrissie.' Her words were echoed by the others.

In her father's study Christina found him leaning against the mantelshelf of the cast-iron fire grate. One foot on its black fender. His eyes were closed, his head tilted backwards. His eyes opened and his gaze slowly swivelled towards her when Christina entered.

'My dear,' his sonorous voice boomed out. 'Let us pray.'

He grasped the back of the nearest chair and stood as if nursing the pulpit in front of him with his broad spread of hands. He was dressed in his usual clerical grey suit, white dog collar and flowing black robe with its broad purple ribbon. His eyes closed again. 'Dear Lord, you know how much it saddens us, saddens us all, to know that our Chrissie is to be united with a man who is not a committed Christian. But we thank you for the comfort that his father is such a loyal churchgoer and friend. Dear Lord, have mercy on Moses Monkton in this his hour of need. Bless him and comfort him and, if it be thy will, raise him from his bed of sickness. And, dear Lord, help our Chrissie to be a good Christian wife – a good Christian wife who will be able to influence her husband and bring him safely into the fold. Safely into the fold. For thine is the power and the glory for Jesus' sake. Amen.'

After a murmuring echo of Amen, Mrs Gillespie peered through her black trellis of veil.

'Is everything all right, William? Has Simon gone next door?' Next door meant the Martyrs Church.

'I believe,' the Reverend Gillespie said, 'that everything is in order, or as much in order as it can be in the circumstances.'

He sailed from the room and Christina followed, head lowered. Normally they used the space in the bushes near the back door of the manse to reach the church. Today, however, decorum decreed an exit from the front door and a walk down the manse drive. Then it was necessary to go through the pillared gates of the church and up the church driveway. This afforded the waiting crowd a chance to admire the bride. Fortunately the rain kept away for her journey from the manse to the church, but it was bitterly cold.

Through the milky haze of veil she saw a crowd of Girl Guides in their navy-blue uniforms. They hastily spread out in a guard of honour as soon as they spotted her approach. There were some children she'd taught at Sunday school, their faces gazing from nests of woollen mufflers. Parents were nudging their offspring and pointing at Christina. Some of them waved. There were uniformed servants from Monkton House, a few strange faces caught Christina's attention, and then she had turned and was walking, trying not to shiver, towards the ancient church door.

The stones of the rough drive pierced the soles of her satin slippers and made little crunching sounds echo up into the cold air. The church door with its wrought-iron hinges, locks and latches, the work of some medieval smith, lay open. Inside two young bridesmaids stood waiting, their arms goose pimpling the same shade as their pink taffeta dresses.

As soon as Christina stepped into the porch Miss Price attacked the organ. The familiar strains of 'Here Comes the Bride' swelled up to reverberate around the high vaulted ceiling. Miss Price was a spinster with withered, drooping bust and face that looked as if it had been made of melted candlewax. Unhappiness reflected dully from her eyes at all times except when she was seated at the organ. Music transformed her, albeit temporarily, into a wisp of pathetic passion. I could have been like that, Christina reminded herself. The thought reassured her and gave her enough strength to take her father's arm and begin the dignified walk down the aisle.

In the far distance in front of the altar were the backs of two tall men. One of them turned and her brother Simon smiled at her. His moustache, neatly trimmed, matched the smartness of his officer's khaki uniform. Monkton did not move. Her father led her to Monkton's side, then stepped up to lift his holy book and position himself in front of them.

'Dearly beloved brethren, we are gathered here together in the sight of God and in the face of his congregation to knit these parties together in holy matrimony which was instituted and authorized by God himself.'

It was then that Christina felt the hatred emanating from the man at her side. It was so strong, so passionate that all her panic returned. Somehow she managed to contain it, to push it down into the deep strong core she'd discovered in herself with the secret knowledge that for better or for worse she was glad of what she'd done.

Chapter Five

The immediate problem was that she might not be able to get into Aunty Murn's. Aunty Murn daren't let her in if Hugh Gordon, Aunty Murn's brother and Annalie's father, was in. Hugh Gordon was a bricklayer by trade, a big man, brown and weatherbeaten from working outside all the time. A quiet, plodding kind of man most of the time with a clay pipe jutting from underneath a big walrus moustache. He'd a violent temper when he was roused however, and when he discovered that Annalie was pregnant he had raged at her for disgracing the family and bringing shame on herself and everyone who knew her. There was no talking to him, no explaining. He had literally run her out of the house by the back of the neck and warned her she'd better never set foot over his door again, otherwise she would be flung bodily down the stairs not just run outside onto the landing.

Aunty Murn had tried to argue with him, tried to stop him putting her out, all to no avail. Later Aunty Murn had angrily told Annalie, 'He's a fine one to talk about disgracing the family. Him that's married that dirty tinker.'

Aunty Murn always referred to Saviana behind her brother's back as a dirty tinker. She didn't dare say a thing in front of his face. It was her revenge and it gave her a sense of satisfaction to allow Annalie to visit the house when her father was out either working or at the pub. She would never admit it, of course. Nor would she have admitted that she missed Annalie, especially since Annalie's two younger brothers had run away and joined up. Annalie could still hardly believe they had done such a thing. They were under age and barely out of school.

Cumberland Street cut across the end of Commercial Road, and reaching it Annalie joined the bustle of shoppers, mostly women wrapped in shawls like herself, though some from the more prosperous end of Cumberland Street wore

34

hats and coats. Cumberland was considered the best street in the Gorbals for shops. It ran across Main Street, along to the south of the busy Gorbals Cross. The busiest time at Gorbals Cross was on Sunday when all the Jewish shops were open and crowds of Jews, the men in traditional dress, gathered around the Cross to exchange news and views.

During the week the best place in the Gorbals to shop was, without doubt, Cumberland Street. There were drapers' shops, pawn shops, shoe shops, butcher shops, dairies, wool shops. Outside the wool shop at the Corner of Cumberland Street and Crown Street the men of the Salvation Army band played every Saturday Night. There were bakers' shops and fish shops, Co-operative shops, undertakers', and a pub at every corner. In between shops were the tunnel-like entrances of closes from which stairs at the back would lead up to the tenement flats, – or houses, as all dwelling places were known in Glasgow. At the back of some closes were also stairs leading down to dunnies where there was either access to a communal back yard or dungeon-like windowless houses, or both.

As Annalie turned into Aunty Murn's close she prayed that her father would not be in. Aunty Murn's two-roomed flat was her bolt hole now. Without it she felt she would go absolutely mad. She tried to feel grateful for the place that she had found to live after she had been flung out of Aunty Murn's but it was such a dreadful dump of a place it was impossible to manage it. And yet, without Mrs Rafferty, the woman who had taken her in and indeed had looked after her and even delivered her baby, she didn't know how she would have survived.

That day she had been put out she had no idea where she could go or what she could do. She'd wandered blindly along Cumberland Street. Then she'd turned down Commercial Road past the narrow Errol Street that branched off it on the left and Spring Lane on the right. There tenements backed onto each other, with washing strung from windows of one building to the back windows of the other. She had just reached the corner of where Rutherglen Road cut across Commercial Road with the B.B. Picture-

house at one side of the narrow Commercial Road and the
stables at the other. She had stopped, not knowing where
to go next, whether to cross Rutherglen Road and carry on
down the wider end of Commercial Road or walk down
Rutherglen Road with its clanging tramcars and rattling
horses and carts. Then suddenly Mrs Rafferty appeared
from the close next to the stables, the only close, in fact, in
that part of Commercial Road and just opposite the B.B.

By this time Annalie had started to cry and Mrs Rafferty
inquired sympathetically, 'What's up, hen?'

Annalie had blurted out the whole story.

'See men!' Mrs Rafferty said. 'Never mind, hen. You're
all right now.'

'All right,' Annalie echoed. 'How am I all right? I've no
money and nowhere to go.'

'Aye you have,' Mrs Rafferty said. 'You can stay with me
until you get on your feet.'

Annalie eyed the close from which Mrs Rafferty had
emerged. Having been brought up in Cumberland Street
she knew the area well. She and the other children who
lived nearby were particularly interested in this part of Commercial Road because of the stables. It was here the carters
stabled their horses. The entrance to the stables was actually
in Rutherglen Road, but they took up the whole corner.
She'd often peered down the dunny next to the stable
entrance in Rutherglen Road and this dunny in Commercial
Road. In both you could hear the noise of the horses and
even smell them, but she never had the nerve to venture
down the dark pits of stairway.

In response to Mrs Rafferty's reassuring 'Come on, hen.
Just follow me. You'll be all right' Annalie did as she was
told. There didn't seem to be any alternative. Both she and
Mrs Rafferty made a slow, groping descent into the inky,
foul- smelling blackness. At the foot of the stairs Mrs Rafferty turned left along a corridor. There was still no form
of lighting. There were no windows either because now
they were underneath the ground. Mrs Rafferty felt along
the wall until she came to the first door. Annalie learned
later that there were two or three other doors further along,

but they were used by shops for storage purposes. The woman opened her door and Annalie could see the faint glimmer of a gas lamp.

'Come on in, hen,' Mrs Rafferty said and led her into the small, windowless area that was home to her, her husband and eight children.

It had an uneven stone floor, rough stone walls, a black iron sink and fireplace and two hole-in-the-wall beds or what were supposed to be beds but looked more like shallow black caverns heaped with rags. The airless place reeked of horse dung, sweat, urine and stale cabbage. Annalie was appalled and sickened. Aunty Murn's place was always spotlessly clean and tidy.

'I was out looking for the weans,' Mrs Rafferty said. 'But och, they'll turn up soon enough I suppose. We might as well enjoy a wee bit of peace while we've the chance. I don't suppose you've a penny on you, hen? See the wee peep the gas is down to.'

Annalie fumbled in her pockets and produced a penny.

'Oh, here. You're a godsend so you are.'

Delighted, Mrs Rafferty went to the cupboard under the sink and fed the gas meter with the penny. Then she went over and turned the gas up.

'Take your shawl off. Make yourself at home, hen.'

Annalie looked bleakly around. The room was even worse with the gas turned up. A table in the centre of the floor was covered with newspapers and crowded with dirty dishes crusted with the remains of a variety of dinners, by the look of them. There was part of a loaf, an open packet of tea and a chipped enamel jug containing some milk in which small floating globules of yellow signalled it was already souring. The ceiling was low and black, and bulged down as if at any moment the stables above and the heavy Clydesdale horses would crash on their heads. Annalie felt suffocated and had a panic-stricken urge to run from the place. She would have done so had it not been for a sudden violent urge to vomit. She just reached the sink in time, her stomach muscles cramping, slamming together to throw up hot acrid vomit. Mrs Rafferty was unperturbed.

'I was the very same, hen. Spewed my guts out every day.'

Annalie would never forget that first night at the Raffertys', lying crushed among the Rafferty children, listening to the squeaking and scraping of the rats and not knowing exactly where they were in the pitch blackness. The next day she bought candles with her last few coppers. She lit them that night and found to her horror that the rats were all over the room. On the side of the sink, or as Mrs Rafferty called it, the jawbox, on top of the coal bunker, on the chairs, on the table. She even caught the shadow of one skulking low legged along the mantelshelf. She had wept with distress and fear. Despite the anguish of her feelings however, she had eventually collapsed into an exhausted sleep only to waken in the early hours with a heavy, hot feeling on her head. When she moved, by the light of the guttering candles she saw a rat slink along the pillow and realized that it had been lying on her head. She had jumped up screaming hysterically, wakening Mr and Mrs Rafferty, the twins Nellie and Theresa and the younger girl Mary who had been in the bed along with her, and the other children who had been sleeping on the floor. Everyone came crowding around her.

Mrs Rafferty inquired solicitously, 'Were you thinking the baby was coming, hen? I wouldn't worry if I was you. I don't think your time's near yet, and I should know.' She gave a hearty burst of laughter. Her body, which was like a pile of loose cushions under her nightie, wobbled in all directions.

Somehow Annalie managed to bring her hysteria under control and told them the cause of her distress. Mrs Rafferty said, 'It wouldn't have bitten you, hen. They're used to us.'

Annalie was outraged.

'Well I'm not used to them.'

There had been the odd scraping in the pot cupboard at Aunty Murn's in Cumberland Street in the past, but her daddy had soon put a cage in and caught the intruder, and Aunty Murn had spent the next day scouring the pots and scrubbing out the cupboard.

'You'll have to put cages down and catch them.' Annalie told the Raffertys.

'We haven't got any cages, hen.'

'I know where there's at least one,' Annalie said. 'Please try and get some more. Surely you can get one or two from somewhere or somebody.'

Mr Rafferty, as naked as the day he was born and not in the least self-conscious about it, said soothingly. 'If I have to tramp all the way to Ireland and back, I'll get your cages, hen.'

Patrick Rafferty worked as a navvy on the roads. He was a good-natured man when he was sober and even more good-natured when he was drunk, insisting on giving every-one a song. Mrs Rafferty, ever calm and philosophical, never seemed to upbraid him for wasting so much of his wages.

'He needs a drink,' she explained.

The rats had gone with the lighting of the gas and the stampeding of everybody coming to see what was wrong with Annalie.

'Leave the gas on, oh please,' Annalie pleaded.

'Och well,' said Mrs Rafferty. 'It's nearly time to get up now anyway.'

Mr Rafferty had been as good as his word and managed to get two cages in time for the next night. She had got one from Aunty Murn who had promised to ask around all the neighbours and see if she couldn't borrow another one or two. Aunty Murn had also given her a pile of pennies to make sure she could keep the gas on for the next few nights.

One cage was put in the cupboard under the sink, another in the cupboard beside the fireplace, another over beside the bunker and one under each bed. Before sleep claimed her Annalie heard the snap of the cages shutting and the squeaking and wild scraping at the bars. On subsequent nights more rats were caught until Mrs Rafferty assured her that they were all gone.

'At least the crowd we had,' she told Annalie. 'But there's always plenty more.'

So the cages were still put down every night. They still

caught rats, but at least the place was no longer overrun with them, or so Mrs Rafferty said. But Annalie could never feel sure. What upset her most, however, was having to bring up baby Elizabeth in the Raffertys' hovel. Elizabeth's rightful place was being brought up like a lady in Monkton House.

Annalie suffered agonies of spirit every time she returned to the dark dunny in Commercial Road, and every time she could hardly credit what had happened to her. Even before she'd ever met Adam Monkton she had always felt that she didn't belong in the Gorbals. She'd always nursed secret dreams of being a lady, of marrying a gentleman and bringing up her children as ladies and gentlemen. Despite the fact that her more sensible side told her that it was ridiculous, the romantic part of her nature still clung tenaciously to this dream.

The immediate struggle, however, was for survival. Somehow she had to get a job and earn enough money to feed herself and the baby. Pride would not allow her to continue living on charity from Aunty Murn and Mrs Rafferty, neither of whom could afford to be giving her anything.

Chapter Six

The wedding supper was a subdued affair. The fact that there was nothing stronger to drink than Ada Gillespie's home-made rhubarb wine might have contributed to the restrained atmosphere. It hardly seemed decent to the small party of wedding guests, however, to make very merry with the spectre of the dying father of the groom hovering over the wedding table.

The mother of the groom was not present. This seemed to confirm the rumour that she too was in a state of collapse. Was it any wonder, it was whispered at the table, that the bridegroom looked so stony faced? He was obviously making a brave attempt to hide his feelings from the assembled company. It came as no surprise when the minister announced that owing to the sad circumstances the usual speeches would be dispensed with. They would simply break bread and drink wine together before parting. He made it sound like the Last Supper. In truth, however, the meal could not be described as simple. Mrs Kelvin the cook had slaved conscientiously, not only for hours but for days as she explained to everyone, 'To do Miss Chrissie proud'. There was a boar's head garnished with aspic jelly, mayonnaised fowl, an ornamented tongue, an elaborate trifle, an epergne with fruit, an iced savoy cake and biscuits. The guests did justice to the meal, chatting in fairly subdued undertones while they ate, except old Mrs Monkton, the very one who ought to have been subdued considering it was her son who was at death's door. Dressed in an ancient, not at all respectable hat piled with enormous feathers, she gabbled away in her usual loud and common fashion. Beatrice Monkton had often bemoaned the fact to Ada Gillespie in private that her mother-in-law was as common as an Irish peat bog except that old Martha Monkton was a Glaswegian and proud of it.

'My man and I started our married life in a single end in the Gorbals and I don't care who knows it,' she was often heard to boast. Or 'I brought up our Moses in one room over a pawn shop in Cumberland Street and it never did him any harm.'

The fact that her husband Daniel died of tuberculosis at the age of forty-eight was always brushed aside with 'Och. He was never a strong man. Moses takes after me.'

Mrs Gillespie was hanging desperately onto her sympathetic expression as she listened to the horrors of Cousin Kate's latest operation. The bridegroom was talking, sometimes even smiling, with his best man. Only the bride and bride's father were silent.

Usually there was plenty of room at the long mahogany table in the manse dining room. This evening however, chairs had to be jammed as close as possible to each other and the starched white linen table cover was overcrowded with cutlery, china and glasses. Sometimes while Adam ate or when he turned to speak to Simon his arm or leg would brush against Christina, making her tremble.

After the meal, Christina made the first cut in the wedding cake. It sat in all its glory on a small table in a corner of the room, its pristine whiteness glowing through the shadows. It was Mrs Kelvin's pride and joy and represented much energetic stirring and beating and patient tongue-chewing efforts with the piping and icing sugar to create the loops and lovers' knots and rosettes that made the many decorations. She had carried the cake upstairs herself, helped by the maids Gladys and Millie. The small table had been covered in readiness with a hand-made lace tablecloth. They had stood for some time admiring the ornate confection topped with its china replica of a bride and groom standing stiffly under an arch of sugar rosebuds. Mrs Kelvin's only regret was that the cake could not have been set to more advantage under a gas light. The only gas light in the room however, was a central one over the dining table and even that was not as bright as Mrs Kelvin would have liked it.

The cake was eventually returned to the kitchen to be

42

expertly cut into pieces and put into individual coloured bags with drawstring tops to be given to each guest to take home with them. Mrs Kelvin said she'd probably just managed to make the cake in time. Rumour had it that sugar was going to be scarce. If Christina had been getting married this time next year a cake would perhaps have been impossible, although no one really believed that the war could last that long. As the guests took their leave and their bag of cake, good wishes were given like condolences. Then everyone had gone and the manse sank further into its funeral gloom. Simon kissed her, her mother held her in her arms while giving her a comforting pat on the back, then she released her with one of her brave 'have courage' looks and a sympathetic squeeze of Christina's arm. Her father shook her solemnly by the hand.

She had already discarded her veil and headdress and now her mother put a coat over her shoulders, saying, 'You've probably caught your death of cold already dear, going round to the church wearing only that dress.'

Clutching the coat collar round her throat with one hand and struggling to hold up the train of the wedding dress with the other, Christina left the manse with Adam to walk along Queen's Drive to Monkton House. Nothing was said between them nor did Christina expect anything to be said in the teeth of the blustering wind that kept throwing sharp pellets of sleet in their faces. It was as much as she could do to concentrate on keeping a grip of her coat.

The maid Doris opened the door to them and after a respectful bob said, 'The master wants to see you, sir.'

Christina followed Adam up the stairs. Unlike the manse this hall and stairway were brightly lit with a crystal chandelier. The woodwork was painted white and made a startling contrast against the crimson and fawn floral-patterned carpet. All the doors had china door handles and finger plates decorated with dainty bunches of flowers. Paintings in heavy gold frames decorated the wall of the stairs and a small table was cluttered with Staffordshire ornaments. In the master bedroom it was also obvious that Beatrice's taste prevailed. The main pieces of furniture, the wardrobe, chest of drawers, dressing table and wash stand were relatively plain and functional. The dominant feature in the room, however, was the colourful drapery covering windows, cushions, chairs, quilts, the frill along the front of the mantelshelf and the fringed linen runners on top of the chest of drawers and dressing table. All of this combined with a patterned wallpaper and a profusion of ornaments made the effect overwhelming. The dressing table in particular reflected Beatrice Monkton's taste with its sumptuous display of accessories in cut glass and richly decorated silver. Over in the cast-iron bedstead Moses Monkton, propped up with pillows, looked out of place among the feminine clutter. His coarse features had taken on a grotesque twist like a brown gargoyle against the ivory satin pillow.

'Is that the pair of you wed then?' he asked as soon as they entered the room, his mouth working hard to push the words out.

'Yes.' Christina said. 'Everything's all right now.'

'Huh!' Adam gave a sarcastic laugh. 'You think so?'

'Remember your father's condition,' Christina whispered. Adam laughed again.

'Oh, I suspect father will live for many a long year yet. He wants to live and he always gets what he wants, one way or another.'

'I'd like to be here to see my grandchildren. That's true enough.'

Christina found it distressing to watch the painful contortions of her father-in-law's mouth.

Adam said, 'Yes, so you can make sure the business of Monkton Builders continues.'

'What's wrong with that?' Moses wanted to know. 'I've worked hard enough to build it up.'

'You've not to get excited,' Christina warned. 'Maybe we'd better go now and let you rest.'

'Where's Beatrice? If she's stopped having her hysterics send her in.'

'I'm sorry she's been so upset,' Christina said. 'I'll try to make it up to her.'

Adam raised an inquiring brow. 'In what way? By having the marriage annulled?'

Moses glared over at his son and it was a second or two before he managed to chew words out. 'You behave yourself, do you hear? It's high time you settled down.'

'Good night, Mr Monkton,' Christina said hastily.

The first thing Christina noticed about the bedroom she was to share with Adam was the two single beds. She was deeply shocked. Never before had she either seen or heard of a married couple who did not share a double bed.

Adam saw her helpless stare and while loosening his tie remarked, 'My choice. All at my own expense, and worth it.'

Tears gathered and became a dead weight in Christina's chest. She removed the coat from her shoulders and hung it away in the wardrobe. At the side of the wardrobe lay her suitcase that Gladys had brought round from the manse the day before. Christina felt ashamed that Gladys would have seen the beds, then it occurred to her that the maid would probably not have been allowed to come upstairs. The case would have been handed to Doris, who would have taken it to the bedroom. This did not, however, make Christina feel any better. She knew only too well the gossip grapevine among the servants.

The dark, masculine decor of the room closed in on her. She felt an unwelcome intruder in a stranger's very private place. It was panelled in dark oak on which hung a few sporting prints. The carpet was patterned in black, grey and rust, and above the heavy ornate fireplace a glass case displayed two long-barrelled pistols. On the mantelshelf under the case was a row of silver cups and trophies for a variety of sports. Books crammed a flat desk. Beside them lay a folded copy of the *Glasgow Herald*, a box of cigars and a pair of cigar scissors, a brass ashtray and a pen holder. At one side of the fireplace sat a black leather winged and deeply buttoned armchair and matching footstool. Close to the arm of the chair there was a small, round, three-legged table on top of which lay a whisky decanter, a crystal glass

45

and an ashtray on which a half-smoked cigar had been stubbed out.

The fire had been lit and was crackling with logs but Christina could feel no heat. She was aware however of the pungent mixture of wood and cigar smoke. She felt it invade her nostrils, her mouth, her clothes. Eyes lowered she began to fumble with the row of tiny buttons down the back of her dress. She knew it wasn't possible for her to undo them all and she longed for Gladys and the familiar routine of the manse.

She wondered about the propriety of sending for Doris to help her but didn't have enough courage to risk Adam's displeasure. He was unbuttoning his shirt with swift confident movements. As he removed it and she saw his broad-chested, muscular body she was reminded of the time they had made love, the surprising gentleness of his touch and the comfort as well as the thrill of being in his arms. The tentative thought came to her that his most passionate feelings had been aroused by seeing her undressed. Perhaps he would have the same reaction now. Her breathing quickened with the thought.

'Adam . . .' Her voice sounded tremulous despite her efforts to calm it. 'Could you help me take this dress off, please?'

His eyes held hers as he walked across the room, came behind her and stood very close. She felt the heat of his hands move up over her shoulders to the nape of her neck, then suddenly he jerked at the dress with both hands, ripping it down the back until with a final wrench it slithered over her hips and onto the floor at her feet. Then he went over and picked up a robe that was lying across his bed.

Putting it on, he said, 'I'm going for a bath now, I'll expect you to be in bed out of my way when I return.'

Chapter Seven

The kitchen in the two-roomed flat in Cumberland Street was so small that Annalie had to twist sideways to move around it. She sat down in one of the spar-backed chairs that crowded round the table. There were two other bigger chairs, one on either side of the fireplace, a high-backed leather winged or leather lugged chair as it was more commonly called. It was her father's favourite. Its leather had a myriad of hairline cracks from continual usage. The other was a wooden rocking chair on which bulged a large cushion embroidered with purple thistles and green stems. This was the one used by Aunty Murn. When the boys were young they loved to play horses on it, rock it wildly back and forward, whipping it and clicking their teeth at it as if they were riding a Derby winner. Aunty Murn always boxed their ears with the warning, 'If you break that chair I'll murder you. Your life'll not be worth tuppence.'

A dark green horsehair sofa in front of the hole-in-the-wall recessed bed, as these small areas so often found in Glasgow tenements were called, had been used many a time by Annalie as a stepping stone to reach up onto the piled-high mattresses. If it was a very cold, draughty night Aunty Murn would pull the brown chenille bedcurtains across the front of the bed and Annalie would feel cosy and warm cuddling into Aunty Murn's back. Davie and Eddie slept in with their daddy in the front-room bed. Annalie thought longingly of Aunty Murn's bed. Everything about the place had become so much more precious. She savoured the black fireplace that Aunty Murn had polished with such energy, attacking the iron parts with a brush and black lead, and the steel edges with emery paper. The brass fender and the antimacassar-shaped brass fronting to the mantel-shelf were sparkling after her labours with Brasso. On top of the mantelshelf sat Aunty Murn's fat toby jugs, an alarm clock, a dish of spills to light the gas mantle and a red toffee tin in which she kept the rent money. A square wad of cloth, hung from the corner of the mantelshelf, was always used when lifting the kettle off the fire. On the opposite wall above the coal-shelf on which perched Aunty Murn's china dogs. It always seemed to Annalie that there was a look of Aunty Murn herself about these ornaments. It was the way their heads stretched so high on top of such rigid backs. Their marley blue and white colour also reminded her of Aunty Murn's favourite wrap-around apron. The dogs sat at either side of the shelf and in between them were displayed two china soup tureens in a rusty fawn pattern, with some dinner plates to match.

Annalie watched with darkening eyes as Aunty Murn poured boiling water from the kettle into the brown enamel teapot.

'I should have gone, I wish I'd never listened to you.'

'Havers! If you hadn't listened to me, my girl, you wouldn't be sitting there happy as a bug in a rug. You would be behind bars.'

'Happy? Me? What have I got to be happy about?'

Aunty Murn marched over to the sink and refilled the kettle from the swan-necked tap. She then replaced it on the fire before thumping her big body down at the table beside Annalie.

'You've only got yourself to blame.'

'I should have gone today,' Annalie repeated. 'And presented her with the baby and given her a right showing up.'

'Give yourself a showing up, more like. What were you thinking of, lassie? It was bad enough working in that house for a start knowing how your daddy felt about the Monktons. He's never forgiven Monkton for sacking him like that without a minute's notice.'

'Where else could I have got a job? All the other mistresses didn't like the look of me. One of them told me to my face. Just didn't like the look of me, she said. I wouldn't have got started in the Monkton place if it hadn't been for the old woman. She wasn't so bad, Adam's granny.'

Aunty Murn shook her head. 'It's always stuck in your

daddy's throat. And then for you to go and let that man put a hand on you and disgrace yourself.'

'I loved him and he loved me.'

'Havers,' Aunty Murn scoffed. 'He took you for a right fool. He's no fool, though. He's brains to burn, that one, brains to burn,' Aunty Murn repeated.

In a sudden rush of bitterness Annalie said, 'I know where I'd like to burn him.'

'Watch your tongue.' Aunty Murn gave a knowing glance over at the sleeping child in the bed. 'Walls have ears.'

'She's only a few weeks old, for goodness' sake. I should've taken her with me today and handed her to that woman.'

'What would you be spoiling the lassie's wedding day for? It wasn't the minister's lassie that got you into the family way. Now drink up your tea and get out of here before your daddy comes home.'

'He doesn't love her,' Annalie said. 'He loves me.'

'Will you never learn?' Aunty Murn said. 'I can see you still being as daft as this when you're ninety, if you live that long.'

'He told me he did.'

'And if he told you the moon was made of green cheese you would have believed him as well, I suppose.'

'It's me he should have been marrying today.'

'How many times have I got to tell you?' Aunty Murn's voice strained with exasperation. 'Masters never marry servants. Never. Do you hear me? It just never happens. And never will.'

'The minister's daughter of all people,' Annalie said half to herself. 'She and her mother used to visit Monkton House, you know. Many a time I've served her coffee in the morning or afternoon tea, and never a moment did I suspect. You would have thought butter wouldn't melt in her mouth the way she sat there. Such a good Christian. Such a good daughter sitting there saying 'yes Mother, no Mother, three bags full Mother', her eyes lowered and her hands clasped demurely on her lap. The sly two-faced bitch.'

'Your tongue'll strangle you yet. The minister's daughter sounds like a real lady, which is more than you are my girl, or ever will be.'

'I will so!' Annalie gave an indignant toss of her head. 'I will. Do you hear?'

'There you go again, Annalie,' Aunty Murn said. 'Blethering a lot of nonsense. Your head's full of fairy tales. You've always been the same. The trouble with you is you've read too much. Your nose always in a book, even when you were a wee lassie. I knew it would come to no good.'

Annalie sighed. 'I've been looking for a job.'

'Aye, and fat chance you've got. Without a character and a baby to look after into the bargain.'

'Mrs Rafferty said she would help look after Elizabeth.'

'Oh aye. She's got nothing else to do, I suppose. I wouldn't trust that wee bachle with a dog.'

'She's awful kind.'

'She's just plain awful, you mean.'

'I've heard they're needing girls to sort rags over in the coffin works.' Annalie said. The coffin works was aptly named because of its shape and because it backed on to the Gorbals Graveyard.

'Well, I suppose it'd be better than nothing. But mind you'd have to wear every stitch you possess and a lot more besides if you want to survive the cold in there. I've an old pair of woollen gloves you could have. The fingers are all frayed but I could cut them off and make them presentable as mittens.'

'Thanks, Aunty Murn. At least it would be quite handy.' Annalie said. 'Being on that end of Commercial Road. It would only take a few minutes to get there and get back to Mrs Rafferty's at night.'

'Aye, well . . .' Aunty Murn said. 'Drink up your tea.'

Annalie took a drink of the comforting beverage and then nursed the warm cup between her palms.

'It's an awful thought going there though, after me being used to better things. Monkton House was such a lovely place.'

'Well I've said it before and I'll say it again, you've only got yourself to blame.'

Annalie sighed. 'No word from Mammy?'

Aunty Murn cast her eyes heavenwards. 'What good do you think she'd do you? She's no better than any of the dirty tinkers she roams the country with. What your daddy saw in her I'll never know. He must have had a brainstorm.'

'You know fine she's a gypsy, not a tinker.'

'Six and half a dozen. What good could she have done you?'

'If she'd known I'd needed help she would have taken me away and seen that I got a decent roof over my head.'

'Huh!' Aunty Murn scoffed. 'Your imagination will be the death of you, yet. What roof could she have given you, may I ask? A worm-eaten old caravan full of dirty tinkers for company. That's all she could have given you, my girl.' Aunty Murn tugged her apron down for extra emphasis. 'But if she had found out you were in trouble she would have run an extra mile, more like.'

'Nobody's ever given her a chance, and Daddy never gave her her place. He's let you rule the roost right from the start. That's why she keeps going away.'

Aunty Murn banged her cup down onto the table, making tea leap up and splash over. She rose to her full five feet ten inches and pointed towards the kitchen door.

'Out.' She was a formidable character with her rock-like features, wiry grey hair screwed back in a massive bun and her big-boned figure solidly encased in corsets.

'I'm going, don't you worry,' Annalie said, but didn't move. Aunty Murn busied herself getting a cloth from the sink and mopping up the spilled tea on the table.

Annalie sighed. 'It's terrible in that place in Commercial Road. The horses have better conditions in the stables.'

'You've made your bed, now you'll just have to lie on it.'

Reluctantly Annalie rose and went over to collect the baby from the bed. She tucked it into the big tartan plaid, then wrapped the other end firmly round herself, pinning the baby's warm body against her own.

'Well, I suppose I'd better go.'

51

'Aye,' said Aunty Murn. 'And just you remember. It was me that brought you and your two wee brothers up while that dirty tinker was stravaging away all over the country. Not that any of the three of you've been any credit to me. You getting yourself into trouble and the two of them running off to the army.'

'Have you told the recruiting place that the twins were under age?' Annalie asked.

'Of course I have. And a lot of help they were. They said the boys would be in France by now and them hardly out of school. I'll give them France when I get my hands on them.'

'Have you any candles about the place you could give me, Aunty Murn? That place in Commercial Road's like the pit of hell.'

'If your daddy comes in and finds you here he'll bring the roof down. But already she was squeezing her way sideways into the cupboard in the corner between the fireplace and the window. The door of the cupboard could only half open without moving Aunty Murn's fireside chair.

'Here's three.' She stuffed the candles into Annalie's bag then saw her to the door.

'Haste ye back,' she said automatically, forgetting that Annalie wasn't supposed to come at all.

Annalie didn't kiss her as she would have kissed her mother. Aunty Murn wasn't a kissing kind of person. The door closed abruptly and Annalie trailed away forlornly down the stairs and out into Cumberland Street. Turning left outside Aunty Murn's close she reluctantly made her way towards Commercial Road. On the corner of Cumberland Street was a wet fish shop, so called because the fish had been freshly caught. At the other corner was the police station. The first thing in Commercial Road on the side wall of the fish shop was a big advert proclaiming the big picture now showing in the B.B. Picturehouse further along the road. J.J. Bennet was the founder and sole proprietor of the B.B. Pictures and one of the pioneers of the Saturday matinees. He had acquired a hall like a huge warehouse with windows all round from the Good Templars Association in the Gorbals and from there in Commercial Road he launched his 'bright and beautiful' pictures. Hundreds of children were squeezed into the hall on Saturday afternoons. Annalie remembered the crush and excitement when she had been young. Mr Bennet went round pulling down all the blinds to shut out the light. When he came to the last blind a huge roar went up because everyone knew the pictures were about to go on. First, though, Mr Bennet always came on the stage and led the mass of children in song:

> 'B.B. Pictures, they're all right,
> Come and see them every night,
> We will sing with all our might,
> B.B. Pictures, they're all right.'

Sunday was the day she was dressed up in her best white starched pinafore, and with boots that had been energetically polished by Aunty Murn she set off proudly to Sunday school. If her mammy was at home she would brush Annalie's hair and polish it with a silk scarf until it gleamed and she'd say, 'You're a real lady so you are. A real lady if ever I saw one, dearie.'

Thinking of her mother brought a pain of longing. Despite all that Aunty Murn said, Annalie thought her mother to be not only a warm, loving and caring person, but absolute magic.

Memories of her were not only laced with kisses and cuddles, but with wafts of heady perfume, the jangle of golden earrings and the dazzle of brightly coloured clothes. It had been her mother who had filled her head with tales of Cinderellas being transformed into princesses and handsome princes always coming to the rescue in times of trouble.

Her mother had once read her palm and with a husky mysterious voice had told her that she saw a big house. 'That's where you belong, dearie, and with a handsome gentleman by your side. Oh, handsome as a prince he is. Yes, that's where you belong, dearie. I see you as such a fine lady by this gentleman's side and he loves you more than anyone else in the whole world. You mark my words. It's your destiny to be loved by this man.'

She had only been a little girl of twelve at the time and still at school when her mother had told her fortune. She had been so hypnotized by her mother's great dark eyes she had never forgotten it. Her mother was the seventh daughter of a seventh daughter and so had been born for the *dukkerin*. *Dukkerin* was the Romany word for fortune telling.

Now the big house had evaporated as if it had never been anything more than a dream, and with it had gone the handsome prince.

Annalie prayed every night for her mother's return. Her mother's magic would surely make everything all right. She longed to have her fortune told again.

Chapter Eight

It was unbearable for Annalie to think about Monkton's wedding night, yet she could think of nothing else. In her mind's eye she saw Christina and Adam undressing each other, caressing each other, making love to one another in a comfortable feather bed in Monkton House.

She tossed and turned in the hole-in-the-wall bed in Commercial Road which caused the Rafferty twins to moan and groan in sleepy protest and kick out at her. Mrs Rafferty was awakened by the noise and thrashing about.

'Is there anything wrong, hen?' she called round from the next bed.

'He got married today,' Annalie said.

'Were you fond of him, hen?'

'I loved him.' Her voice grew louder with defiance. 'And he loved me.'

'Wheesht,' Mrs Rafferty said. 'You'll waken the weans.' They both knew there was no danger of wakening Patrick Rafferty who lay snoring deeply by Mrs Rafferty's side. There were three kinds of labourer, she had explained to Annalie, the digger, the hod carrier and the cement mixer, and the digger was the hardest worked of the lot. That was why Mr Rafferty was so exhausted and always slept so soundly, although Annalie could have said, but didn't, that Mr Rafferty never seemed too tired to make love to his wife judging by the rhythmic bumping and creaking of the bed every night.

'I can't bear it,' Annalie said. 'I can't believe this has happened to me.'

'I'll get up and make us a wee cup of tea,' Mrs Rafferty said.

'I'm sorry to have wakened you,' Annalie said.

'Och, I wasn't asleep.'

Annalie propped herself up on one elbow and watched

by the feeble flickering light of the candle as Mrs Rafferty's shapeless figure emerged from the next bed, scratching with both hands, heaving up and down and wobbling about. Bedbugs had been almost as bad a problem as the rats. Annalie had rubbed paraffin all over the walls in the cavity bed where she slept, but Mr Rafferty had objected to her doing the same in his.

'That stink'll gas the pair of us as well as the bugs,' he protested.

'The fire's still red. I'll give it a bit of a poke up and it'll soon bring the kettle back to the boil.'

It took a bit of manoeuvring to climb over the truckle beds and squeeze round the side of the table. Annalie struggled into a sitting position.

'I could have made it. I'm sorry to be causing you so much trouble.'

'Trouble?' Mrs Rafferty laughed. 'What trouble can you be after all this lot?'

Taking care to avoid the child sleeping on the stone floor in front of the fire Mrs Rafferty managed to reach for the poker and ease it between the bars of the grate. Some cinder clanged into the ashpan underneath.

'Funny how everything sounds louder at night,' she remarked, nestling the kettle down among the red embers.

'If he'd known he'd never have married her.'

'How do you mean, hen? Known what?'

'About me having his baby.'

Mrs Rafferty laughed again.

'You're an awful lassie. You're living in cloud-cuckoo-land, hen.'

'He loved me. I know he did.'

'Och. They all say that.'

Annalie rubbed her hands wildly through her hair. Hair about which Mrs Rafferty had often remarked wistfully, 'You've enough hair for two folk on that head of yours.' Mrs Rafferty's own hair was very scant and straight and hardly worth tying back because it always escaped to hang in limp strands around her face.

'If he had known it would have been different,' Annalie insisted.

Mrs Rafferty put tea in the pot and filled it with the boiling water.

'Listen, hen, half the weans running about Glasgow are weans like yours. Have you ever heard of a master marrying a maid? Now tell me, have you?'

They sat in silence for a moment before Annalie managed to speak.

'He was different.'

'No he wasnae, hen. The quicker you realize that, the better you'll get on. You've your own life to live.'

'I'll have to take that job in the coffin works. I can't live off you for nothing. You've enough on your plate.'

'Now I'm no rushing you, hen. Something better might turn up if you give yourself time to have a good look around.'

'Without a reference? No. Anyway I can't take anything with too long hours or anything that's too far away and certainly not living in, even if I got the chance. Not when I've got the baby to consider.'

'Now you know I can look after wee Betty.'

Annalie opened her mouth to correct Mrs Rafferty but didn't have the heart. All the same it annoyed her to hear her daughter called Betty. She had been christened Elizabeth and that's what she wanted the girl to be called. It annoyed her even more when Mrs Rafferty called her Annie instead of Annalie. She had corrected her several times about that.

'I'll go over to the coffin works tomorrow.'

'Well, I can't deny I'll be glad of the extra shilling or two for your keep. As I say, I wasn't rushing you, hen.'

The coffin works was a terrible comedown. She had worn two smart uniforms at Monkton House, one cotton dress for mornings and a black dress with a frilly apron and a perky frill of a cap with two ribbons dangling down the back for afternoon wear. She'd had room to breathe in Monkton House. The coffin works, like everywhere in the Gorbals, was overcrowded. There was not only a crush of people, there was a vast sea of old clothing waiting to be sorted, being sorted, having been sorted, ever moving, ever increasing waves of rags threatening to drown the human sorters. The air was choked with dust and wool fibre and constantly reverberated with the sound of coughing. The long high-ceilinged building with its rough stone floor had no heating whatsoever. Annalie was forced to copy the other women and wrap herself up with as many clothes as she could lay her hands on. The cold, however, could seep through woollen cardigans, woollen socks, woollen mufflers, woollen gloves until, at the end of each day, everyone was blue and stiff as if they were encased in icy water. The only consolation for Annalie was that she didn't have far to go after her day's work was finished. A few minutes along Commercial Road took her back to the tunnel of a close and the dunny where Mrs Rafferty would have a hot cup of tea waiting for her.

Annalie still clung to the idea of taking the baby and tracking Monkton down either at his home or office or building site. She still treasured the dream that it all had been a misunderstanding and once Adam knew of her predicament he would, like the handsome prince in so many of her mother's stories, come and whisk her away. But more and more she was becoming uncertain and confused.

The coffin works exhausted her spiritually and emotionally as well as physically. Returning to the Raffertys' windowless cave of a room, packed and noisy with children, did nothing to alleviate her tiredness and depression. It was as much as she could do to bind the baby to her in the plaid and go along to Aunty Murn's in the hope of getting a few minutes' peace and a proper wash. She could never have a wash down in the Raffertys' place because of Mr Rafferty being there or his brood of growing and ever curious male offspring.

Sometimes though, after Annalie had trailed round to Cumberland Street and up the stair, Aunty Murn would come to the door and flap her hands in silent command for Annalie to go. This meant that Hugh Gordon was in. After Aunty Murn had shut the door again, Annalie often sat down on the stairs for a while. It took all her effort not to weep with disappointment and fatigue. The thought of returning to Commercial Road and descending into the blackness under the stables was unbearable. She longed for her own flesh and blood in the form of her brothers. She and the boys had been very close. They confided in her and she confided in them. They comforted and supported one another. It was three of them against the world. She wept with the pain of missing them and the normal routine of life they had once enjoyed together, the safe haven they'd shared in what had once been their home. Sometimes she wept remembering, and the baby sensing her distress, would weep along with her. Then she would cover the tear-stained face with kisses and make soothing noises and rock with it to and fro until they both felt comforted.

Things became worse instead of better when Mr Rafferty was persuaded to go away and fight for King and Country. It wasn't what the newspapers and magazines said that persuaded him. When Mr Rafferty had read things about the Germans being the Frankenstein of iniquity, hideous monsters whose fangs dripped with the blood of millions, the cruel, pitiless, ruthless, murderous Hun, he'd say, 'Now what would you make of that? And us having had such a good help from Mr Steinbeck?' Mr Steinbeck was a German-born owner of a local grocer's shop and had been kind to them when Mr Rafferty had been unemployed and Mrs Rafferty had no money to pay for food. It hadn't been Lord Kitchener's words either. 'Be honest with yourself,' the posters had commanded. 'Be certain that your so-called reason is not a selfish excuse. Enlist today.' It hadn't even been the many parades of khaki heroes, as they were known, headed by their recruiting sergeant. Nor the military bands playing with great gusto in Glasgow Green to drum up recruiting enthusiasm. What had made Mr Rafferty march in anger to the recruiting office and take the King's shilling was a middle-class woman in furs who had come up to him in the street and presented him for all to see with a white feather, at the same time telling him that he ought to be ashamed of his cowardice. Mrs Rafferty was pregnant again and vomiting violently from morning to night.

'This is the worst one yet,' she told Annalie. 'I feel fit for nothing.' Indeed this was the case because nothing was done. The children became completely undisciplined. They swarmed about the floor, the stairs, the streets like an army of cockroaches, impossible to catch. Despite her exhaustion and depression Annalie struggled to help as much as she could. She lit the gas in the morning and made the tea. She spread hunks of bread for the children's breakfast and saw that they were dressed and ready for school before she left for work. She was becoming increasingly anxious about leaving baby Elizabeth. Not that she believed that Mrs Rafferty would purposely neglect her or be unkind, but Mrs Rafferty had to spend so much time running to hang over the sink. The worry was what the children might do to Elizabeth while Mrs Rafferty's back was turned. It didn't bear thinking about.

Dealing with Mrs Rafferty's problems had become overwhelming. And Annalie often thought, lying awake in the stuffy earthy smelling bed, that she could never allow Adam Monkton to see her in the state she was in now. She had too much pride for that. Even if she saw her father coming along the road she always hid in a close until he passed so that he wouldn't see her in the dirty neglected state to which she'd been reduced. She was painfully conscious of her stained and matted shawl, frayed fingerless gloves and down-at-heel boots showing under her shabby skirts. To add to her distress and exhaustion baby Elizabeth began screaming every night. Annalie became distracted, worrying about whether the baby was ill or one of the Rafferty children had been tormenting her or whether or not she'd been fed properly. It became more and more agonizing to leave her every day and go to work.

After one particularly bad night, Annalie couldn't bear it any longer. She went to work as usual, but before very long slipped out again and hurried back across Commercial Road. She flew into the close but had to slow her pace when she reached the dunny. Descending into the inky blackness her feet had to shuffle to feel for each step. And also to stamp as noisily as she could in an attempt to chase away any rats. On reaching the bottom her hand fumbled along the damp wall of the corridor until she came to the first door. She could hear the baby's sobs before she opened it. There were other sounds too. A man's voice was raised in anger and Mrs Rafferty's had a pleading tone. Annalie made straight for the bed and snatched up the baby.

'What's going on?' she asked Mrs Rafferty while trying to soothe and comfort Elizabeth. 'Who's this?' She jerked her head in the direction of the man.

'It's Mr Fintry, hen. The factor. I'm a wee bit behind in my rent with Patrick going away like that. What I get from the army isn't that much. Separation Allowance the army calls it. More like Starvation Money. I was trying to explain to Mr Fintry the rent swallows up most of that. And having to keep the gas on all the time eats up an awful lot of pennies. We're spending a fortune on candles as well, aren't we, hen? I don't know how we're going to pay this increase.'

'Increase?' Annalie jeered. 'For this dump? You should be paying us to live in it!'

'You won't be living in it,' the factor said. 'If she doesn't pay what she owes.'

He was a weed of a man with an undulating shape, a narrow slit of a mouth and steel-framed spectacles.

'I'd like to see *your* house,' Annalie flung at him. 'I bet you don't need to put up with rats and bugs and stinking cesspools.'

He started towards the door but turned back to say, 'I'm giving you two more days and when I come back then you'd better have the money, otherwise I'm sending the bailiffs in. We'll soon see if you like sleeping in the streets any better.'

Chapter Nine

By some miracle of good fortune Annalie managed to slip back into the coffin works without the gaffer seeing her. She hardly knew what she was doing for the rest of the day, however, so abstracted was she by the latest of Mrs Rafferty's problems. At the end of the day she hurried back along Commercial Road, but had to wait until one of the carters manoeuvred his giant Clydesdale horses up the ramp and into the stables beside the lemonade factory. The horses pulled huge two-tiered lorries, their feathered hooves slipping and stamping on the steep ramp. The driver sat high up in the centre front while a boy sat at the back to guard against any of the bottles of lemonade being stolen.

Annalie managed to get past. Commercial Road was narrow from Cumberland Street until it reached Rutherglen Road. Once it crossed Rutherglen Road it became much wider until, at its widest, it reached Adelphi Street and the River Clyde. Apart from Mrs Rafferty's close all the other dingy and dilapidated-looking buildings were used for commercial purposes and stables. Annalie supposed even the B.B. Picturehouse almost opposite the close could be classed as commercial premises, although it gave so much pleasure to so many people. Already a queue had formed outside the door of the B.B. awaiting entry to the evening's performance. As Annalie reached the close a tramcar clanged along Rutherglen Road, blocked that end of Commercial Road and disgorged more people to join the queue. There was a Charlie Chaplin film showing and he was everybody's favourite. There was nothing like a good laugh to make you forget your troubles and cheer you up. Annalie would have far rather been going into the B.B. to see Charlie Chaplin than down the dunny to Mrs Rafferty. However, she had no choice.

As she entered the close and carefully descended into

the dunny she could hear bursts of high-pitched whinnying and the clomping, clattering and slithering of horses' hoofs. The smell of dung mixed with the fousty stench of damp earth clogged her nostrils.

When she reached the single end she found Mrs Rafferty retching over the sink and the children creating bedlam all over the floor, the beds and even on top of the coal bunker. Mrs Rafferty straightened up with an exhausted sigh and wiped her mouth with the back of her sleeve. Sweat glistened on her brow and matted strands of hair plastered against her face.

'I'm that done out,' she told Annalie, then as an aside to one of the twins, 'Nellie, give the wean a wee bit nurse, hen. That'll maybe quieten her.'

But Annalie had already reached the baby who was being bounced about at the back of the bed as a result of the energetic wrestling of two of the boys at the front of it. She punched them aside and pulled the baby into her arms.

Elizabeth was crying with terrible broken-hearted hiccoughing wails and seemed to gaze up at Annalie with broken-hearted reproach.

'This won't do,' Annalie said to Mrs Rafferty. 'I'm sorry, but this just won't do.'

'What do you mean, hen?' Mrs Rafferty said, scratching under her bosom with one hand and pouring a cup of tea with the other.

'My baby's not happy,' said Annalie.

'I know fine how she feels,' Mrs Rafferty said. 'I'm not very happy myself, hen. Will I pour you a cup?'

Annalie nodded and sat down at the table, hugging the baby, patting her back and rubbing her cheek against her own. At last Elizabeth quietened down, her eyes closed and in a few seconds she was asleep with exhaustion, her head lolling against Annalie's shoulder. Annalie swallowed down a mouthful of tea.

'I'll have to find another place.'

Mrs Rafferty's faded blue eyes looked stricken. She stared at Annalie in loose-jawed silence.

'Don't worry, I'll stay until you have the baby,' Annalie

said hastily. 'And I'll give you a few shillings extra to help you clear your arrears. As soon as I finish my tea I'm away along to ask Aunty Murn to keep her eye open for somewhere.'

'You're quite right, hen.' Mrs Rafferty heaved a shuddering sigh. 'I don't blame you.'

Impulsively, Annalie bent forward and kissed the older woman on the cheek.

'I'm sorry,' she said. Tears welled up in Mrs Rafferty's eyes. She rose and, clumsy because of her swollen belly, knocked against the table and nearly overturned her chair.

'Oh, see you!' She smacked one of the boys across the head. 'You'll be the death of me yet.'

As quickly as she could, Annalie tucked the baby into her shawl and left the house. The queue at the B.B. was still standing outside. A shabby man with a flat bunnet on his head and a white scarf knotted round his collarless throat was singing 'It's a Long Way to Tipperary' and rattling teaspoons against his knee as a musical accompaniment. Some of the queue were joining in the singing. As Annalie went along towards the Cumberland Street end she thought with longing of the small toffee shop in Earl Street and was sorely tempted to spend a penny on a bag of home-made toffee balls. It was a treat in itself just to walk along Errol Street and loiter at the window and around the door of the shop to savour the sweet aroma. Another smell in Errol Street was enjoyable in its own way. That came from the kipper-smoking factory. On pay day sometimes she had a kipper for her tea. She might have treated herself to a cake of toffee or a kipper today had it not been for her promise to help Mrs Rafferty clear the money she owed the factor.

I'll never get out of the bit if I stay there, she thought bitterly. I'll have to find somewhere. She prayed that her father would be out having a drink at the pub with his friends. There were plenty of pubs to choose from, one at nearly every corner in the Gorbals, not that her father overindulged in drink, but as Aunty Murn said, a man deserves a wee refreshment after working so hard. Aunty

Murn always maintained that her brother was a well-doing, hard-working man except for the time he had his brainstorm and married his dirty tinker, Saviana.

Annalie, unlike her Aunty Murn, could well understand why he had married her. Saviana was an exceptionally good-looking woman with her black hair and bold, dark eyes. She had a way of walking that turned all men's eyes in her direction. It was a kind of provocative swinging of the hips and tossing of the head and sideways glances that seemed to promise wicked excitement. Everything about her was exciting, different and entrancing.

Annalie felt quite faint as she climbed the stairs to Aunty Murn's house. She'd had nothing to eat since the slice of bread and cheese eaten in the coffin works in the middle of the day. She waited with eyes closed, holding her breath and praying after she knocked on Aunty Murn's door.

When it was opened Aunty Murn said, 'You just missed him. You can come in for a minute or two.'

Annalie headed automatically for the kitchen which most of the time served as a living room. There was a room where her father slept which was used as a parlour, but only on special occasions. His bed had wooden shutter doors that could close over the bed and hide it. Aunty Murn was proud of the fact that the room had a square of carpet in the middle of the floor, something that put them a cut above most of their neighbours. Every year at spring cleaning time the carpet was taken outside and put over a rope or the wall of the back yard and beaten viciously with a carpet beater. The rag rug in front of the kitchen fireplace was taken down every day and beaten in this way to get rid of the dust. The kitchen floor was covered in linoleum. Aunty Murn had allowed her to make chalk marks all over it when she was young in order to play ball beds and peever. It didn't matter about the chalk marks because the floor was scrubbed daily by herself.

'If you put them on you can take them off,' Aunty Murn told her. But Annalie had not minded going down on her hands and knees with a scrubber after having enjoyed her games. Sometimes she played skipping, the rope rhythmically skelping the linoleum at one side of the room while Eddie and Davie wrestled on the floor at the other. Or had a noisy game of marbles. The only drawback was the lack of space in the kitchen and more than once there had been an accident where the rope had knocked something off the bunker or the table onto the floor. Then Aunty Murn would drop what she was doing – sewing, darning socks or peeling potatoes – and she'd march over to Annalie with a threatening outstretched hand.

'Right,' she'd say. 'I've had enough. I'm up to the gunnels. Hand them over.' And Annalie would have to hand over the skipping ropes. Or the boys would be forced (usually by Aunty Murn twisting their ears) to hand over their mottled glass marbles.

She had memories of her mother skipping along with her, even on occasions playing with her at ball beds and peever, much to Aunty Murn's enormous irritation and disapproval. Saviana loved to dance and often she'd cross the poker and tongs on the floor and dance a wild sword dance over them. The boys would giggle and clap their hands or fool about trying to dance along with her. Her extrovert behaviour embarrassed Aunty Murn most acutely. She couldn't bear to look at Saviana 'carrying on like a mad thing'. Instead she would turn her back on Saviana and busy herself peeling potatoes or scrubbing the draining board. But Annalie loved to watch her.

So did Hugh Gordon. He seemed to come to life in her presence and became a different man from the quiet plodder who kept himself to himself, only bursting out occasionally with explosions of anger.

Through in the room there was a bit more space, where Saviana would whirl into gypsy dances and Hugh Gordon would clap his hands and stamp his foot, his eyes sparkling with happiness. Each time Saviana disappeared it was as if a light went out in his eyes.

'Give me the wean,' Aunty Murn said. 'You look as white as a sheet.'

'She's asleep, thank goodness.'

'I'll lay her over on the bed.' Aunty Murn carried Elizabeth over to the hole-in-the-wall bed and tucked the patchwork quilt over her. Annalie had collapsed into her father's chair beside the fire. She found herself suddenly shivering with cold and exhaustion.

Aunty Murn didn't say any more until she'd poured out a cup of hot tea and put it between Annalie's palms.

'Drink that. Have you had anything to eat?'

Annalie shook her head.

'Has the wean been fed?'

'I don't know.'

'What a disgrace!' Aunty Murn tugged her apron down. 'You get more like your mother every day. I'll put a wee pan of milk on to simmer and have bread saps ready for the poor mite when she wakes up.'

The hot tea was beginning to revive Annalie again.

'I'm doing my best.'

'Well it's not good enough,' Aunty Murn said as she busied herself pouring milk into a pan and setting it down at the side of the hob. Then she cut a slice of bread and broke it up into a bowl and sprinkled sugar over it.

'I'm up to the gunnels worrying about the lot of you. There's not a peep about the twins yet.'

'I can't imagine them as soldiers,'

'I know. If it wasn't so serious it would be a joke.' Aunty Murn banged the frying pan on top of the fire. 'Could you go a wee bit sausage?'

'Thanks, I'm starving.'

'It's enough to make a cat laugh. These boys were as bad as you. They had to have a light beside their bed every night, they shouted for their mammy if anybody laid a finger on them. Fight the Germans? I'll German them when I get my hands on them.'

'I'll have to get out of there,' Annalie said.

'You should never have gone there in the first place.'

'What could I have done? I didn't have anywhere else to go.'

'You could have looked for a better place. That's what.'

'No I couldn't have. I hadn't any money. Anyway, I'm looking now. Could you look as well, Aunty Murn?'

'What do you think I've been doing since you've been there? Down among that crowd of Irish heathens.'

'They're not heathens. They're Catholics.'

'Six and half a dozen,' said Aunty Murn.

'Have you seen anything yet?'

'There might be a single end going to let up the wet-fish shop close.'

'Oh, Aunty Murn!' Annalie jumped up, clapping her hands like an excited child.

'Behave yourself,' Aunty Murn commanded. 'It's Mrs McWhirter. The poor soul's had a telegram saying that her man's been killed. She's thinking she might give up the house and go back to stay with her mother. But there's nothing definite yet. She's in shock if you ask me.'

'Will you tell her that I'll take the house if she gives it up?' Annalie said.

'I'll do nothing of the kind. The poor woman's got enough to bother her without being pestered by you. I can crack an egg with this sausage if you'd like.'

'Oh, yes please. She wasn't that long married, was she? And she can't be much older than me.'

'Aye,' said Aunty Murn. 'He was just a laddie as well. And him so far away from home, not even getting a decent burial.'

The egg was sizzling in the pan beside the sausage now. The sound cheered Annalie up. She felt almost happy.

'That's a real nice wee single end.'

'Aye. And young Mrs McWhirter will probably be living in it for years yet.'

But the hope that had lifted Annalie's spirits would not be quelled. There was Mrs Rafferty to consider of course, but if the single end became available she would have to take it. Her first duty and responsibility was to her baby, not to Mrs Rafferty. Annalie felt convinced of this. She was sorry for the poor woman, of course. But that was life, or at least that was life in the Gorbals.

Chapter Ten

The Martyrs Church was quiet and shadowy, lit by gas jets
turned low. Soon the doors would be opened and the
church officer would go along the pews turning up the jets.

Christina was sitting alone, in a front pew, staring at two
large, brass candelabra on the pulpit without seeing them.
Her baby was due very soon and she felt enormous, unat-
tractive and depressed. No small measure of depression was
caused by the many long hours that she sat by her father-
in-law's bedside. He liked to speak to her about old times
and how he had started his business, but it was such a
difficulty for him to articulate the words that it made her
feel tired and sad watching his struggle as well as listening
to him.

At other times she read to him the bible as well as from
his favourite newspapers and periodicals, mostly about the
building trade. She'd become familiar with terms like 'babby
it up'. Babby up, she learned, meant a wee temporary repair
that you did here and there and 'nailsick' meant that the
nails on the roof were rotten although the slates themselves
could be in comparatively decent condition.

Despite the depressing hours by her father-in-law's side,
she was glad of the opportunity to be there. She could relate
to Moses Monkton, and had always admired his down-to-
earth way of talking and his steely determination. Beatrice
was so frothy and superficial in comparison, with her petty
snobbishness, her many extravagances and self-indulgences.

Most afternoons Beatrice lay on the chaise longue in the
drawing room, eating chocolate peppermint creams and
sugared almonds and reading the romantic novels of Elinor
Glyn. Often she'd ask Christina to read to her because she
had one of her headaches or her eyes were too weak. And
she'd lie back in a froth of chiffon, fluttering her fan and
listening to the story. Or she would talk to Christina about

the old days when she lived in Ireland, but her reminiscences were always so boastful and snobbish that Christina avoided being with her as much as she could. More than once recently she had refused to pander to Beatrice's whims. This 'cruel behaviour' as Beatrice called it, had been duly reported to Ada. Many sad remonstrations had resulted.

'Honour thy father and mother,' according to Ada, was supposed to include mothers-in-law. This depressed Christina because she felt her mother was being disloyal to her. At the same time she chided herself for having such thoughts. After all, her mother and Beatrice had known one another for so long, even before Christina was born. They were as close as sisters. This bond had been strengthened by the proximity of their homes and the regular social interweaving of their lives.

Christina kept telling herself these things, but could never quite convince herself that her parents were being fair in showing more loyalty to and concern for Beatrice than herself. Even sitting in the church Christina could not control the resentment that weighed heavily inside her along with her unborn child. It was because of the child and the harm she might do it with this negative emotion that she had come into the church to pray for God's help, but somehow she couldn't concentrate. Memories of her own childhood wandered in and out of her mind.

While her brother was away at private school thoroughly enjoying himself, she was forced to endure silent Sundays except for prayers and hymn singing. Even on weekdays there were long prayers, led by her father, before breakfast and school. Prayers at lunchtime, prayers at dinner, prayers at night.

A hymn that had been often sung in the past floated back through the years:

> Hushed was the evening hymn,
> The temple courts were dark,
> The lamp was burning dim,
> Before the sacred Ark.

70

She cringed at the sound of voices all around her in the shadows.

'Our master, as this day closes and passes from our control, the sense of our shortcomings is quick within us. Help us to show mercy to those who have grieved or angered us. Suffer us not to cherish dark thoughts of resentment or revenge.'

Yet, there was no one there. The grey walls, the crimson and purple of the coloured glass windows was shrouded in a ghostly mist. The whole atmosphere of the church made her feel worse, crushed her spirits – as, she realized, it had always done. Or was she confusing the church with the overzealous minister and his wife?

She felt more lonely and depressed now than she had when she came in. Deciding not to wait for evening service she heaved herself up and dragged herself wearily back down the aisle towards the door. She didn't know where to go. Moses Monkton would be sleeping. His wife would be in the drawing room reading or languidly toying with the knitting for soldiers that all the middle-class women in Glasgow were so busy with. Both in Monkton House and the manse a table was kept in the drawing room covered in several pairs of half-finished khaki socks, mufflers and balaclavas so that when visitors arrived she could get on with the knitting while chatting to her hostess. The war which everybody had so confidently prophesied would be over by Christmas 1914 now looked as if it might not even be over by Christmas 1915.

For a minute or two Christina loitered at the end of the drive between the pillared gateposts. To her right was Monkton House, to her left was the manse. She did not believe that it would raise her spirits in any way to go into the manse. Her mother's conversation was becoming quite morbid. It looked to Christina as if Ada almost found pleasure in reading and discussing the lists of dead, wounded and missing servicemen in the Glasgow Herald. Christina felt guilty viewing her mother in this unflattering light. Perhaps she fell on the paper every morning with such alacrity and devoured it so eagerly to find out who in the congregation had been affected. Then she could lose no time in going to comfort and sustain them. It could be, too, that her mother was fearful of finding Simon's name on the lists, although she never appeared fearful. At times a little agitated perhaps, but nothing more.

Christina suspected that her mother believed, as she did, in Simon's lucky star. Perhaps she felt that Simon, as a son of the manse, had and was entitled to some divine protection. It seemed, Christina often thought bitterly, that both her parents believed that God was always on Simon's side, whereas in comparison he kept a constant and severely critical eye on her.

Simon's letters were typically cheerful and read more like records of a holiday abroad that was turning out to be a bit of a disaster, and quite an amusing disaster at that. He never mentioned trenches but spoke about living close to nature. He compared French forests to Scottish ones and the lethal potential of French wasps as opposed to Scottish midges. They would never have had any idea what the realities of war were like had it not been for other sources. Nor was it only from newspapers that they learned about the winter battle in Neuve-Chapelle. So many of the Second Scottish Rifles lost their lives there. Even worse had been the battle of Ypres. The British lost ninety thousand there, so it was rumoured. Ten hundred thousand wounded too and over seventy thousand missing. At the disaster of the Gallipoli landings it was said that the sea was red with the blood of British soldiers. The civilian population were becoming more aware of the seriousness of the war by what soldiers on leave told them, by hearing word-of-mouth reports. There was also the sight of wounded soldiers arriving in overcrowded special trains. Central Station in Glasgow was still regularly packed with young men in khaki and tartan leaving for the front. The atmosphere had changed, however. It was no longer as it had been in 1914, a cheering, flag-waving, exciting occasion. Now Central Station had become a tearful place of sad partings. Instead of the troops leaving in good voice, singing songs like 'Pack up your Troubles in your Old Kit Bag' or 'It's a Long Way to

Tipperary' they were now singing words like 'If you want the old battalion you know where they are. They're hanging on the old barbed wire.'

On the civilian front there were food shortages and queues everywhere and one of the most common topics among people of Beatrice Monkton's and Ada Gillespie's class was the shortage of domestic staff. So many women were leaving domestic service and going to help the war effort in munition factories and other even heavier and most unlikely jobs. Fortunately, at least a few of the servants at the manse and Monkton House were either too old or too set in their ways to be so adventurous. Gladys had been grey haired as far back as Christina could remember and Mrs Kelvin had always seemed middle-aged. It was the same with Mrs Bishop and Doris in Monkton House.

Ada Gillespie had told Beatrice the other day that she'd actually seen a woman delivering bags of coal.

'A woman,' Ada had repeated. 'Black faced and disreputable, carrying a bag of coal on her back.'

Both Ada and Beatrice were torn between their need of domestic servants and their enthusiasm for doing everything possible to help the war effort.

Christina decided that she did not want to turn into the manse and visit her mother any more than she wanted to return to Monkton House. She did not feel like going for a walk either, although it was quite a pleasant evening. Her personal problems and resulting depression had been made a hundred times worse by the weight of all the tragedies taking place in the world around her. As if all the dreadful battles weren't enough, she had been reading about the worst disaster that had ever happened on the railway. A troop train conveying a regiment of the Seventh Royal Scots from Larbert to Liverpool from where they had been destined to go to Gallipoli had been involved in a crash at Quinton Hill. The precise number of men who lost their lives in the troop train could not be established. One, because so many had been burned to ashes and two, because the roll of the Royal Scots was lost in the accident. It was estimated, however, that at least two hundred and fifteen officers and men were killed. Simon, but for his lucky star, might have been among them. He was an officer in the Royal Scots.

Ada had gone around the manse wringing her hands and crying out, 'Oh what a tragedy, what a terrible tragedy. And for no reason whatsoever. Oh what a waste, what a tragic waste. Had they been killed in Gallipoli they would at least have died a hero's death in defence of King and Country.'

Christina couldn't help feeling that death was death. What did it matter to the poor men *where* they'd lost their lives? What mattered was that they had.

She trailed dejectedly along Queen's Drive to Monkton House. She longed for comfort but had lost hope of getting any from her husband. He was in the drawing room when she entered, lounging back in an easy chair by the fire and reading the *Glasgow Herald*. He glanced over at her, but only for a second before his attention returned to his newspaper. Adam didn't speak – he never at any time said anything to her if it could be avoided.

'Where's your mother?' she asked, going over and lowering herself into the chair opposite him.

'Out at her Tipperary Club, I believe,' he replied without moving his newspaper. Tipperary Clubs were one of the many kinds of voluntary organizations that middle-class women formed to help soldiers' wives, refugee funds, prisoners' funds and soldiers' canteens. Other clubs were set up to help the wounded and others again took the form of war economy leagues. The knitting mania was part of most of these efforts. Jessie Pope, the popular poet who wrote for the *Daily Mail*, even invented a poem about knitting:

> Soldier lad on the sodden ground
> Sailor lad on the seas
> Can't you hear a little clickety sound
> Stealing across on the breeze?
> It's the knitting needles singing their tune
> As they twine the khaki or blue
> Thousands and thousands and thousands strong
> Tommy and Jack for you.

'I suppose my mother will be there too,' Christina said dully.

'No doubt,' Adam agreed.

A terrible sense of desolation almost swamped Christina. She longed to plead with Adam to take her in his arms. The need for him had been growing day by day. There was a vast sea of grief gathering in strength all over the land and she was part of it. Only her grief was not for a dead man but for one who was only too vitally alive.

She felt so sad that their marriage wasn't working out, so sorry that she'd caused the only man she had ever loved to harbour such coldness and bitterness towards her. She had always loved Monkton. Even as a child her heart had warmed towards him. She had been quite content then to sit in the background while all his attention had been directed at Simon. She had hovered gratefully on the edge of their relationship, their close friendship warming her. Now there was no warmth anywhere. She was frozen in her loneliness, cast adrift in an ocean of desolation.

Chapter Eleven

'He takes after my pater of course,' Beatrice said. 'You never knew Pater, Adam, but oh, wasn't he the fine-looking man?'

Beatrice was leaning admiringly over the cot, wearing a tea gown of crepe de chine in a pretty shade of powder blue with a dainty fichu of fine paris lace gathered from the low V neck and hanging over her bosom and shoulders.

She was a good-looking woman with a clear complexion, big brown eyes and wavy grey hair swept up in curls at the back of her head. She had a youthful, china doll look about her, despite her grey hair, a look accentuated by her preferences for frills and flounces and floaty materials and delicate pastel shades. Her tea gown reached the floor.

Lying in the bed beside the cot, Christina was aware of the tangy smell of her mother-in-law's eau de cologne blending with the sweeter smell of the baby's talcum powder. Her attention clung to Adam, however. He too was admiring the baby. Christina was filled with new hope. Her depression had lifted. She felt fit, even energetic. She was impatient to be up and getting on with her life, a life that she was confident would be completely transformed now that the baby had arrived.

For a few moments as he gazed at his son, Adam had lost his stony-faced look and his big hand gently caressed the baby's head. Christina tentatively imagined him looking at her with the same tenderness. Despite the ways in which he had caused her hurt and humiliation since their marriage she was more than ready to forgive him if he made any conciliatory move towards her. Such had been her humiliation that she could not bring herself to make the first move towards him.

Monkton's coldness towards her had a devastating effect that had not in any way diminished over the months of her marriage. Indeed, her suffering had increased. Had it not been for her music she believed she would have gone mad. There was a grand piano in the upstairs drawing room of Monkton House at which she would sit for some time of every day and allow her emotions to have release in the sad strains of music like Sibelius's *Valse Triste* or Beethoven's *Moonlight Sonata*. Then as often as not Beatrice would flutter into the room and break the spell.

'Can't you ever play anything more cheerful? Cook says even the scullery maid's getting depressed.'

However, it didn't seem appropriate from any point of view to be playing happy tunes. The master of the house was just along the corridor lying like a frail corpse in his big black iron bed. It was also anything but a happy situation to lie every night in her own bed with her husband so near and yet with an icy wasteland stretching between them. She longed to speak to someone, to unburden her anguish, to seek advice, anything to help her in her impossible predicament. But there was no one. She could not even confide in Moses Monkton any more. He was no longer fit to share any burden of worry although they did still talk together. Sometimes he spoke of his boyhood and how he had started work as an apprentice to a jobbing slater at a very young age. He had worked night and day. Weak as he was, a determined glint could still harden his eyes. He spoke of his ambition to succeed and build up his own business.

'I started with nothing,' he told Christina. 'I proved that it could be done. It wasn't just an ordinary business either, but a firm with a good reputation in the town. I don't want all that I've worked for to be lost. I want it to go on growing and prospering, generation after generation.'

'And so it shall, so it shall,' Christina repeated soothingly in an effort to calm his mounting agitation.

The doctor had said it was a miracle that Moses was still alive. It was only his spirit that was keeping him going. He was determined to live to see his grandson born. She had not believed that his now wasted body would last out, but it had and this very morning Mitchell, the new nanny, had carried the baby through to the master bedroom for inspection. Now Moses was vowing that he would see his grandson christened. His joy in the child strengthened and cheered him. It had surprised her, however, to see Adam's pleasure. He didn't express it verbally, but she could see it in his face.

'Time I was away,' he announced at last.

To Christina, Adam's coming home at lunchtime was another indication of his changed attitude. Usually he had a drink and something to eat in a local pub, or if he was in town, he went to his club.

Before leaving he turned to Christina.

'I told Mitchell to move the baby into the nursery.'

'Oh, I like him here beside me,' Christina protested.

'Don't be so selfish,' he said. 'Mitchell tells me that everything the baby needs is in the nursery and it will be more convenient for her to look after him there.'

Christina sighed her acquiescence, then as soon as Adam and Beatrice had gone she got up and sat on the side of the bed to admire the baby. Eventually she lifted him from his cot and nursed him close against her, only returning him to his nest of blankets when Doris appeared with her lunch tray. She began to feel cheerful again. After all, the nursery was only up another flight of stairs. It wasn't a thousand miles away. She was suddenly quite looking forward to her lunch of finnan haddies, clapshot and for dessert a fluted glass dish of crannochin.

Finnan Haddie came from the east coast of Scotland from the village of Finnan some miles south of Aberdeen. They were noted for their distinctive smoked flavour. In Finnan the haddocks were split and the flesh smoked to a golden yellow colour. The skin of the Finnan Haddie always showed the unusual marks of St Peter's thumbprints by which they could be easily recognized. Cook had grilled them and they were accompanied by clapshot – potatoes and turnip mashed together with plenty of butter. Christina enjoyed them and then enthusiastically tackled the very Scottish dessert of crannochin which was made of toasted coarse oatmeal soaked in whisky, double cream and brambles, the Scots blackberries.

Strengthened by the good meals with which she was being provided and her growing sense of optimism, she was able to get up and back to normal within a few days. Very soon, however, her first flush of good cheer was considerably cooled. It appeared to Christina that the starch-aproned Mitchell was yet another person intent on undermining her. Seeing that Beatrice was the mistress of Monkton House, the snobbish Mitchell not only deferred to the older woman, but fussed over her and encouraged her selfish and hypochondriac tendencies. Christina thought that at times Mitchell was as much Beatrice's nurse as the baby's.

To Adam, Mitchell was so deferential she was almost flirtatious. Christina grew to hate the woman. She had to fight a minor battle of wills with her every time she set foot in the nursery. According to Mitchell, Christina never arrived at a convenient time. She never came right out and said so, of course, but used more subtle methods to make it awkward and uncomfortable for Christina to be in the nursery. She always seemed to be interrupting some important routine that would result in the baby's suffering. By looks, by sighs, by slight shakings of the head, by impatient hoverings Christina was made to feel guilty at taking pleasure in nursing or spending time doing anything with the baby. At one point, in exasperation and desperate longing to have freedom to love her baby in her own way, she tried to dismiss Mitchell. She'd actually given the woman notice. Beatrice had taken hysterics. Adam had been coldly furious.

'Mitchell is a trained nurse with first-class qualifications and references. She adores the baby and he is contented and happy with her. Why should his care and wellbeing be put at risk just because you've taken a spite at the woman? Either you reverse what you've done or I will.'

She argued that Mitchell had an impertinent and possessive manner. She argued that, as the child's mother, she had the right to decide who and what was best for her own son. As usual, however, she was unable to communicate to Monkton her deepest and truest feelings. There was a longing inside her. A need to love and be loved. She had failed with her husband, now she was terrified of failing with her son.

She could not, for any reason, bring herself to tell Mitchell that she'd changed her mind about the dismissal, and so Monkton did. It was obvious to Mitchell, of course, that in fact Christina had not changed her mind and Monkton had simply overruled her. As a result the woman's veiled insolence increased. So did her possessiveness with the baby. It had been an added distress to discover that Adam's tenderness and pleasure with his son had not changed his attitude towards Christina in the slightest. Sometimes she was tempted to pour everything out to her mother, but her introverted nature would not allow her to do so. A sense of shame too prevented her from revealing her invidious position at Monkton House. She even thought on occasions of confiding in old Mrs Monkton, Adam's grandmother, but in the end felt it would be too unkind to worry the old woman. After all, she was in her eighties and was suffering the terrible experience of seeing her son fade away before her eyes. She visited Monkton House nearly every day, coming in her carriage from her cottage in Pollokshields. She'd always refused her son's offer to build her a bigger house or to come and live in Monkton House. She preferred her independence, she insisted, and also liked her little cottage, the house her husband built and moved her to from their original slum dwelling in the Gorbals. Not that she ever complained about where or how she'd lived in the Gorbals. Indeed, she boasted about it. Nevertheless, she was very fond of her cottage and nothing and no one could make her budge from it.

The old woman never stayed long on her visits to Monkton House. She would go straight to the master bedroom and sit by the bed as rough and loud-spoken as ever, trying to bully some life into her son. Then eventually, seeing Moses' eyes close and sleep overcome him, she would stomp away downstairs and out to her carriage where the horses were pawing the ground and snorting impatiently.

It was decided that the baby was to be called Jason and he was to be christened in Monkton House by the Reverend

Gillespie. Normally the child would have been christened in the church, but Moses Monkton wanted to see the christening and was unable to leave his bed. Meantime, far from becoming warmer or more tender towards her, Adam if anything had become more irritable and bad tempered. She had learned however, from Beatrice's brother, Magnus Doyle, who was a regular Sunday visitor with his wife and son and also a member of the board of Monkton's, that there were business difficulties worrying them all. The war had caused building to come almost to a complete halt – a general trend all over the country. Christina had learned about the general situation from her reading of the building periodicals, and began to miss out items on this downward trend when she was reading to her father-in-law in order not to worry him. It was obvious that Adam was also hiding the true state of affairs from his father.

Nevertheless, Moses said to Christina one day, 'I'm worried about the business. Adam's never had the same interest in it as me. It's never meant as much to him.'

Christina was taken aback. 'Oh, surely that's not fair. Adam does a good job. He's always been a hard and conscientious worker. You must know that.'

'Aye, it's always been just a job to him,' Moses said half to himself. 'It was different to me. I had real poverty to goad me on. He's never known that.'

'He's served his time,' Christina protested. 'What more could he do?'

'He needs something to goad him on,' Moses said. Despite the weakness of his body his eyes were still pebble hard and calculating. They hooked onto hers, making her feel uneasy. She wondered what he was thinking.

Chapter Twelve

Dear Aunty Murn,

I hope you're not still angry with us for running away and joining up.

Eddie and I were thinking that maybe you hadn't reported us to the authorities to teach us a lesson. We thought maybe that would be your way. We remember you brought us up quite strict. Not that we're complaining. You were perfectly right. We were thinking, looking back, what a handful we must have been to you. Believe me, Eddie and I would give anything now to be back in that wee kitchen in Cumberland Street with you giving us a row or even chasing us around the table trying to catch us to give us a thumping. We're really sorry for what we've done. We just thought, you see, it would be a bit of a laugh and an adventure, like a holiday. You know how we've never been away on holiday except once when Daddy took us down the water to Rothesay. I know it sounds daft now, Aunty Murn, but honestly that's what Eddie and I thought. We've always been a bit daft, haven't we? You once said we needed our heads knocked together we were that daft and you'd do it, if you could get your hands on us. Do you remember that? You chased us all round the house that time and never caught us. You never could catch us. We were too quick for you, the pair of us dodging about. We just wish you could catch us now. We wouldn't mind a bit if you knocked our heads together. We deserve it for being as daft as this. Fancy Eddie and I talking about going to France in the same breath as our holiday to Rothesay. They've told us that we've to go up front tomorrow. Up front and over the top. That's what they said. We just thought Eddie and I, that we'd write you this wee note while we had the chance, to let you know how we were getting on.

Tell Daddy and Annalie we were asking for them and love to you all from Eddie and me, but especially love to you.

From Davie and Eddie.

P.S. If you happen to see our mammy tell her we send our love to her as well.

'What does that army think they're playing at?' Aunty Murn said to Annalie.

'Did you tell them?' Annalie asked.

'Of course I told them. I told them months ago. I don't know what they were playing at taking these young lads in the first place.'

'Well,' Annalie said unhappily. 'I suppose they're big and well made for their age.' Although she was remembering the freckled faces of her young brothers and thinking how despite their tall, husky bodies their faces had never lost their baby roundness nor the wide-eyed innocence of youth.

Aunty Murn got up from the table and tugged down her apron.

'I'm away to that army office to give them a right sherrakin'. The whole street'll know. The whole of the Gorbals'll know what I think of them before I'm done.'

'I'll come with you,' Annalie said.

'You'll do nothing of the kind. It's time you went back to Commercial Road and got that wean fed.'

As Annalie was trailing dejectedly towards the door Aunty Murn called after her. ' Your daddy will still be away tomorrow. If you come round then I'll let you know how I get on.'

Annalie had been so worried and upset by the letter she couldn't fight back the tears as she went down the stairs. Furtively she wiped them away on the back of her sleeve in case Aunty Murn would make up on her and see them. Aunty Murn never had any time for tears. What was the use of them? She alway said. Her philosophy of life was to get on with it. Annalie struggled to banish Davie and Eddie from her mind but failed abysmally. The empty place where her stomach had been was now a knot of fear. To think that only yesterday she'd felt quite cheered up. The sun had been shining, she had felt cleaner and better than she'd done for months, having thoroughly washed her hair and body in the big zinc bath in front of Aunty Murn's fire. Her daddy had been sent to work on a job up north for a few days and she was able to relax and indulge herself in the luxury, the privacy, the blessed quiet of Aunty Murn's warm kitchen.

It was now September and she'd still never found a place of her own. Mrs McWhirter had decided to struggle on by herself in her single end. The disappointment had been terrible. Annalie was beginning to feel that staying down the dunny in Commercial Road would be the death of both her and Elizabeth. Mother and child looked pale and listless. Several times Elizabeth had been ill with sickness and diarrhoea. Often they both cried together, the noise of their weeping seldom noticed in the midst of the Rafferty bedlam. If it hadn't been for Aunty Murn and the occasional visit to her house Annalie believed she and the baby would have died. Mrs Rafferty's new baby was due at any moment and Annalie dreaded the event. Another child seemed an impossible burden. There was no food for it, no clothes for it, no space for it. Annalie dreaded too the fact that she might be the only one there to help Mrs Rafferty. They had no immediate neighbours. These past couple of days when Mrs Rafferty hadn't felt well and labour seemed about to start Mrs Rafferty's Rutherglen Road friends had taken turns to come round and sit with her during the day. Every one of Mrs Rafferty's children had come into the world during the night, however, and Annalie feared that this would happen again. She had terrible visions of not being able to get to Mrs Rafferty's friends in time and therefore having to cope by herself. It was an anxiety that had been haunting her more and more as Mrs Rafferty's time drew near. Since her own pregnancy Annalie felt she'd aged far beyond her years. Her life between the coffin works and under the earth among the Raffertys was so far removed from Adam Monkton's Glasgow, it was another world, a veritable hell sucking her further and further down each exhausting day, each squalid night.

Earlier in the year, like most people, Annalie had felt her spirits lift at the sound of the recruiting bands drumming through the streets and marching in Glasgow Green, and at the sergeant majors' rallying cry that echoed all over the city and added to the general air of excitement. Gradually, however, a dark cloud was forming, there was an increasing feeling of tension and foreboding. A hush would come over the street as people watched the telegram boy in his blue uniform and pillbox hat carrying the buff-coloured envelope which held the dreaded news that someone's brother or father or son or husband had been killed in action or died of wounds.

More and more mourning clothes were being worn. Black dresses, black coats, black veils, black suits and black armbands were everywhere, darkening the streets. Two of Mrs Rafferty's friends had lost their men and Mrs Rafferty often took time to go round and see them.

'I just sit with them, hen,' Mrs Rafferty explained. 'I don't know what else to do. I've offered to look after the weans or run a message or anything at all, but they seem to just want me to sit with them and talk about old times. We all went to school together, you see. Their men as well. Oh I remember them fine as wee laddies. It's hard to believe they're gone.'

Annalie had been affected to some extent by the death cloud and the anxiety felt by the women around her for their men away at the front. But with her brothers' letter, the reality of the war knifed into her heart. She had a terrible premonition. She tried to banish it from her mind, to scoff at herself, after she left Aunty Murn's close and made her way along Cumberland Street, but it had so taken over her mind she hadn't been paying attention to where she was going. She literally bumped into Mrs Gibson, one of Aunty Murn's neighbours.

'Oops!' Mrs Gibson laughed.

'Oh, I'm sorry, Mrs Gibson. I nearly knocked you down.'

'Never mind, hen. Better you than a horse. You'll have been up seeing your Aunty Murn.'

'Yes, Daddy's up north just now.'

'Are you still in the coffin works, hen?'

'Worse luck.'

'Have you not been looking for something else?'

'I never seem to get a minute, and anyway who'd give me a job without a reference?'

'Lots of places nowadays.'

Annalie was surprised.

'Do you think so?'

'Och aye. With all the men being away at the war, some places are glad of anybody. I heard Hurley's the grocer would be needing somebody soon. Jamie Saunders that works there has joined up.'

Excitement brought colour to Annalie's pale face and hope gave her a surge of renewed energy.

'Do you think I should try for it?'

'Why not, hen?'

'Oh thanks, Mrs Gibson. You've fair cheered me up.'

The very next day she washed and dressed herself at Aunty Murn's in her coat and hat and went along to Hurley's. She kept the precious coat and hat at Aunty Murn's because it was the only place they could be clean and safe. She was trembling with excitement. Oh, to be free of the coffin works. She felt like death all the time she was in it. Everyone looked like miserable ghosts picking at piles of bones all the time. It was a place of no hope. But now she had hope of a job at Hurley's. She flew along Cumberland Street to the shop, hanging onto her straw boater, its ribbons flying, long skirts flapping in the angry wind, boots clattering on the cobbles. Mrs Hurley ran the shop with her son Malcolm. He did not have a good reputation with women, but so desperate was Annalie to get the job she wouldn't have cared if he was a werewolf. Anyway, Mrs Hurley was pleasant enough and it was she who spoke to Annalie and gave her the job.

On her way back to Aunty Murn's to change into her shawl Annalie wept unashamedly with relief. She wasn't to start for two weeks yet, but already she was counting the days.

Chapter Thirteen

The thought of working in the shop was the only thing that kept Annalie in the coffin works. She had hated the place from her very first day there and her hatred had burned like the fires of hell ever since. Her desperate loathing of the squalor in the dunny where she had to spend the rest of her time added fuel to the flames.

Sometimes her hatred could not be contained and exploded out in screaming at Rafferty children, punching and pulling at them just to get them into some sort of order and discipline. Mrs Rafferty, sitting like a helpless buddha in the dark dunghill of a place, never objected to this rough treatment of her children. Her eyes and face would crinkle up in what could have been sympathy, embarrassment or apology, but she never said anything. Only after Annalie's tirade had been exhausted would she venture a mild 'Would you like a wee cup of tea, hen?' A wee cup of tea was Mrs Rafferty's panacea for all ills.

Nellie and Theresa, the twins and the oldest in the family, having been instructed to make themselves useful, found Saturday jobs helping local Jewish families. Saturday was the Jewish Sabbath and their religion forbade them to do any work at all on that day so they had what was called a Shabbos boy or girl from among the Gentiles to rake out their fires, empty the ash-pan, set the fire again and, if necessary, light it. Nellie attended to Mrs Greenbaum's fire and Theresa went to Mrs Greenbaum's next-door neighbour, Mrs Solomon.

Neither Mrs Greenbaum nor Mrs Solomon would even light a match or turn on the gas ring to heat the evening meal for their family. Sometimes, the night before, they would put a pot of whatever they intended to eat on the side of the fire. There it would cook slowly. Or because they were fortunate enough to have a gas ring they would sometimes light it the night before, leave it at a peep and allow it to remain like that. Then when Nellie or Theresa came in on the Saturday morning they would put the gas up and finish off the cooking process. The coppers the girls earned helping their Jewish friends were added to the Rafferty income and went some way to help alleviate the growing hardships of finding enough for food and rent.

Sunday was the best day of the week for food. After all the Rafferty children had attended Mass they would troop straight down to the Mission Hall and join in the Protestant hymns because afterwards plates of hot soup and hunks of bread were distributed. This procedure was beginning to worry Theresa, who was in her first adolescent years and seemed to be developing a religious conscience. Nevertheless, hunger drew her along with her brothers and sisters and if she didn't sing the Protestant hymns quite as lustily and enthusiastically as they did, she did at least join in. She asked her mother on one occasion if this was a sin.

'Och, you're not doing any harm, hen. As long as you go to chapel first.'

The third and only other girl in the family was twelve-year-old Mary, who might have been a pretty child if she'd been cleaned up, with her neat features and curly hair. Once when she and all the Raffertys had been talking about what they would most like in the world if they had plenty of money Mary had piped up with 'A clean pinny.'

The boys showed no such delicacy of thought. For the most part snotty-nosed, dirt-smeared, ragged and impudent-faced, they were often caught, especially at night, using the sink as a urinal. Annalie always boxed their ears if she caught them, and screamed at them what disgusting, dirty little devils they were. Secretly, she couldn't blame them. Going along the corridor in the dark to the unlit and stinking lavatory was something she dreaded doing herself. The dustmen came every now and again to collect the ordure, but as often as not before they arrived the place would be overflowing with pestilence. It was yet another difficulty in the uphill struggle to be clean and decent.

Annalie could see only too well how easy it would be to

give up the struggle. Sometimes she'd sit out in the front close with baby Elizabeth in order to get a breath of fresh air and she'd think tiredly, what was the use of caring about herself, what was the use of caring for her baby? Behind the high grim walls of all the grey tenement buildings in all the narrow side streets like Commercial Road, in neglected and derelict courtyards, in winding cavernous closes, the scores of children played among rotting refuse, always in shadow because the sunlight could not reach them. It terrified Annalie that Elizabeth, like so many other children, might become infected with measles, diphtheria, scarlet fever, rheumatic fever or any of the other diseases that were rife in the area. At other times though, Annalie's wild, fighting spirit would flash into life again and she would vow that some day, somehow, she and Elizabeth would escape from their sordid surroundings. At times like these she would remember what life was like for those who lived in Monkton House and she would feel such anger at the unfairness of life that her heart would pound against her ribs and the blood would swell in her head until she felt it was going to burst with the pain of it. She remembered the beautiful silver candelabra, the china dishes, the crisp white linen, the sweet smell of lavender floor polish, the comfort of carpets underfoot, the feel under her fingers of satin quilts on Mrs Monkton's bed and dresses in the wardrobe as light and gauzy as a butterfly's wing. But most of all she remembered the sweet-smelling cleanliness of the place. Her anger was directed at Adam Monkton as well as at the rest of his family, yet often in the foul-smelling darkness of the hole-in-the-wall bed her anger would be confused by physical longing and she would howl to the moon in silent anguish.

Any thought of seeing him again had become unreal. Time had distanced him into another world. While she had still been in some way part of that world she could face up to him, or his mother or to anyone. Her pride had been intact. Now even if she managed to have a decent wash at Aunty Murn's and was wearing her coat and hat she felt she still carried the squalor and pestilence of the dunny inside her. She did not believe that now she would be able to toss her head and stare Beatrice Monkton straight in the eye with an impudent 'I'm every bit as good as you' look. She just hated her from a distance instead.

Annalie hated Adam Monkton's wife too. She remembered the minister's mousy daughter when, before her marriage, she had visited Monkton House with her parents. Little had Annalie guessed at the time what scheming must have been going on behind the quiet, modest exterior.

Annalie took pleasure in cursing her. Saviana Gordon had not taught her any curses. She had promised to one day, along with the secrets of palm reading, the crystal ball and the tarot cards. Annalie prayed for Saviana's return, but until that day she made do by conjuring up Christina's pale, placid face and vehemently aiming at it every bad wish, every misfortune, every torment she could think of.

Chapter Fourteen

'Have you seen that beautiful poem by a young soldier?' Ada Gillespie asked her daughter as they sat in the manse drawing room knitting khaki body belts.

Christina had been glad to get out of Monkton House for a time and sit with her mother rather than Beatrice Monkton. Beatrice never failed to irritate her and it was as much as she could do at times to control her tongue and prevent herself from being impertinent to the older woman. Christina despised her weakness and hypochondria and the way she kept running to Mitchell for help and advice.

'He's called Rupert Brooke,' Ada said, adjusting her glasses and picking up a paper from the small table by her side.

'Yes, Mother,' Christina interrupted. 'You showed it to me the other day.'

Ada sighed. 'It's so beautiful. Your father's going to read it out at church. He and I were just saying, pure patriotism had never found a more noble expression. There's another one too, called 'Into Battle' by Julian Grenfell. Your father says they will provide consolation for those whose relatives have fallen.' Her knitting needles began to click again, but she said, 'Have you read the one about the dying horse? It's called "Goodbye, Old Pal".' She looked around. 'I think I have it somewhere.'

No, not just now please, Mother,' Christina pleaded.

'Very well, dear,' her mother said. 'Maybe I'll read it tonight. You'll be coming to the sewing party?'

Christina lowered her eyes. 'I may not manage.'

'Chrissie! The poor soldiers need shirts and nightshirts. We must all carry on and do our bit, you know.'

This had become the general cry in the land now. 'Do your bit! . . . Carry on! . . . A pamphlet advised the Home Front on how to behave. 'Carry on,' it said, 'your duty in wartime. There must be pluck in the office and the shop and the factory and in the house ... The ships that sweep the seas, the khaki cohorts that march in glory, the unnamed heroes trampled dead to make a bridge to victory, they thrill you with pride in the majesty of human power. But you too may be ... a combatant in the great cause, comporting yourself as a hero or a craven ... Your part is to live plainly, pay promptly, apply your mental and physical powers to the benefit of the commonwealth ...' Posters were everywhere and one of them portrayed two women watching soldiers marching away and the slogan: WOMEN OF BRITAIN SAY *GO*!

All this could not be making life easy for Adam, Christina knew. His family and close associates knew how hard he had tried to join up and also how he was needed to run the business, but people who did not know him had no doubt included him among those known as slackers, laggers and shirkers. He had been given white feathers in the street. Even she had on occasion been looked upon with contempt because she was with a man in civilian clothes. Accusing songs were sung in music halls: 'Oh, we don't want to lose you, but we think you ought to go ...' Other songs like 'Goodbye Dolly, we must leave you ...' and 'Keep the home fires burning ...' echoed continuously throughout the land. The novelist Baroness Orczy had formed an active service league and in a letter to the *Daily Mail* had defined its purpose: 'Influencing sweethearts, brothers, sons and friends to recruit. Pledge – I hereby pledge myself most solemnly in the name of my king and country to persuade every man I know to offer his services to his country and I also pledge myself never to be seen in public with any man who, being in every way free and fit has refused to respond to his country's call.'

Christina had voiced her indignation when she'd either witnessed Adam being unfairly treated or heard Beatrice relate incidents to Ada Gillespie. Ada was terribly sympathetic. Her previous disapproval of Adam had mellowed, and she no longer seemed to resent him for so unexpectedly removing from the manse the prop and comfort on which she and the minister had depended for their old age. After all, their Chrissie was still a dutiful daughter and was still very handy, living as she did just at the other side of the church.

'I have a dozen ladies coming tonight,' Ada said.

Christina was about to comment on this when suddenly Gladys came into the room looking agitated.

'Miss Chrissie,' she said. 'You've got to go back round to Monkton House at once. I think it's Mr Monkton. He's taken worse.'

Both Ada and Christina rose.

'I'll come with you, Chrissie,' Ada said. 'No doubt my words of comfort will be needed.'

They found Adam in the downstairs drawing room of Monkton House.

'Mother's lying down upstairs,' he told them. 'The doctor and nurse are in with Father.'

'I'll go straight up to Beatrice,' Ada said hurrying away. Christina removed her hat and coat.

'Is it bad?' Christina asked. He was standing with his broad back towards the fire.

'Yes,' he said abruptly.

'I'm sorry. I feel for you.'

He was silent, and working up courage she said, 'That's all your father has ever wanted, for us to feel for each other.'

Adam stared across at her with a mixture of incredulity and sarcastic amusement.

'I've felt more,' he said deliberately, 'for one of the servants I used to sleep with than I've ever felt for you. You remember her. A stunner with raven-black hair and flashing eyes.'

She was so shocked for a minute she stood perfectly still just staring at him. People had always spoken of her as a very calm person. She always spoke quietly and evenly. All her movements were neat and carefully controlled. This occasion appeared to be no exception. She walked slowly across the room and sat down on one of the fireside chairs.

Just then the door opened and Doris cried out, 'Sir! The doctor says you've to come quickly.'

Christina didn't move but Adam strode quickly from the room. She was still sitting like that when she heard he mother say, 'Chrissie, Chrissie.'

Christina looked round with blank eyes.

'He's gone, dear.' Her mother's voice hushed with sympathy. 'Passed quietly away, the doctor said. God, in his infinite mercy, has released him from his suffering.' She gave Christina's shoulder a squeeze. 'He was always very fond of you, dear, and I know you were fond of him too, but you must try not to be too upset. It is God's will, remember.' Her voice suddenly quickened without losing its sympathetic softness. 'I'd better go, Chrissie. I must tell your father to put a date in for the funeral. You know his diary gets full so quickly nowadays.'

Christina was not thinking of Moses Monkton. She was still trying to save herself from drowning in the whirlpool of her husband's insult. She remembered the servant all right. She even remembered her name. Annalie Gordon. Remembering her, she felt a sickly hatred for the girl, but what affected her most was the deep and terrible wound of Adam's insult in talking so openly about the subject – and to his wife of all people. This proved to her beyond any doubt the extent of Adam's contempt for her and how much he despised her. She folded into herself in layers of hardness and self-protection.

She shed no tears at the funeral and did not join in the murmurs of sympathy when Ada remarked that the poor man had not after all lived to see his grandson christened. In fact, as Ada told everyone in a low dramatic voice, the christening was to have taken place that very day.

Beatrice had to be supported by Adam and given regular administrations of smelling salts. After the funeral service she had to retire upstairs and lie down. Already Moses' favourite black iron bed had been removed and a more fashionable wooden one replaced it.

A sudden emergency arising on a job up in Aberdeen meant Adam had to rush away to attend to it. As a result, the reading of Moses' will had to be postponed until he returned. The reading, as it turned out, fell on the same day as the baby's christening; since the family was all gathered, it seemed appropriate for the will to be read that afternoon.

The christening of Jason Moses Monkton took place in the Martyrs Church and the ceremony was performed by his grandfather, the Reverend William Gillespie.

Christina felt distanced from the child. The nursery was an alien place in which she had been made unwelcome. Right from the start she'd had difficulty with her breast milk, which seemed to harden in lumps inside her and refused to flow out. Eventually the doctor had given her medicine to dry it up, and the baby had been put on a bottle which was fed to him by Mitchell.

At first Christina had gone into the nursery every day to lift the baby and hold him in her arms for a few minutes. She still went into the nursery, but only stood quietly, silently looking down at the child. Since the day of Moses' death she had not even done that. Mitchell brought the baby down to the drawing room every evening for a short time but it was mostly Adam who held him and made a fuss of him. She was still shocked, locked in, alone with herself.

The first thing that sharpened her thoughts into awareness was the reading of Moses' will. To her own and everyone else's astonishment he had left her not only equal half shares with Adam in Monkton House, but a substantial number of shares in the Monkton building business. There was a stunned silence around the table. Then the atmosphere became electric. The fury so intense it could almost be seen burning in the air.

At last Magnus Doyle spluttered out. 'Beatrice, Adam, you must contest this.'

'How could he?' Beatrice had to resort to her smelling salts again. 'If he felt he had to leave only half the house to Adam, surely the other half should have come to me? This has always been my home. Oh how could he? I . . . I cannot believe it. Can you, Adam?' Before Adam could reply Magnus Doyle said, 'The stroke obviously affected his brain.'

'Yes,' Beatrice agreed with her brother. 'Moses would never have done this to me had he been in his right senses.'

'To hell with the house, Mother,' Adam said at last. 'It's the business, it's the business that matters.' Then he glared across at Christina and said, 'I'll get papers drawn up for you to sign.'

'What papers?' Christina asked quietly.

'Saying that you will give up the shares, of course.' Then he turned to the solicitor. 'Get these papers made up at once. I want this matter put right without delay.'

A new feeling, one that she had never in her life experienced before, took root and immediately blossomed inside Christina. She examined it with her inner eye, recognized the malicious satisfaction as being wicked, but could not deny herself the pleasure of nurturing it. Let this day pass. Let all the Monktons think and feel as they wished. When the day came for her to sign the papers she would quietly and politely refuse. A faint hint of a smile hovered around her mouth at the prospect.

Chapter Fifteen

When Mrs Rafferty gave birth, Annalie found herself alone with her, just as she had feared. The older Rafferty children were at school and the youngest were out somewhere, so there was no one to send for Daisy or Lexy, Mrs Rafferty's two friends from Rutherglen Road. Annalie had considered running out herself to find help, but she had just reached the door when Mrs Rafferty said apologetically, 'I think it is already on its way, hen.' She was crouched in the bed among the rags that served as covers, kneading her hands together and making little grunting and moaning noises.

'My God!' Annalie squealed, pushing her hands up through her hair.

'Don't worry, hen.' Mrs Rafferty managed, not without considerable difficulty. 'You'll be all right.'

Annalie came back to the bed.

'What am I supposed to do?' she asked. Mrs Rafferty was sweating profusely. 'Will I wipe your face?'

'I tell you what, hen.' Mrs Rafferty squeezed the words out. 'You could bring over that pile of old newspapers in the corner. Tommy in the chip shop gave them to me. He's a right gem, that man.'

Annalie had rushed over and grabbed the pile of newspapers as Mrs Rafferty was speaking.

'Aye, that's right hen. Just put them on the bed and maybe if you could give me a wee hand up so that you can slide them underneath me.'

For the next few minutes the two women struggled together, Mrs Rafferty clinging round Annalie's neck and Annalie wrestling to get the newspapers underneath Mrs Rafferty's mountain of fat.

'I'm that sorry to have put you to all this trouble, hen.' Mrs Rafferty gasped breathlessly.

'It's all right, I've managed it,' Annalie said.

Mrs Rafferty's concentration had switched to her contractions. She was going red in the face and shuddering with them.

'It's for the afterbirth,' she managed eventually. 'If you just wrap it up and put it in the pail, hen, I'll empty the pail myself later on.'

'Oh God!' Annalie shouted out in panic. 'I think that's the gas going out.'

Mrs Rafferty gave a half-plaintive, half-apologetic little gasp.

Annalie fumbled in her pockets and rushed across to the mantelshelf where sometimes they kept a penny ready for the meter, but nothing was there.

'We haven't any pennies.' Annalie was sobbing now. Mrs Rafferty gasped again.

'Candles, candles.' Annalie stumbled around trying to find one before the gas, which had shrunk to a faint flicker, petered out all together. There wasn't even a glimmer from the fire because they had just paid the rent and there had been nothing left this week to buy coal. With nothing to heat the kettle on, Mrs Rafferty had even been denied the comfort of her wee cup of tea.

The gas went out. The shadowy cave with its pitted stone walls, low flaking ceiling and uneven stone floor, disappeared in suffocating blackness. Suddenly Annalie was angry, wildly, madly, recklessly angry. She felt outraged. She stamped her feet and beat the black air with her clenched fists and screamed out, 'This is terrible, this is an absolute disgrace! Nobody should have to live like this.' Her screaming wakened the baby Elizabeth who had been sleeping in the other bed and she began to scream too. 'Oh shut up, shut up,' Annalie shouted at her.

'Oh, I'm that sorry, hen.' Mrs Rafferty's voice sounded far off. 'I can't tell you how sorry I am for putting you to all this trouble.'

Annalie felt her way blindly towards her. 'It's not your fault.' She managed to reach the bed and Mrs Rafferty. 'Hang on to me,' she told her. 'Hang on to me.'

'Thanks, hen.'

The baby was born before the young Raffertys arrived home and started complaining about the gas not being on.

'Away you go to Lexy and Daisy's,' Annalie shouted at them, 'and tell them what's happened. They'll give you a penny if they have it, if not, get a candle and be quick about it or I'll box your ears for you. And after I get the gas lit,' she added, 'you can all keep out of here until I get your mammy cleaned up and as comfortable as I can make her. Oh, and ask Daisy and Lexy if they couldn't spare us a lump or two of coal so that I can get the fire going and make your mammy a wee cup of tea.'

Annalie felt much in need of a cup of tea herself. Her feelings went beyond exhaustion or harassment or even concern and sympathy for Mrs Rafferty. She kept thinking that they had just paid rent for this place. The words burned in her brain like red-hot pokers. Rent! They paid money for this cave, this disgraceful stinking putrid hole in the earth that wasn't fit for a dog to live in. Somebody, some-where, was making money out of her own suffering, out of the suffering of dozens and hundreds and thousands of women like them.

The factor, she knew, made money, but behind him was the man or men who owned the slums in the Gorbals and other places like it. Somebody had insulted their fellow human beings by building places like this in the first place and expecting people to live in them, had insulted and degraded people, had robbed them and deprived them of their dignity. It was then, for the first time, she made the connection between the firm of Monkton's Builders and the virtually uninhabitable accommodation in the Gorbals. From listening to the servants in Monkton House, from overhearing family conversations and more directly, from Adam himself, she had learned that the tenements that the Monkton firm had built were nearer to where the Monktons lived themselves, in the suburb of Queen's Park. They had also built other places like pubs and warehouses and even a church of two. When somebody wanted something built, Adam had explained to her, different building firms put in a tender, that is, they worked out what it would cost to construct the building. Then they would offer their price to the client who would usually choose the firm that had put forward the lowest tender.

However, Adam had told her that the Monkton firm had such a good reputation for dependable tradesmen and good workmanship that they were often engaged to do the job despite the fact that they did not always offer the lowest tender. Once the building was erected, it was usually the end of the firm's association with it, unless employed later on the maintenance side, but that tended to happen only on older buildings. After a new building was completed, the owner then let the premises out and collected rent for ever after. Or rather his factor collected rent for him. The factor often had a seat on the board of the owner's firm, however, and so he had his share of the profits. He did the dirty work. He was the one most hated. But who were the owners of the Gorbals property, Annalie wondered? Where were they? What did they do?

No doubt they lived in even bigger and more luxurious houses than the Monktons. No doubt they were regular and pious attenders of churches, burying their heads in Christian sand. Well, it was time somebody dragged their heads out and opened their eyes to exactly how they were making their money.

She felt feverish sick with rage. She'd show them, she vowed. She'd show them what a disgrace they were to humanity. While men like Patrick Rafferty and the husbands of Daisy and Lexy were away fighting for their country, their wives were being worried to death trying to pay rents for miserable, unsanitary slums. Something had to be done.

She didn't know what until, only a few days later, Mrs Rafferty got her notice from the bailiffs telling her they were coming to evict her because she'd got into arrears again.

Chapter Sixteen

The board meeting had been well in progress when old Mrs Monkton had nodded off to sleep as she quite often did. Or at least they thought she had until suddenly she spoke up in her loud, Glasgow voice.

'He's been in everything except a Co-op meat pie.'

'Grandmother,' Adam said. 'That remark adds nothing useful to the discussion on hand.' He was obviously trying to sound severe, but the hint of a smile twitching at his mouth betrayed him.

'Aye, it does,' Mrs Monkton said. 'It puts the man in his place and stops you lot getting the wrong impression of him.'

'Point taken,' Adam said. 'Now go back to sleep, Grandmother.'

'Don't be so cheeky,' she shouted at him. 'I'm a shareholder the same as any of the rest of you. I'm entitled to my say.'

'All right,' Adam groaned. 'Now perhaps we can get on to the next item on the agenda.'

Round the table of the small dusty room that was used for meetings in the offices of the Monkton construction firm in Pollokshaws Road sat the chairman, Adam Monkton, his grandmother, old Mrs Monkton, Christina – the only other woman present – Magnus Doyle, his son Brendan, the lawyer Duncan McCaully, Logie Baxter, the son of old Mrs Monkton's brother, and Hector McAllister, the secretary.

Christina had been surprised at her first board meeting when Adam had opened the proceedings with a brief prayer. Later she learned that his father had always done so and old Mrs Monkton insisted that the tradition should be continued, at least as long as she was there.

There was other evidence in the boardroom of Moses

Monkton's religious leanings. There was a scripture text framed and hanging on the wall opposite Christina:

> Except the Lord built the house,
> They labour in vain that built it
> Psalm 127 verse 1

The room was small and stuffy. The table they sat round was rickety. Two bookcases against the wall were crammed with dog-eared files, piles of papers and books. From somewhere outside came sounds of sawing and hammering.

'Right,' Adam said. 'The question is, and it's the most important one before us today, the situation in the building trade and how we can get more work, not only to continue making a profit, but to make sure that we survive.'

'It's the war,' Magnus Doyle said moodily. 'It's nothing we're doing wrong. We were doing perfectly well before.'

'We all know the war has caused the building trade to come to a virtual standstill,' Adam said. 'The question is, what are we going to do about it?'

Christina was fingering a pencil and she did not raise her eyes from it when she said carefully, 'Am I right in thinking that the firm tenders for contracts for building different premises on the one hand, and the other line of business is carrying out maintenance on older premises? But both these kinds of premises are owned by someone else? We don't own any buildings?'

'I've already made it quite clear,' Adam said, 'that stating the obvious is not what is needed. The question we must address is what we are going to do, how we are going to find more contracts.'

'You've just said,' Brendan Doyle piped up, 'that building has come to a virtual standstill, so it strikes me that there're no contracts to be had.'

'It strikes me,' Logie Baxter said, 'that what will keep us from going under is the maintenance work. We'll have to concentrate on that until the war's over.'

Adam said, 'That seems the only thing for us to do at the moment.'

'I don't agree,' Christina ventured mildly.

'That doesn't surprise me,' Adam said. 'You know nothing about the building trade.'

'I'm learning,' she said.

This was true. She was not only avidly devouring every publication on the subject, every file in the office, but she was also going out onto sites and talking, when she could, to workmen. Admittedly, the latter was difficult, well-nigh impossible in fact, because the workmen were most uncooperative – not because they were bad workmen, but because they were men.

Adam gave a humourless laugh and eyed her sarcastically.

'You are going to do as my father and I and most of the people here have done, are you? You're going to serve your time? You're going to work up from the ground and really be able to know what you're talking about?'

Christina said, 'I was thinking about that. Surely you don't need to be the type of person who can take their jacket off and roll up their sleeves and saw wood or lay bricks or fix a roof slate or lay water pipes to be able to run a business of this type?' Although she was not showing it even by the flicker of an eyelash, she was excited. She was communicating with Adam at last. He was finally paying attention to her. Not in the way that she had once dreamed of and longed for, nevertheless they were now bound together in vital and important issues that he could not ignore. Although, of course, he tried.

'If you must attend these meetings,' he said now, 'for goodness' sake try not to talk nonsense.'

'In what way is it nonsense?' Christina persisted. 'Surely there's room for different kinds of people in a business to concentrate on different aspects of it.'

Adam was growing impatient as well as angry. 'We've a lot of business to get through here. We're not going to be finished by midnight tonight if we allow you to continue rabbiting on like this.'

Old Mrs Monkton woke up again. 'A man has to have a trade and this firm runs on tradesmen. I can't see what you're talking about either, Chrissie.'

Adam said, 'Now can we get on with the business in hand?'

'Just a moment please,' Christina said, still with eyes down, still rolling her pencil carefully, slowly, round and round between thumbs and forefingers. 'What I'm trying to say is, there are other sides to this business than building and maintenance.'

'These are the only things that concern us,' Adam said.

'But they needn't be.' Christina looked directly into his dark, angry eyes. 'Why can't we buy property and let it and add to our income in that way?'

'God!' Adam smacked his brow. 'Tell her, somebody.'

Duncan McCaully cleared his throat. He was a neat little man with a neat little moustache and thin hair plastered against his scalp with pomade.

'We do not have the capital for such a venture. It would be a grave error, in my opinion, to embark on any risky ventures at this stage or indeed at any stage in the business.' He favoured Christina with a small, patronizing smile. 'I'm sure you know that to keep a proper balance of housekeeping books you do not spend more when you are needing to economize.'

'But I don't believe it would be an error,' Christina said. 'I believe it would be a worthwhile investment. Buy property and let it. Or buy it with sitting tenants and reap the income from it. Or buy property and sell it and get a profit that way. Or do all these things.'

McCaully shook his head. 'I repeat, buying and selling of property needs a vast amount of capital expenditure. You don't understand, Mrs Monkton, the very high risks involved.'

'What I don't understand,' Christina said, 'is why you are messing about with all the problems of building and construction and getting X per cent return on capital investment with all the risks of jobs going wrong when there is a lot more money with less risk, as far as I can see, on the property side.'

'Look,' Adam said, 'this is a construction firm. It's always been a construction firm. It was started by a tradesman, it's

105

been built up by tradesmen who knew every side of the business and it's been a good business. There's no question about that. It's been built on solid foundations. It's grown steadily over the years and it'll continue to grow. The problems that we are facing today are not of our making and are no reflection on the way the business has been run. There is no reason why we should change our thinking or our good business methods. The difficulties we're facing today are due to the war and the war won't last for ever.'

Logie Baxter spoke up then. Christina knew he was also a time-served man. Before Moses Monkton would allow him or any other member of the Monkton clan into the business they had to 'work on the ground', as Moses used to say, and Logie had done so for many years as a plumber. Now at fifty-four, shrunken and gnarled with rheumatism, he glared out from a bewhiskered face that looked like a silver-grey feather duster.

'What I can't understand is, why cousin Moses left her all these shares. I told you, Adam, we all told you that you should have contested it. He couldn't have been right in the head when he did it. Now it's too late.'

Suddenly old Mrs Monkton cackled. 'He didn't think she'd have the nerve to come on the board. He didn't think she'd have enough gumption.'

Brendan Doyle grinned. 'You've surprised us all, Christina.' Both he and his father had worked for some years as plasterers but they had worked for the family firm and as workmen had had a much easier time than Adam, who in his day had been forced to cope with hatred and jealousies in another firm in which he had no privileges.

Magnus Doyle spoke up then. 'The building trade is no place for a woman. The quicker you get that into your head the better it'll be, Christina. There is no place in the building trade for a woman,' he repeated. 'Not in the construction side, not in the maintenance side, not in the property side. You keep talking about property, Christina, but you're not a property man any more than you're a builder.'

'No,' Christina agreed, 'I'm not a property man, but I think I'd know a good deal when I saw one.'

'For God's sake, Christina,' Adam said and she experienced a thrill at the sound of her name spoken by him. 'What can you know about deals or anything connected with any business? You're a minister's daughter. You've been brought up since birth in the manse. Nobody could have led a more sheltered existence. You've never had the slightest thing to do with business, so will you stop this nonsense and get back to your knitting?'

Christina looked up again. She looked him straight in the eyes, and her eyes told his that her knitting was very definitely a thing of the past.

Chapter Seventeen

Annalie had passed the word around that as many women as possible should meet together in Lexy's back yard. About twenty of them turned up to stand around Annalie and find out what was going on. Washing lines criss-crossed the yard and clothes flapped and cracked in the strong wind. The women were all wearing aprons over their dark, shabby dresses. One or two of the younger ones wore grubby cotton pinafores, another couple had coloured wrap-arounds, similar in style to Aunty Murn's.

Annalie stepped up onto an upturned wooden box, tossed her hair and stared around at the tired, bedraggled-looking crowd.

'Does everybody here know Mrs Rafferty?'

'The wee woman down the dunny in Commercial Road?' someone piped up. Someone else said, 'She's just had another wean, hasn't she?' and the woman standing next to her nodded. 'That makes nine the poor soul has now.'

'Yes,' Annalie said. 'And it would be bad enough trying to cope with nine children, as you very well know. In fact, each and every one of us know only too well what a struggle it is to try and make ends meet. I'm having to struggle enough to look after just the one, and I'm working.'

There were general murmurs of agreement and sympathy.

'Aye, I know. Food and coal ... Everything's gone sky high. And so many poor souls losing their men as well.'

'Another thing we're all aware of,' Annalie said, 'is what a struggle it is to pay our rents.'

'I know,' someone said. 'The houses aren't bloomin' worth it.'

'They've been worth it to the owners, though,' Annalie told them. 'Just think of all the years these houses have

108

been up and providing rent. They've paid for themselves a hundred times over and they're still earning money.'

'Now they're taking advantage of poor souls while their men are away at the war. War profiteers. That's what they are.'

The tide of sympathy now swelled with anger and there were cries of 'An absolute disgrace, so it is' and 'Poor folk getting put out in the street when they can't scrape up enough for the factor'.

'That's what I wanted to talk to you about,' Annalie interrupted. 'They're going to come and put Mrs Rafferty out.'

'Oh, isn't that terrible?' a woman said. 'And her with that newborn wean.'

'I'm not going to let them do it,' Annalie said.

'But how can you stop them, hen?' a woman asked.

'I can't,' Annalie told her. 'Not on my own. But we could if we all tried together.'

There was silence for a minute and then somebody said, 'I still don't understand, hen. How do you mean, exactly?'

'I've been thinking about it,' Annalie said. 'In the first place if we all crowd into the close, really crowd in and jam pack it, the factor couldn't get past us, could he? He would give up eventually. You know how short-tempered the man is. But I'd like to do more than just crowd him out. Just tell me if you disagree with this, but I was thinking of making bags, you know, paper bags filled with flour and any other kind of missiles you like and we could pelt him with them.'

There was a stunned silence which was suddenly broken by a loud guffaw of laughter, then the laughter swept through the crowd like a huge blast of relief as well as enjoyment.

'It'll serve him right,' someone shouted. 'I'm all for it.'

'Me too.'

Shouts of agreement came from all sides. Excitement that was almost hope brightened their eyes and lifted, for a time at least, their tired, defeated look.

'We'll do it,' Annalie shouted, shaking her fist. 'We'll

show him. Just let him try to lay a finger on Mrs Rafferty. Just let him try to put a foot near her door.'

'He'll be sorry,' someone in the crowd shouted.

'By God, he will,' someone else agreed, and they crowded excitedly together to discuss exactly what each of them intended to do.

When the day came the word flew round the streets and closes faster than the wind that the factor was on his way. By the time Mr Fintry arrived in Commercial Road, Mrs Rafferty's close was packed and overflowing onto the cobbles. Each woman was armed with something, a bag of flour, a brush, a wooden spoon, a ladle, a spurtle, a carpet beater and, much to the hilarity of the others, one woman had even armed herself with a chipped enamel chamber pot.

Mr Fintry was at first disdainful, then discovering that his initial efforts to pass were being blocked he became sneering and insulting. That was all the women needed to release years of pent-up fury at all the injustices they had suffered, all the rudeness and insults from this man and others like him. With a howl like a war cry they set upon him. Bags of flour burst over his head, he was showered with brushes, carpet beaters and a wide variety of kitchen utensils. Then the woman with the chamber pot rammed it on top of his head and immediately the fury dissolved into uproarious laughter.

Big Donald, the six-feet-four policeman from the Isle of Skye, had been passing along Rutherglen Road at the time and had witnessed the disturbance. He could have, without the slightest problem, waded in and nipped the rammy in the bud before it had taken off. That Big Donald would have been vastly outnumbered would not have deterred him in the slightest. Well known, well thought of, and well respected in the area, if he had ordered them to behave themselves and get away home the chances were that they would have obeyed him. But Big Donald, who knew everything that went on in his patch, also knew Mrs Rafferty. She had often apologized to him for her children. He felt sorry for her. He decided to turn a blind eye on this occasion. He continued his leisurely stroll along Rutherglen Road, concentrating his attention instead on some of the rooftops. There was always the chance, albeit a faint one, of spotting the Swan-Necked Kid in the act of purloining lead. The lad had taken his nickname from the shape of the lead pieces that he stole from rooftops. It was common knowledge that the Swan-Necked Kid set out every morning five feet nine inches in height, but by the time he returned home he was only about five feet two. This was caused by the weight of the stolen lead hooked around him underneath his wide coat. It was Big Donald's dream to catch him in the act and arrest him. The prospect added spice to Big Donald's daily routine.

Big Donald usually took his time about everything, yet he could be quick off the mark when he wanted to. He noticed, for instance, the dishevelled, floury and furious Mr Fintry emerge from Commercial Road and immediately concluded that the factor would be looking for the assistance of the law. Big Donald stepped smartly into McKay's dairy where he was always made welcome by the saucy, fresh-complexioned Mrs McKay, a widow woman of over a year now.

'A wee cup of tea would be very nice right now, I was thinking.'

'Come away through the back then.' Mrs McKay smiled flirtatiously up at him.

Further along Rutherglen Road, Mr Fintry was fuming about how you could never get a policeman when you wanted one. He gave up eventually and returned defeated to his office.

The women were jubilant. The day had been saved and Mrs Rafferty would now at least have some breathing space to regain her strength and decide what she could do for the best.

No one felt more elated than Annalie. It was as if her heightened spirits had caused fate in general to turn in her favour, because the very same day she heard that she could get Mrs McWhirter's wee single end after all. It wasn't such a happy turn of events for Mrs McWhirter, of course. As if it wasn't bad enough that the poor woman had lost her young husband at the front, now her father had been killed in France, and her mother was absolutely broken-hearted. The younger widow had decided that she had better go and stay with her mother and try to be of some comfort to her.

Annalie was in seventh heaven about the single end in Cumberland Street. It was the close nearest to Commercial Road and was very smelly because of the wet fish shop, yet it was like a perfumed garden compared with down the dunny.

The thought of escaping from the underground cave that she had shared in such squalor with the Rafferty brood seemed too good to be true. But it was true, she kept telling herself. It was true, it was true. She ran all the way up the stairs with the key clutched in her hand and the baby bouncing about inside her shawl. She was choking for breath by the time she reached the landing. The baby was big now, and heavy. She savoured the thrill of putting the key in the door, of opening it, of stepping inside, of shutting the door behind her, of walking across the small, cupboard-sized entrance lobby and into the kitchen. And there facing her was the most wonderful thing. A window.

Annalie danced around the room making the baby giggle until it developed a noisy hiccough.

'We're alone, Elizabeth. We're alone,' Annalie shouted. 'We're private. It's just us. It's our own home and it's LIGHT! Oh blessed, blessed light.'

There was even a window on the landing halfway up the stairs and there was a gas mantle above the door of the single end for when it was dark. The single end was in the middle of the landing with a door on either side that led into flats consisting of a room and kitchen.

Annalie began to cry with happiness. She cried loudly and unashamedly until she was exhausted. It was then, as she wiped her tears away with an edge of her shawl, that it occurred to her that poor Mrs Rafferty wouldn't feel so happy. Annalie knew that she couldn't bring herself to stay one other night down the dunny. She had no bed for the new house, no blankets, nothing, but if necessary she would sleep on the bare boards.

She would have to tell Mrs Rafferty, of course. The poor woman had been so grateful to her for saving her and the children from Mr Fintry.

'And to take the afternoon off your work, hen. Oh, I'm that grateful. I don't know what I've done to deserve all this kindness.'

Aunty Murn had sent a neighbour's boy along with the key and a written message to tell her about the single end. Annalie had been so excited she'd rushed right out without explaining to Mrs Rafferty.

Now, reluctantly, she turned back down the stairs and headed into Commercial Road. She had begun to shake at the thought of telling Mrs Rafferty, but it had to be done.

'Nothing's wrong, hen, I hope?' Mrs Rafferty greeted her as soon as she arrived in the house. 'You rushed away that quick I thought your Aunty Murn's place must have gone on fire or something. She's all right, is she?'

'Yes,' Annalie said. 'Actually it was just a note to let me know that there was a single end for me. Just round at that first close at the wet fish shop. I know it's a bit quick, Mrs Rafferty, but I'm going to move in tonight. There's no point in waiting, is there? I mean, now that I've got a place of my own I'd better get settled in right away. There'll be a lot to do, you see.'

Mrs Rafferty was staring at her like a stricken deer. Her eyes wide and helpless had the obedient attentiveness of a child. Annalie could have wept. At the same time she felt angry at the world that had put both of them in such a heartbreaking situation. She hated a world that had made Mrs Rafferty helpless under the dark earth, without even a window to cheer her.

'I'll be back to see you of course,' Annalie promised.

'Often. And I'll keep my eye open for a nice wee place for you in a close like that. With neighbours on either side and upstairs from me, I'll have a better chance to hear what's going on and if there's a wee place going vacant . . .'

Mrs Rafferty still stood like an obedient child, listening

113

intently and slightly nodding her head as if trying to learn Annalie's words off by heart.

'You'll be all right,' Annalie said. 'I'll see to it.'

And she meant to. She meant to go round the very next day and she would have had if not been for the telegram which put everything else out of her head.

Chapter Eighteen

Mr Abercromby was a tree trunk of a man, bushy bearded and restless with robust health and energy. He was such an enthusiastic golfer his wife said she never saw him at weekends. This was not delivered as a complaint, quite the reverse in fact. Mrs Abercromby was a frail, gentle, little woman much subject to breathlessness and hot flushes. To be with her husband was an ordeal. A walk in the park, for instance, meant her gasping to keep up with his long, fast strides. From her quiet, still shell Christina observed him from where she sat at the other side of his giant flat-topped desk. He swung about in his swivel chair, drummed his fingers on the desk, then suddenly thumped his arms down on to it and leaned forward across them.

'Forty-eight per cent, you say?'

'Yes,' Christina agreed. 'I'm the biggest single shareholder, but I repeat, Mr Abercromby, I'm only offering forty per cent as security for the loan.'

Abercromby said, 'And at a flat rate of seven per cent per annum on the money borrowed.'

'Yes,' she said. 'I'll have to agree to that. I haven't much choice there, have I?'

'You're obviously not au fait with bank pratice here Mrs Monkton. You've nothing to complain about. I'm granting you a holiday period of the first five years of your loan of non capital repayments. In other words you won't start repaying capital on the loan until after five years and then pay it over the next ten years by which time your rental will have increased per annum. But you are quite clear? The bank is providing capital for purchase of freehold tenemental property, but your shares in the building company will be held in security to be taken up on failure to meet interest charges over a maximum period of six months.'

'Yes. I understand that.'

'You'll need an adviser. Someone who know the business and has his ear to the ground. I know the very one. Clever chap, he's a valuation surveyor. Name of Scott Mathieson. I'll put him in touch with you. You'll also need a good property factor. No doubt Mathieson will be able to advise you on that, but if there's any difficulty on that score you can get back to me and I'll see what I can do for you.' He suddenly propelled himself to his feet. 'Right. No doubt I'll be hearing from you again.'

Christina rose too. 'I'm glad I've talked things out with you. I feel confident now to go ahead with my plans.'

Into Mr Abercromby's eyes came the hint of sly calculation.

'Each scheme must be considered on its own merits, you understand, Mrs Monkton, and for each one I must first of all consider the advice of the agent and the factor. The property business is a very high risk one and it's not the bank's policy to take risks.'

Christina accepted his proffered handshake and smiled sweetly up at him. 'Oh, I'm sure you know as well as I do, Mr Abercromby, that while you're holding forty per cent of shares in such a well-established and successful business as Monkton's the bank at least is protected against risks.'

One or two of the bank employees raised their heads from ledgers to look at her as she passed through the main trading part of the building. She suited the slight flush that the excitement of success had brought to her cheeks. The beginnings of self-confidence too had a flattering effect on her, raising her chin, straightening her shoulders, giving her an aura of dignity and importance. Her clothes too had improved. She no longer allowed Mrs Duffy to make her clothes, a decision which had greatly offended Mrs Duffy. Christina had come to see that the dressmaker made garments that were for the most part old-fashioned and dull. Moreover Mrs Duffy had always been influenced by her friend Mrs Gillespie in what she made for Christina. Christina wanted to break away from this image. Not that she had any desire or intention to go to the opposite extreme and bedeck herself in riotous colours or gimmicky fashions.

116

What she had in mind was a smart, businesslike yet expensively elegant look. It was no longer absolutely necessary to have a good dressmaker. Ready-made clothes could now be had from the new department stores. However, Christina had known for some time of a young woman in the Martyrs Church congregation who had quite a flair for dressmaking. She'd often wanted clothes made by this woman in the past but her mother would never hear of it. Maisie Saunders had done a bit of sewing as a hobby at first and also to make her own clothes. Christina had found out about Maisie's talent when she had admired the elegant way that young woman was always dressed, and Maisie had confessed that the dresses and coats she wore with such style and good taste were of her own making. More recently however, she had become one of the growing number of women who had lost their husbands in the conflict and was now having to earn a living with her needle. She was a bright, friendly woman and was taking great interest and pleasure in providing Christina with a new wardrobe.

All the way back to Monkton House Christina thought over her interview with the banker and her plans for the future. She could hardly wait to get things under way and was glad when a meeting with Scott Mathieson was arranged very promptly.

She met him in his small office in Hope Street, surprised first of all to see how young he looked. She had been expecting another Mr Abercromby, a man in his fifties. Scott Mathieson was perhaps in his late thirties, tall, lean, and so relaxed he barely raised himself from his seat when she entered. His hair was creamy fair and his lashes and brows so fair they were almost invisible. The eyes that met hers held a kind of mock innocence until he smiled most charmingly and innocence narrowed into cold calculation.

'Mr Abercromby has given me the general idea,' he said once she'd settled comfortably into a seat. 'I'm intrigued.'

'With my business ideas?' Christina asked. 'Or because I'm a woman with business ideas?'

He laughed. 'A bit of both. You're serious, are you?'

117

She felt a needle of irritation. 'Would you ask that question of a man?'

He shrugged. 'Maybe.'

'I don't think so,' she said. He lit up a cigarette and blew a spiral of smoke upwards.

'Hang on,' he said. 'It does make a difference, you know, you being a woman. You must face that if we're going to get anywhere.'

'Exactly what do you mean?' she asked warily.

'Well, a lot of property goes on rumour. A word here, a word there. Especially round in the pub about half past five or in one of the clubs, gentlemen-only clubs. You'd be surprised at the amount of information that's picked up in the pubs and clubs.'

'I see,' Christina said. 'But surely there are other more straightforward means to find out what property is on the market?'

'In terms of property.' Mathieson said, 'there's investment and development. There's also trading and dealing. To put it simply my advice to you is to buy land. The essence of property is land and the reason for that is that they've stopped making it.'

Christina smiled but her eyes were serious. 'But that's putting out money without getting an income from it.'

'Ah,' Mathieson said. 'This is where keeping your ear to the ground is so important. You see, ideally you buy a site knowing that a manufacturer or somebody needs land.'

Christina's eyes began to light up with interest and understanding.

'I see. So I buy land at a low price and I sell it to the person who needs it for a much higher price. That way I make money.'

'Exactly,' Mathieson said. 'And you don't need to do anything. That's trading and dealing and it can provide a lot of bread-and-butter capital profit. You could build up profit within your own property company. That way you could also build up a capital base so that within a short time you could say to your banker, 'I've got this capital base. You no longer need my shares in the building side of the company as security so I want them back. I can now offer you all the security you need.' Because, you see, you will have been taking profits and at the same time paying back the banker. Do you follow me?'

Christina favoured him with a slow smile in return. 'Indeed I do, Mr Mathieson. Indeed I do.'

'Something tells me, Mrs Monkton,' he said, 'that you are going to enjoy this high-risk business.'

'Right again,' she said.

'Good. I wanted to be sure of that because it would be much safer and easier for you just to relax and enjoy the interest from your shares. You would have enjoyed a very comfortable living from your husband's business even though you did not have any shares in it. It's not a big business but it's solid and dependable. It had the reputation for doing a good job of work. Comparatively speaking, it's not a high-risk business, nor are the directors the type of people who would want to take risks. I knew the late Mr Monkton and I know your husband. Both admirable, hard-working men.'

'I've no wish to deny that,' Christina said. 'But, as I've already told my husband, rolling up one's sleeves and straining the muscles and sweating in the effort is not the only way to be successful and to make money.'

'I think, Mrs Monkton,' Mathieson said with another charming smile, 'you and I are going to get on very well. Very well indeed.'

Chapter Nineteen

I deeply regret to inform you that the Privates David and Edward Gordon of the Scottish Rifles were killed in action. Lord Kitchener expresses his sympathy.

Signed, Secretary, War Office.

Annalie wept broken-heartedly over the telegram.

'That's enough,' Aunty Murn said eventually. 'Acting like somebody demented won't bring them back. Nothing'll bring them back and there's an end to it.'

Aunty Murn's face was grim and white and rock hard. It amazed Annalie how she could contain her grief. She knew Aunty Murn had loved the boys in her own way, so for her sake Annalie fought to control her sobs. She went over to the sink and turned on the tap and splashed her face with the icy water.

'It's time you got back to your wean,' Aunty Murn said. 'You can't just leave her every time it comes up your humph.'

'Do you not want me to stay?' Annalie said. 'Surely Daddy wouldn't make a fuss at a time like this?'

'What would I want you to stay for?' Aunty Murn said. 'And it's the last thing your daddy needs is to be upset by seeing you here when he comes in from a hard day's work. Away you go back to your wean where you belong.'

Annalie dried her face then nursed her head in the towel.

'I don't know how I can stand it. I can't bear to think. I can't accept it. It's so unfair.'

'What's fair in the world?' Aunty Murn said. 'There's always someone worse than yourself. Look at all these Belgian refugees. Now away you go. You've got your own wee place now and that's where you belong.'

'Have the police found Mammy yet?'

'No. I've laid this blanket out for you. You can't have the wean sleeping with nothing on top of it.'

'But that's off your bed,' Annalie said.

'I'll pick up something at the Barras.' Aunty Murn did most of her shopping for household goods at the market known as the Barras.

'It's a disgrace,' Aunty Murn said. 'You out working and leaving your wean with a stranger every day.'

'What else can I do? Would you have me on the Parish or in the Poor House?'

'Lots of decent folk have to go on the Parish. You're too proud to do that but you weren't too proud to let that man lay a hand on you.'

Annalie sighed. 'There's no comparison between a Parish inspector who comes and pokes around, treats you like dirt and grudges every penny, and a handsome man making love to you.'

'Do you not think he's treated you like dirt?' Aunty Murn said. 'Like he's treated many a poor servant lassie before you, no doubt. Now take that blanket and away you go, and just you behave yourself when you start in Hurley's tomorrow. And never you mind sitting there enjoying yourself, taking dinner when you get your half-hour off. You get up those stairs and see that your wean's all right.'

'I've arranged it all with Mrs Hurley. She's been very good.'

'Aye, Mrs Hurley's a decent enough woman. But just you watch that son of hers.'

In fact Annalie didn't expect to see much of Malcolm Hurley if things worked out as Mrs Hurley had planned.

'Malcolm needs a few hours at night to be with his family,' she'd told Annalie. 'I can't expect him to be here all the time. He's a good son to me and very willing but I mustn't take advantage. But I need to keep the shop open till late, like anyone else, to get in enough money, so what I thought was, Annalie, if you came in every night about five and stayed till eleven or sometimes maybe a wee bit later, that would suit me fine.'

It suited Annalie too, because it would mean that the

baby would be asleep for most of the time when she was out and Flo Blair, one of her next-door neighbours who'd promised to take her in every night, shouldn't have any bother with her. It also meant that Annalie could be with the baby and see to her during the day when she was awake. Her life revolved around Elizabeth. She had gladly given up her youth for her. She saw other girls of her own age parading and giggling along Cumberland Street, eyeing the talent. And she did not envy them, hardly even noticed them. All her concentration was on survival for herself and her baby.

For Annalie it was as much a question of sustaining her spirit as a day-to-day physical survival. The most crushing blow she'd had in her young life was this most recent one, the loss of her brothers. As she descended Aunty Murn's stairs and emerged into Cumberland Street to mingle with the crowd of beshawled and hatless women, she was longing so much to see her brothers again she would willingly have died to be with them. Only the thought of leaving Elizabeth made her struggle desperately with herself to find courage to go on.

Even during the days that followed, however, while she looked after the baby and tried at the same time to convert her barren room into some sort of a home, her mind was still obsessed with the past and memories of Davie and Eddie. They had always been so full of life and mischief that she kept thinking they couldn't be dead. Then the reality of the telegram would sweep over her, leaving her feeling sick and hardly able to stand up, what with the weak trembling in her legs. She was thankful to get out to Hurley's in the evening and to have her time and her mind fully occupied with work.

Mrs Hurley gave her a big, white apron that tied round her waist and reached down to her ankles and she had hardly got the apron tied on when she had to attend to her first customer. The small, gaslit shop was cosy because of the heat coming through from the fire in Mrs Hurley's back kitchen.

The shop was so crowded with groceries that there was

hardly any room for customers, although plenty of them kept pushing in. On the floor there was a pyramid of canned fruit from California. There were stacks of Ovaltine and Horlicks and tins of treacle and the latest breakfast cereals called Force and Grapenuts. A panelled counter ran along the length of the shop topped with polished wood. Behind the counter, running the length of the wall, was a marble-topped shelf. On the marble sat the cheese board with its cutting wire, the bacon and ham slicing machine and the mountain of butter that had to be patted into shape with two wooden butter pats. There was also a basket in which nestled dozens of eggs. On the wooden counter were caddies of tea and large glass jars filled with aniseed balls, humbugs, liquorice allsorts, bags of sherbet, lollipops, strips of everlasting toffee and penny chocolate bars. On other shelves were packets of tapers, candles, Bisto, custard, porridge oats and pipe clay. There were tins of Huntley and Palmer's biscuits and loaves of bread and tins of Zebo and black lead. On the floor was a large flour bin filled with flour and a flour scoop made of painted tin with a wooden handle. On higher shelves that had to be reached by climbing small steps were jars of honey and jam and condensed milk. Mrs Hurley also sold paraffin oil and gas mantles as well as peas, lentils, barley and the sugar that she kept under the counter.

'Things are that scarce now,' Mrs Hurley explained. 'And getting scarcer every day.'

Mrs Hurley, Annalie soon discovered, was as Aunty Murn said a decent enough wee woman, but Malcolm Hurley was a different kettle of fish altogether. He had explained to Annalie, not in the presence of his mother however, what he called the 'tricks of the trade'.

'For instance,' he told Annalie, 'never cut the cheese or bacon exactly to weight. Make it an ounce or two more, then overcharge for this extra piece. You see,' he explained, 'there's very few who can do the sums before you take the stuff off the scale and there's still fewer who can weigh it up again when they get back home. They've nothing to weigh it on, you see.'

Annalie ignored his dirty tricks and followed instead his mother's lead and instructions. She suspected that Malcolm Hurley was not only cheating on the customers, but cheating on his mother. It often worried her that any suspicion on Mrs Hurley's part would be wrongly directed towards her. To be branded as dishonest was something that her pride could not contemplate.

On more than one occasion she saw Malcolm taking money from the till and slipping it into his pocket. She worried constantly about whether she should tell his mother. The only reason she didn't was that she suspected Mrs Hurley would be outraged at any accusation against her son. He was, as far as Annalie could make out, the light of her life. She was constantly telling Annalie how Malcolm's wife wasn't good enough for him, and Annalie was regaled day after day with her daughter-in-law's faults and failings. For everything that went wrong in Malcolm Hurley's marriage, and it seemed that everything was going wrong, Mrs Hurley blamed her daughter-in-law.

Malcolm Hurley was a skinny, round-shouldered leek of a man with a face that slithered into his neck without any chin to stop it. He had dandruff-speckled hair, brows that met bushily in the centre over a long nose and furtive, lecherous eyes. He had a habit of slowly crushing past her behind the counter and pushing himself against her. She would often feel his hands accidentally on purpose, brushing against her bottom. One of the happiest moments of Annalie's life was the day when she accidentally on purpose jammed her knee up into his groin and brought tears to his eyes. He was a terrible worry all the same and completely spoiled her job at Hurley's. As Aunty Murn said, however, 'Nothing's easy in this life and you'll just have to cope with it as best you can.'

It was the anxiety of trying to cope with Malcolm Hurley and her grief for Davie and Eddie that at first had put Mrs Rafferty completely out of her mind. When Annalie did remember her, and felt concerned for her welfare, she couldn't face the prospect of going to visit her at the dunny as she had promised. She was so glad to be away from the place, so relieved of the horror of having to go down through the rat-infested stairs and passage, that she really didn't want to go back there again.

She knew she would have to. She wanted to see Mrs Rafferty, and as each day passed she worried about her more. She would go tomorrow, she kept telling herself. Then when tomorrow came there was so much to do she somehow never got round to it.

She began to feel so guilty and ashamed, however, that one forenoon she wrapped her shawl round the baby and herself and set off along Commercial Road. Then taking a deep breath, she plunged into the darkness of Mrs Rafferty's close and made the necessary shuffling and stamping descent down the stairs and along the corridor. She opened Mrs Rafferty's door, calling out as she did so, 'It's only me, Mrs Rafferty.'

The gas was down quite low and at first she thought there was nobody in. Certainly none of the children were there.

Then she heard Mrs Rafferty say in a broken-hearted voice, 'Oh my God, hen, I'm awful sorry.'

Mrs Rafferty was in bed with a man. He was naked and he got up when he saw Annalie. He hastily pulled on a shirt and trousers, wrapped a muffler round his neck and put on his cap before grabbing his jacket and disappearing.

'I had to do it for the money,' Mrs Rafferty said. 'They were coming back again to put me and the weans out and I didn't want to bother anybody, hen. You were all that kind to me before.'

Annalie didn't know what to say. Mrs Rafferty's baby began to cry. It was at the back of the bed.

Then Mrs Rafferty, a mound of heaving, helpless fat, began to cry too.

Chapter Twenty

As soon as Mathieson mentioned land Christina had thought of Mrs Gray, the oldest member of her father's congregation. She was a widow of eighty-nine and lived in solitary state in a large villa about a mile from the church.

Mrs Gray had a reputation for being miserly. The Reverend Gillespie always maintained she kept a stock of buttons, one of which she placed in the collection bag every week. He had long since tired of aiming at her sermons and texts like 'It is harder for a rich man to enter the kingdom of heaven than for a camel to pass through the eye of a needle' – all to no avail. People were sorry for her maid of all work, her cook/housekeeper and gardener/handyman. These three servants were expected to do the work of the army of servants who ought to have been employed in the running of such a large establishment. Needless to say, despite the conscientious efforts of the servants, the house had a neglected look and the garden had long since become overgrown, as the gardener/handyman was so often needed for jobs in the house.

The large garden was surrounded by a thick wall of trees as well as a high brick wall, and at the back, reached through a gate in the wall, was a large meadow also sheltered by trees.

It was quite easy to appeal to Mrs Gray's greed. Christina did so by offering to buy the meadow land but conducting the negotiations in a way that she knew would please the old miser and convince her that she had got the best of the bargain. She first of all offered the old woman a ridiculously low price, and could see by the gleam in the eyes that the offer of any sum of money interested her.

Christina allowed the old woman to play the game of refusing at first. She pointed out too that the meadow was of no use to Mrs Gray and hinted, as if she was talking on behalf of the Martyrs Church although never actually saying so, that the land could be put to good Christian use. She allowed Mrs Gray the pleasure of believing she was putting one over on Christina and slyly manoeuvring an unexpected windfall for herself. Mrs Gray had reached that stage of senility when she could feel gleefully superior to anyone else. She haggled and pushed the price up while Christina wrung her hands and protested that Mrs Gray drove a hard bargain.

When the price was approaching the one which Christina originally had decided on, she sighed and appeared to capitulate to the other woman's far superior business acumen.

'All right, Mrs Gray,' she said. 'You win. It's double the good price that I came here to pay you and I'll probably get into trouble for allowing you to talk me into this deal, but I'm not a very experienced business person, I'm afraid.'

Mrs Gray was delighted with her success and the unexpected addition to her bank balance. She could not have experienced as much secret delight, however, as Christina did after the deal was safely completed. Mathieson already knew of a buyer desperate for such a prime site and she sold the land, not, as Mathieson suggested, for five times the price paid for it, but for a daring ten times the price. Mathieson was full of admiration.

'You're a natural, Mrs Monkton,' he said. 'A natural. At one stroke you've made yourself a tidy little fortune.'

'I'd still like something that would bring me in a regular income. Tenemental property, it seems to me, would be the most profitable in this respect. I want to buy a property that is old and therefore will be cheap. One with plenty of tenants who are paying sufficiently high rents to make it a long-term profitable proposition.'

Mathieson shrugged. 'Well there's plenty of old property in Glasgow.'

'Not always for sale though,' Christina observed.

'True,' Mathieson said. 'But there are always a few here and there. I'll find out what's on the market at the moment.'

'No,' Christina said. 'Find out what might be liable to

come on the market so that we can get in there before anyone else. Find out too, who might be persuaded or pressurized to sell even if they have no intention of doing so at the moment.'

'Now that you mention it,' Mathieson said thoughtfully, 'I do know of someone with whom a little persuasion might go a long way. Rumour has it he's in deep financial trouble over another business he's been dabbling in.'

'Give me his name and address and phone number,' Christina said. 'I'll make an appointment to see him right away.'

Mathieson lolled back in his chair.

'You don't believe in letting the grass grow under your feet, do you?'

'Write out the address now,' Christina said impatiently.

'Certainly.' Mathieson smiled and in a minute had passed a piece of paper over to her. She gave it a quick glance before rising and stuffing it into her purse.

Mathieson rose too. 'I'll get the details of other tenemental properties to you as soon as possible.'

'Don't post them,' Christina said. 'Deliver them in person to Monkton House.'

'Your attitude intrigues me,' he said. 'You seem to believe strongly speed is of the essence. May I ask why?'

'No you may not,' she said quietly.

'Only natural curiosity. You give the outward impression of such a calm, careful person, not somebody who would rush at anything.'

'I'm not rushing carelessly into anything,' she told him. 'I've worked out my every move very carefully.'

She turned at the door. 'By the way, I was thinking. I really ought to have an office of my own.'

'I agree,' he said. 'Did you have in mind something large and luxurious or would one of the rooms here do? I've three fair-sized ones and I really only need this one. There's the reception room at the front where you came through. My secretary/receptionist is there. Far too big an area for one person, I've always said. It could accommodate two secretaries quite easily. I'll show you round now if you wish?'

'Very well,' Christina agreed.

The third room was not large and she could imagine it being somewhat cramped with a desk and bookcase and anything else she might need. But it was big enough and it had a nice high window looking down onto the busy Hope Street below.

'What rent would you be asking for this?' she wanted to know.

'I tell you what.' He gave her one of his most charming smiles. 'You can have this rent free plus my services in exchange for a percentage of your profits.'

She eyed him cautiously and could see that despite his smile he was serious.

'You mean instead of your introductory fee of two and a half per cent of the purchase price of any land or property?'

'Yes,' he agreed. 'I'd be looking for something in the order of ten per cent of the annual rental.'

'Hmmm. I'll think about that,' she told him, 'and I'll give you my decision when you come to Monkton House to deliver the information about the tenemental property.'

'Fair enough,' he agreed.

She thought about his proposition all the way home. She was very wary of cutting anyone else in, yet at the same time it would surely pay off for Mathieson to have a special stake in her business. For a start it would prevent any danger of him playing her off against another client. By the time she reached Monkton House she had decided that she would offer Mathieson a small percentage, as small as she could get away with, but certainly no more than ten per cent, and she would accept his offer of the office room.

She was just crossing the hall in Monkton House when she heard Adam's voice raised in anger.

'I knew nothing of this.'

In a softer tremble of a voice Beatrice said, 'She's been nothing but trouble from the start. It's just been one thing after another. But she's your wife, Adam, and you're responsible for her. It doesn't matter what you say now, people are still thinking that you did know, you must have known and it's your responsibility what she does.'

Christina hesitated outside the drawing room door. She was tempted to continue further along the hall and go into the morning-room that looked out onto the long back garden. She often went in there and sat alone reading or writing. She had come to regard it as her own private sitting room and would look up in cool disapproval if anyone else entered. On this occasion, however, she felt it would be an act of cowardice not to go into the drawing room and face Adam.

'What the hell do you think you're playing at?' he asked as soon as she entered the room.

Beatrice's slim, white hand went to her forehead.

'I must go and lie down. I've been so upset today with all this tittle-tattle and accusations and blackening of our good name.'

Ignoring her, Christina went over and sat in one of the fireside chairs.

'I repeat,' Adam said after his mother had left the room, 'what the hell do you think you are doing?'

'I gather,' Christina said, 'you are referring to the property deal with Mrs Gray?'

'No, I'm talking about you cheating an eighty-nine-year-old woman. Cheating her out of a fortune.'

'I didn't regard it as cheating,' Christina said. 'Business is business and as far as I'm concerned buying low and selling high is good business.'

'Well let me make it plain to you, Christina, that is not my idea of business nor my way of conducting business.'

She felt a deep thrill at the sound of his voice uttering her name. It had been so long since he had actually said the word. She had blessed Moses Monkton a hundred times for leaving her the shares and she blessed him again. Had it not been for her involvement in the business and her attendance at board meetings she and Adam would have continued to be stiffly encased in the iceberg of their lives together, seeing one another yet unable or unwilling to communicate at all. Her communications with him were now heated, antagonistic and full of conflict, but at least they were communicating.

She shrugged. 'All right, so we have different business methods.'

'No, it is not all right, Christina,' Adam said. 'I will not have you going about Glasgow cheating elderly ladies.'

'I told you, I didn't regard it as cheating.'

'Don't lie to me, Christina. You knew you were taking advantage of an old woman who's not right in the head. She's senile, she doesn't know what she's doing. It was absolutely despicable of you. Although, of course, it doesn't surprise me. You've quite a penchant for cheating, haven't you? You've always been devious and calculating.'

'That's quite an unwarranted personal attack,' said Christina. 'I thought we were talking about business.'

'We're talking about you,' Adam said. 'And what I'd like to know is , where did you get the capital to buy that land?'

Christina's hands tightened in her lap.

'I went to a bank in the city and gave them some of my shares in the building firm as security for a loan.'

'You what!'

He was a fearsome sight. His eyes had a mad gleam and the scar pulling down one brow gave him a satanic look.

'You what?' he repeated in a lower, incredulous tone.

She forced her eyes up towards the muscular figure towering over her without actually meeting his eyes.

'It's perfectly normal business practice,' she managed. 'And the shares are mine to do with as I wish.'

With one quick movement he had grabbed her by the shoulders and whipped her to her feet. The unexpected violence of the moment forced her head back and up to meet his eyes.

'Do you realize,' he said, 'that you could ruin my business? The business that my father worked hard to maintain.'

His words meant nothing to her. She was conscious only of his fingers digging deep into the flesh of her arms and his body hot against hers.

'I won't ruin your business,' she said quietly. 'Trust me.'

'Trust you?' Adam echoed. 'That's one thing I'll never do, Christina.'

If the truth were told she didn't trust him either. People

might say that no relationship could be built on such negative foundations. But people had said she could not succeed in business because she had no foundation of knowledge or experience, and yet she was determined to prove them wrong.

Chapter Twenty-one

She'd thought Adam was going to strike her. She believed he had thought so too. He suddenly flung her aside and strode from the room, saying, 'I'll talk to you later.'

She'd felt stimulated and excited. Later they had talked, but Adam had not been able to make her give up her property business any more than he had previously managed to force her to give up her shares. What he had succeeded in, though, was persuading her not to set up her office on Mathieson's premises.

'Even if it means locking you in this house,' Adam told her, 'You will not go and share an office with Scott Mathieson. If you must have your own room there is extra space in my office building in Pollokshaws Road. At least there I can keep an eye on you.'

Christina decided that on this issue discretion was the better part of valour. She knew Adam had been well schooled in the basic elements of gentlemanly behaviour, and therefore she believed he would not strike her, yet at the same time her instinct warned that she had better not push him too far.

When Mathieson called at Monkton House she informed him about her change of plan, but also said that she would agree to his proposal of a percentage of any profits she made. He accepted this with a little bow and then went straight on to tell her about a property owned by a man who was on the verge of bankruptcy.

'If you get in there quickly with an offer,' he told her, 'you could make a very good killing. By the way, have you seen the man yet that I told you about?'

'Oh yes. I saw him the other day. I didn't bother to get in touch knowing you'd be over today. I had a meeting with him and I bought his tenement building for this.' She passed him over a paper. He looked at it and laughed.

'I don't know how you do it! I could almost feel sorry for him. That building is crowded with tenants. Overcrowded actually, like most of the slums in that area. They've ticketed houses there but it doesn't make any difference.'

'What's that?' Christina asked.

'Oh, it's a bright idea from the sanitary department. Well, that's not strictly true. It's actually from the Glasgow Police Act of 1862 which gave powers to the Medical Officer of Health to enter and inspect all small houses in the city.' He lit a cigarette. 'What that means in practice is that the houses are raided in the middle of the night by the Public Health inspectors who have powers to bring surplus people to court. Each pair of sanitary inspectors is expected to make a hundred visits per night.' He laughed. 'Can you imagine it? These men creeping about between midnight and four o'clock in the morning with lanterns and books taking notes.'

'How very odd,' Christina said.

Mathieson strolled across the room in search of an ashtray. He was an elegantly dressed man and always looked as if he had stepped straight out of the bath into pristine clean and pressed clothes.

'Ticketed houses, they call them. They put a metal disc on the door saying how many bodies are allowed in the square yardage of the house. The inspectors check their numbers against that.'

Christina was already studying the papers he had given her.

'These tenement properties do bring in a good income, don't they?'

'Property is about people. I mean the people one has to negotiate with. It's about people, land and money. But, as I've told you before, it's a very risky business. Don't imagine that every deal you make will necessarily be as successful as the ones you've made so far. You've always got to have either the foresight or the guarantee. Also the knowledge and the information. So far we've been lucky, you've had information about the people we've had to negotiate with, information that's been useful to you in the making of a profitable deal. You might not always be as lucky as that.'

'I don't see it as luck,' Christina told him. 'It's as you say, foresight and information. It's also about nerve, wouldn't you agree?' It was also about acquiring things, owning things. This was an instinct, a need in her as powerful as the need for food or water. She could not have articulated it. Even to herself.

He smiled at her through a cloud of cigarette smoke. 'Oh yes, and the keeping of one's nerve. That's very important.'

They discussed then the possibility of further deals. She was interested in finding more land but, as Mathieson said, land was at a premium and not easy to come by. At present he didn't know of anything, but he'd keep on the lookout. Meantime she would concentrate on acquiring more tenement property. This he could help her with and they discussed the property he had in mind.

Eventually, noticing the time, she brought the discussion to a close. Adam was due home at any time now and she did not think it wise at this stage to risk a confrontation between the two men. Adam, she knew, resented Mathieson's involvement. She would like to have thought that his resentment stemmed from jealousy but knew in her heart that his only concern was about the property business and how it might adversely affect the building side of Monkton's. She had tried to explain to Adam when they attempted to discuss the situation, that the property side of the business was not a threat or a danger but could, on the contrary, be a financial advantage to the construction side of Monkton's. She had to admit of course that there were dangers. 'But I believe,' she told him, 'that you can't get anywhere unless you take risks.'

'There are enough risks in the building trade without adding to them,' Adam said. 'You take on a job, you lay out a large sum of money buying material, you do your sums to include men's wages et cetera for a certain length of time. You reckon to finish on a certain date and that's what you've budgeted towards. Then a hundred things can go wrong. The weather can turn hellish for one thing and hold up a job for days, weeks or even months. The man for whom you're building the premises could go bankrupt. Any one of a hundred things could happen to leave you with a fortune laid out and nothing coming in.'

'But couldn't the fact that the property side is making good money be used if necessary as security for the building side?' Christina said. 'I mean if some emergency like that happened again and you were in difficulties wouldn't it be easier for you to borrow money for your needs?'

The stiffly controlled manner in which he had been conducting the discussion snapped into anger.

'The horrific risks involved in what you're doing far outweigh any advantages that you imagine there might be for my side of the business. How often must I tell you that? Can't you get it into your head? There is a very real danger that you could ruin Monkton's. But quite apart from anything else I have been running the business and have always coped very successfully with any difficulties that have arisen. I intend to continue doing this without any so-called help from you.'

She couldn't make him understand her vision. He was blinkered in terms of business construction. He couldn't think of anything else, but at least they were talking now. Not as easily or as often as a normal married couple, but at least he didn't ignore her, which several people in the church now did.

She still attended church service on Sunday morning, but now, in contrast to the dull little mouse she had once been she appeared in elegant dresses and coats much wider than the draped hobble skirts that were still worn by most of the female congregation. Older people especially were shocked by the fact that her skirts no longer decently covered her ankles. They also considered the soft colours she wore to be disgraceful in view of the fact that most decent people now were wearing black, at least on Sundays. This was in sympathy with the bereaved of the growing lists of dead in all the newspapers. A distressing number of young men who had belonged to the Martyrs Church, who not so long ago attended Sunday school and bible class were now lost for ever. The Reverend William Gillespie had made pointed reference to wearing coloured clothes on Sundays in more than one sermon in which he spoke of respect for the dead and grieving families. Both the Reverend Gillespie and his wife had spoken to Christina directly. They had told her how sad her behaviour was making them. Her father said a prayer over her in the manse drawing room in which he asked God to forgive her and guide her in better ways.

Her mode of dress, of course, was not the only thing about which her parents were concerned.

'Your place is at home in Monkton House attending to domestic matters and supervising the work of the servants,' her father told her, and her mother agreed with him. 'Your sole ambition in life should be to see to the efficient running of your home and to create a comfortable haven for your husband and family.'

'Father,' Christina said, 'the time has passed for women to sit at home all day twiddling their thumbs and waiting for a pat on the head from their husbands.'

Her mother's face creased in sympathy.

'Is it because it's still Beatrice's home, Chrissie? Is that the root of the problem? Perhaps if you and your husband got another house, a place of your own, dear, you would settle down better then. I hear that nice villa just across the road – you know where we attended the Appleford soiree – is going up for sale soon . . .

'Monkton House is my home, mother, in more ways than one. I own half of it for one thing.'

'What about your lovely little boy?' Ada said. 'Do you not care about him?'

'Of course I do,' Christina said. 'But Mitchell looks after him very well and Beatrice spoils him whenever she gets the chance. Jason's thriving without me fussing over him all the time.'

Her mother sighed. 'It's not as if you need the money, Chrissie. Your father and I just cannot understand you.'

They never could, Christina thought, or surely they would not have subjected me to such anguish in my childhood, such fear, such self-denial, such emptiness. Giving up, giving up, giving up all the time. Hiding inside. Building a protective shell. But in the end she could not hide her love of music. As a result she had been forced to give that up too. At least as a career. All the same it seemed to have turned out for the best, for the career she now had was not only deeply satisfying but exciting as well. She still had her music. It was her relaxation, her escape. She often sat lost in musical delight at the piano. Now, however, she did not choose tragic themes so often. The characteristics of a Beethoven scherzo, the rapid tempo, the grand triumphant march-like theme seemed more to suit her mood. Although Mozart remained her favourite composer, and his music could still bring a lump of sweet appreciation to the throat. She tried to avoid playing the piano in the evening, however. It did nothing to help an unhappy situation for her to be emotionally aroused and then go straight to a bedroom and a man she found physically attractive but who wanted nothing to do with her in that way. On the occasions that she had allowed herself to be emotionally aroused she had undressed in full view of Adam instead of performing her toilet more discreetly. She nursed the tentative hope that her now more glamorous underwear with its embroidered chemise and knickers threaded with blue or pink or white silk ribbon and lace might arouse his sexual desire and tempt him to approach her. When each time she failed, shame overcame her and she lay stiffly in bed, her face turned away from him.

These and other blows to her self-esteem would have proved completely disastrous had it not been for the admiring glances of other men, and Scott Mathieson in particular. Sometimes Mathieson would gaze at her with his open innocent look and say things like 'You're looking particularly attractive today, my dear' or 'How could anyone refuse your offer in a hat like that?'

She had told him more than once that she disapproved of his personal remarks. Business was business and she did not want the fact that she was a woman to interfere with it. She realized that Mathieson knew she was lying when she told him she didn't like his compliments, despite his round-eyed innocent look. Not too often but every now and again he would slide in another flattering comment about her appearance. At times she felt uneasy about him. Although she secretly liked his flattery she wasn't sure that she liked him. She sometimes wondered why he was not doing military service. The new Military Service Act made it compulsory for all single men between eighteen and forty-one to have enlisted. As far as she knew Mathieson came into that category.

She'd heard him make no mention of being a conscientious objector either. The press at the moment was full of howls of protest about the conchies or cuthberts, as they were known. The press also referred to them as sickly idealists, flimsy sentimentalists, pasty-faced curs and anarchists. It was claimed they suffered from fatty degeneration of the soul and that they were men with as much pluck and brains as the rabbit and as much conscience as the skunk. Horatio Bottomley in *John Bull* had spoken about conscientious objectors as a fungus growth, a human toadstool which should be uprooted without further delay.

Perhaps, of course, Mathieson had, like Adam, tried to join up but had been turned down because of medical grounds. She had the feeling, however, that if Mathieson did not think it was to his advantage to go and fight in the war he would manage one way or the other to slip smoothly and charmingly out of his obligation to do so. He had told her more than once that they were two of a kind. She hoped she was not like him.

Chapter Twenty-two

Her mother had a point suggesting that Beatrice was in charge of the household, but on reflection Christina decided she preferred it that way. She had no particular interest in interviewing the cook every morning to discuss daily menus and whatever shopping was necessary, nor did she have any urgent desire to supervise the servants and check on their daily work. It was bad enough having to listen to details of servant problems from Beatrice. They were fortunate in having the old faithfuls of Mitchell, Mrs Bishop and Doris, but they'd lost McKendrick to the army. Now, most importantly, they needed an under parlour maid, housemaid and scullery maid, but decent, trained girls were becoming increasingly difficult to find.

Beatrice had found that the girls from the local orphanage had been worse than useless. They tended to be dull and heavy, never having had any experience of freedom. Even the sight of any luxury seemed to demoralize them. They were unable to resist gobbling food from the larder that was not meant for them. They picked up Beatrice's pretty possessions that they weren't supposed to touch. They even tried on clothes that they found lying about. They had learned how to scrub floors, but didn't know how to clean carpets. They could handle heavy crockery but not crystal tumblers or fine china. Beatrice had thought that, at barely fourteen, the girls would have been young enough to train, but Mrs Bishop, Doris and Beatrice herself had found the task quite impossible.

'I'm now looking for a young girl with a home and family, some sort of normal background,' she told Christina.

'Good,' Christina said, and was glad that no more was needed from her than a word of approval.

If she was honest with herself, she had no particular interest even in the feminine accomplishments of knitting or sewing. She felt she'd performed enough domestic duties and accomplishments in the manse to last her a lifetime.

As for Jason, she enjoyed seeing him when Mitchell brought him down to the drawing room every evening. He was rather sweet and she didn't mind making some attempt to amuse him. What she enjoyed most, though, was seeing how fond Adam was of the child. Jason was their real link. He was part of each of them and there was nothing Adam could do or say to change that. She was always quite relieved when Mitchell took Jason back upstairs to the nursery. She would never have admitted it, of course, but that was the truth of it. She was fond of the child and was conscientious in making sure that everything was done for his health and welfare. However, the idea of haunting the nursery all day and devoting all one's time to pandering to the needs of a child and a husband, as some women did, remained an anathema to her.

All her life she had been forced to put other people's needs first. She had been taught that it was selfish and wicked to think of oneself. It was supposed to be her Christian duty to put others first at all times. So much so that she had developed an instinctive resistance to it. As a child she'd been so often called upon to give up her penny's pocket money to 'feed the starving children in Africa'. She had always been gently forced to give up some precious belonging to the 'poor orphans' including, on one occasion, her much-loved teddy bear.

The most crushing lesson she had been taught since childhood however, was the text: honour thy father and thy mother. This, she realized now, had been used spoken or unspoken as a form of emotional blackmail to secure absolute obedience all her life. Looking back and trying to be fair, she didn't think that her parents had meant any harm. They were good-living people and no doubt would have been horrified had they thought they were oppressing her, denying her any form of self-expression, individuality or freedom of spirit. Fortunately, deep inside her there had been a core of strength, a very secret determination to keep her own space.

In recent years that determination had begun to surface. Sometimes she even wondered if it was stronger than her love for Adam. She loved Adam as much as she was capable of loving anyone. At the same time that secret, cautious part of herself was always ready to take evasive action. It would seem on the surface that the career into which she had now launched herself and the risks it entailed was a contradiction to the type of person she was, but on the contrary she found the challenges and dangers exhilarating. They gave her the very sense of freedom and self-expression that she needed, and this, she suspected, was more important to her, affected her more deeply than anything else.

Other concerns affected her but were not such a deep integral part of herself. She was worried about her brother, for instance. There had been no letters from him for quite some time. Not to herself, not to Adam, not even to her mother or father. Now it was not only her mother who tensely scanned the newspaper lists of dead and wounded, her father had acquired this daily habit. He had also taken to discussing the war with Adam. The Reverend Gillespie had never previously had any interest in world affairs, nor much knowledge of them. His attention had been wholly taken up by the affairs of the spirit and the welfare of his congregation. Now in his talks with his son-in-law it was almost as if he were trying to make up for lost time and gain as much knowledge and understanding as he could through Adam.

Sometimes, despite his usual solemn, lordly manner – he always spoke as if he were standing behind the pulpit and looking down at his flock – a note of barely concealed anxiety would creep into his voice. He would ask Adam where he thought Simon would be and in what battle he might be involved, and when Adam thought the whole sorry business might end.

Adam tried to reassure him by saying that because Simon was a doctor, the chances were he would not be anywhere near the front line. He would be further back in a medical station or hospital where the wounded would be taken. The Reverend Gillespie would nod as if in agreement, but still his eyes remained anxious and unconvinced. On these occasions Christina would sit in the background talking in quiet undertones to her mother while they both knitted the inevitable socks, mitts, balaclavas or body belts. It was no use objecting to the knitting – her mother would have been too upset. She had tried protesting but Ada had reminded her that it could be Simon who was cold and needing woollen comforts, and if not Simon some other poor mother's son or some girl's brother. It was wicked and selfish to sit with idle hands at such a time.

She knew her mother was right, but nevertheless felt irked at being forced constantly to comply with this duty. She believed she loved her parents, it would have been quite unthinkable to believe otherwise. She worried about them and was sorry for them in their present state – but still they always needled her into a mood of suppressed irritation. Often she wished she could be as open and uncomplicated as Simon. There had never been anything repressed about him. He had never been emotionally frustrated. Not that he behaved in an unbalanced or feminine way. He had been taught in his private school to keep the proverbial stiff upper lip. But he had always been very open in his affection for both his mother and his father. They pretended to object to the disruption of their dignity.

'Behave yourself, Simon,' her mother would say when he would pounce on her, lift her off her feet and dance round the room with her. 'Put me down at once. What way is this for a young gentleman to behave?' She'd cry out in a show of great harassment. But the glow of happiness and pride in her eyes always betrayed the love she felt for her son no matter what he did.

Simon had never been overawed or crushed by the Reverend Gillespie's solemn, religious dignity. Not content with a handshake with his father when leaving, he had affectionately hugged the older man.

Often over the years Christina had wished she could be so relaxed. She had tried, she had struggled with herself. She had never succeeded however in bringing herself to behave in such an uninhibited manner. Even her soul shrank from exposing herself to such vulnerability.

Since her marriage to Adam, despite the risk of rejection she had tried, on occasion and with nervous apprehension, to discard her protective shell and reach out to him. Each time he would rebuff her, and to ease her humiliation she would fling herself into her work with relentless determination. But there were times when she even ceased to fear failure in her professional life. In failing she might ruin the business – and thereby hurt Adam in return.

The thought would flit through her head that she could not only hurt him but she could destroy him. That was power. Then, immediately ashamed of herself, she would conquer the thought, push it away, bury it deep in her subconscious.

There were other equally desperate thoughts. She would try to fathom ways of making Adam love her. Not just to attract him sexually but to make him really care. She kept trying to change his attitude towards her in a business sense because it was in this area that so much of the antagonism between them was sparked off. But she found it impossible to either impress him or persuade him. Then unexpectedly, she did have one small breakthrough.

She had gone to see some property in the Gorbals, not to examine it in detail – that was the job of Mathieson and the factor. She just cruised along the street in a taxi-cab to get some idea of the situation and appearance of the building. Women were standing at close mouths chatting and although hatless and wrapped in dingy-looking shawls they looked well fed and happy enough. It was the children who shocked Christina. All of them were barefooted, dirty and inadequately dressed. They crowded the streets with apparently nothing better to do than stare in awe at her taxi-cab.

She hadn't been able to get the children out of her head, and later when she'd noticed a large empty shop as part of the tenement she was thinking of buying, she had an idea. She had put it to Mathieson as soon as she reached his office.

'A gymnasium right in the centre of the area would keep

at least some of the children off the street. It would give them something to occupy their minds and be good for them in a physical sense too.'

Mathieson was less enthusiastic. 'It's up to you, but you could get a good rent for those premises as a shop.'

She shrugged. 'I'll get plenty of rent from the flats around it. I'll ask Adam how we should fix it up. He'll know how it should be converted and what sort of equipment the children would enjoy using.'

Adam had looked surprised then impressed when she'd told him about her idea. They had discussed the conversion with some warmth as well as enthusiasm. It was then she remembered the warmth that had existed before their marriage when they had been friends.

She prayed that the present faint glimmer was something she could build on.

Chapter Twenty-three

The shop had been particularly busy and Annalie was exhausted by the time she left to walk along to her close. It was dark and foggy. Gas lamps were faint amber smudges around which snowflakes whirled like a million moths. Annalie shivered and drew her shawl tighter around her shoulders.

From out on the River Clyde a foghorn boomed a deep melancholy message. It was a haunting, eerie sound that seemed to accentuate the bleakness of the night. Usually there was most light in the close mouth, but when she arrived it too was shrouded in foggy gloom.

She climbed the stairs slowly. On the first landing at the top of the stairs there was no light and she had to pat the walls to feel her way as she went along. It was here on the landing that there was a lavatory shared by the first three families in the building.

It was still pitch black at the first storey because the gas light was broken. She carried on up another flight of stairs to the second landing where there was a lavatory for another three families. Each lavatory had a huge keyhole and a strong stench of urine. On the second storey the gas was working and shone a yellow light onto her door but it was to her neighbour's door that Annalie went first. She prayed that Flo would not be in a chatty mood, and her prayers were answered. Flo came to the door carrying the sleeping Elizabeth and simply handed her over with a whisper:

'You look tired, hen. I'll let you slip right in.'

Annalie smiled her gratitude and said nothing. With great care she put her key in the door and carried the baby inside through the darkness and over to the bed recess. She wasn't even going to bother lighting the gas. All she wanted to do was to undress and climb into bed beside the baby.

She spread her plaid on top of the blanket Aunty Murn

had given her and then slipped underneath the covers to cuddle in beside Elizabeth. She kissed the child's soft, downy head and smoothed her cheek against it, purring with love and pleasure to be united and alone with her, and looking forward to the luxury of the few hours they would have together the next day before she had to go to work.

Despite her fatigue it was some time, due to the cold, before she was able to fall asleep. The fire had long since gone out and the winter's chill had seeped into the small room with the fog. The first thing she would have to do in the morning would be to rake out and light the fire before Elizabeth became too cold and hungry.

She tried to warm herself by thinking of the times she had lain in Adam's arms after he'd made passionate love to her. She kept every nuance of every memory fresh by concentrating very hard on each tiny aspect of it. The heat of his skin, the jagginess of the hairs on his chest and sometimes, if he needed a shave, the roughness of his jaw and chin. Then she'd touch his face and say, 'You're prickly. You'll have made my skin all rubbed and red.'

His hand would fly self-consciously to his face and he'd apologize.

'I'm sorry. I should have shaved.'

Or if her finger explored his scar he would cringe away very slightly and say, 'Do you mind that very much?'

'Mind?' she'd asked gently. 'Why should I mind?'

'It's ugly.'

She particularly treasured those intimate and revealing moments when she caught glimpses of the sensitive human being behind the aggressive, sometimes arrogant outer shell of the man.

'There's nothing ugly about you,' she told him as she tenderly kissed the scar, his eye, his cheek, his mouth. 'You're a lovely man, perfect in every way.'

He'd smiled lovingly down at her.

'Darling, I'm only that way to you. That's because you look at me through biased eyes.'

'I look at you with love, that's all,' she said. Oh, and how she loved him. And how her heart ached for him now in the dark icy tenement room.

Flo had offered to keep the fire going by popping in now and again to give it a bit of a rake and put another lump on. Annalie had been too proud to admit, however, that she could not afford the coal to sustain it all night. She was hard pressed, once she had paid her rent, to buy any coal at all let alone feed herself and Elizabeth. Each week too she had been forced to go to the Barras and spend some money on second-hand household goods like a kettle and a pot, a couple of cups, saucers and plates, a minimum amount of cutlery and a poker for the fire.

She had not yet been able to afford sheets or pillow cases or any more blankets or a rug for the bare floor, curtains for the window or a zinc bath in which to wash by the fire, or indeed, any of a hundred necessities. Aunty Murn helped out when she could, and only the other day had come round with a three-legged stool that she'd picked up for next to nothing – or so she said. She'd also brought a jug of hot soup.

Annalie knew that Aunty Murn would have done even more, but she was struggling herself with the rent eating into so much of her meagre housekeeping money. It was becoming a constant anxiety for everyone to find enough money to pay their rents. More and more people were finding it impossible. The spectre of arrears and of being made homeless haunted everybody. Annalie could see worry in the eyes of the women who came into the shop. They tried to be cheerful. They clung valiantly to their Glasgwegian sense of humour. There was as much laughing and joking as there ever had been and just as many ribald and hilarious remarks about factors, but despite their tough cheerfulness a shadow of concern continued to grow in their eyes.

She thought she heard a scraping sound, realized it might be a mouse or rat, but was too fatigued to care. She'd only seen one rat since she'd come to live in her own single end. She'd been on her knees on the floor in front of the fire changing the baby's nappy when she'd happened to look up

148

and see a rat on the draining board by the side of the sink. Its eyes were beads of malevolence staring over at her. Her scream died in her throat before it was uttered for fear of frightening the baby. She'd immediately gathered Elizabeth up and gone next door to Flo's house. Erchie, Flo's man, was a wiry wee plumber and able for anything. He had caught the rat and tried his best to fill in the hole through which he thought it had entered.

'I'll plaster up two or three of these other wee holes I see you've got, hen, while I'm at it. That'll keep the mice out as well.'

She hadn't heard or seen any vermin since then, at least not inside the house. Nobody went down to the back yard to empty their bins in the dark if it could be avoided. They were all sorry for the bin men. They had surely the worst job in the country.

Erchie had a big powerful torch that he used at his work and sometimes if he heard the bin men coming he would go down and help them by shining it on the bins while they emptied them. If you happened to look out of your window then onto the back yard you would see rats all right, and plenty of them.

'What angers me, Erchie' Annalie had said to him, 'is that we have to pay good money every week to live in places like this. It wouldn't be so bad if the landlords or the owners or whoever is responsible did something to the buildings, kept them in decent repair. Our lavatory's all right because you're a plumber and you fix it in your own time, but look at all the others around here, all overflowing and sewage spilling all over the place. How can children keep healthy playing about in cesspools like that? No wonder the fever van's never out of the Gorbals.'

In her exhausted state she allowed thoughts of rats and fever vans and all unpleasant things to drift into the back of her mind. Again she tried to ignore the icy air around her and concentrate on warm and pleasant memories – memories of being held in strong arms, of being kissed and caressed, of sweet words of love, of mounting passion that made her cry out in ecstasy. With the memory, however, came the tears. She wanted to toss about, to cry out, to scream and kick at cruel fate that had denied her the man she loved. She thanked God for Elizabeth. At least she had not been left with nothing. She showered the baby's head with kisses again until exhaustion overcame her completely and she slept.

Next morning she awoke very early and as quietly as possible lit the fire to take the chill off the air before she had to wash and dress Elizabeth. The gas mantle was lit because it was still pitch black outside. The fire was crackling merrily. She had just made a pot of tea and was about to pour herself a cup when to her surprise she heard a knock at the door.

Annalie went to open it. There was no mistaking the fine-looking woman who stood on the doorstep leaning one raised arm against the lintel, her brown skin, her golden earrings, her bold dark eyes and black, straight hair unevenly cut, straggling over one side of her face and reaching to her shoulders.

Annalie was speechless with joy.

'Well *rakli*,' her mother said, 'stand aside and let me in.'

Red skirts with flouncing frills of petticoats showing underneath swished about. High-heeled black buttoned boots beat a tattoo on the floorboards. Annalie never failed to be enchanted by her mother's appearance and the strange Romany words she used. She knew quite a few herself. She knew for instance that *rakli* meant girl, *juvals* meant woman, *chavvies* were children and *romes* were men. A *gaujo* was a non gypsy.

'They found you!' Annalie cried out incredulously.

'Nobody finds me unless I want them to,' her mother said, throwing her sheepskin shawl over at the stool and looking around with her hands on hips. 'You've nothing,' she said. 'You would have been better with me. I wanted you to come, you know. But your father wouldn't hear of it.'

Her dress had a tight bodice and sleeves puffed to the elbow. Over the long wide skirts she wore a *jodaka* or apron of white satin with two deep side pockets embroidered with flower patterns and coloured threads. She wore massive gold rings in the form of a strap and buckle on one hand and a gold sovereign on the other. Round her neck hung strings of red coral and her gold earrings were crescent in shape.

'My poor *chavvies* would have been better with me too. My poor Davie and Eddie,' she said. 'I came as soon as I heard. I had to burn their belongings, although they didn't have much either.'

Her mother had often told her in the past of the gypsy funeral rites where they burned the van and destroyed the possessions of the dead. The origin of this custom lay far back in time, but Annalie suspected it was somehow related to Romany fastidiousness and a superstitious fear of the *mullo* or ghost.

'Burned them?' Annalie echoed. 'Where?'

'Out in the back court,' Saviana replied. 'That gave them all something to talk about. All hanging out their back windows they were, their faces lit up with the flames like rows of old devils.'

She was pacing around the room, the heels of her boots clipping against the floor, her hips swaying. 'And I wailed and wept for my poor wee *chavvies* the whole night long and all the time old Murn raging at me to be quiet. But I had my grieving despite her. Don't just stand there. Show me your wee *chavvie*.'

Annalie had been open mouthed and shining eyed with admiration. Suddenly she jerked herself as if out of a dream and ran across to the bed. Elizabeth was still asleep but Annalie lifted her and carried her across to her mother. As she did so the child wakened and, still flushed and starry eyed with sleep, smiled up at her grandmother.

'She's a year old now,' Annalie said proudly. 'And quite big for her age, don't you think? Hasn't she got a lovely skin too and beautiful eyes?'

'And why shouldn't she?' Saviana asked. 'Hasn't she got a beautiful grandmother?'

Annalie laughed. 'Oh, Mammy, I'm so happy you're back. You'll stay, will you not? Oh please say you'll stay?'

Her mother shook her head. 'Once a traveller, always a traveller. But you and this wee beauty could be travellers too. She deserves better than this, and so do you.'

It was wonderful to think of being with her mother and the temptation to agree was very strong. Annalie tried to think why she was being so hesitant. It was mostly because of Aunty Murn, she decided. How could she worry Aunty Murn and leave her, especially so soon after Aunty Murn had lost Davie and Eddie? But at the back of Annalie's mind there was something else. Something that no matter what happened and no matter how much she tried to banish it from her mind still remained. She believed she was meant to be with Adam Monkton again.

Chapter Twenty-four

Monkton had just sacked his foreman. Joe Dalkeith had been in charge of the local jobs. Fortunately Monkton had been supervising the work on government contracts himself. On recently turning his attention to the local jobs to check what was happening he discovered a situation of chaotic incompetence involving the installation of a new bathroom and kitchen in a house that a Mrs Graham had just bought. It soon became obvious to him that in the first place Dalkeith had given a wrong estimate and in the second place the plans for the Public Health inspector had been late. The inspector told Monkton brusquely that the drawings of the proposals should have been in a week before the work started. He said he'd told Dalkeith that if he hoped to connect the new WC into the existing old vent pipe that he was going to be disappointed. It was substandard. He'd also warned Dalkeith that his committee would require a complete new soil stack and probably twenty feet of new drain. As a result of this, of course, a new estimate had to be calculated. This had naturally infuriated Mrs Graham. Dalkeith, he discovered had smoothed things over with Mrs Graham and blamed the capriciousness of health inspectors. Then there had been the complaint from Mrs Graham after the inspector from the Electricity Board had told her that the main feeding the new power points was inadequate for the increased load.

'If he hadn't come round,' Mrs Graham told Monkton, 'your firm would have left me to blow myself up or have the house catch fire. I could have been burned in my bed. I liked your foreman at first, but now I don't believe a word he says. He's always blaming the labourers or somebody else for the bad workmanship. And certainly,' she added indignantly, 'the laziness of some of the men is shocking. They seem to spend half the day gossiping and making tea.

It would do most of them good to be away in France. An army sergeant major's what they need, it strikes me.'

Monkton was furious. After assuring Mrs Graham that he would see to it personally that everything was put right and finished to her satisfaction he sought Dalkeith out and asked him what the hell he thought he was doing. Just as Mrs Graham had told him, Dalkeith immediately blamed the men.

'They're a right crowd of lazy, idle buggers we've got just now,' he told Monkton. 'I'm never done shouting at them and accusing them of being lazy, feckless, incompetent. It makes damn all of a difference. I don't know what else I can do. After all, I can't do every part of every job myself.'

'If you don't know what else you can do it means I'll just have to get someone else who does know,' Monkton had told him abruptly. 'Your services are no longer required.'

It only took a few days of being on the job himself to discover another man who was better foreman material than Dalkeith, the man who had been originally hired by his father. Dalkeith's behaviour had an obvious impact on how the group of workmen under him had behaved. His unwillingness to plan had discouraged everyone else from looking for the best way to organize their work. There had only been one man who had struggled against the general lowering of standards. He was a painter called Jim Dawson. Without wasting any time Monkton promoted him to works foreman.

Monkton realized that the growling and shouting and general abuse of the men that had been Dalkeith's practice had also been the way the old man had run the business. Monkton was determined, however, that this would not be his way. He believed that a man's willingness to work depended not only upon the rewards he received but also the various kinds of personal satisfaction that he derived from performing his tasks. He believed in fact that people who are constantly told they are of a low status begin to behave in low-status ways. They find it difficult to understand their work instructions. As a result they become muddled, lazy and uninterested in the success of the job.

Although tough, Monkton was never abusive. At least,

he hadn't been until tensions had built up between himself and Christina. Sometimes he wished he could purge his frustration by knocking her about as many a man would. Wife beating, particularly in Scotland, was fairly common. He wanted to. God knows he wanted to beat the living daylights out of her at times. Something in his nature prevented him from actually putting his wishes into practice. Instead he would go out and do some jabbing at the punch bag in the gym until he was exhausted. Sometimes he had a few rounds in the ring with big Geordie. Sometimes he got steaming drunk. Sometimes he shouted at the men.

His tension was now becoming exacerbated by something else. Christina had always been in his eyes quite an attractive woman, but since their marriage she'd blossomed in this respect. She had become more self-confident, more elegant and infinitely more attractive. To share a bedroom with her, to watch her undressing at night had become a sexual agony to him. He wasn't in love with her, but after all he was a normal man and any normal man would feel sexual arousal in such intimate circumstances. He'd never felt so sexually aroused since his affair with the servant Annalie Gordon. Annalie had been a very different person from Christina, of course. The main thing about Annalie had been that she was so exciting. Exciting in every way, not just sexually. She had been so different from anyone else he had ever known. He had been absolutely enchanted by her. He would never forget his feelings of utter devastation when on returning from a job he'd discovered that Annalie had gone.

When he inquired about her his mother had shrugged and said, 'Oh she and her family have emigrated somewhere. Australia, I believe. Anyway, she's gone and certainly won't be back.'

He had thought they had been so close. He had thought they had loved one another. It wasn't just a physical attraction. They had been confidants, soulmates. They had been everything to each other. At the same time, of course, he'd always known it was an impractical dream. No doubt her decision to leave had been for the best. No doubt it would never have worked out. It was strange though how she kept coming back to his mind even now. He tried to banish her from his thoughts. It wouldn't have been sensible to do otherwise. Nor did his occasional lapse into thoughts of the past affect his feelings towards his wife, which were much more complex than those he'd ever had for Annalie. For one thing he had known Christina for so much longer. She'd always been part of his life in one way or another. Now there was the tender trap of his son. He hadn't realized how different it could make you feel to produce another being of your own flesh and blood. He loved his son, cared passionately about his welfare and his future and could not imagine ever doing anything that would in any way harm the child.

There was also no getting away from the fact that as Christina's husband he had a duty and a responsibility towards her. And yet what most troubled him was the effect she might have on his business. His gut contracted into a hard knot of tension every time he thought of this. The business and the money he earned from it were a kind of freedom, a kind of independence. The thought of everything being jeopardized by Christina made him furious. He could recognize and appreciate that she had certain entrepreneurial skills, but there was no place for them in his business. He had no patience or interest in all the wheeling and dealing upon which she seemed to thrive. It smacked too much of trickery for him. More than that, it all seemed to be done on paper, and paperwork was certainly something that gave him no pleasure at all. Any business involved a certain amount of administration, of course, but Monkton's had always been a building firm and it was in the different aspects of the actual building that Adam's interest and satisfaction lay. He was a time-served joiner and believed that the joiner's work was the most crucial part of building. Most people assumed that it was the brick-layer who would be top of the list of importance when a building was going up, but in fact the bricklayer had to work to the joiner's specification. The bricklayer would always have to ask the joiner, for instance, what size the windows were to be. Similar types of consultation had to be made by the slaters, electricians, plumbers, plasterers, painters. Each and every trade was vital, of course, and cooperation between all the trades was what he liked to aim for on a job. There was nothing to beat a good team creating something solid from nothing. It gave him a special kind of thrill to see a building take shape, rise out of the ground, and he felt a rare sense of achievement and satisfaction to be able to say to himself: I built that.

If only he could make the same sort of success of his marriage. For the child's sake, if for no other reason, he knew he ought to try. If he could just get Christina to stay at home and be a wife the same as everyone else they knew, it might be easier. He admired her intelligence and enthusiasm even though he objected to her methods. If only she would concentrate that intelligence and enthusiasm on charity work (she had shown she had a head for this by her generous gift of a gymnasium in the Gorbals) or on running her home and bringing up her family. If only she would spend her time on anything except business.

He sighed to himself. Christina was not like the wives of other men he knew. Women like her mother and his mother were more the norm among their neighbours, friends and acquaintances.

He felt out of his depth. He had always been more at ease in dealing with men. He didn't know what to do about Christina.

Chapter Twenty-five

'I just told him' – Saviana tossed her hair back – 'the *rakli*'s suffered enough. You'll allow her to visit and make her welcome and no more of your nonsense.'

Annalie threw her arms around her mother and hugged her.

'Oh, Mammy. You've no idea how much this means to me. It was awful having to sneak up there and worry all the time in case Daddy would come in and throw me down the stairs. He warned me he would if he ever caught me in the house again. Aunty Murn tried everything to get him to change his mind, but he would have none of it. I don't know how you managed it.'

Saviana winked at her. 'You'd be surprised, *rakli*.'

Annalie laughed, then turned serious again. 'I was really dreading New Year, being on my own, you know? Although I suppose the neighbours would have made sure I had some company. They're all awfully good.'

'But it's better to be among your own family.'

'Oh yes,' Annalie agreed.

'And so you shall be.'

'I'll be working until quite late, but I'll come along to Aunty Murn's after that. I'll collect Elizabeth first, of course. She'll be with Flo.'

'No she won't,' Saviana said. 'She'll be with me. I'll look after her now that I'm here. You just come straight from the shop. Darklas and I will be waiting for you at your Aunty Murn's.'

Saviana had insisted that the baby should have a gypsy name and had christened her Darklas. Annalie couldn't pinpoint exactly why, but she felt uneasy and apprehensive about this and continued possessively to call the child Elizabeth.

Aunty Murn always set the table in readiness for the bells

that pealed out all over the city to herald in the New Year. The table boasted her best linen table cover, dishes and glasses, shortbread, home-made fruit cake and sandwiches. At one time they would have had a meal of steak pie, but they could no longer afford such a midnight feast. Aunty Murn was dressed in her Sunday long black skirt and high-necked Edwardian-style blouse. At her throat was the cameo brooch which had belonged to her mother. She did not seem to fill her clothes as she had once done and Annalie noticed for the first time that her aunt had lost weight and had a gaunt look about her face.

Hugh Gordon was also dressed in his best, as befitted the occasion. His Sunday-best suit had become somewhat shiny and threadbare over the years, but Aunty Murn had sponged and pressed it, and it looked quite presentable. In his waistcoat pocket was the watch which had belonged to his father and his grandfather before him, and his gold watch chain looped over his stomach. His moustache had been neatly clipped and his hair well brushed.

Annalie could see that her father only had eyes for Saviana when she said, 'Come now, dearie. Say welcome to our Annalie.'

Gordon's face closed as he turned towards to Annalie but he said, 'Welcome.'

'And wee Darklas,' Saviana said. 'Would you look at her? What a beauty.'

Annalie put Elizabeth down on the floor and the child sat looking around, delighted at being the centre of attention. Hugh Gordon stroked his moustache.

'I can see a definite look of you in her, Saviana.'

'And why not?' Saviana said. 'Isn't Annalie the image of me too?'

'No,' he said. 'She couldn't match your beauty.'

Saviana laughed loudly and dashed over to fling her arms around his neck and shower him with kisses, then she sat on his knee with her arm around his neck. Aunty Murn tutted and turned away.

She told Annalie later, 'I was fair affronted. That woman has neither modesty or shame.'

Aunty Murn's room and kitchen was spotlessly clean. It was always clean at the best of times. On New Year's Eve, however, it was a tradition even to run down at the last minute before the bells and empty the ash can so that not a scrap of ash would taint the spotlessness. The black grate gleamed like ebony, its steel edging silver and glowing with the reflection of the gaslight. The fender competed in warm sparkle. The draining board, the bunker and the linoleum had been scrubbed. The reddish-brown chenille bed curtains had been washed and pressed and the fawn bed valance had been starched.

There was an air of excitement, of importance, of anticipation. Hogmanay was always an event.

'Quick,' Aunty Murn said. 'Where're your bottles, Hugh? It's nearly time for the bells.'

Slowly, reluctantly, Gordon removed his wife from his lap, rose and went through to the front room. He returned carrying a bottle of whisky and one of wine. Aunty Murn brought a bottle of Iron Brew out of the kitchen press, for young people or teetotallers.

'Did you open the front window?' Aunty Murn asked.

'Yes, yes.' Hugh Gordon said.

'Get this one open then. Annalie, you run and open the door. I'll pour out the drinks.'

It was the custom to open all windows and doors to let the old year out and the new in. Then a few minutes before the New Year they all crowded to the open back window and strained out as far as they could, and every window now was bright with gaslight and the figures of the occupants leaning out. It was a time for silent contemplation of all that had passed in the old year. This contemplation was given a depth of sadness that reduced everyone to tears when blind Alex at his window played 'The Last Post' on the trumpet. Its sad strains mingled with and then were drowned by the bells of all the Glasgow churches ringing out and the cacophony of hooters from the ships on the Clyde. Then everybody dried their eyes and laughed and shouted out 'Happy New Year' before withdrawing into their houses, embracing and shaking each other by the hand. Then drinks were raised and toasts made and plates of cake and shortbread handed around.

Annalie kissed her mother first and then ventured a quick peck on Aunty Murn's cheek before turning to her father and giving him a warm hug and kiss.

He patted her back and said, 'Aye, all right, all right.' And she knew then that everything was forgiven.

The baby had long since fallen asleep and been tucked safely into Aunty Murn's bed under the colourful patchwork bedspread.

'There's no point in you trailing back down the road tonight,' Aunty Murn said. 'You and the wean can sleep with me.'

Saviana kept running over to the bed and gazing at the child and crying out, 'Darklas, Darklas, my beauty.'

Aunty Murn was outraged.

'Will you stop calling the wean that heathen name? She was christened Elizabeth.'

But Saviana only laughed and sang out, 'Darklas, Darklas,' like some kind of incantation.

'You must come with me and bring her to the *achin' tan* tomorrow. I want to show everyone at the gypsy camp what a beauty my Darklas is.'

An anxious look strained at Aunty Murn's gaunt face.

'You'll do no such thing,' she told Annalie. 'No good can come of that. Do you hear me? That dirty tinker's going to bring you nothing but bad luck.'

'Watch your tongue.' Gordon warned his sister.

Aunty Murn stuck to her guns. 'I say what I think. She hasn't exactly brought you any good fortune. You've taken your spite out on Annalie, but in fact it was your tinker that was the cause of you losing your job. It should have been her you told that you would fling down the stairs if she ever came back. But not you. Since you've got mixed up with her you've had a slate loose on your top storey.'

'Be quiet, woman!' Gordon commanded.

'No I will not be quiet,' Aunty Murn persisted, tugging down her blouse for emphasis. 'Our mammy would birl in her grave if she knew how you'd been carrying on.'

Saviana swaggered round the table with swishing skirts and swinging hips.

'So this is how the *gaujos* start the New Year,' she said, pouring herself another glass of whisky.

'I'll *gaujo* you.' Aunty Murn said in a threatening fist of a voice.

'Show me your palm, Murn,' Saviana said, 'and I'll tell your fortune. I'll tell you if there's a tall, dark, handsome man waiting to become your lover.'

'I'll have no more of your snash. Do you hear?' Aunty Murn said. 'You're nothing but a cheeky bisom.'

'There's somebody at the door,' Annalie cried out. 'First Foots, Aunty Murn.'

The custom was that it was luckiest if the first person or First Foot over your door in the New Year was tall and dark and carried a piece of coal as well as a customary bottle and perhaps a piece of shortbread or cake.

It was a group of their neighbours who burst in noisily with loud wishes of Happy New Year and Happy 1916, although Annalie thought, once the initial greetings had been dispensed with and they all settled down, that compared with previous years, the proceedings had an underlying restraint about them. It was difficult to be otherwise when everyone was so continuously conscious of the war and the number of men from the district who had been killed or terribly wounded. There were frightening stories of poison gas and the effects it was having.

Nevertheless it was a good party despite the fact that some of the songs like 'Keep the Home Fires Burning' and 'It's a Long Way to Tipperary' kept the war in the forefront of their minds. However there were more cheerful songs too like 'Alexander's Ragtime Band', 'I Want a Girl Just Like the Girl', 'The Spaniard that Blighted my Life' and 'Ragtime Cowboy Joe'. As everyone except Aunty Murn and Annalie got drunker, however, the songs became sadder. Big Sandy McLellan from the top flat gave a tearful rendering of 'Memories' and an encore of 'They Didn't Believe Me'. Sandy had a reason for his melancholy, the rest of the party learned. There was a tradition in industry in Glasgow that the last man to enter the workshop on the last day prior to the New Year was classed as Skittery Winter. As he walked down the workshop everyone clattered their hammers and made as much noise as possible to draw attention to him. It was a terrible humiliation and the title stuck to him the whole year through. To his workmates at least, he would be known as Skittery Winter until New Year 1917. It had been a terrible blow to big Sandy's pride because normally he took trouble to be a good timekeeper. He was often seen at the head of a crowd of men stampeding through the streets to beat the works hooter.

Annalie enjoyed the warm companionship of everyone at the party. The highlight of the evening for her was when her mother got up on top of the table and with stamping feet and swirling petticoats did a wild gypsy dance. Except that poor Aunty Murn was hard put to it to rescue all her good china. Best of all though was when everyone left and Annalie was cuddled into Aunty Murn's bed with the baby nestling comfortably between them. But just as she was drifting into a euphoric, trouble-free sleep, Aunty Murn said, without turning round, 'Don't let that dirty tinker call your wean Darklas. Do you hear? No good will come of it.'

Chapter Twenty-six

In response to Annalie telling her of the problems with Malcolm Hurley and how much the man upset her, Saviana said, 'You should get out of there.'

'But I need the money, and the hours suit me,' Annalie explained.

'There's other ways to make money. Gypsy ways.'

'What could I do?' Annalie said. 'I'm not like you. I haven't been brought up a gypsy.'

'I'd teach you everything you need to know. You could learn how to make and sell clothes pegs, artificial flowers, wicker and cane articles. Then there's fruit picking in season. Mostly you go "calling". That's round the doors selling.'

'Go round the doors selling things?' Annalie echoed in a shocked voice.

'Oh ho,' Saviana said. 'Proud are we?'

Annalie flushed. 'I couldn't bring myself to do that some-how.' She didn't say so to her mother, but to her it would feel like begging.

'How about the *dukkerin*? You can make plenty of money at that.'

Annalie's face brightened. 'Oh yes, the fortune telling. You always said you would teach me that one day, but do you think I'd have your gift? Is it something you're born with, do you think? Or can it really be taught?'

Saviana flung back her head, making her earrings swing about. Her laughter racketed about Annalie's small kitchen. It had an element of coarseness about it that grated slightly on Annalie's sensibilities.

'There's no gift about it, dearie. The first thing you've to learn about the *dukkerin* is some of the things you must always say.'

Annalie was puzzled. 'I don't understand.'

Saviana leaned forward. 'Give me your hand, *rakli*, and I'll show you.'

Annalie did as she was told and Saviana leaned over it, her black hair falling forward and shadowing her face. She looked black eyed, mysterious, almost frightening.

'You've got no common hand, girl.' Suddenly she winked at Annalie. 'That's the first one. Then there's this.' She peered close to Annalie's face. 'There's luck in your lovely face, lady.' She winked again. 'This is a good one: You'll always remember your whole life long what the poor gypsy girl tells you this day.' Then you can lower your voice every now and again and say, "You understands what I mean, my dearie?" or "I'm telling you the God's truth, ain't I now?" '

Annalie felt more upset than words could say, but she managed, 'You mean . . . You mean it's all just a trick? Just a whole lot of lies?'

'Oh, there's a skill to it. Gypsies have a special skill in this. A clever gypsy can know what kind of person sits before her, can know the kind of experiences that person has had and is likely to have. It's the keen eye and the intuition. It's the feeling you get from the person just by touching them. That's why the palm is better than the crystal. *You* could do it, dearie. I can see you've got the eye for it and you've got the instinct too. You can't deny it. Now come on, it's time we were away. I'll carry Darklas.'

Annalie had promised her mother that she would go with her to visit the *achin' tan* that was at present on Glasgow Green for the annual fair. Glasgow Green, across the other side of the river, was one of the great historic sites of Scotland, in some respects as important as Bannockburn or Culloden. The sustained fight for political freedom and social justice was largely conducted on Glasgow Green. It was also used intensively for leisure and recreation and political and religious meetings by all classes of people. The use of Glasgow Green was considered to be the birthright of every Glaswegian, and the heroic struggles of the nineteenth century to stop encroachments or alienation were familiar to everybody. The fights to retain free speech on the Green were also well known. Traditionally the Green belonged to the people of Glasgow and they zealously guarded their right to it.

It was early morning and the fair had not yet come to life but there was plenty of life in the *achin' tan* which was some way across the Green from the fair under some trees. There were two covered wagons, several horses, two bender tents and a knife-grinding machine. It was at fairs like this or horse fairs, race meetings or crop harvesting that the gypsies gathered and the tribes came together to exchange news, to celebrate or to mourn. Those were the times when marriages were made, friendships and feuds formed, renewed or ended. Occasions like these had a special air of zest and festivity and were the travellers' equivalent of holiday times.

The morning mist was still clinging to the Green but a fire had been lit. It was glowing warmly and sparking and casting huge ghost-like shadows in the mist. Children were running around laughing and playing but at the sight of Annalie they turned shy and stood silently watching her. Groups of women were standing about too, all dressed in bright-coloured clothing, though none so striking as Saviana who wore a sparkling white satin pina underneath which her bright tartan skirts stopped just above the ankle. On her head was a silk scarf of orange and green knotted at the back which set off her glossy hair, her copper-brown face and heavy crescent earrings of embossed gold.

An old woman was sitting near the fire with soap-stiffened locks that seemed raked forward from her head like rams' horns over her brow and wrinkled cheeks. There were *romes*, gypsy men, sitting around and Annalie noticed one man in particular who stood back against one of the wagons and seemed to have his eyes fixed on Saviana in a hypnotic stare. He was strikingly handsome, with long black hair, and his yellow silk *diklo* knotted around his neck. For the first time it occurred to Annalie to wonder if her mother had another man when she was travelling. The thought shocked her. She felt herself tremble inside. All the beliefs she'd so fondly held for a lifetime began to crack and crumble, leaving her feeling unsure and afraid.

166

'Look at these two beauties,' Saviana cried out. 'Annalie and Darklas.'

The younger women crowded round but it was at the baby their attention was directed. Looking around, Annalie's eye was caught by rows of dead hedgehogs. Her mother had told her in the past of this favourite gypsy dish of *hotchiwichi*. The spines of the hotchiwichi were shaved off, the remaining hair singed, then it was opened out, cleaned and put to soak in salt water to be later roasted on a spit or stewed. Annalie had always taken it as a joke and had screwed up her nose and laughed at the mere idea. Now, seeing them, it became a reality and she determined not to share a meal with the gypsies.

She remembered then the other meal her mother had told her about. It was made with *bauri*, or snails. Bread of course was the staple diet and the respect for it was almost biblical, but even this did not tempt Annalie to stay. If she'd had moments of indecision about travelling with her mother and the other gypsies, that indecision was now gone. She didn't feel at home among these people and their way of life.

After a time she made the excuse that she had many things to do before going to work that day and was relieved when eventually she and her mother returned to the more familiar surroundings of Annalie's single end in Cumberland Street. She felt so unsettled and upset by the visit to the gypsy camp that she wished she didn't have to leave Elizabeth and go to work. Somehow she would have felt better if she could have left the baby with Flo rather than her mother. Saviana seemed to take everything to such extremes. Her mother's love was so noisy, so exuberant, so intense, so dramatic that Annalie was beginning to feel Saviana was swamping the child with emotion and attention. She crooned it to sleep. She clapped her hands and acted like a clown to make it laugh. She did a slow snakelike dance to capture its hypnotized attention. She covered it in kisses and extravagant words of love.

Annalie began to sink into dark corners of jealousy. She experienced growing feelings of possessiveness and protec-

167

tiveness towards the child. Her feelings weren't helped by Aunty Murn's constant warnings of, 'That dirty tinker's putting a spell on that wean.'

Annalie had never paid any attention to what Aunty Murn said about her mother before, particularly the fact that she called her a dirty tinker. She knew that the gypsies, and her mother in particular, were very fastidious about cleanliness. Her mother had thought that she and Aunty Murn were *mockadi* or unclean because they washed themselves in the sink and that was the same place they used for washing the vegetables and the food utensils. Gypsies had a separate bowl for each and every operation. Only good-quality china was used and any dish that was chipped or cracked was destroyed. However, although Annalie knew that Aunty Murn was wrong in calling Saviana dirty, she began to wonder if there could be some truth in some of the other beliefs that her aunt so strongly held about her mother.

Chapter Twenty-seven

The streets were full of soldiers – soldiers in khaki, soldiers in strange trench clothes, soldiers in tartan, Dominion soldiers, tall, lean, springy in their walk, wearing broad-brimmed khaki hats decorated with feathers. Trains full of fresh troops returning to battle steamed out. Hospital trains full of shattered victims glided ominously in to take their places. The wounded in their strange bright blue, red and white uniforms were becoming all too familiar in the town. Huge banners saying 'Quiet for the Wounded' hung over straw-covered streets outside hospitals. Soldiers drilled on Glasgow Green, town squares, school playgrounds. The parks were full of drilling khaki.

The conscription of men to the forces increased the employment of women. They were now seen everywhere doing every kind of job. They were at the wheel of cars and vans. They were conductresses on buses and trams. They were handling the reins of horses. They had become what were called land girls, working as farm labourers. They were working in munitions factories, and this job was proving dangerous as well as unpleasant. Despite the use of masks or respirators and facial grease, the fumes from TNT turned the girls' faces a hideous yellow and because of this they were nicknamed the canaries. Women who varnished aeroplane wings were doing dangerous work. They were often overcome by toxic fumes and had been seen lying sick in rows outside the workshops. Even more perilous were the monkey machines. A heavy weight was dropped to compress explosives into shell cases. Already there had been more than one explosion in which some female workers had suffered terrible mutilations.

In the circumstances it seemed to Christina all the more ridiculous for Adam to object to her involvement in business, either on the construction and maintenance side of

Monkton's or on her own property side. He had never actually said so, but she had the feeling that it wouldn't have mattered what she had been engaged in, he would have taken this attitude – that a woman's place was in the home. He was a very masculine man in the very Scottish sense. Scottish men believed the man was the undisputed head of the house. The woman was part of his goods and chattels. A man could do what he liked with his wife. Her promise in the wedding ceremony to obey was taken very literally and seriously.

Christina felt sure that if, at any time in the future, men were going to change their attitudes to women, Scottish men – and particularly Glasgow men – would be the very last to do so. She believed Scott Mathieson was different because he was an Englishman. He had gone to school in England and did his training there as a valuation surveyor. His father had worked for a law firm in England and had only moved to Edinburgh a few years ago to join a more lucrative practice. Mathieson had initially come up with him just to look around. On assessing Glasgow, however, he had decided that there were better prospects for him there. As a result, instead of joining his family in Edinburgh, or what some witty Glaswegians called the Far East, he rented a flat and settled in Glasgow.

Christina often puzzled over this because, in a way, he seemed more suited to the clever legal atmosphere of Edinburgh. That city was also known as east windy, west endy – a place full of lawyers, a place of outward show but little heart.

Certainly, Edinburgh seemed on the whole more genteel whereas Glasgow tended to be rougher and tougher, with a bouncy vitality about it. The Glasgow man, especially the Glasgow working man, had a kind of swagger about him reminiscent of a jaunty sailor's roll. Monkton was Glasgow born and bred. He had come from stock that had been originally working class. He'd been knocked into shape and acquired a sturdy resilience by serving his time and working on building sites along with the toughest. He was not one of those in the building industry who were now being defeated by the adverse circumstances caused by the war. Firms were going bankrupt and going out of business because building had virtually come to a standstill. Christina could see Monkton harden with determination before her eyes although she hadn't been seeing a lot of him recently. He was travelling so much, further and further north and south in his efforts to obtain contracts.

He had discovered that because khaki-clad men from every part of the country were being transported across the Channel the existing camps and barracks were totally inadequate. As a result a contractor was needed to work fast. He began by building vast lines of wooden hutments but it soon became evident that a timber ring – a group of men making vast profits from timber – was exploiting the serious moment. As a result prices soared. Supplies of wood became erratic. Monkton, suspicious of the amount delivered on one site, set a man to measure up each and every truck and found that by artful packing each load was very much underweight.

Monkton saw that every foot of timber was made good. He was supported by his joiners in helping to beat the ring and the joiners worked long hours to house troops waiting to occupy the camps. The dedication of the workforce coupled with Monkton's determination not to be bound by any ring of war profiteers or to bow to exorbitant demands, meant they were able to construct the camps at a cost of twenty-five per cent below the average. Government official figures gave the standard cost per man as twenty pounds. Monkton's figure was fourteen pounds nine shillings.

Christina had mixed feelings about Monkton's inflexible principles of business conduct. She had grudging admiration for this type of strength of character. On the other hand she knew that she would have preferred him to take the chance to make as much money as possible. Many government contracts were given on a basis of time and materials plus profit, and it was common practice to carry dummy men and make extra, although admittedly illegal, profit in this way. Whenever possible Monkton refused these terms altogether, preferring to submit a tender in the usual peacetime manner.

During one project the chemical manufacturing company who had given Monkton's the contract ran short of funds. The scheme, which was important to the war effort, would, necessarily have been abandoned if Monkton had not agreed to carry on without payment and undertook a liability of thousands of pounds with only a remote possibility of being repaid. This had caused many fiery exchanges in the boardroom, particularly between Christina and Monkton.

'You've got a nerve,' she'd accused him. 'You criticize me for putting the firm at risk by my business ventures and my business decisions. What do you think you're doing?'

At first she'd thought that there would be no problem in swaying the other board members to throw in their vote with her to defeat Monkton's proposition. But Adam had defended it so fiercely and for so long that he gradually persuaded the others to his view. Everyone that is except old Mrs Mokton, and one person's vote was all Christina needed to defeat him. The gaslight in the boardroom had to be lit and one of the office staff sent out for bread and cheese to make sandwiches. Much whisky was consumed by the men and gallons, it seemed, of strong tea by Christina and old Mrs Monkton, who valiantly stuck it out to the end.

Christina had thought she had secured the old woman's vote, especially when she'd pointed out that Moses Monkton would never have agreed to what his son was proposing.

'You're right,' Mrs Monkton had said, 'Moses would have flung it out, no doubt about that. And it wouldn't have mattered a tuppeny toss what that Brigadier General whatever his name is explained in that letter. Of course a brigadier would say it's urgent for the war effort. Everything's urgent for the war effort. But even an ordinary soldier gets paid for what he does. No. Moses would have flung that letter into the waste-paper basket. My man ran this business not just on hard work but on money. Not on high-falutin' phrases or empty promises, but on money, on hard cash.'

Nevertheless, as time went on, perhaps because the old

woman became exhausted despite the strong tea, Monkton managed to beat her down in argument and eventually he won the vote. Christina was furious.

Back at Monkton House she tackled him again.

'To think,' she said, 'of the abuse and insults I suffered from you about the way that I had treated Mrs Gray and got her to sell me her land.'

'You don't know what you're talking about.' Monkton lit a cigar and held it between clenched teeth. 'There's absolutely no comparison between the two business deals.'

'There's no comparison in this respect,' Christina said. 'I didn't bully and browbeat old Mrs Gray into such a state of exhaustion that she didn't know what she was doing.'

'Don't talk nonsense,' Monkton said. 'My mother knew what she was doing all right. I know her better than you do. For one thing she's as tough as an old boot.'

'You're a bully,' she persisted. 'You're a selfish, domineering swine who would do anything to get your own way. What you've done today is far more likely to ruin the business than anything I've ever done.'

'They'll pay up eventually.'

'How do you know that? I wouldn't if I were them. Everything's fair in war and business, and business, as far as I'm concerned, is about making money and making it in whatever way you can.'

He took the cigar from his mouth, blew a spiral of smoke upwards, then shook his head.

'What a philosophy. And you're the one that goes to church every Sunday.'

'You've had the nerve to criticize me,' Christina persisted. 'You've made my life miserable. You've tried every way to get me to stop being involved in any side of the business, and yet you can do a ridiculous thing like this?'

'I thought I'd made it perfectly clear at the board meeting that I knew what I was doing.'

'Oh I'm sure your patriotism is very noble and commendable,' Christina said sarcastically. 'You'll probably get a knighthood after the war's over. If you manage to survive in business, that is, which now seems to me very unlikely.'

173

'You don't know what you're talking about.'

'Don't keep dismissing me like that. You've put the business at an enormous risk and you know it. As if there weren't enough problems with labour shortages. I'll tell you one thing,' she added. 'You'll never get the better of me like you did with your mother today. My side of the business at least is going to continue and prosper and nothing you can ever say or do will affect that or me one iota.'

Suddenly, almost as she spoke, she thought she detected a different expression in his eyes. Darkly shadowed by his scarred brow, they glimmered with what could either have been amusement or sexual awareness. The heat of her anger dissolved into uncertainty and confusion. He had never stared at her like that before.

She tried at first to stare him out, but was forced to avert her eyes. At the same time she was unable to control the flush that she felt rising from her neck to suffuse her face. She had never been able to fathom him, never understood him, and she did not understand him now. She wondered if he found conflict and challenge sexually exciting. And yet, they had argued before. They had been arguing more and more often these past few months. Whenever they were in each other's company now conflict was inevitable.

He sauntered towards her, still with his cigar clenched between strong white teeth. He came very close, making her heart thunder through her body, then he reached across to the table at her side and put his cigar out on the ashtray. After straightening up again he placed a forefinger lightly under her chin and said, 'It's been a long day. Time for bed.'

Chapter Twenty-eight

'Why are you doing this?' Christina asked.

He smiled. 'You're my wife.'

'You know what I mean.'

They were in the bedroom and he had unbuttoned her blouse, peeled it slowly off and smoothed his hands down over her shoulders and her breasts. She was struggling to keep herself closed in, aloof, but her defences melted away when he took her in his arms and kissed her. She had been so in need of him.

'Put out the light,' she said. She didn't want him to see the tears that were rising to her eyes and in danger of spilling over. In the dark before he came into bed beside her, she hastily dabbed her face with the sheet.

She could hardly believe that it was really happening. Her hands fluttered over his body as he kissed her again. She gradually allowed herself to relax and absorb each sensation thirstily, gratefully, not making a sound but clinging to him as if she'd never let him go. She had to eventually as he rolled away from her, got out of the bed and thumped over on to his own one. She was just beginning to struggle with the pang of disappointment that he hadn't stayed and held her after the lovemaking when he said, 'Touché.'

After a moment's silence she said, 'What do you mean?'

'You tricked me in this manner once,' he said. 'Now I've returned the favour and for the same reason.'

Another longer silence followed. Eventually she managed, 'You mean you hope I'll get pregnant and that will put me out of the business?'

'I'm beginning to think it's the only thing that would.'

She had turned to ice. Hard, brittle inside. She didn't move in case she should crack and crumble to pieces.

'You're a real bastard,' she said.

'Tut tut. Such language from the minister's daughter.'

'This isn't going to work.'

'You mean I might have to try again?'

'Don't you ever touch me again, you bastard,' she said.

He laughed and she heard the creak of the bedsprings as he turned to settle himself to sleep. She remained rigid. She was still lying like that long dark hours later, but she must have fallen into an exhausted sleep eventually, because when she did awake he was no longer in the room. The maid was drawing the curtains.

'Are you all right, madam? I was getting worried when you didn't come down for breakfast with the master.'

'I've just got a bit of a headache.' Christina said.

'Will I bring you up a cup of tea or breakfast on a tray?'

'I don't feel hungry but a cup of tea would be very nice, thank you.'

At first when she wakened, she had a vague feeling of a nightmare still clinging to her. For a few seconds she couldn't remember what it was about. At first when she opened her eyes she was momentarily relieved that she had awakened from the nightmare. Then suddenly she was flung into anguish when she remembered. Then defiant disbelief, then anguish again, until eventually there was only cold rage.

After she had sipped her tea she got up and took a very hot bath and scrubbed herself with an obsessive thoroughness, as if determined to remove from her body not only Monkton's sperm but also his touch. She resolved to find out how one could prevent a pregnancy, and realized that the only person she knew who might be able to help was Maisie the dressmaker. She would go and see Maisie this evening. First of all she had business to attend to in her office.

Her office room was next to Monkton's and they shared the same reception area. If Monkton was in the building they often saw each other in passing. She determined that in no way would he be allowed to feel that he had got the better of her. She dressed very carefully in a peacock-green velvetine suit with black fox bands on the collar, cuffs and edging of the long, wide-skirted jacket. Her hat was black plush with a beige cloth brim and an amber ball pin. Underneath the wide skirt was a daring show of the cloth uppers on her black leather boots. The reflection in the long mirror showed a very prosperous-looking, expensively and elegantly dressed lady whose posture was dignified if perhaps a little too stiff and straight backed. The pale face with its smooth, even features was somewhat spoiled too by the steely determination staring from the grey eyes and the slightly bitter twist to the once softly vulnerable mouth.

There was a yard at the back of the Monkton office building where a variety of vehicles were parked. Part of the building was used as a large joiner's workshop, and always reverberated with the noise of sawing and hammering. The floor was fawn-coloured with wood shavings and the air thick and dry with wood dust and the pungent aroma of pine sap. There was an entrance to the building both at front and back. Going through the front way one had to pass the offices of different members of the firm. At the end of the corridor on the left was a stair going up to her office, Monkton's and Logie Baxter's, and two smaller rooms used by her own and Monkton's secretaries. At the foot of the stairs on the right the corridor led to a back door to the yard and to a door into the joiner's workshop.

From Pollokshaws Road Christina decided to cut down the lane that led into the yard and enter the building from the back door. She was in no mood to engage in conversation with any of the other members of Monkton's she might meet in the front corridor. She also wanted to see if Adam's car was in the yard. It was. She steeled herself against the prospect of meeting him.

After picking her way past high honey-coloured walls of timber, mountains of dark blue-grey slates and other builder's debris, she entered the back door. She had just reached the top of the stairs when Monkton emerged from his office to cross over to his secretary's room. Catching sight of Christina he gave her a wink which absolutely infuriated her. She could hardly believe his impertinence.

He called into his secretary's room, 'I'm off to the Shettleston job. I'll be back about four.' Then just as Christina was passing him he said, 'And how are we this morning?'

She gave him a withering look before turning into her own office.

'Perfectly well, thank you.'

'Good,' he said and clattered away down the stairs.

Inside her office she took off her jacket and sat down on the chair behind the desk. But she couldn't settle. Suddenly she grabbed the telephone and dialled Mathieson's number.

'Christina here,' she said. 'Have you anything interesting on your books?'

'Not really.' he said. 'Unless you want another tenement property.'

'All right,' she said. 'I'll go for that.'

He laughed. 'You'll own most of the Gorbals before you're done.'

'So?'

'Nothing,' he said. 'Just an observation.'

'Anything else?'

'Hmmm . . . Could be. Nothing definite yet though. I'll keep you informed.'

'I want to know now,' she said.

'In the first place it's not something I think it's wise to talk about over the telephone.'

'Over lunch then.'

'I'm sorry, Christina. That's impossible. Today anyway. I'm just on my way out to another appointment. Make it tomorrow.'

'Oh very well,' she said. 'But give me the details of this tenement property and I'll get going with that.'

'I could have discussed that tomorrow too.'

'I want it now,' she said, pen poised over a notepad.

He sighed, but gave her the necessary details.

After she put down the telephone she immediately lifted it again and dialled the number that Mathieson had given her. Before the day was out she'd struck a bargain for another tenement property.

She was still restless, still wanting to do something, anything to keep her mind from her personal life and the angers and anguishes that she was barely managing to freeze into the far distance.

She began to pace back and forth in her office. Then suddenly she decided to pay another visit to the Gorbals to view the tenement buildings. It was all very well taking advice from Mathieson and Neil Fintry, the factor. It was all very well studying facts and figures on paper or arguing over prices and beating them down, but she felt it was also important to see the property that was being negotiated. With some relief she lifted her jacket and buttoned it on, at the same time crossing the corridor to tell her secretary to phone for a taxi-cab. But she'd hardly stepped out of her office room when she saw, coming along the corridor, a tall young man in khaki. She could hardly credit her eyes.

'Simon!' she cried out. 'Is it really you?'

'You look exceptionally prosperous,' he said. And it was then she noticed that there was something different about him. She felt a stab of concern but could not break through her aura of cool sophistication.

'Yes,' she said with a kind of puzzled laugh as she stared at him. 'I'm a successful businesswoman now.'

'Mother told me. She doesn't seem too pleased about it. Can't say I feel very thrilled either.'

'Well, I'm thrilled about seeing you,' she managed. 'It's wonderful to have you back. Come into the office, I've some whisky in the cupboard here. We'll drink to your return.

'Why aren't you pleased at my success?' she said as she was getting the bottle and glasses out.

'Oh, I'm sorry, Chrissie,' he said. 'But from the moment I arrived down south Britain has seemed like another world somehow.'

She was intrigued.

'What do you mean?' she asked, handing him a glass.

'There seems to be a kind of war madness. Everybody's so damned enthusiastic about it as if it's some sort of a game.'

'Oh, it's not so bad now.' Christina said. 'It was very much like that at first, I admit, but . . .'

His voice turned bitter and he continued as if he hadn't

heard her. 'A jolly old sport. They don't know what they're talking about. I've seen things in newspapers and heard talk that would . . . Oh, I don't know. It would sicken anyone who really knows what war's about. In all the papers and magazines I've seen, the soldier is represented as invariably cheerful and revelling in the excitement of war and finding sport in killing other men and hunting Germans out of dugouts like a terrier hunts rats. We're depicted as merry assassins rejoicing in the opportunity of a scrap. It's disgusting.' He lit a cigarette and drew deeply at it. 'Certainly, for a time at least, I tried to be cheerful in my letters to Mother. For one thing I didn't want to worry her. I can't even write now. I don't dare. I'm in too much danger of telling the truth. Then I come home on leave from that hell and I see everyone going to fat on big money at home.'

She tried to smile. 'I'm not fat, am I?'

'No. You look beautiful and I'm sorry. I'm detaining you. You were just on your way out.'

'Not at all,' she said. 'It was nothing important.'

Chapter Twenty-nine

It was late as Annalie entered the close and was absorbed into the eerie sounds and flickering shadows of the gas light.

As she crept through the shadows she stumbled over a man sprawled in his doorway, too drunk to crawl through it. She was greeted by a stream of oaths from the body that she had jerked back into consciousness. Before he had said anything Annalie knew it was Joe Cowley, who got drunk every Saturday night on Red Biddy, the local cheap and lethal wine.

Annalie was keenly sorry for Sadie Cowley, his wife, who had recently given birth to her twenty-third child. On the second or third day after each birth she was always up and about and back to work washing stairs for the people who could afford to pay for the service in more prosperous tenements. Often Annalie saw her plodding along the street with her bucket under her arm. Her customers provided the soap and the white pipe-clay that she used to decorate the sides of each step and the sides of the close.

Mrs Cowley, although tired after her long day's work, still took her turn of washing her own stairs. It was a hopeless task, however, because of the number of people who went up and down, the hordes of children who played on it and the overflowing toilet on the first landing.

It was a mechanical duty to her, as was her childbearing and ultimate delivery. She accepted with quiet resignation the burden of duties which she as a woman was expected to. Annalie's strong sense of rebellion arose inside her every time she saw Mrs Cowley. She felt sure that if she were married to Joe Cowley she would have murdered him years ago, or at the very least taken great pleasure in castrating him.

Climbing the stairs in the hollow hours of the dark

winter's night, she could hear sounds of snoring, children crying and screaming, husbands and wives squabbling. Then she heard the music. When she entered her house she saw her mother sitting on the stool with a piano accordion strapped over her shoulders. Her head was leaning forward, her black hair glistening in the glow from the fire but shadowing her face. She was softly singing a gypsy song to the music. On the floor in front of her sat Elizabeth.

'Mammy!' Annalie cried out. 'Elizabeth should have been in her bed asleep hours ago. What do you think you're doing?'

She snatched up the baby and nursed her against herself.

'My Darklas *chavvie* was in bed hours ago and sleeping, but woke up crying, so I've been entertaining her until she felt sleepy again. She does now. She was nodding off there just before you came in.'

'If you had to play to her you surely could have played to her while she was still in bed.' Amnnalie said, going over to the bed and gently laying the half sleeping child down on it. She tucked the covers over her.

'She wanted up.' Saviana said. 'She likes to watch me.'

It was understandable, Annalie supposed, that the baby should be so hypnotized by the sight of Saviana. She was such a splash of vivid colour in this drab place. Still, she felt angry.

'You might have had some tea made,' she complained. 'I've been on my feet for hours and I'm absolutely exhausted.'

Her mother was still filling the small room with the strange haunting music.

'And for goodness' sake stop that noise,' Annalie said irritably. 'You're giving me a headache. It's time you went back round to Daddy.'

Her mother was wearing a dress of bright tartan, with crimson flannel petticoats short enough to reveal her high-heeled, buttoned boots. Her earrings, rings and bangles, even the accordian all glistened and sparkled in the light from the fire and from the hissing and flickering gas mantle above the fireplace.

'You've a quick temper, *rakli*,' Saviana said, getting up and fixing her dark eyes on Annalie's face. 'Be careful with it. There could be death in it.'

Annalie tossed her hair. 'You don't frighten me. Keep your *dukkerin* talk for the fools that part with money for it.'

After a night's sleep Annalie felt sorry for speaking so sharply to her mother. After all, she was being kind enough to look after Elizabeth for most of every day and evening. Annalie determined to apologize to her next time they met. She was in the habit of taking Elizabeth round to Aunty Murn's most days and leaving her there with Saviana. She had to pass Aunty Murn's close to get to her work at Hurley's.

This day, however, when she arrived at Aunty Murn's it wasn't Saviana who came to the door.

'Have you time to come in, hen?' Auntie Murn asked as she took the child from her arms.

'No, I'm going to be late as it is,' Annalie said. 'Tell Mammy I'll see her when I come home.'

'Aye, all right.'

Not that Annalie was looking forward to this day in particular. Mrs Hurley was going off to Edinburgh to visit her sister and was staying overnight with her. Malcolm was going to be in charge of the shop while she was away.

Fortunately the shop was very busy the whole evening and it wasn't until after they were closing and she had gone to the back kitchen to collect her shawl that the trouble started.

She heard the bolt go in the front door, and called to him, 'Just a minute, I've to get out first.' But when she came running through he was standing with his back to the door and a hungry look in his eyes.

'Open that door and let me out at once,' she commanded.

Without saying anything he came towards her. Her hand felt the flour bin at her side and she grabbed the small metal scoop. Before he could lay his hands on her she'd brought it up and crashed it against his face. He gave a howl, his nose and mouth spurting blood.

'You come near me again,' she bawled at him, 'and I'll

tell your wife what a dirty swine you are, as if she didn't know. And if that doesn't work I'll kill you. I'm warning you, I'll kill you.'

While he was nursing his face and mumbling something she couldn't make out she managed to open the door and get away. She flew along Cumberland Street in panicky distress, feeling sick every time she thought of the hungry lascivious look in Malcolm Hurley's face. She flew in the close and up the stairs, only stopping for breath when she reached her door. Still struggling for breath, she stood in the dark kitchen, the fact that the light was not lit and the fire had gone out not registering at first. For a few seconds she just stood breathing heavily, her mind blank.

'Mammy?' she called out.

Once before when she'd come home Saviana had fallen asleep in the bed with Elizabeth. Irritation at her mother for letting the fire go out needled over Annalie's nerves as she groped towards the mantelpiece and felt blindly along it for matches to light the gas mantle. The mantle hissed and puttered and burst into flame. Annalie could now see that the room was empty, and realized that it had felt empty the moment she stepped over the threshold. She felt harassed. Her mother had obviously stayed at Aunty Murn's and put the baby into her bed. Saviana had been far too possessive with the child for some time now.

'My Darklas,' she kept saying. 'My *chavvie*.'

Annalie sighed. It was an ordeal to have to go out again when she was so fatigued, but without taking off her shawl or making herself a cup of tea she hurried along to Aunty Murn's.

Aunty Murn came to the door in her long flannelette nightgown, her wiry hair in two long pigtails.

'What do you mean bringing me to the door in my goony at this time of night?' she demanded.

'I've come for the baby, of course.' Annalie said. 'I wasn't going to go to my bed and just leave her here all night, was I?'

Aunty Murn's face went a sickly grey. 'The wean's not here.' Suddenly in a panic Annalie pushed past her.

184

'She must be. She'll be in bed with Mammy and Daddy.'

'I knew it,' Aunty Murn said. 'I just knew it. That dirty tinker's gone and taken your wean away with her. I've never seen her for hours.'

'She's not here?' Annalie said.

'I'm telling you. She's never been here for hours. She left with the wean not long after you went to work.'

'Oh no.' Hysteria began to whirl around her like a tornado. 'No. No. She couldn't do that. She wouldn't do that to me.'

'It's time you stopped fooling yourself.' Aunty Murn said.

'I'll go to Glasgow Green. I'll get her back. I'll go right now.'

'I said it's time you stopped fooling yourself,' Aunty Murn repeated. 'Do you think she'll still be there? Not on your life. That dirty tinker's well away now. She's always been the same. She disappears and that's her away and nobody'll find her unless she wants to be found. Do you not think your Daddy's tried often enough to run after her? He's never caught her and nor will you. That poor wean.' Aunty Murn shook her head. 'God only knows where she is by now.'

'I've got to go to the Green. I've got to try.' Annalie was sobbing violently now. 'Oh my baby, my baby.'

Suddenly Aunty Murn's big hand smacked across her face, leaving a vivid splash of red on the chalk-white skin.

'Calm down. You're not going to run out there in a state like this. Calm down, I said.'

Annalie felt broken-hearted. She didn't know how she was going to cope with the pain and the emptiness. Aunty Murn was right, Saviana would be far gone by now. She wiped her eyes on the corner of her shawl.

'I've got to go,' she said in a calmer but still trembling voice.

'All right,' said Aunty Murn, holding the door open wide. 'Go then, I'm telling you, you're wasting your time.'

Annalie ran demented and weeping stormily through the streets. Fog which had been gathering all evening had settled densely over the river. Ships in the distance were groping ghosts in a cavern filled with wailing and strange cries. Street lights were dim, disembodied glows floating above the street. Even without any lights, however, she would have known her way to the Green. There, through the grey veil of fog the moon was struggling to penetrate.

She ran to the place where the wagons and bender tents had been but there was nothing but the burnt-out remains of a fire and a few clothes pegs dropped from someone's basket. The gypsies had gone. Her baby was gone.

Annalie's sobbing loudened to a crescendo. She tore at her hair and howled wildly at the moon. But her baby was gone.

Chapter Thirty

'Hasn't your daddy done this a dozen times before? Searched here, searched there, asked everyone including the police. He's never been able to find her. And *they've* never been able to find her. So how do you think you will? You'll just have to content yourself until she comes back.'

'But will she come back this time?' Annalie said. 'When she's taken the baby? Would she have the nerve to come back?'

'Oh, she'd have the nerve all right,' Aunty Murn said. 'Bold as brass she is, that dirty tinker. Nerve for anything, she has. She'll come back all right. But just when it comes up her humph.'

Annalie felt as if she'd had an operation without an anaesthetic – as if part of her had been torn from her body. She was in agony from the raw pain of it. She went to work oblivious of Malcolm Hurley and his now smouldering hatred of her, his black looks and sulky, drooping mouth. The hours that he worked hardly overlapped Annalie's hours and after he was gone, Annalie in a short, quiet spell in the shop, burst out to Mrs Hurley about the awful thing that had happened.

Mrs Hurley said, 'Och well, she is the wee girl's granny and she must have been fond of the child, otherwise she wouldn't have taken her, so she'll be all right. And she'll be back. She's done that sort of thing before, hasn't she, that woman? I remember your Aunty Murn saying something one time she was in the shop. And you'll be a lot freer now. You won't need to be always worrying so much. You're always worrying that much about hurrying home at night.'

Annalie stared at the older woman incredulously. All Mrs Hurley was apparently thinking about was her being unfettered for working in the shop to all hours of the night.

She could see that Mrs Hurley had no idea of the absolute agony she was in, and felt enraged. It was on the tip of her tongue to tell Mrs Hurley that all she cared about was squeezing the last pennyworth of work out of her, but the shop suddenly filled with customers and she didn't get the chance.

Afterwards she was so tired she didn't see the point. Anyway Mrs Hurley had her own problems and no doubt was so obsessed with them that she hadn't any emotional energy to feel too deeply about anyone else. She was nice enough on the surface and that would have to do.

But it didn't do. After work Annalie walked along Cumberland Street, hugging her shawl tightly around herself, nursing herself, trying to comfort herself, but that wouldn't do either. She dreaded the thought of going up to her house and being alone yet she knew that Aunty Murn wouldn't be very pleased if she was wakened up for no apparent reason at this time of night. Aunty Murn would tell her to get away home. She'd say things like 'You've made your bed now you'll have to lie on it' or 'I told you what that dirty tinker was like. I warned you but you'd never listen. You never listen to anybody.'

Annalie reached her own close and hovered at the close mouth trying to force her feet in, but it was as if there was a barrier she couldn't break through. Impulsively she started to run round into Commercial Road. Reaching Mrs Rafferty's close she felt her way along and, crying loudly now and automatically stamping her way down the stairs, she reached Mrs Rafferty's door. Opening it she called in, 'Mrs Rafferty, are you awake? It's me. Annalie.'

'Aye come in, hen. I'm not even in bed yet.'

The gas was lit and Mrs Rafferty was sitting by the fire in her nightgown. She got up in agitation when she saw Annalie.

'What's up, hen? What a state you're in.'

'My Mammy's taken my baby. She's gone away and I know I'll never find her. My baby. She's gone.'

'Oh my.' Mrs Rafferty's eyes immediately filled with tears. 'You poor wee lassie. Is that not awful?'

Annalie flung herself into Mrs Rafferty's arms and they clung to one another, Mrs Rafferty patting Annalie's back every now and again in an effort to comfort her.

Eventually Mrs Rafferty said, 'I'll pour you a wee cup of tea, hen. I've a pot made there. I'd just finished a cup myself, but I'll have another to keep you company.'

'Thanks, Mrs Rafferty.'

Annalie's sobs had sunk to hiccoughing exhaustion. She rubbed at her eyes and face with the sleeve of her blouse.

'I'm sorry for making such a racket,' she said. 'I might have wakened the children.'

'Och, it would take a bomb to waken that lot.' Mrs Rafferty said. 'Once they're out for the count that's them till the morning. Even then – remember the job we had to get them up?'

'Why were you sitting here not sleeping?' Annalie said. 'Do you not feel well or something, Mrs Rafferty?'

Mrs Rafferty sighed, reached for a piece of paper from the mantelshelf and passed it over.

Annalie read: 'Deeply regret to inform you that Private Patrick Rafferty was killed in action.'

'Oh, Mrs Rafferty,' Annalie cried out. 'Oh, you poor thing. I'm so sorry. And here was you being that sympathetic to me. You should have said right away.'

'There's your tea, hen,' Mrs Rafferty said. 'Drink it up. We'll both feel better after a wee cup of tea.'

'This war's terrible,' Annalie said. 'I keep hearing of people being killed. Every day in the shop there's somebody lost their man or knows somebody that's lost their man or their son or their father or someone. It's just terrible. But I can't believe it about Patrick, somehow. I mean, knowing him. What a fine, big strong man he was.'

Mrs Rafferty nodded and took a gulp of her tea. 'Yes, he was a fine man, my Patrick – hard-working fellow and that good to me and the weans. There's many a woman not been half as lucky as me. If you'd just seen him as a young man, Annie, when I first met him. Oh, he was that handsome. And as strong as an ox as well.' Suddenly tears overflowed from Mrs Rafferty's eyes and she sat like a helpless child staring at Annalie.

'I hope they didn't hurt him, hen. I can't bear the idea of my man being hurt.'

'I'm going to stay with you tonight,' Annalie said. 'Come on. We'll go to bed and I'll cuddle into you and you'll be all right. We'll both be all right.'

'Oh thanks, hen,' Mrs Rafferty said. 'You're an awful good wee lassie. You've always been that kind to me.'

Next day before she left Annalie said, 'Now you'll come and see me, Mrs Rafferty? You'll come for your tea one day?'

Mrs Rafferty flushed with pleasure. 'Oh, I couldn't do that, hen.'

'Why not?' Annalie wanted to know.

'Och well, you don't want the likes of me in your nice wee place.'

'Don't be daft.' Annalie said. 'I wouldn't have asked you if I hadn't wanted you. And there's nothing very special about my place. I've only newly managed to get a table and I was lucky to get that at a knock-down price at the Barras. Aunty Murn's been very good, right enough. If she sees anything she'll get it for me if it's cheap. She's got me one or two nice wee bits of linen things.'

'Oh my,' said Mrs Rafferty.

'She got me a white table cover the other day with crocheted edging. She said it was second hand and next to nothing at Paddy's Market, but it looks pretty good to me. I'm really proud of it. I'll put it on when you come. Come tomorrow afternoon.'

'Oh my,' said Mrs Rafferty. 'Are you sure, hen?'

'Of course I'm sure. I'll look forward to it. Now that's settled then. You're going to come tomorrow. Come about half past two and stay for your tea. It'll have to be an early tea I'm afraid, because you see I go to work.'

'Aye, I know, hen. I won't stay long. I'll really look forward to seeing your tablecloth and your nice wee place.'

Annalie looked forward to the visit too. Her anguish over losing Elizabeth had not lessened although everyone seemed to think it would only be a temporary loss. Her suffering was no longer noisy and uninhibited, however. It was a pain deep inside her. It could still flare up and overflow in tears, but only when she was alone. Even then she struggled to control herself and do something to take her mind off her suffering.

Usually if she was in the house and it was during the day she ran next door to Flo's. Once, she was there after work because Flo and Erchie had been having a party, and their parties always went on well into the early hours. They had a big family, some of whom were in their teens. Flo's old father lived with them as well and he, like the rest of the family, enjoyed a bit of a do.

Flo had the door open ready for her arrival when Annalie finished work. She'd been considering whether just to go into her own place because she was tired, but Flo, hearing her come up the stairs came out and said, 'Come on in, hen. You're just in time for our wee number.'

Flo and Erchie's wee number was the song that they always sang, one by Burns called 'John Anderson, My Jo' and they sang it standing arm in arm:

> 'We clamb the hill thegither,
> And mony a canty day, John,
> We've had wi' ane anither:
> Now we maun totter down, John,
> And hand in hand we'll go,
> And sleep thegither at the foot,
> John Anderson, my Jo.'

This night they did another Burns favourite as an encore and it wasn't only Flo and Erchie who had to wipe their eyes and blow their noses afterwards. 'Ae fond kiss and then we sever, ae fairweel alas for ever. Deep in heart wrung tears I'll pledge thee waring sighs and groans I'll wage thee.'

Flo and Erchie's rooms were packed. Neighbours and friends were sitting on chairs round the walls, children and young people on the floor.

It was the custom for each in turn to sing a song or recite a poem or do something to add to the entertainment of the evening. Old Sandy, Flo's father, always recited, and wee Cathy, the youngest of the family, always sang 'Jesus Wants Me for a Sunbeam.'

To feed the crowd Flo always made a big cloutie dumpling. This was a huge round affair with, as Flo said, 'everything in it but the kitchen sink and if I could get that in as well I'd put it in, hen.' It was rich with spice and fruit, and Flo always wrapped it in an old tablecover, tied it very securely and boiled it up in the boiler in the wash-house down in the back yard. When the cloth was cut off eventually there was a lovely shiny skin round the pudding and the steam rising from it with the smell made everyone's mouth water. It put some heart and energy into Annalie and when her turn came she was able to get up and do one of the wild gypsy dances that she had seen her mother perform so often. Everyone clapped their hands and stamped their feet in time to it and afterwards there was great applause and appreciative laughter and yells of 'Encore, encore!'

The dance had proved a welcome expression and way of releasing her strong emotions and so she was glad to whirl into another dance and indeed to keep going until she was exhausted.

She slept well that night, but again the next day she awoke to stare bleakly at the roof of her bed. Alone with her thoughts she wondered where Elizabeth was, what was happening to her and if she was missing her mammy. She thought of how much she'd enjoyed the previous evening's merrymaking, and was thankful to have good people around her.

She was very lucky with neighbours really, except for the drunken Mr Cowley downstairs. Most of the men were away in the army now and the women were having to manage the best way they could. The biggest and growing problem was the rents. They were all finding them a terrible struggle and more and more people were getting into arrears.

Then she heard the bailiffs were coming to put the Cowleys out on the street. All the neighbours were talking about it and sympathizing with poor Mrs Cowley.

'Here,' Annalie said to Flo, 'Remember how we got together and stopped them flinging Mrs Rafferty out? Well, why couldn't we do the same for Mrs Cowley? Why can't we, in fact,' said Annalie, 'do it for any of the poor souls that get into arrears and get flung out on the street? And keep doing it.'

'Do you think it'll work?' Flo said.

'If there's enough of us, why not?'

'I'll pass the word around everybody right away.'

'Are you game to help me, Flo?'

'You just try and stop me.'

'Right, I'll tell everybody on this side of the street. You cross the road and do that side and get some of the others to do the other streets. You know, Hospital Street, Thistle Street, Mathieson Street. I'll go down Commercial Road and do as much of Rutherglen Road as I can as well.'

'Right,' Flo said grabbing her shawl and making for the door while Annalie did the same.

Annalie laughed as they both ran down the stairs.

'Into battle!' she cried out.

It was the first time she'd laughed since she'd lost baby Elizabeth.

Chapter Thirty-one

Maisie told Christina to take hot baths and drink gin. There was also something called slippery elm root that could be used if necessary. As it turned out it wasn't necessary. Either her bleeding had come naturally or the hot baths and gin had worked.

Christina's relief was intense. She had enough on her mind at the moment without having to worry about becoming pregnant. She didn't think she could ever forgive Adam for his callous treatment of her. Sometimes, however, she suspected that she was more enraged at herself for being taken in by him. She had allowed herself to be thrilled by his touch and he had sensed her excitement. She was furious at herself for betraying to him such a weakness, such a vulnerability. She had no intention of ever doing so again. Yet all the time she knew that beneath the hard casing she was building around herself, she still thrilled to him.

She felt it was the opposite with him. He now spoke to her quite freely about business. He became heated in talk with her, indeed he could speak to her now with passion, but it was a passion about the business and his fight for its survival. Underneath he was icy cold and indifferent, although it wasn't his nature to be so. His frigidity was directed only at her – he had greeted Simon like a brother.

They had both been enthusiastically demonstrative and affectionate. One night when the two men had been out on a pub crawl, Adam had returned the worse for drink. She heard Simon and Adam before either man had reached his home, singing a bawdy song at the top of their voices. She was embarrassed and ashamed as well as annoyed. It was now the early hours of Sunday morning, and she could just imagine how shocked her mother and father would be at Simon's behaviour. No doubt they would blame Adam,

194

probably with some justification. After all, Adam had always been the irreverent one.

She hadn't been able to sleep and had gone downstairs in her nightgown to watch for him. After Simon turned into the manse, still singing, Adam also continued with his tuneful bawling until he reached the door of Monkton House. She got to it before he rang the bell. There was no point in wakening the servants at this hour.

'Quiet,' she hissed at him as soon as she opened the door. 'You'll waken the whole house.'

Entering the hall he flung his arms wide and shouted a quotation from Burns:

> 'When chapman billie leave the street,
> And drouthy neebors, neebors meet,
> As market-days are wearing late,
> An' folk begin to tak the gate . . .'

'Be quiet,' Christina repeated, but he continued unabashed.

> 'While we sit bousing at the nappy,
> And getting fou and unco happy,
> We think na on the lang Scots miles,
> The mosses, waters, slaps, and styles,
> That lie between us and our hame,
> Whare sits our sulky sullen dame,
> Gathering her brows like gathering storm,
> Nursing her wrath to keep it warm . . .'

She pulled his arm towards the stair then pushed at him as best she could to hurry him up.

'Are you not pregnant yet?' he asked.

'You're a disgrace!' she said.

'No doubt you'll say a prayer for me the next time you're in church. You'd better pray that you're pregnant as well because no way – no way, do you hear? – am I going to allow you to ruin my business.'

'I'm not going to ruin your business,' she told him, managing to guide him into the bedroom and shut the door. He pulled off his jacket and flung it onto the floor and then started peeling off the rest of his clothes, dropping them as he walked unsteadily about the room. She followed him, picking up the garments and folding them neatly over a chair.

'Always tidy and methodical, dear,' he said.

'You say that as if it were a fault,' Christina protested. 'What would the servants think if I left all your things lying about the floor like this?'

'That's so typical of you as well,' he said with a short laugh, although in fact he had gone completely serious. 'Always worrying about what other people might think.'

'There's nothing wrong with that either,' she said. 'We have a position to maintain.'

'What kind of position will we be in and what might people think if we went bankrupt?'

'Oh, don't be silly,' she said. 'We're not going to go bankrupt.'

His eyes darkened with hatred. 'Don't you dare use that tone of voice to me.'

'Well, you've got an obsession about me ruining the business and you've absolutely no justification for it.'

'For a start,' he said, 'I don't trust you nor do I trust your partner, Scott Mathieson. You're two of a kind.'

She flushed with annoyance. 'Don't say that. I'm nothing like Scott Mathieson. We've nothing in common in our natures except business acumen.'

'Let me be the judge of what's business acumen or not,' Monkton said. 'I've had a lot more experience in business than you have.'

'My side of the business is quite different from yours,' she said. 'And it takes a different kind of person from you.'

'Oh I can believe that,' he said. 'That's probably why I've never had any interest in trading and dealing. But quite apart from personalities, it never has been the Monkton kind of business.'

'Obviously not, but I'm a Monkton now, remember, and I felt and still feel it's right that we expand into this area and it's my place in the business, my area of expertise.'

'Your place is in the home,' he said.

196

'Oh,' she said. 'I wondered when you were going to come out with that. There's hardly a woman in the land now, except perhaps the elderly, who isn't out of the home doing something. They're even working in shipbuilding and engineering. How can you say now that women's place is in the home?'

'You're talking,' he said, 'about a temporary wartime situation. Come the end of the war when all the men return, these women will be back where they belong, running their homes and rearing their children.'

'Your mother runs this home,' she said. 'And Mitchell rears our child.'

'So I've noticed. Mother and Mitchell have little choice in the matter, have they? You're never here to do either.'

'I was the one that had no choice,' she said. 'They took over right from the start. I've never had a chance to do anything in this house. But now I don't care. I'm not interested in it any more.'

'Well, let's give you a chance now, then. Let's make sure that you have another infant and this time you'll be the one who'll look after it, not Mitchell.'

'I don't want another child, and most certainly I don't want a child by you.'

'Well, I've news for you. If it takes every single night from now until Christmas I'm going to continue trying. Whether you want it or not, I'm going to make sure you do have another child by me.'

'You'll have to rape me first.'

'Well, if that's the way you want it.'

'It's not the way I want it.'

'You can have it any way you like, but make up your mind.'

Suddenly his fingers jarred into her shoulders, making her stumble backwards onto the bed.

'Don't you dare touch me,' she said, kicking out at him. But despite kicking and punching as hard as she could she couldn't prevent him from coming on top of her.

She continued to struggle desperatley, but his brute

strength was too much for her. Afterwards she dug her face into her pillow and lay for long hours, unable to sleep.

Next morning, without turning round to face him she said, 'I've already taken the necessary steps to have an abortion once and I'll do it again and again and again if necessary. Even if it means killing myself in the process. If you're determined to stop me continuing in my business you'll have to think of a better idea than making me pregnant.'

He didn't say anything. She heard the bedroom door open and shut and he was gone.

She got up and put on a soft wool dress in a delicate lavender shade. Fine gold chains went round her neck, and a black hat with a lavender ribbon and a high buttoning coat finished the outfit. She passed Doris as she was going downstairs.

'Don't you want any breakfast, madam?' Doris asked.

'No thank you, Doris. I'm not hungry this morning and I've an important engagement in the office.'

She decided to walk. She needed the fresh air and the time to gain proper control of her thoughts and feelings. One thing she had no intention of controlling and that was her ambition to get involved as soon as possible in a really big deal, bigger than anything she had attempted before. If it was risky, all the better. Let Adam sweat. Let him suffer agonies of suspense. The more business anxiety she made him suffer the better she would be pleased.

She phoned Mathieson as soon as she reached the office.

'We've got to talk,' she said. 'Can I come over to your office?'

'Of course,' he agreed.

She took a taxi-cab into Hope Street. Mathieson was waiting for her with a pot of steaming coffee and two cups ready on his desk. He poured the coffee and they both settled back and enjoyed a few sips.

'Well?'

'I want us to put together a package,' she said carefully, 'That will bring us in our biggest profit yet. I think we've got to get a hold of land first of all. I was thinking of the river front on the Clyde. I believe that's a potentially good location. In fact I've come to see that there're three things about land and the principle in each case is location, location, location. There are quite a lot of rundown, derelict warehouse areas on the river front. Now if I could get a piece of land like that for buttons and if we could, at the same time, find someone like the Co-operative movement who are expanding and who need more offices or store-rooms or warehouses or a depot or all of those things combined, we could persuade them that that area would be the most convenient. Or it could be a large engineering works or a substantial coal merchant. We could purchase the land on the basis of a legal missive, that is a contract gaining legal control of the site with a settlement date say two or three months later.'

'You'd need,' Mathieson said, 'to have it coupled with a planning application for consent to carry out a new or differ-ent form of land use. And remember, whether its residen-tial, commercial, industrial or whatever, land values are effectively created by the granting of a planning consent.'

'I know,' she said.

The thing about trading and dealing, or indeed any kind of property deal, was that it was like juggling several balls in the air at one time. Different things had to be done concurrently and were dependent on the success of each other. It took nerve to do this. Of course, Christina always had the safety net of her income from the tenement property to meet the interest on her capital loans from the bank.

'The railway might be another good bet,' Mathieson sug-gested. 'But I think you might be better to try the Fordyce Munitions Company first. They're obviously doing well at the moment and I wouldn't be surprised if they wanted to expand onto a bigger site.'

Christina nodded. 'I'll aim for getting the biggest river-side site that I can possibly lay my hands on.'

Mathieson said, 'I suppose you're hoping to meet another Mrs Gray?'

'Why not?' Christina said. 'There's one born every minute, they say.'

Chapter Thirty-two

The gym in Pollokshaws Road was spartan. Its bare floor-boards echoed with the rapid drumming of men's feet training with skipping ropes. There was also the rhythmic thumping on the leather punchbags. The only decorations on the walls were posters with the strongmen who went round showgrounds and theatres displaying feats of strength and challenging all comers. The posters advertised when the next visit of each man was to take place, men with names like The Terrible Turk, Bulldog Barton and The Scottish Lion.

There was a raised boxing ring in the centre of the floor where, at the moment, Monkton and big Geordie were having a bout of jujitsu. Geordie attacked first with a low kick. This was quickly evaded by Monkton, who immediately leapt on his opponent and seized him round the waist. Then with a knee stroke placed under the right thigh, and left hand squeezing the back muscles of Geordie, he swung the navvy over and caused him to fall heavily on his back. Monkton followed him down, held him by the throat and was able to seize Geordie's right hand. Turning himself over onto his back, Monkton passed a leg over Geordie's neck and squeezed the carotid artery. Then he pulled violently against Geordie's arm joint. This hold, which can dislocate an arm, provoked such pain in Geordie that he offered little resistance before letting out a terrible cry, and giving in.

The jujitsu lock that had defeated him was called the *ude-shi-ghi*. Monkton had relaxed the hold as soon as he heard Geordie cry out, and both men stood up and shook hands.

Geordie said, 'Mr Monkton, it should be you that's going in for the contest – not me, by the looks of things.'

'You'll do fine, Geordie,' Monkton said, walking away from the navvy over to one of the punchbags.

The air in the gym was thick with the smell of horse liniment and sweat. Bandages were lying about. Another couple of men wearing only long johns were doing bagwork.

After flinging off the special canvas jacket worn while practising the art of jujitsu, Monkton began thumping at one of the bags. Thump, thump, thumping as fast as he could till the sweat was running down his face and chest. He wished it was someone thumping him. In his opinion rape in any circumstances was despicable, no less so when the woman was the man's wife. He could think of no excuse for himself, certainly not that he was drunk at the time. He had wanted to apologize to Christina but next morning she had spoken about abortion in such a cold-blooded way that he had been shocked into silence.

More and more he longed to communicate with her, to talk as they'd once done when she was a young girl, but the woman she had become was so icy cold at times. There were occasions when she managed to surprise him. Her apparent concern for the children of the Gorbals, for instance, and the success of her gymnasium there. But for the most part it was well-nigh impossible for anyone to get through to her. Mixed with his fury and hatred at the anxiety and threat she caused him in business, however, the memories he had of her as a girl persisted. It was when he remembered her as she had been, completely crushed by her environment, that he had to admire the fighting spirit that had got her out of her predicament in the manse. He had fought against the restrictions and frustrations that his background had imposed on him. She in her own way had done the same with hers. But even if he'd hated her without any qualifications there was still no excuse for the rape.

Eventually, after pushing himself to punishing limits in the gym, he returned to the office. Still restless, after a few minutes he went down to the joinery workshop. He found Al Brownlee there on his own.

'Have you heard that Jackson's joining up, Al?' Monkton asked. Brownlee nodded.

'So many changes. Men come and go all the time these days.' Brownlee was a man in his early fifties, a steady, conscientious worker.

'How would you like to take over from Jackson?' Monkton asked.

Brownlee smoothed a big hand over a piece of wood and dusted off some sawdust.

'Foreman?' he queried. 'Do you think I fit the bill, Mr Monkton?'

'As a sort of joinery and jobbing foreman for the smaller jobs, yes. You could be responsible for the measuring and estimating of the joinery, and looking after the other carpenters who work out of the shop here. And perhaps helping on the carpentry work on some of the larger jobs?'

'Will I stay on the tools in here when I'm not estimating and things?'

'No,' Monkton said. 'I'm getting another van so you could drive my old one, and have a desk up in the office too and go on the weekly staff salary. I'll give you a bit more money. What do you get now?'

Brownlee told him and Monkton said, 'I'll give you a pound more than that and of course, there are various other perks when you're on the staff.'

Brownlee scratched his head.

'It doesn't seem much more for all the extra responsibility, Mr Monkton. I don't want to seem greedy but could you make that two pounds?'

'Yes,' Monkton said. 'But not for a couple of months. Let's see how you do first?'

'Fair enough,' Brownlee agreed.

'Now do you understand exactly what the job entails?' Monkton asked him. 'You've to be a sort of roving joinery foreman. If someone rings up and wants something made you go round and talk to the client, estimate the job whether it's for a cupboard, a bookcase or whatever. Do the job, help to make out the bill, and talk the client into paying if he's reluctant. In fact, see the whole project through so that I don't have to be worried about every small job that's going on.'

Brownlee cleared his throat. 'Would you mind talking to the lads, sir, to tell them about my new position?' He faltered. 'It's a bit awkward for me.'

'Don't worry,' Monkton said, 'I'll see to it.'

He returned back upstairs to his office, made a few phone calls and then sat tapping his fingers impatiently on the desk. There was a lot to do but somehow he just couldn't settle to get on with anything. He not only cursed himself now, but Christina as well. She was a real thorn in his side. Always had been. He longed to pluck the thorn out. Get rid of it. Discard it so that he could be left in peace. He knew, however, that his strong sense of duty would prevent him from doing this.

'Till death do us part,' he had promised. He had given his word, and that, as far as he was concerned, was that.

Suddenly he banged his elbows onto the table and nursed his head in his hands. Damn the woman. If she just had some warmth and responsiveness about her it wouldn't be so bad. Her coldness repelled him. The way she shut everyone out was abhorrent to him even though he could understand how her particular type of character had originated and been formed in her childhood. She wasn't a child now. She was a cold, calculating bitch of a woman. Thin ice seemed her natural habitat. She obviously enjoyed skating on it, especially in a business sense. Admittedly he found her physically attractive and apart from when he raped her, she seemed uncharacteristically vulnerable and totally submissive during lovemaking. But even then he couldn't call her responsive.

He ran his hands through his hair. He was a hot-blooded man and needed a woman to match his passionate moods. Not just in sex either. He longed for someone uncomplicated. Someone he could be natural with. Someone with whom he knew where he stood. Someone warm, open, honest, passionately responsive. There was only one woman he'd known who had ever been like that.

Remembering Annalie Gordon again, he closed his eyes and took a deep, shuddering breath.

Chapter Thirty-three

'Matthew, Mark, Luke, John
Ask the Proddies where they're gawn
If they say they're gawn to Kirk
Whack them wi' a great big stick!'

The children were playing in the back court, the girls skipping backwards and forwards, arms crossed, two jumps to
a turn, red faced, breathless and gasping out their rhyming
chants like metronomes.

'A hundred and ninety nine
My father fell in a bine
My mother came out with the washing clout
And skelped his big behind.'

Other girls were bouncing balls off the cobbles onto the
wall in different ways, under their legs and birling round
and clapping between bounces and singing out.

'One, two, three aleery
Four, five, six aleery
Seven, eight, nine aleery
Ten aleery post man.'

Ragged boys were hunkered down playing marbles, shouting and arguing with each other. Above the children, criss-
crossing the back yard were washing lines with wet clothes
fluttering and snapping about in the wind. Higher up,
several of the tenement windows were open and housewives
were leaning out on folded arms viewing the scene below
– or having a wee hing, as this pastime was known as
Glasgow.

A tramcar could be heard rattling and clanging along
Rutherglen Road, mixing with the clip-clop of a horse, the
trundle of a cart and the hoarse, rasping voice of a back

court busker giving a passionate rendering of 'Moonlight Bay.'

Annalie glanced down at the back court while she was washing her dishes at the sink. She could see Mary Rafferty among the crowd of young people. The child must be about thirteen now, Annalie reckoned, and her fair hair was reaching almost to her waist, but tangling all over and matted with dirt. Like all the other children she was bare-footed, but unlike the others she was not participating in a group game. She was a little apart, intent on playing peever, hopping earnestly about edging a Cherry Blossom boot-polish tin along with a dirt-caked foot. On a sudden impulse Annalie jerked the window up and called out, 'Mary, Mary Rafferty. Come here a minute.'

Mary immediately grabbed her peever and disappeared through the back close. In a few minutes she was knocking at the door. She quite often ran a message for Annalie, fetching something she'd forgotten from the shops. At other times Annalie would wrap a piece of bread and jam in newspaper and throw it out of the window for her if she saw her in the back court, a jeelie-piece delivered this way being another Glasgow tradition. And the Rafferty children were always hungry.

'I was just wondering Mary,' she said to the girl once she was in the kitchen, 'If you'd like to wash your hair. I've got a big kettle of water on the boil there. What do you think?'

There was silence for a minute as Mary's face registered first of all disbelief, then wonder, then excitement.

'Oh here,' Mary said, 'I'd love to see what my hair was like when it was washed and you've got a mirror, haven't you?'

'Yes,' Annalie said. 'And I've got a nice hairbrush as well. Right, I'll put the plug in the sink and we'll put in some hot water and then cool it down out of the tap, and I've got some nice scented soap here from Hurley's. It was a special delivery they had the other day.'

'Scented soap!' Mary echoed indredulously.

Annalie found it was no easy task to get either the tangles or the dirt out of Mary's hair, but after a long and strenuous effort she managed it and at last they were both sitting in front of the fire, Annalie on the stool and Mary at her feet. Annalie was brushing the long hair and admiring its golden glow.

'I just knew it, Mary,' she said, 'your hair is absolutely beautiful. Now here you are. Have a look at yourself in the mirror.'

She passed the hand mirror to Mary who gazed at it in disbelief and then delight.

'Oh here, it is nice.'

Annalie nearly said that Mary's face was beautiful as well now that it had a proper clean, but she stopped herself in time. There was no use spoiling the girl and making her big-headed. But she said, 'I tell you what, Mary, I'm here on my own all the time. How would you like to come up here once a week, say on a Friday afternoon before I go to work, and have a bath.'

'A bath?' Mary echoed.

'Yes. I could have the water heated up beforehand and I've got the zinc bath here and I could have mine first. But I won't dirty the water because I have a wipe down every day so that the bath water would be all right for you after me.

'A bath.' Mary repeated.

'Well is that settled then? Friday afternoon straight from school. You could wash your hair then as well. I mean you could do it yourself now that it's got the worst of the dirt out.'

'Oh yes, I could do it myself, I'd love to do it myself.' Mary said. 'Oh thanks, Annalie.' Her hands were clasped tightly together and she was almost dancing with delight. Annalie laughed.

'We might as well go the whole hog and wash your pinny as well.'

She *is* beautiful, Annalie thought, seeing how the young face was glowing with happiness, making the blue eyes sparkle and the cheeks flush a rosy pink.

'The thing is,' Annalie said, 'if you get properly cleaned up and looking smart it means that when you leave school you'll be able to get a decent job. You could go into service in a nice house, like where I used to work. The chances are you would get a nice clean bedroom to yourself and you would see how the toffs live. You would see lots of lovely things that you've never seen in your life before. The main thing is though, Mary, it would get you out of here.'

'Oh Annalie,' Mary said. The words strangled in her throat and she stood staring up at Annalie unable to say any more.

Annalie laughed again.

'Away you go. And if I don't see you before I'll see you next Friday afternoon.'

Helping Mary raised Annalie's spirits a bit. The pain of being separated from Elizabeth was always in her mind and heart, but by occupying herself as much as possible with other things she was able to survive and continue with day-to-day living, to outward appearance at least, as if nothing had happened.

The bath was a great success. Mary savoured every minute of it. Closing her eyes in exquisite pleasure, she dribbled handfuls of water down over her shoulders and young newly formed breasts while Annalie washed and dried her own hair at the sink. Afterwards Mary helped Annalie to lift up the zinc bath and empty it into the sink. Then they both sat in front of the fire, heads bent and hair curtained forward towards the heat.

'Your hair's beautiful too,' Mary said. 'Like shiny, black liquorice.'

'Eugh.' Annalie made a face. 'Doesn't sound very beautiful to me.'

'You know what I mean.'

'Annalie laughed. 'I suppose so.'

'Everybody says you've got gypsy blood in your veins and that's how you're so dark. You've got very dark eyes too, haven't you, and what lovely, long black lashes. I wish I had long lashes like that.'

'You have long lashes.' Annalie said. 'It's just they're so fair you don't notice them so much as mine. And yes, I have gypsy blood in my veins. My Mammy's a gypsy.'

'Gosh.' Mary was impressed. 'Where does your mother live? Along the road at your Aunty Murn's place?'

'Sometimes. Mammy always says, once a traveller always a traveller, so she keeps travelling around.'

'Where is she just now?'

A shadow crossed Annalie's face.

'I don't know. I wish I did.'

'Can I walk along the road to the shop with you?'

'If you like,' Annalie said, then she smiled. 'I know why you want to go parading along Cumberland Street. You want to show off that lovely hair, don't you? To show off how pretty you are from head to toe, in fact.'

Mary flushed with pleasure and Annalie said, 'Oh here, I nearly forgot. I asked Aunty Murn if she could find any of my old pinnies that I used to have when I was your age, and she did find one. I've got it here somewhere. Here you are. Try it on for size.'

The pinafore, white and crisp and smelling of lavender, fitted Mary perfectly. Mary was struck dumb.

'Come along then. Let's parade along Cumberland Street if that's what you want. You can hold your head high now,' Annalie said. 'Because you, like me, are as good as anyone, do you hear?'

Mary nodded, still bereft of words that could adequately express her joy.

Just before they reached the shop Annalie stopped, fished in her purse and gave Mary a ha'penny.

'You can come in and treat yourself to some broken biscuits or whatever you like.'

Mary stared in silent wonderment at the ha'penny before following Annalie into the shop. She stood in front of the counter like a burst of golden sunshine amidst the dark clutter of the place.

Annalie went through to the back kitchen to leave off her shawl. When she returned Malcolm Hurley was serving Mary. Annalie felt immediately dismayed and apprehensive at the way he was looking at the child. She hurried over and elbowed him out of the way. He glared murderously at her but said nothing.

'There are you then, Mary.' Annalie put the broken biscuits in a bag and handed them across the counter. 'Away you go now.' Obediently Mary took the biscuits and left the shop looking, even from the back view, like some sort of Alice in Wonderland.

Mrs Hurley said, 'Was that one of the Raffertys?'

'Yes,' Annalie said.

'My word. She's turning out quite a wee beauty, isn't she?'

'Not so wee,' Malcolm said.

Annalie eyed him with disgust. It looked as if the thought of Mary was making his mouth water.

'You keep your dirty paws off her, do you hear?'

The words were out before Annalie could stop them.

'Here!' Mrs Hurley was shocked. 'Don't you dare speak to my son like that. What a terrible thing to say. Just shows you what's in your mind.'

'It's not what's in *my* mind that's worrying me,' Annalie said. 'Mary Rafferty's only thirteen.'

'We know she's only thirteen,' Mrs Hurley said. 'What's that got to do with my Malcolm? My Malcolm's a decent lad, a good man with a nice family. He's got a lassie of that age at home.'

Malcolm Hurley sighed. 'Don't upset yourself, Mother. I'm used to this sort of thing from her. I never liked to say to you before. I'd rather suffer anything than see you upset.'

'Do you mean to tell me, son, that this isn't the first time she's been nasty to you?'

'Och don't worry about it, Mother.'

Annalie gave a humourless laugh. 'Me nasty to him? Listen, I'll tell you why I said that to him just now. It's because he's never got his dirty paws off me. I've had to fight him off every day since I worked in this place.'

'Oh you wicked liar!' Mrs Hurley gasped. 'You go through there and get your shawl on at once and get out of my shop. Never you put your foot over this door again.'

'Oh don't worry, I'm going. I knew it would come to this sooner or later. I knew one way or another he'd get his own back on me for not letting him touch me.'

She went through to collect her shawl with a nonchalant swing of his hips and toss of her hair as if she didn't have a care in the world. In fact, she was deeply distressed at losing what was her only means of livelihood.

Tossing her shawl over her shoulders she said to Mrs Hurley, 'Right. Pay me up to date then.'

Mrs Hurley practically flung the coins at her. Annalie picked them up and strolled towards the door.

Malcolm was holding it open for her with the pretence of being a gentleman. She could see the gleam of malicious pleasure and triumph in his eyes.

Passing close to him she said, 'Thank you, Malcolm,' and brought her knee up as hard and as viciously as she could.

Howling in agony he staggered back, tripped over the lid of the flour bin and tumbled onto the floor, banging his head on the bin as he went down. Mrs Hurley was screaming as she ran to his assistance.

'I'll have the police on you, you wicked creature you. I'll have you in jail. I'll have you behind bars for this!'

Annalie stopped in the doorway and turned round. She bent her head forward, letting her hair hang like a dark curtain shadowing her face in the same way as her mother had done when she was showing her what to do and what to say when dukkerin.

'There's an old saying, Mrs Hurley, that every gypsy woman is a witch.'

Clinging onto her son, Mrs Hurley, stared white faced at Annalie. 'Get out of here, I said.'

But her voice was no longer loud and strident. There was a quaver of fear to it now.

'Every gypsy woman is a witch,' Annalie repeated very slowly. 'And you know as well as I know, Mrs Hurley, that I have the *Kaoulo Rati*. That's the dark blood, Mrs Hurley, and I'm warning you now. You can go to the police. You can do what harm you wish to me. But I'm warning you now it will mean there will be a death in your family. Someone close to you will be taken away in death very soon. I see death in your face, Mrs Hurley.'

Mrs Hurley began to whimper and sob, at the same time trying to stifle her sobs in her bunched-up apron.

'You'll call to memory,' Annalie said, 'all your life long what the gypsy girl tells you this day.'

Chapter Thirty-four

With intense satisfaction Christina approached the area of her new site in a slow-moving taxi-cab. Part of the area had been described at one time as a practical harbour constructed by businessmen for businessmen. True, it was a working kind of place rather than a picturesque one. Huge cranes towered upwards, like long black beaks stabbing the sky. Underneath them lay a long line of sheds. Behind the sheds, tall, grey tenements jostled together, half hidden in sooty smoke and grime.

The dark pall of smoke and the tenements, the cranes, the sheds, the jumble of ships – some in various stages of noisy construction because Glasgow was best known and most proud of being a ship-building city – were all contained by the hills rearing up on every side. At one time a traveller looking down from these hills would have seen only beautiful rolling countryside, a tapestry of greens and gold, the sparkling blue ribbon of the Clyde used only for salmon fishing.

It had taken Christina some time and a great deal of work before she had found and bought this site. She'd had to discover who owned every part of the sites along riverbanks and inquire into every one of them. She had eventually found that one area had been owned by a wealthy coal merchant who had died some time ago. The benefactors of his will were his only relatives, two spinster ladies living in a flat in the genteel West End district of Hyndland. According to the solicitor – an elderly gentleman who, it seemed, could hardly totter about – the ladies wanted nothing to do with the coal business, so the land and everything on it was being left to go rusty and derelict.

Although Christina did the deal through the solicitor, she made a point of going to visit the ladies personally. The result was that although she did not get the land for buttons

– the ladies were not as foolish as Mrs Gray – she still felt that the price she paid for it would prove well worthwhile in the end. At the same time as negotiating this part of the deal she had been having meetings with the Fordyce Munitions people, and sold on the land to them for a whacking great profit. She was absolutely elated and as soon as Mathieson stepped into her office she rushed over to tell him the news.

'My God!' he said. 'You're an absolute wizard, absolute magic.'

Laughing with shared pleasure they impulsively hugged one another. Until suddenly Mathieson was jerked from her grasp. It was then she saw that Adam had Mathieson by the scruff of the neck.

Mathieson cried out, 'What do you think you're doing?'

'I think that should be my line,' Monkton said. 'Now get out of here before I lose my temper. I want to talk to my wife in private.'

'Fair enough, old man,' Mathieson said. 'There's no need to resort to violence.'

'Get out,' Monkton repeated.

'This is my office,' Christina protested indignantly. 'You've no right to barge in here like this.'

Monkton waited a few seconds until Mathieson had left, closing the door behind him.

'You listen to me,' Monkton growled. 'This is my office. This is my building. This is my business. You're just having the use of this place. Now, what's this I hear about a deal with Fordyce Munitions Company?'

'Where did you hear about that?'

'People talk in clubs and pubs.'

'Anyway,' Christina said. 'It has nothing to do with you. The business that's carried on in this office, whether or not the building belongs to you, is my business, my property business, not yours.'

'It concerns me and the other directors what you do, because what you do could have an adverse effect on us and our side of the business.'

'I've just made a whacking great profit in the deal with the munitions factory.'

'There's many a slip, as they say,' Monkton told her. She laughed.

'Oh, you don't know how anxious this firm is to get that land. No. This is one of the best deals I've made.'

'I wasn't thinking of the firm,' he said. 'I was thinking of public opinion and objections that could be lodged from various sources.'

'What on earth do you mean?'

'There are tenements crowding right up to the edge of that site. Do you think the people there look forward to being that close to a munitions factory? What if there was an accident? An explosion. Think of the danger, the disaster that could cause in such a built-up area.'

'You're just trying to confuse the issue,' Christina said irritably. 'The munitions business is the concern of Fordyce Munitions, not mine.'

'Listen. I've told you before and I'll tell you again, I've been in business longer than you and so I've had more experience of the things that can go wrong. You've been lucky so far. As a result you've no idea of the pitfalls in a situation like this.'

'I'm beginning to think,' Christina said, 'that you and the other directors are just jealous.'

'I'll treat that with the contempt it deserves,' Monkton said. 'I came in here just now because the foreman on a maintenance job among some of the tenements down there came to me and reported that word has got round about the munitions factory and already people are getting up a petition.'

Christina shrugged. 'Let them. As I've said, it's not my concern.'

'Isn't it?' he asked. 'Didn't it come into your calculations at all that there could be reasons why this wasn't the best place for a factory dealing in gunpowder?'

'I keep telling you,' Christina said. 'Where they want to put their munitions factory is up to them.'

'People will override a lot of considerations and take a lot of risks to make a lot of money, as you well know.'

'It's their business what they do.' Christina repeated.

'You don't think you've any moral obligation?'

'No.' she replied abruptly.

'Quite apart from the dangers of it being in such a built-up area,' Monkton said, 'it is also the waterside, which would mean that in the case of a Zeppelin raid there the river would mark out the place very clearly and conveniently for any air pilot.'

'Zeppelin raids,' she scoffed. 'What'll you think up next? There haven't been any Zeppelin raids up here. You know perfectly well they've only been down south. To me that says they can't reach up here. Anyway, the war'll be finished any time now, I would think.'

'People were saying that a year past last Christmas,' Monkton reminded her.

'I don't want to talk any more about this,' Christina said. 'The deal's gone through and that's an end to it.'

'You never cease to amaze me,' Monkton said. 'You really aren't a bit concerned, are you?'

'I've just made a great deal of money,' she said. 'I'm very pleased about it and so should you be.'

He shook his head.

'I have to go out now. I'll see you later at home.' And with that he left.

Most of Christina's elation was now swamped with irritation, not so much because of what Adam had been saying, but by her own reaction to his words. She had become very self-defensive in his presence, quick to prevent herself from showing any weakness in case he took advantage of it. She had in fact had some worries about the munitions factory and had voiced them during negotiations with the company. Her anxieties had been exactly those that Adam had spoken of: the tenements crowding right up against the site, the easy marker of the river, the danger of Zeppelin raids. She wasn't certain in her own conscience if these items on the agenda would have prevented her from going through with the deal, but they were certainly concerns.

The munitions factory people had assured her that their safely precautions were of the highest and that their reputation for safety was second to none. As for Zeppelin raids, they had put forward a very convincing argument against the efficiency and long-range capability of the Zeppelins. They went so far as to say that indeed the Zeppelins were finished. An explosive bullet had been invented to set fire to their gas bags. Armed with these, even the ramshackle BE2C aeroplanes flying to defend London could destroy the raiders. She hoped with all her heart that they were right. She had not seen them herself but had been given graphic descriptions by more than one family at Church who had been into England and actually seen Zeppelins. They were very frightening, huge, dirigible airships some six hundred and fifty feet long, their great hulls lifted into the air by two million cubic feet of hydrogen. They could carry a weapon load of twenty-seven tons, but they were dangerous to fly and crews had to wear padded boots to avoid the fatal spark that might set off the gas, petrol and explosive that surrounded them. Slow and clumsy, they were certainly very vulnerable too in strong winds.

Mr and Mrs McKay had been in East Anglia during a raid, and had told Christina that they had been astonished to hear first of all an anonymous and ominous grinding growing in volume, throbbing, pulsating, filling the air with its sound. Then there were huge shattering, deafening reports and great flashes of light leapt up as the bombs fell. They didn't see much of the airships themselves except two bright stars moving apparently thirty yards apart, but Mr McKay insisted that he had seen one and it looked like the biggest sausage he'd ever seen in his life, like a church steeple sideways. During their stay there they had grown to fear dark, moonless nights.

Another couple in the congregation, Mr and Mrs Paisley, remembered an odd chunkety-chunkety noise. It sounded as if a tram with rusty wheels were travelling through the sky, Mrs Paisley said, and Mr Paisley told her it was like a long, narrow object of a silvery hue and had given the impression of absolute calm and absence of hurry. At first people had gone out to the streets to look up, overcome with curiosity, but after there had been damage done to buildings and several people had been killed, there was fear and panic when the Zeppelins returned, and people were running through the streets with the warning cry, 'Zeps! Zeps!'

It all sounded very frightening and disturbing, and she had felt a keen concern about it. Her irritation at herself now for not admitting this concern to Monkton grew to such proportions it gave her a blinding headache.

She tried to recapture the mood of happy triumph that she'd been enjoying before he entered the room, and failed miserably. Sitting at her desk she leafed through some papers and straightened different items on its already immaculately tidy surfaces. Then resting her elbows on the desk she nursed her head in her hands.

I don't care what he thinks of me, she told herself. I don't care. But all the time she knew that she did.

Chapter Thirty-five

Annalie said to Mary, 'Don't you ever go near that shop when Malcolm Hurley's serving in it.'

'Why not?' Mary said.

'Because he's a horrible man and he's got his eye on you.'

'Do you mean he fancies me?' said Mary.

'You shouldn't know anything about that sort of thing at your age.'

Mary tossed her golden mane of hair. 'A lot of horrible men fancy Mammy. She needs the money to pay the rent, she says.'

'Never you mind that. You keep clear of Malcolm Hurley, do you hear?'

'If I got some money from him I could save it up and it would help me get away from here. Far away.'

'No. It wouldn't work like that. You would just get horrible too,' Annalie said. 'And you'd have less and less chance of getting away from here. Believe me.'

Annalie worried about Mary. She was such a lovely child. The thought of Malcolm Hurley touching her made Annalie feel worse than him laying hands on herself. She was relieved to be away from that danger and glad now that she had flared up and said what she thought of him. She had been nervous before about leaving in case she became destitute and would be forced to go for help to the Parish Council or end up in Barnhill Poor House. This was a fear shared by everybody she had ever known for as far back as she could remember.

It was hard to accept that there was more work now than there had been in the past for women, although there was still resentment from men trade unionists. There was talk of cheap labour, and of course that was true. Even in munitions women's pay was less than half of the men's.

Annalie had thought of trying to get work in the munitions factory. Girls in munitions factories were the most discussed in newspapers. They were called things like 'a brave cama-raderie' and 'most patriotic'. One paper said that a munitions worker was as important as a soldier in the tren-ches and on her his life would depend. But Annalie knew of girls whose faces had turned a hideous yellow and she couldn't bear the thought of that happening to her. Their skin was yellow brown even to the roots of their hair.

She would like to have had a posh job like a shorthand typist working in an office where she could have gone to work dressed nicely and looking her best, but she didn't know how to do shorthand or type and couldn't afford to go anywhere to learn. Even if she could acquire these skills, she doubted if she'd be able to get a job in an office anyway. All the factors' offices had her marked as a trouble-maker and no doubt they would be able to pass the work around other offices.

She had caused trouble for them all right. Thanks to her the women in the district were well organized. Hand bells were rung as signals which brought every woman running to the aid of anyone who was being threatened with eviction. Factors, bailiffs, any man who came to try and put a family out were attacked with bags of flour and rolling pins, wash-ing cloths, buckets of water and by the women themselves. More than one factor had been set upon and carried bodily to the back court where he had been flung head first into the middens – the rubbish bins.

There were hordes of battling, jeering women now. Women crushed up stairs, overflowed from closes, filled whole streets, stopped traffic and created an impossible problem for Big Donald the policeman. All the women, including Annalie, were in a ferment of anger about the housing situation. There were wild rumours flying around that the authorities believed the women had become so out of hand that as well as police reinforcements the army was going to be sent in.

'If they send in a mob of men,' the women had said at a

recent back court meeting, 'what can we do about that? We can't use force against the same number as ourselves.'

Annalie agreed and it was then that she came up with the idea of a rent strike.

'How do you mean, hen?' Flo had asked.

'We stop paying rent at all,' Annalie said. 'We'd better try and put it aside all the same so that it'll be a right protest then. We can say, 'We've got the rent here, but we're not going to pay it until something's done about this situation. Until things are put to rights and poor folks whose men are away fighting and dying for their country aren't treated in this shameful, wicked way.'

'It's terrible, isn't it? To think of the men out there in the front line getting wounded and even dying, and here at home war profiteers are making a fortune out of their poor wives and mothers, even throwing them out in the streets. They've managed it in other places, as we well know. But now the women in other districts are getting themselves organised as well.'

'I think I'll pass the word around that the next step should be what I've just said, a rent strike. Not just in the Gorbals, but all over Glasgow. That's one thing we've found, haven't we? That as they say in the trade unions, "unity is strength". It's true, isn't it? What I think we should do is keep our rents until we get some decent conditions. That is until they do some repairs and improvements on the houses to make them more fit for decent human beings to live in. It's about time they stopped treating us little better than pigs in sties. In fact most animals have better conditions than what we have in our houses.'

She roped Mary in to help her go round the houses and let everyone know what was going on and to come to a meeting to discuss the business of rent strikes and how to be prepared for the increased number of attempted evictions that would result. She thought up all sorts of tricks to make things difficult and confuse the factor and the factor's men. Name plates were changed on houses, placards, oblong in shape, were printed with the words RENT STRIKE. WE ARE

NOT REMOVING and placed in the windows. Sometimes no matter what they did an eviction would take place.

Jessie McLean who lived in Rutherglen Road and had six young children and a husband fighting in the army in France, was thrown out in the street and all her belongings sold before anyone had time to come to her aid. Jessie's household goods hadn't amounted to much, but they had meant everything to her. It had been like taking away her life's blood.

This particular eviction produced a popular uproar and patriotic indignation. The struggle intensified. Street meetings, back court meetings, drums, bells, trumpets, every method was used to bring the women out and to organize them for the struggle.

Every spare moment of Annalie's time now was taken up with the excitement and attention of the strike and it wasn't just the rent issue that had caused the deep-seated anger. The anger had been festering away for years – anger at the atrocious state of the houses they had to live in; anger at every trick from physical force to ideological terror which had been used to oppress the tenants (ticketed houses, for instance, were subject to unannounced raids in the middle of the night, by sanitary police); anger at how you could be victimized if you complained about lack of repairs. How you could be evicted for that too and not be given a factor's line or reference and so you wouldn't be able to get another place to live even though you could pay for one.

'Will we let them get away with this?' was the new war cry resounding in every street in the Gorbals.

'Never!' thundered the reply from the women.

In the streets, in halls, in houses, meetings were held. Annalie was glad to be able to whip herself into a frenzy of emotion over this public issue. It meant that she had no energy or emotion left to feel the pain of losing Elizabeth. She was glad, too, that all the excitement going on had taken up Mary's time and attention. Quite often now Mary would spend a night with her and sometimes she would stay in Annalie's single end for the whole weekend. She told Annalie that she dreaded going back down the dunny every time after she'd stayed at the single end. Annalie understood how she felt. She remembered only too well her own feelings about Mrs Rafferty's place.

Although she would have liked Mary to stay all the time with her she couldn't afford to keep her. Mary was still at school and therefore not earning any money. After Annalie found a job in McClusky's paper shop, however, things became a little easier. She also put in a good word for Mary who got an early morning paper round which earned her a few coppers. Not that Mary gave any of it to Annalie, of course, nor did Annalie blame her for buying pretty crimson and cornflower-blue ribbons for her blonde hair with her first week's wages.

She got Neilly Rafferty the afternoon paper round. He was a couple of years younger than Mary, a painfully thin boy whose ragged clothes hung loosely on him. He had such a recurrent cough, pale pinched face and large dark eyes that sometimes Annalie wondered if he might have T.B. Tuberculosis was common enough in the area. But he was quick on his feet and a willing and eager worker. Mrs McClusky was very pleased with him. Mr McClusky of course, was never pleased about anything. A small, thin, balding man with watery eyes, a moustache and mouth that drooped and straggled, he was continuously grumbling and complaining. Mrs McClusky kept confiding in hushed tones to Annalie or anyone else who happened to be there, 'It's his stomach.'

Annalie was never quite sure what this meant although she had noticed that Mr McClusky consumed a great many Abdine powders. At least he wasn't like Malcolm Hurley. He was a decent, hard-working man and kindly enough in his own way.

Annalie had been thankful to get the job. She had felt almost happy in a strange way, with her wild emotions finding an outlet in her rousing speeches and active involvement with the women of the area against the factors.

She was so involved and her life was so busy between her work in McClusky's and leading the fight for decent housing and fair rents that she was hardly in her own house except when she dropped exhausted into bed. Then one day she'd come home and found Mary pulling a dress over her naked body. The small kitchen was thick with the smell of tobacco smoke and sex.

Annalie was so shaken she had to sit down.

'You've had a man in here,' she accused. 'How could you?'

Mary's face was ashen white, but there was a rebellious hardness about it too.

'I got enough money to buy Neilly a pair of socks and shoes and a pair of shoes for myself as well.'

'Neilly could have saved up his wages until he got a pair,' Annalie said.

'Huh,' Mary scoffed. 'He might have been dead by then. Anyway, he gives all his money to Mammy.'

'You might become pregnant,' Annalie groaned.

'Oh no,' Mary said, looking wide-eyed and suddenly childish. 'I won't do it unless they use a french letter.'

Annalie was horrified.

'You're only a child. You shouldn't know about things like that.'

'A good job I do,' Mary said. 'And anyway, I'm not all that much younger than you. You're only eighteen.'

Annalie felt in fact that she had aged ten years in the last couple, she'd gone through so much suffering and trauma.

'Be that as it may,' she said. 'But one thing's certain, Mary. You're not going to act like this again in my house. I'm locking my door from now on and taking the key with me. You'll only get in when I'm here to let you in.'

'That's all right,' Mary said with a toss of her hair. 'I quite understand.'

She had a proud, hard look about her that made her seem older than her years. Yet as she left in her dress and pinny and long fair hair, she still had the look of an Alice in Wonderland.

Alone in the house Annalie wept for her, and her weeping became angry when she thought of the conditions and environment that were making Mary as she was. And her hatred for the factors and the landlords burned bright.

Then, that very afternoon, when she went into work and the flame was still inside her, she read in the newspaper an article about Christina Monkton, wife of Adam Monkton. The article concerned some sort of dispute about land she'd bought on the riverside, but it wasn't that that caught Annalie's attention. In the article it also went into details about Mrs Monkton's other property, tenemental property in the Gorbals. It was Christina Monkton who owned the property in which so many good people of the Gorbals struggled to exist in such deprivation and squalor. It was Christina Monkton who owned her single end. It was Christina Monkton who owned Mrs Rafferty's hovel down in the dunny.

The flame raged through Annalie now, consuming her.

Chapter Thirty-six

'Well, it's two o'clock,' Monkton said. 'So let's get on with it. The minutes of the last meeting have been circulated. May I sign them as a true record of what took place?'

There was a murmur of 'Aye,' round the table. The secretary, Hector McAllister, then passed a sheet of paper across to Monkton who scrawled his signature on it.

Monkton's eyes swivelled round the group 'Now, are there any matters arising out of those minutes that are not to be dealt with elsewhere in the subsequent agenda?'

There was a murmur of 'No'.

Christina sat stiffly looking at the pencil she was holding and twisting round and round between her fingers. Her stomach was knotted with tension. She knew only too well what the main item on today's agenda was and the one with which everyone was impatient to get to grips. Not that there hadn't been plenty of talk and argument on the subject outside of the board room. She had been badgered and raged at by each of them in turn in the more informal setting of Monkton House, including old Mrs Monkton. She could take their anger and recriminations, their accusations. Her reaction to all of that was a silent vow to herself: I'll show them.

Her outward dignity and self-possession had not appeared in any way ruffled. It wasn't what they could say that worried her, it was what they could do. She had become familiar with each of the board members now and the way they were liable to conduct themselves at these meetings. Old Mrs Monkton was the one who always looked asleep, but could suddenly come out with a shattering piece of logic. Magnus Doyle was the one whose eyes glazed, especially after his customary liquid lunch. His son Brendan was always late and his cry was always 'as for myself person-ally'. The lawyer, Duncan McCaully, invariably countered every proposal with 'but the trouble is', and swept his hand over his head. Hence no doubt his bald patch. Hector McAllister had an irritating habit of continually shuffling papers and moving them about. He also made a big fuss about tiny rules and regulations.

'As for me myself, personally,' Brendan Doyle was saying to Adam. 'I would like to know why we weren't told about this immediately you learnt what Christina had done with her shares?'

'Yes,' his father agreed. 'You must have known she was putting the firm at risk.'

'Your father's firm,' old Mrs Monkton bawled out. 'That he worked hard all his life to build up.'

'I do believe, Mr Chairman,' Hector McAllister said, 'that an extraordinary meeting ought to have been called immediately.'

Christina was somewhat taken aback that an attack should be made on Adam. She had expected them immediately to jump on her.

'When I first discovered that my wife had given her shares to the bank as security for a capital loan to establish her property business,' Adam said, 'of course I realized the dangers and I did my utmost to explain this to my wife and to try to influence her to rethink her position. I believed for some time that I could succeed and that there would be no need to put in a formal report to the directors.'

'But the trouble is,' Duncan McCaully said, smoothing one hand over his head and half folding himself forward as he did so. He always appeared to be squeezing his words out from every part of his body, from his toes right up to his balding head. 'If you had reported to the board immediately you learned of your wife's initial action, we, in a concerted effort, may well have been able to dissuade her where you have obviously failed.'

Anger flashed in Monkton's eyes but before he could reply, Christina said, 'You are quite wrong, Mr McCaully. My husband knows me better than you or any other member of the board could do. Had he made a formal report to you immediately he gained a knowledge about my shares, and

226

had you and other members of the board as a result put pressure on me, I would have responded by going to the opposite extreme from what you desired. I would have given the rest of my shares to the banker rather than recover one of them at your request.'

'Isn't that a disgrace, Martha?' Logie Baxter cried over to old Mrs Monkton, whiskers quivering indignantly all over his face. 'I had her summed up from the start, had I not? Didn't I tell you, Martha, what I thought she was like?'

'Through the Chair, Mr Baxter,' Hector McAllister said. 'Through the Chair at all times, please. That is the proper procedure.'

'Och, to hell with your procedures,' Logie Baxter shouted. 'We're all family here except you and Duncan McCaully and this is a family firm we're talking about and our livelihood into the bargain.'

'The trouble is, Baxter,' Duncan McCaully said, 'if we don't have some sort of order we could be arguing and shouting and bickering all day and all night and still never get anywhere.'

'We know only too well where we're getting,' Magnus Doyle said. 'We're getting ruined, and by her.'

'That's quite enough, Doyle,' Adam said. 'The position as I see it is this. Christina wanted to start a property business, something she was perfectly entitled to do. She needed capital and so used most of her shares in this company as security for a capital loan. From her point of view this was a perfectly legitimate thing to do. You mentioned procedure, McAllister. As we all know perfectly well, this was proper business procedure.'

'Aye, from her point of view,' Baxter shouted. 'But it's not her point of view we want. Whose side are you on?'

'It's not a matter of sides,' Monkton said. 'Now if I may finish. Her deals have so far been very successful. She's had no difficulty in paying the running interest on her loans. This latest deal would have been very profitable had it not been for the unexpected objections of the public, but more importantly as far as the law is concerned, the objections on the grounds of denial of right of way for an adjoining business. That is, Bloomberg's Tailoring Factory. They claim to be doing war work inasmuch as, on government edict, they have turned all their production to khaki and blue uniforms. This means that it must come before a Dean of Guild Court, which takes time. What takes even more time is something my wife has now embarked on, and that is a legal debate and possibly court action because of the attempts of the munitions people to withdraw from the legal bargain with her. This means she's left in the position of being legally forced to purchase the site but has no second buyer to take on the major site acquisition. She now has the added misfortune of having no rental income coming in from her tenement properties because of her tenant's rental strikes. As we are all well aware, bankers are willing to give you an umbrella on a sunny day and take it away when it's raining, and so now, my wife's bankers are confiscating her shares. This puts all of us and the business in a very uncertain and dangerous position. Now, Christina, do you wish to make any more detailed comments before I throw the meeting open for general discussion?'

'Yes,' she said. 'The bank has not yet confiscated my shares. They are threatening to do so but I'm having a meeting with Mr Abercromby tomorrow and I'm hoping to persuade him to give me a little more time. There are one or two things that could happen, given some time to get me out of my difficulties. For instance I can take certain action to bring the rental strike to an end, thereby renewing my rental income. I could accept an offer of another potential buyer for the riverside site. Talks with this alternative buyer are already underway. If I settle this negotiation I will realize a substantial capital profit which can then be lodged with the banker to take the pressure off my building company shares that are held in security. Or I could lodge a nominee account with another bank on deposit. The interest on that account will meet the interest on my capital loans from my first bank. That would take the pressure off the security of my building company shares.'

She sounded perfectly cool and confident, as if, indeed, there was no problem, certainly not one that was worrying her. She gave the impression that she had everything under control. This in fact was far from the truth. She was worried sick. There was a deep gnawing panic fighting to rush to the surface and shame her. If she could stop the rent strike it would be one quick way out of the problem, but how could she stop it? If she could get another buyer for the site, that would also be an immediate solution, but where could she get another buyer? Mathieson was certainly doing his best to find one at the moment.

What had nearly melted her cool was the unexpected support and loyalty that Adam had shown her. The other members of the board didn't matter. In comparison with Adam she didn't care what they thought or what they said. All she cared about was him. And she determined for his sake as much as for her own that she would solve her present difficulties and save her shares.

Meantime she had to suffer, with as much good grace as she could muster, the abuse, sneers and accusations of all the members of the board except Adam who continued to do his best not only to keep order in the meeting but to defend her. He even persuaded them not to pursue any form of legal action against her, and also to give her time to get out of the pit and settle her difficulties.

Later, back at Monkton House, she stiffly thanked him. He lit a cigar.

'You were bluffing, of course.'

'I've no wish to continue the meeting here,' she told him. 'I only wanted to thank you for your loyalty and support.'

'I could hardly do otherwise,' he said. 'Whether I like it or not you are my wife.'

She turned away to hide her hurt. It was then she was taken aback by Beatrice bursting into the sitting room in a state of extreme agitation.

'Adam. Something terrible is happening and it's all her fault. Oh, Adam. She'll be the death of us yet. She could be the death of us right now.'

'Calm down, Mother,' Adam said. 'What on earth are you talking about?'

'I was out in the front garden just now. I was on my way

round to the manse when I saw them. Oh Adam, it's just terrible. They're going to kill us all. I'm sure!'

'Who is?'

'A whole crowd of awful-looking women. A huge mob of them. They're all coming along Queen's Drive. They've got placards and banners and things all about a rent strike and the one at the head of it, I recognized her right away. Another wicked woman. Another woman who wishes nothing but bad to our family.'

Adam had gone over to the window. He was staring outside. Christina could now hear the shouts of abuse and she also went over to the window.

'Get back,' Adam said. 'Don't look out.'

But it was too late. Christina had already seen the desperate-looking mob of shawled women and the woman at the front carrying a pole attached to which was a cage holding a live rat, a huge, ugly, black creature, its tail angrily swishing, amber eyes staring balefully. She could see the mad eyes and the red inside of its mouth as it darted about and snapped at the bars of the cage. Attached to the bottom of the cage and the pole was a piece of cardboard stating 'This is what we have to live with'.

Beatrice was sobbing and crying now.

'Send for the police, Adam. Oh quickly, please.'

'Mother, that's the girl who used to work for us, Annalie Gordon. You told me that she and her family had gone to Australia. Emigrated, you said.'

'Oh never mind that just now,' Beatrice cried out. 'Send for the police, for pity's sake. They're going to break into the house any minute.'

'There's no need for the police,' Adam told her. 'I'll attend to this.'

'What are you going to do?' his mother sobbed.

'I'm going outside to speak to Annalie.'

He left the room and after a minute or two Christina forced herself to turn back round to gaze out of the window.

Another woman was holding the pole. Annalie Gordon had come forward on her own and she and Adam were talking very intently and seriously together.

Christina couldn't hear what was being said, but the sight of Annalie Gordon and Adam standing together made her feel faint with apprehension.

Beatrice said, 'I can't bear another minute of this. I'm going upstairs to my room to lie down.'

Christina went over to a chair beside the fireplace and sat down. She looked a neat, elegant figure in her tailored beige coat-frock buttoned to a fairly high waist with a full, flared skirt showing a daring amount of ankle. She sat very still and quiet. Eventually Monkton came back into the room.

'Where's Mother?' he asked.

'She's gone upstairs to lie down, I think. What's happened?'

'Oh, your rent strike's over,' he said. 'At least for the present.'

'How did you manage that?' she asked.

'By assuring them that something would be done about the worst of the repairs that were needed, for a start. I also promised to speak to you and make sure that something was done about all the evictions they're complaining about. I've arranged for Annalie to come and see me again.'

Christina raised an eyebrow. 'Oh, have you indeed?'

Chapter Thirty-seven

All the women had had a meeting in Florence Street where they discussed Monkton's proposals. Now it was quite late in the evening and they were returning home in small groups like leaves blown in the wind.

Florence Street, on the edge of the Gorbals, knifed across Cumberland Street and stretched further on to cut across Rutherglen Road as well. The whole of the area was in the shadow of the famous Iron Works, known locally as Dixon's Blazes, and they had chosen Florence Street for the meeting because it was never dark there. It was not so much in the shadow of Dixon's Blazes as continuously in its ruddy glow. The flame-coloured light licked the buildings and painted the street and everyone in it with a flickering orange warmth.

Even though it was quite late there were still plenty of children playing outside. Most closes had about seventeen families living in them, with most of the women having an average of seven to ten children. Even toddlers were safe enough, however, as mothers stood at the close mouth with the youngest child wrapped in a shawl and kept a close eye on the other youngsters. Noticing one group of children sitting at the close mouth telling stories to each other, Annalie was reminded how she too used to be part of such a group. They would tell each other ghost stories and afterwards she would be terrified to go up the feebly lit stairs. She would shout loudly 'OPEN' so that Aunty Murn would hear her and have the door open. Some nights they would sing the latest songs, some nights she went to the Band of Hope and was given hot sweet tea and buns. After the singing of hymns there was a lantern show. Its flickering jerky pictures were usually about an alcoholic battering his wife and children, but it always ended up with the man repenting and then the whole family living happily ever after.

She never went with the boys when she was a wee girl because one of their favourite games was going round the middens with their great dogs and a big stick to see how many rats they could catch.

Lizzie Booth was walking alongside Annalie and in the distance they could see a crowd of boys playing cowboys and indians. The indians all appeared to be wearing dazzling white headbands.

It wasn't until they got nearer that Lizzie yelled out, 'My God! Would you look at what my Jimmy's got on his head?'

She pounced on him, stripped off the offending sanitary towel and punched Jimmy all the way to her close.

One by one the other women dropped off at their closes, calling out to each other, 'Cheerio Jessie' or 'Goodnight, Bella. See you tomorrow, hen' or 'See you when I come in for my paper, Annalie'. Annalie liked working in McClusky's despite Sid McClusky's moans and groans and complaints. Far from disliking the man, she in fact felt sorry for him, with his stomach complaint, though he seemed to eat quite well, or at least quite often. He even ate during the night, according to Mrs McClusky. She reported too that he smoked ten cigarettes during the night, and during the day and was seldom without a cigarette hanging from the corner of his mouth. The smoke drifted up and made him keep his eyes screwed half shut all the time. As Mr McClusky was thin and concave so his wife was plump and round. He had a sallow complexion. She, in comparison, had ruddy cheeks. He was fast going bald. Mrs McClusky's hair was grey but she had it in abundance. It was even sprouting on her upper lip and chin. Her teeth were ill fitting and hurt her badly at times, especially when eating. As a result she had a habit of taking them out at mealtimes. Sometimes she couldn't think to put them back in and she'd sit quite happily behind the counter if they weren't busy, chewing her gums and knitting a few leisurely rows of a jersey or a pair of gloves for Mr McClusky, who felt the cold more than most. Sometimes she'd just sit contently, sausage-plump hands clasped on the hammock of her lap.

She would happily knead her gums together and listen to Annalie telling the latest news on the housing front.

As well as the usual cigarettes – Gold Flake, Capstan Navy Cut, Du Maurier, and the green packets of Wills Woodbine – there was also the pleasant aroma of Manikin cigars and the pungent Rubicon Smoking Mixture, Three Nuns tobacco and St Bruno's Flake. One old man always bought Gallagher's snuff. They also sold sweets – Boy Blue liquorice nougat, toffee balls, aniseed balls, dew drops, acid drops and sherbet dabs.

There were household goods too, like powdered bathbrick and Monkey Brand soap and Avon powder. There was the Coal Tar Sheep Dip Disinfectant Tablet, Robin Starch and Carriage Candles, McAllums Thistle Soap, Kitchen Magic Panshine (for everything but clothes), and Reckitt's Bag Blue and many more popular items like Crichton's Magic Corn Cure (the only cure for corns, sure and speedy. Thousands of testimonials, sevenpence ha'penny and one and three per box). This was all over and above the newspapers, magazines and comics that were sold.

If they weren't busy Annalie enjoyed a look at the papers. That way she kept herself up to date with what was going on both locally and in the outside world. She also became an avid reader of *Good Housekeeping* and *Woman*. She was not interested in the more melodramatic goings on of the working-class girls in magazines like *Red Star Weekly*. For one thing she had enough melodrama and traumatic struggles in real life to find any entertainment in reading about them. The more genteel, middle-class and fashionably dressed women of the other magazines however she found totally absorbing. She felt she might learn something by reading about them.

Despite all that had happened she still clung to the remnants of her ambition to better herself and to become a lady, although her feelings in this area were somewhat confused. She despised most of the ladies with whom she'd come in contact. Granted they'd been few in number and she hadn't known any of them that well. Apart from old Mrs Monkton, Beatrice Monkton and the minister's daughter she'd only had brief glimpses of others in the form of Beatrice Monkton's guests. She'd served afternoon tea to them and heard little snippets of their conversations.

Her hatred mainly stemmed from the way she had been treated – either like dirt or as if she didn't exist at all. The other servants didn't seem to mind, but it bothered her. She often thought with great satisfaction of her last encounter with Beatrice Monkton. The old lady hadn't been able to ignore her that day – nor had she been able to today. Annalie had seen her emerge from the front gate of Monkton House then flutter about like a panic-stricken butterfly.

Beatrice Monkton hadn't changed, nor indeed had her son. When Monkton strode aggressively from the house and down the path to meet her she still felt the impact of his strong sexuality. It seemed to take the form of a kind of restlessness inside him. Even the way he stood suggested this, never quite still, never quite at peace, legs apart, he kept making little, jerky, restless movements that to the perceptive or responsive eye were very sexual in origin.

Annalie was responsive all right. Every inch of her body immediately ached for him, longed for him, silently screamed out for him. So strong was the attraction between them that she could almost see the electric sizzle in the air as their eyes met. It had always been there, this powerful, sexual pull between them. That had always been one of the reasons why she could not understand his abandoning of her and his subsequent marriage to the frigid-looking minister's daughter.

She soon discovered Beatrice's hand in the affair and, right there and then, she would have gladly murdered the woman. She and Adam had spoken briefly about why she and the other women had made the protest march to Monkton House. He had made enough concessions to satisfy the women, then he'd said to her, 'Come and see me at my office', and given her the address and the time to come.

She was to go the next evening and she knew that everyone else would have finished work and gone home by then. She literally shook with passionate emotion every time she thought of their next meeting. She had to grip her shawl tightly around herself in an effort to prevent her trembling appearing too obvious to anyone else. She no longer cared what he had done to her or had not done. It didn't matter what position in society he had and whether or not he was beyond her reach as far as marriage was concerned. All she had felt at the sight of him and all she felt now were the strong waves of physical passion that he awakened in her. Her mind was saturated with memories of their lovemaking. The thought of being with him again made her breathing quicken.

As soon as she got home she filled the zinc bath with hot water. There wasn't much room to sit in it and even with knees bent up she was in a very cramped position. She did her best though, to give herself a good wash all over, then she laid out her good skirt and clean white blouse and her one and only coat. Although she wore it only for very special occasions, it had still become faded and threadbare. But her straw hat looked quite pretty with the new blue ribbon she'd sewn onto it.

Everything was laid out ready over the chair so that when she finished work the next day she would come in, have another quick wash-down and don all her clean clothes. Before going to bed, however, she washed her hair and dried it in front of the fire. Then she shook it out and flung her head back and stretched her body like a sinewy cat. It felt good to be alive. It felt good to be a woman.

Chapter Thirty-eight

The next day in the shop seemed never-ending. Customers kept asking her what was wrong. Often she didn't hear what they said and they had to repeat themselves. She gave wrong change. She called people by wrong names. She flushed scarlet at the slightest provocation, then tossed her head and laughed and didn't bother to deny the teasing when it started.

'So this is what just seeing a man does to you? My word, hen, you're going to be floating up into the air before our very eyes if it goes any further.'

'Let us know when you're seeing him again and we'll all come too. You're our lead, hen. Where you go, we follow, remember.'

'Not this time, you don't,' she'd countered laughingly.

By the end of the working day the excitement in her had reached such a peak she could have fainted with it. Or danced with it. Or sung with it. Or wept with it.

The tramcar that took her from Gorbals to Pollokshaws Road trundled along with agonizing slowness. She could have shaken the driver, as if he were purposefully keeping her in agonizing suspense. She longed to leap from the tram and run, race, fly along the road at a hundred times the speed of the noisy old tortoise of a vehicle.

At last they reached the stop in Pollokshaws Road outside Monkton's office.

'I'll leave the back door open,' he'd said, 'and be waiting in my office room at the top of the stairs.'

She raced up the stairs and he came running to meet her. He swept her up into his arms and into his room, noisily kicking the door shut behind him.

After Annalie and Adam had made love slowly, passionately and long, Annalie burst into uncontrollable and noisy sobbing. The past few days had been too much for her.

First the shock to her nervous system of finding out that Christina Monkton owned the Gorbals property. Then the adrenaline boost of excitement from whipping the women into such a frenzy of indignation that they marched behind her to Queen's Park, and the trauma of meeting Adam face to face again. After that the feverish anticipation of being with him, and finally the excitement of their lovemaking.

'Darling, what's wrong?' he asked her. 'Did I hurt you? Tell me.'

'No, no,' she managed, and then it all poured out. Her father's anger. Being flung from the house. The shame, the humiliation, then the horrors of the dunny. Her fears and worries about Elizabeth, her prayerful relief at getting the single end, her grief at the loss of her brothers, her joy at seeing her mother again. Then the disillusionment and finally the tragic and painful loss of her daughter.

'She's your daughter as well,' Annalie sobbed. 'Please help me find her, Adam. Oh, please. I can't bear to think what might be happening to her now. And even though they were being good to her in their own way, I don't want her brought up like that. I don't want her living in a camp and travelling around with no proper education and no settled home.'

'Have you reported her kidnap to the police?' Adam asked.

'To Big Donald and Hamish, our local bobbies. They said they'd see there was a thorough search, but I wonder if they've bothered to do anything. I keep going into the police station to ask. It's practically next door to me, but they just fob me off. They tell me they're doing what they can, but what is that, I'd like to know?'

'Well, calm down. Stop worrying,' he soothed her, stroking her hair and kissing her face and eyes and mouth. 'Everything possible will be done now. You have my word on it. Another thing,' he continued. 'What were your wages when you were working for my mother?'

Surprised, Annalie told him.

'That doesn't sound much.' He sounded doubtful.

'It was quite good compared with some jobs,' Annalie

assured him. 'And of course, I had my room and board. Why do you ask?'

'I want to pay you that sum from now on and we'll see if we can't get you a better house – at least a room and kitchen. Have a look around yourself and see if there isn't anything you like that's empty just now.'

She gazed up at him adoringly. She could hardly credit her good fortune. Along with her wages at McClusky's she would now have no worries about paying the rent. She would even be able to afford some luxuries. A flutter of excitement quickened her pulse and sparkled her eyes. She might even be able to buy herself a new coat. She flung her arms gratefully round his neck and showered him with kisses, making him laugh in mock protest and then gather her up in his arms again and kiss her deeply.

For long after she left his office she felt him warm and strong against her, inside her, all around her. His kisses still tingled every part of her from the top of her head to the soles of her feet. She was saturated with passion, drunk with it, she was floating with it, reeling with it.

Back home she danced with it, hugged herself with it, laughed with it, cried with it. Eventually she calmed down enough to make herself a cup of tea, but she wasn't calm enough yet to sit down. She looked around the single end that was her home. She had done all she could with it. As well as the stool she had two spar-backed chairs now and a table, all of them picked up second hand at the Barrows. There was also another blanket on the bed and some extra cups and saucers, but she still hadn't managed to get any pillowslips or sheets.

The wallpaper had long since faded and in parts was hanging off the wall. There were the bare boards with no linoleum or rugs to cover them, and despite the room being as clean as she could possibly make it, it still had a dreary neglected look. She hadn't realized it at first, but before she had left Adam he had made it plain to her that he intended paying her rent. She shivered with excitement at what this could mean. A room and kitchen? A room and kitchen with a toilet inside? A room and kitchen even with a bathroom inside? The idea of actually having a bathroom in the house was almost too much for her. She began to cry again. She hardly knew why she was crying any more and she was too exhausted to care. She fell asleep the moment her head hit the pillow.

When she woke the next morning she wondered at first if it had all been a dream. Hastily she backtracked on her thoughts, snatching them from her memory and feverishly examining them for validity, praying that everything had been true, fearful that it had all been a figment of her imagination. But no, wonder of wonders, it had really happened. She had been with Adam. He had made love to her. He was going to help her find Elizabeth. She was going to get a new house. Even a bathroom was a real possibility. She scrambled from the bed and dressed quickly, hardly taking any time to wash her face or brush her hair. She would run to the factor's office this very minute and see what they had on their books.

She was flying from the house when suddenly a thought struck her and she turned back in again. What if the factor refused to give a decent house because of her dishevelled and disreputable appearance? She forced herself to calm down enough to have a proper wash, tidy her dress and pin up her hair. She discarded the shawl that she had been wearing and put on her coat and hat instead. As she stuck her hatpin in her hat she noticed her hands were trembling violently and the cracked mirror above the bunker reflected an unusually pale face and dark eyes stretched wide. Nevertheless, by the time she had reached the factor's office she had managed to regain some of her natural courage and boldness. She didn't care if the toffee-nosed girl in the factor's office looked at her with disdain. Who did she think she was? A jumped-up little clerk who would be flung out of her precious job as soon as the war was over and the men came back.

The girl gave her the addresses and keys to three houses that were vacant, in Florence Street, Mathieson Street and Cumberland Street. Annalie knew immediately that the Cumberland Street one was her dream house. She knew by the number that it was at what was considered the posh end of Cumberland Street. One or two of them even had tiled closes. Tiled closes!

She ran practically all the way from the factor's office to the number in Cumberland Street. Hallelujah! The walls were tiled half-way up with the most beautiful tiles she'd ever seen. They were dark maroon and glossy, and then at shoulder height came a row of fawn, with a pattern on them. The painted part of the wall above the tiles was a bit flaky in patches. So was the ceiling, but what did that matter? It was a tiled close.

She ran up the stairs two at a time. Her house was on the top landing. Already she had claimed it as hers. What a lovely door it had, solid and dark and shiny. Her hand shook so much it took her quite a time to get the key in the door. Then she unlocked it and was inside. She found herself standing in a square hall with several doors leading from it. One door led into the front room. It was a good-sized room with shuttered doors to the recessed bed and, joy of joys, a neat little tiled fireplace. There was a wide bay window. You could stand and look up one end of Cumberland Street or down the other end or straight ahead at the houses and shops opposite. It was joy, heaven, bliss, perfection.

The wallpaper was a faded fawn colour, but it looked quite respectable and at least it was all sticking to the wall. The floor looked good and solid, no loose boards anywhere – and she whirled around in a mad gypsy dance to prove it. Out in the hall again she danced across into the back kitchen. Again it was a fair size, quite a few feet bigger, she guessed, than her single end. The black range, the cupboard at the side, the black iron sink at the window with the swan-neck tap and the cupboard underneath, the coal bunker and the hinged shelf above it all were much the same as every kitchen she'd ever seen. To her eyes at that moment, how-ever, no kitchen had ever looked so beautiful.

Back out in the hall again she stood for a moment or two, hands clasped under her chin, heart pounding. The other door, she knew, must lead to the bathroom. Slowly, she pushed it open. She entered reverently as if going into a church.

'Sweet Jesus,' she said out loud, for there before her very eyes was not only a white lavatory with a shiny brown varnished seat, but a wash-hand basin and, holy of holies, a bath!

Chapter Thirty-nine

When Christina went round to the manse to visit her mother she found both Ada Gillespie and Beatrice Monkton in tears. Every nerve in Christina's body tightened with apprehension. She immediately thought that something had happened to Simon.

'What's wrong?' she asked. Beatrice was reclining helplessly back on the chaise longue dabbing at her eyes with a lace-edged handkerchief.

'Our dear Lord Kitchener has been drowned,' she sobbed, clasping her hands and casting a reproachful look upwards as if asking God how he could have allowed such a cruel thing to happen.

Christina relaxed. She didn't feel anything at all for Lord Kitchener.

'Oh dear,' she said. 'How awful. Will I ring for Gladys to bring some tea, Mother?'

Ada leaned forward in her chair to peer solicitously at Beatrice.

'A little tea, dear? It might soothe and refresh you.'

Beatrice fluttered her handkerchief in assent. Christina pressed the bell to summon the maid.

'If such a tragedy can happen to dear Lord Kitchener, what might happen to our poor Simon?' Ada said worriedly. It was the first time that Christina had heard her mother voice any serious concern for Simon. Suddenly the war and the dangers it could mean to Simon had become a reality.

'He wasn't himself, you know, when he was on leave.' Ada said as much to herself as the other two women. 'He was trying to be cheerful, I know, and act as if nothing was amiss, but he wasn't the same. He was a changed man.'

'I thought so too, Ada dear,' Beatrice said. 'But I didn't want to worry you by commenting on it.'

Beatrice gracefully eased into a sitting position when the

maid entered the room with a tray on which sat rose-patterned china and a matching teapot.

Christina too had been worried about Simon since his last leave. There had been a haunted look about his eyes and he had admitted to feeling a sense of alienation from people at home. He also drank more than usual. Not just the couple of binges he'd had with Adam. On several occasions when she'd gone round to the manse to see him she'd found him drinking alone, sadly, moodily. His cheerful, joking manner no longer seemed natural to him. When he behaved in a cheerful way it was almost always an embarrassment, it was so brittle and insincere.

The day he had gone back had been like that. He had joked with them all, been so cheerful that it had been painful. At Central Station, while others shuffled towards their train with a crucified look, Simon smiled and chattered and then sauntered away with assumed unconcern. The only apparently serious comment he made at the leave-taking was when he heard a young group further along the platform lustily singing the popular song 'Goodbye Dolly I Must Leave You'. His mouth had taken on a bitter twist, he'd jerked his head towards them and said, 'They've obviously never been to the front before.'

Every week in church she prayed that he would be all right and every night when she remembered to say her prayers she included pleas for his wellbeing. She didn't like to dwell on the war and what might be happening at the front; she automatically shied away from the emotional distress, and avoided reading articles about the fighting, or going to films that had anything to do with conflict. She didn't even like listening to popular war songs although it was very difficult not to hear when, as D.H. Lawrence said,

And the war news always coming, the war horror
Drifting in, drifting in, prices rising, excitement growing,
People going mad about the Zeppelin raids and
Always the one song,
'Keep the Home Fires Burning,
Though Your Hearts be yearning . . .'

She had enough conflict in her own life and needed all her emotional energy to deal with that. She suspected that Adam was not only seeing Annalie Gordon, but making love to her again. Day after day, night after night she longed to plead with him to tell her it was not so. Yet she knew in her heart it was. The pain was a sharp knife twisting continuously in her heart. She could not even glance in a mirror without being reminded of Annalie Gordon's vivid beauty compared with her own pale, closed face. She would have given anything to have even a hint of the fiery passion reflected in the gypsy girl's looks. She did not blame Adam for being so attracted to her. Yet surely he must know there was no future in such a relationship. His future was with his wife and child. Their lives were bound together in a much more practical and lasting way. She could make him a good wife and she could make him happy if he would only give her the chance.

Despite knowing that she could not compete with the gypsy girl in dramatic beauty she spent a considerable sum of money on fashionable clothes and glamorous underwear. A great deal of time was spent too at the beauty salon and hairdresser in her attempts to look as attractive as possible. She tried to tell herself that it was for her own pleasure. Or to look smart for business purposes, but knew it was only one desperate and futile attempt after another to attract her husband.

She wondered if anyone else knew of his affair with Annalie Gordon. She prayed that they did not. She did not know how she could cope with the pity and the gossip that such a knowledge would bring. She felt vulnerable. She felt insulted. She felt hurt. She wept oceans of bitter tears but they were always shed in her protective armour.

Fortunately she was at least resolving the business muddle she had been in. The Co-operative movement, in terms of their stores and offices and retail outlets, were very aggressive in land purchases and acquisition and she and Mathieson had managed to do a deal with them. They wanted to establish themselves on the river front with a large warehouse and depot. She was able, therefore, to realize a substantial capital profit after all, part of which she lodged with the bank to take the pressure off her building-company shares. Part of it she lodged under a nominee account with another bank on deposit. That way she accrued interest that could meet interest on her capital loan from her first bank. Since the rent strike had ceased, however, the interest payments had stopped being a problem. Of course, she was going to have to pay bills for the repairs that Adam had promised would be done to her property. He wasn't going to allow the building side of the business to do anything for nothing. She would have a fight on her hands to keep this cost down to the minimum. She was already insisting however that only absolute emergency repairs need be done.

It had been a very wet winter and there had been some pretty bad storms which had caused slates to fall from roofs and rain to penetrate into houses. She had given orders that those jobs were to be given priority. They were to be patch-up jobs, though, rather than complete re-roofing. Patch-up jobs still cost a considerable amount. However, at least people would not have to suffer dampness in their houses now.

She was on her way to a meeting with Mathieson at his office in Hope Street.

'Aren't you staying for tea, dear?' her mother asked.

'No thank you, Mother. I haven't time today. I just called in to see how you were. Where is Father?'

'He's out doing his sick rounds, dear. There are so many poor people nowadays in need of comfort and Christian reassurance. Remember in your prayers, Chrissie, to ask God if he'll allow this war to finish soon and to let us have Simon back safe and well.'

'Oh yes, I do, Mother.' Christina replied. 'It's time I was away. Will you be all right?'

'Yes, thank you, dear. The point is, are you all right?'

'What do you mean, Mother? I feel fine.'

'You may feel fine, Chrissie. It's your appearance I'm worried about. And appearances are important, you know. A woman in your position should give a good example.'

'I still don't know what you mean, Mother.'

'Well dear, you may think you're wearing a smart suit, but that skirt I'm sure must be nearly six inches from the ground. It's not only showing your ankles, but more than that.'

Christina laughed. 'Oh, Mother. That's the fashionable length these days. I wouldn't be surprised if the skirts go much shorter. After all, with women doing so many jobs now, it's not convenient to have skirts too long.'

'That skirt is not too long Chrissie, it's too short.'

Christina sighed. 'I'd better go, Mother. I'll pop in tomorrow. All right?'

'Very well dear,' Ada said somewhat stiffly. 'I just hope your father's not too shocked if you wear something like that. He's concerned enough as it is – we both are at the number of clothes you seem to have. No good will come of such vanity and attachment to material possessions. I thought that was a lesson we'd taught you long ago. Obviously we weren't successful.'

Christina wished there was a full-length mirror in the hall so that she could have given herself a reassuring glance on the way out. Her parents' criticism or disapproval, no matter how gently or kindly delivered, could still erode her self-confidence. She struggled against this by remembering how smart she had looked in the wardrobe mirror in Monkton House. She had checked from the upturned brim of her straw hat down over the high-necked buttoned linen suit with its long jacket and full skirt to her fine leather shoes with their pointed toes and high louis heels. She had found herself safely immaculate, elegantly fashionable but in quiet good taste.

Mathieson was waiting for her when she arrived at his office. She had come to discuss, among other things, the Co-operative deal. There were still some loose ends to be tied up. As she sipped her coffee, however, he remained silent. She glanced curiously across at him. The sun was glistening in his blond hair. It occurred to her that he was not only handsome, but strikingly unusual in a Glasgow setting where most men were dark haired like Adam. She

247

wondered idly if Mathieson had any Nordic ancestors. He was staring at her with equal interest.

Eventually she said, 'Well?'

He lit up a cigarette, took several leisurely puffs and then said, 'Do you know about Monkton and that floosie from the Gorbals?'

She felt the colour drain from her face and didn't dare lift the cup to her lips again in case it revealed the trembling of her hands.

She said calmly, 'You obviously do.'

'Some time ago,' he continued, 'I went over to see you in your office. You weren't there so I went along the corridor to ask Monkton if he knew where I could contact you.' He took another puff of his cigarette and gazed at her with one of his wide-eyed, blank looks. 'I'm a quiet mover. They obviously hadn't heard me approach. When I opened the office door they were locked in an embrace. I just shut the door again and came away. I wasn't sure whether I ought to tell you or not. On the one hand I thought it was none of my business. On the other hand, it could affect me.'

'In what way?' she asked.

He shrugged. 'For one thing, what concerns you concerns me too. This knowledge might come in handy from a business point of view.'

'Blackmail, you mean?' she said.

'Oh . . . Harsh word,' he mocked.

'It wouldn't work,' she said. 'I know him.'

A hint of a smile turned up one side of Mathieson's mouth. 'You're a cool customer,' he said. 'I admire you.'

'I admire you too,' she said. 'Now can we get down to work? By the way,' she added, 'I've taken up smoking and I've come away without mine.'

Mathieson flicked open his cigarette case and held it over to her. She selected one, then bent over his proffered cigarette lighter.

'That should cause more of a scandal in the manse than your husband's little peccadillo,' he said.

'About the Co-operative deal,' she said coolly, but inside tears were surging up, desperate for release. Her head was

248

pounding: How could he touch that girl within a few feet of her own office? She was his wife. How could he wound her and shame her like this?

But more than anything she felt fear. Fear of losing him. Her thoughts changed to cries of How can I keep him? How can I keep him? . . .

Chapter Forty

'I'll take my *Peg's Paper*, hen', Flo said. 'And five Woodbine for Erchie.'

'Erchie?' Annalie echoed in surprise. 'Aye, did you not know? He got wounded in the leg. He's back home. He'll be back to work soon, he says, but he's limping like I don't know what. You'd think he'd developed a wooden leg. I thought he'd be fair dumped, but between you and me, hen, he's as happy as a wee lark.'

'Because he's got wounded?' Annalie asked in surprise.

'Aye, well he's hoping to get out of the army. You know, invalided out? You must come round one night and hear some of his stories.'

'Right,' Annalie said. 'You're on. Is there anything else now?'

'No. That'll do me just now, hen. He's got wee Peter started his apprenticeship in the plumbing. We're hoping the war'll be finished before he's due to be called up. Peter's such a sensitive wee laddie. He's awful frightened of rats and Erchie says the trenches are teeming with them, and the sight of those trenches would kill our wee Peter. It'll be bad enough for him in the plumbing.'

'Right enough,' Annalie agreed. 'Anyway, be seeing you, Flo.'

'Right, hen. Cheerio just now.'

There were no other customers for the moment and so Annalie followed Flo out and stood, arms folded, leaning up against the frame of the shop door. It was a warm summer's evening and Mrs McClusky had taken her favourite basket chair outside and was sitting knitting and watching the world go by while her husband fussed about in the back of the shop. Mr McClusky could always find something to be done.

'Would you look at these weans,' Mrs McClusky greeted Annalie. 'It's great to be young, eh?'

Annalie laughed as she watched the children following a two-wheeled vehicle with a huge barrel on it and a sort of spray attachment at the back. As the horse walked on, the water showered along the street and barefoot children were dancing behind what was locally known as the water scoot, their trousers pulled up to let the water spray onto their knees.

'Look at Big Hamish,' Mrs McClusky laughed. 'He looks as if he'd love to be in there along with the weans. That uniform must be hot on him, right enough.'

'I saw him giving Francis Rafferty a kick up the backside last night,' Annalie said.

Mrs McClusky began a new row, pushing the crush of stitches along her needle to spread them out a bit. 'He's a right wee devil, Francis Rafferty. What had he been up to?'

Annalie shrugged. 'Dear knows.'

'He's needing to give Mary Rafferty a kick up the backside as well, if you ask me.'

'I haven't seen her for a wee while. I was wondering how she was.'

'Have you not heard?' Mrs McClusky asked.

'Heard what?'

'Oh aye, it was last night she was in. That was your early day, wasn't it?'

'Who was in?'

'Mrs Hurley. She was telling me that wee Mary's staying with her now. She says Malcolm, you know what a saint she thinks that sleekit big leek is? – anyway, she said that Malcolm was that sorry for wee Mary. She comes from such a terrible dump, he says, and she's such a well-doing wee girl. He's persuaded her to take Mary in and give her a home in return for Mary helping in the shop. She's still at school, you know, and not fourteen yet. But she'll help when she comes home and then when she leaves school altogether she'll be working there full time. Mrs Hurley says he treats her like his own daughter and he feels that if she's there he can keep a better eye on her.'

'Huh! Keep a better hand on her,' Annalie said. 'And a lot worse besides'.

'I know. Everybody knows. Except Mrs Hurley, of course. But I blame Mary. She's all there, that girl.'

'That creep's old enough to be her father,' Annalie said indignantly.

'I know, I know. I'm not excusing him,' Mrs McClusky said. 'But she's old enough to know better and it's not as if she likes him. Nobody could like Malcolm Hurley but his mother. Mrs Rafferty shouldn't have called that one Mary, she should have called her Eve, like the original temptress.'

'I could kill that feeble excuse for a man,' Annablie said. 'You'll notice he doesn't come in for his paper when I'm around. He and his mother are both frightened of me, you know.'

'That girl,' Mrs McClusky said. 'She'll end up at the Trongate if you ask me.'

'How? What goes on at the Trongate?' Annalie asked. She knew of course that the Trongate was the area at the east end of Argyle Street and she'd learned at school that it was the oldest area in Glasgow. That and the High Street leading off it was where Glasgow had begun. The city had been a model of strictness and devotion at that time. The inhabitants had been remarkable for their public and private worship of God, and a stranger going past their doors of an evening would hear so much singing of psalms they'd imagine themselves in a church. Changed days now. And not only in Glasgow or Scotland. She'd read several times in the newspapers of a government minister denouncing drunkenness in England and saying things like 'Drink is doing us more damage in the war than all the German submarines put together', 'the men who drink at home are murdering the men in the trenches' and 'we are fighting Germany, Austria and drink'.

She'd also read about the liquor regulations. Public houses were now closed in the mornings and afternoons. Treating – that was buying drinks for other people, especially soldiers – was now forbidden and beer had been reduced in strength and made more expensive. Spirits had been luxuries which were hard to obtain, especially in munitions areas. King George himself had taken the King's Pledge to abstain from alcohol. The newspapers had begun publishing recipes for non-alcoholic drinks. Changed days indeed.

She'd been a few times along Argyle Street to look at the shops. It had been during the day, and as well as being busy with people it had been chock-a-block with tramcars and horse-drawn traffic. She had enjoyed the visits but had been quite glad too to get back to the more familiar home territory of the Gorbals. Most people kept to their own territory for most of the time.

'Friday nights,' Mrs McClusky said, 'that place is a cess-pit of sin.'

'How do you know?' Annalie asked.

'Sid told me. He says on a Friday night the place is strewn with bodies, even women lying prostrate in the street. Everybody drunk as newts.'

'I can't imagine Mary ever drinking,' Annalie scoffed. 'I don't know what makes you think that about her.'

'The women start with selling their bodies. They go with the men to pubs and they drink themselves silly so that they don't know what they're doing.'

'I hope Mary never comes to that,' Annalie said.

'Listen, hen,' Mrs McClusky said, 'if she can go with Malcolm Hurley then she can go with anybody.'

Annalie sighed. 'I wish I could do something. I did try, right enough.'

'She's not your responsibility. She's Mrs Rafferty's, although a lot of good she's been to the wean. What an example! She's an absolute disgrace, that woman.'

'Och, but she's a kind-hearted soul,' Annalie said. 'I can't help liking her. It's being forced to live like an animal down in the bowls of the earth like that has made her what she is. It shouldn't be allowed. People like Christina Monkton should get put in jail for making money off poor folk like that.'

'Och. She lives in a different world, hen. She'll no even know what kind of places she's getting the rent off.'

'You're right,' Annalie said. 'I used to work in Monkton House before she went to live there. She lived at the other side of the church in the manse. I know her world all right.'

'Fancy,' Mrs McClusky said. 'What was the house like?'

'You couldn't have described it better,' Annalie said. 'It's another world all right, believe me. If Mrs Rafferty had been brought up in that house she wouldn't have ended up in the state she's in today.'

'Maybe you're right, then. I don't know. I've never been in any place like that. Can't say I want to either. I'm quite happy with my two room and kitchen. Sid's got it really nice. He finished papering the kitchen just the other day, and of course he'd whitewashed the ceilings before that and everything looks that nice and fresh. Sid and I are as proud as punch of that house. Not that he'll admit it. You know what he's like. It's his stomach of course.'

'Bobby's whitewashing mine just now and he's going to help me with the papering tomorrow.'

'Is that Flo Blair's eldest boy?'

'Yes.'

'He must be eighteen now. Has he not been called up?'

'No, it's not his birthday yet, but he'll be getting his papers any day now, he thinks.'

A sudden influx of customers brought the conversation to an end and both Annalie and Mrs McClusky went back into the shop and behind the counter. The evening papers had come in and Mr McClusky had them all sorted out along the counter in preparation for the regular demand. Every day, morning and evening, the usual crowd of women would buy the papers, open them immediately and anxiously scan the lists of dead and wounded.

'Nothing today, hen?' Mrs McClusky would inquire of each of them. 'Oh, that's good. What a relief, eh?'

The busy time tailed off again and eventually Mrs McClusky said to Annalie, 'You can go now, hen. There's nothing much else now till we shut.'

'There's plenty for me to do, though,' said Mr McClusky, who was fussing miserably about with a mouth like a piece of chewed string drooping down at both ends. 'This shop would go to wrack and ruin if it wasn't for me.'

'Away you go, hen,' Mrs McClusky repeated. 'It's just his stomach.'

Annalie went away along Cumberland Road to her own close, happiness in every movement – in her bouncy step, her swinging hips and the tilt of her head was full of hope for the future. She had a good job, a nice wee house, and a wonderful lover who was going to get her baby back.

His aggressive self-confidence had inspired her with total trust. He would get Elizabeth back all right. She knew it.

He was coming to see her next week. Perhaps he would have good news then. He had wanted to come sooner but she had persuaded him against it. She had wanted to get the house looking nice first. She wondered what everyone would think of his car. The only motor car that anyone had seen in the Gorbals belonged to the doctor and everyone knew the doctor's bull-nosed Morris. Adam's car was so beautiful she was afraid that the children might scramble over it and accidentally damage it in some way or even just dirty it.

Bobby had finished whitewashing the ceilings when she arrived back and was peeling paper off the front-room wall. The kitchen walls had been originally whitewashed the same as the ceiling, but Annalie had decided that, as well as the main room and the hall, the kitchen must be papered too. Bobby had never heard the likes of it and thought she was being very posh.

'That'll do you for today,' Annalie said. 'You've really done well, Bobby. Thanks a lot. Come on through to the kitchen and get a cup of tea. I'm going to make one for myself anyway.'

Suddenly Annalie felt a pang of sadness and for a moment wondered why. Then it occurred to her that Bobby's freckled face reminded her of her brothers.

'No word from the army yet, Bobby?' she asked once they were seated with their cups of steaming hot tea.

'No,' Bobby said. 'And I don't want to get any. But that would be too much to hope for.'

'I don't blame you for not looking forward to it,' Annalie said. 'Changed days from the beginning of the war, eh? Do you remember how everybody was so excited and couldn't get away quick enough? They were queuing up in their thousands to volunteer.'

'I wouldn't have felt so bad,' Bobby said, 'If it hadn't been for my dad's stories. Make your hair stand on end, so they would.'

'The rats, you mean?' Annalie said.

'Poor wee Peter's the worst with them. I don't like them either,' Bobby said. 'But it's not just that. It's all the horrible ways you can die out there. Da was telling us that there was one young bloke arrived and he was that excited to see what was going on he looked up out of the trench and a sniper put a bullet right through his brain. He wasn't five minutes in the trench. Not even two minutes, Da said.'

'Well, if you've to go out there, Bobby, you just keep your head down, do you hear?'

'Don't worry.'

After Bobby had left she washed and dried the cups and put them away, gave the table a wipe over, then stood back to admire the kitchen for the millionth time. Tomorrow after she came home she would put up the cream bedcurtains and valance and the cream blind on the kitchen window. The next day or the day after, when the room had been papered and scrubbed out, she would put up pretty floral curtains at that window. She'd already bought a rug at the Barrows and scrubbed it spotlessly clean. The scrubbing had brought up the pretty colours of it and the lavender, pale blue and pink would nicely match the tiles in the fireplace. She'd also managed to find quite a good armchair so that Adam would have something comfortable to sit on and there was a little table to put beside it with an ashtray, just like he had in his own house. There were also a couple of upright dining chairs which she supposed had originally been part of a set. They were in good condition, with dark polished wood. The seats and backs were padded and covered with a golden, slightly khaki colour in plush velvety material.

She had crisp white sheets and pillowcases for the front-room bed. These she vowed would be kept only for when Adam came and the bed used only for their lovemaking. Meantime she slept in the kitchen bed and without sheets until she could afford another pair.

She was tired after her day's work. Nevertheless she busied herself sweeping the kitchen floor and then scrubbing it thoroughly. She had no linoleum or rugs yet for the kitchen. Most of her money had gone on the main room because that's where she would take Adam. But if he insisted on seeing the kitchen, at least it would be clean.

At last she collapsed into bed, utterly exhausted but totally happy, blissfully unaware or uncaring of any complication or hindrance to their relationship. She could only dream of being in his arms again.

Chapter Forty-one

'You stupid bampot,' Annalie screamed up through the skylight of the top landing. 'You've put your brush down the wrong chimney and covered my house in soot. Do you hear me up there? You're in the wrong chimney.'

'No,' a man's voice bawled back down. 'You must be in the wrong house, Missus.'

'Don't you be funny with me,' Annalie shouted back. 'My kitchen's in a right mess and I'm just after cleaning it. Call yourself a sweep? You obviously can't tell one chimney pot from another.

'If you don't be quiet I'll charge you for yours,' the voice shouted back.

'It's not funny, I'm telling you.' Suddenly Annalie burst into tears. 'I was expecting a visitor and I wanted everything to look nice and now it's all spoiled.' Her sob climbed to a howl. 'Even I'm covered in soot. What'll he think when he sees me?'

Suddenly a man's head appeared at the rim of the sky-light.

'Never mind, hen. Me and my mate'll come down and help you clear it up.'

Suddenly another door in the landing opened and Mrs Baxter appeared. She was a small dumpling of a woman whose hair was so tightly screwed back in a bun that her face looked as if it were going to burst. She'd had rickets when she was a child and this had caused her legs to bend outwards so that she was like a heap of dumplings increasing in size one on top of the other and tied in the middle with the strings of her big apron. Mercifully her apron and skirts were so long they hid her misshapen legs.

'Is he still up there?' she asked Annalie, then aiming her voice at the now empty skylight she bawled up, 'My man's going to get in for his tea soon and everything's still covered with sheets.

'Any minute now, hen,' a voice replied from the high distance.

'I wish I had everything covered with sheets,' Annalie sobbed.

'Oh here,' Mrs Baxter gasped in sympathy, noticing Annalie's tears for the first time. 'Don't tell me.'

'Yes,' Annalie said. 'He's gone down my chimney instead of yours.'

'That man should be drawn and quartered and hanged from the chimney, so he should.'

Just then they were joined by Mrs Reid, a wiry wee woman with silver hair. She was hurrying breathlessly up the stairs carrying two heavy shopping bags. Mrs Reid was always breathless and always in a hurry. She was Annalie's other neighbour on the top flat.

'I saw when I was coming along the road,' she said. 'I saw and I knew he was on the wrong chimney. I just knew it. Oh, you poor soul. That's terrible. Never mind, hen. I'll come in and help you if you just give me a minute to put these bags in the house.'

'I'll be in too,' Mrs Baxter said. 'Just as soon as he's done mine and I get these sheets lifted.

'Oh thanks. It's awful good of you both.' Annalie dried her eyes when her apron.

'Don't be daft,' Mrs Reid said. 'You'd do the same for us.'

Before long Annalie's kitchen was a hive of activity with Mrs Reid scrubbing and sloshing a wash cloth around the floor and the chimney sweep and his mate getting rid of the worst of the soot which had fallen into the black range and the fireplace. Mrs Baxter and Annalie were dusting and wiping the surfaces, the mantelshelf, and draining board, the top of the bunker, the chairs, the table. All the time the chimney sweep and his mate were whistling cheerfully and the three women's tongues were as busy as their hands. Mrs Reid and Mrs Baxter, indeed all the neighbours, thought Annalie a great wee girl. It was because of her efforts in organizing their militant protest that not only had the evictions stopped, but quite a number of much needed repairs had been done. Admittedly there were still other problems that were in urgent need of attention – blocked lavatories and drains, broken stair gaslights, dangerously worn stairs, broken stair banisters, broken windows and a thousand and one other items which conspired together to make life difficult still waited to be dealt with. Annalie's success had not completely banished everyone's natural cynicism about what the factor could or would do, but at least now something was being done. And so far there hadn't been any more evictions. As a result there was a spark of hope in the air.

At last the kitchen was sparkling clean again, and Mrs Reid gathered up her enamel bucket and big floor cloth and bustled away, hardly taking time to give Annalie a backward wave.

Mrs Baxter moved more slowly. She picked up her own bucket and cloths and said to Annalie, 'You'll be all right now, hen. All you need to do is give yourself a wee wipe down. I'll away and see to my man's tea.' She waddled off with the side-to-side rocking motion, dictated by her rickety legs.

The chimney sweep and his mate went cheerfully on their way after calling to Annalie the usual 'Don't do anything I wouldn't do, hen.' And she gave the usual reply, 'That gives me plenty of scope.'

As soon as the door was closed behind everybody she rushed to the bathroom, turned on the bath taps and stripped off her clothes while the bath was running. After giving her hair a thorough brush and her face and body a good wash in the bath she felt totally recovered. Dressed in clean clothes, she went through to the front room and peered out of the window. Impatient to have a better look she lifted the lower sash and sat leaning forward over her folded arms so that she could get a better look down and along each side of the street.

There was no sign of Adam's car. She felt under the circumstances that it was a blessing he was late, but she prayed he could come now – she was eager for him, ripe for him, hot and impatient for him. She tried to remind herself of his warning that he could never be sure that he would be on time for any meeting or even that he could come at all when he promised. This was owing to the nature of his work. He could be away at a job and not able to get back to Glasgow at all until the following day or even longer. An emergency might arise at the last minute that required his attention. Something might go wrong at home or with his grandmother, who was a very old lady and constantly seeking his attention.

He told Annalie, 'I'll come if and when I can, but never wait around for me, never be disappointed if I don't turn up.

'I won't be able to help being disappointed,' she said.

'Well don't be surprised,' he said. 'Or imagine it's because I don't want to come.'

From somewhere over the rooftops in some other street she could near the thudding and fading, thudding and fading of soldiers feet. The sound had become so familiar, so part of the background to everyday life she was hardly aware of it. It was the same with Dixon's Blazes. The thundering scream from steam valves, the donging of giant hammers, and spewing and belching of steam and smoke, the hideous smells, were all part of the vivid, colourful tapestry of Gorbals life. The whole area was alive with sound from the tramcars and horse traffic in Main Street leading to the Gorbals Cross, from the railway at Gorbals Junction, from the thousands of children playing in the parallel streets. All along Cumberland Street the buzz of sound from the shops and cries of street traders added to the cacophony.

Earlier on there had been a fight between the Cumbies, the gang from Cumberland Street, and the Billy Boys from Bridgeton. Each gang had consisted of about forty youngsters aged from fourteen to sixteen. For a few minutes there had been a noisy and glorious free-for-all before one side admitted defeat by retreating from the fray. As soon as the combat had ended Mrs O'Reilly, who lived in the bottom flat on the corner of Florence Street and Cumberland Street, opened wide the lower sash of her window, which attracted a long queue of youngsters nursing cuts and abrasions. In turn they perched on the sill with their heads over Mrs O'Reilly's sink while she washed their wounds.

Gang fights had to be short and sharp in case they fell foul of Big Donald or the other minion of the law, equally big Hamish McCulloch. Big Donald and Big Hamish did not take kindly to their Friday or Saturday evenings being disturbed by rowdy youngsters. Any gang member captured by either of these large Highlanders would be likely to have his ears boxed all the way to the police station.

Annalie was not the only woman having a hing out her window. The grey tenements in every street in the Gorbals were dotted with women enjoying this pastime. She was well aware that all the women relaxing, arms folded on cushions on their open windows on Cumberland Street, would enjoy the sight of Adam's car drawing up and would watch with great interest when the occupant of the car alighted and disappeared up her close. Annalie felt no resentment at this, however. She was as curious as anyone else about comings and goings in the street. It was part of what made life so interesting, and the shared interest gave everyone something in common. It was like being a member of one huge family whose members always had something new and lively to talk about. But there was no sign yet of any car coming along Cumberland Street.

It was getting late. Women in aprons and slippers were standing talking in little huddles. Some were calling to their children from closes or windows, telling them it was time to come in for bed. Howls of protest rose up from groups of playing youngsters. Threats of 'if you don't come here at once I'll murder you, I'm warning you,' were automatically delivered and automatically if somewhat grumblingly obeyed. Sometimes a half-hearted punch or slap was given to hurry along a particularly reluctant child.

Annalie was beginning to feel worried and anxious. It was Friday night, the end of her early shift. She was seldom off early on a Saturday night. The shop was too busy then with people buying cigarettes and sweets on the way to the picture houses. She didn't know how she could bear the pain of disappointment if he didn't come.

The pubs were beginning to empty now and the usual drunks were reeling down Cumberland Street, some singing in mournful chorus. Downstairs Mamie Patterson would be nursing her wrath to keep it warm. She was a wee, nebby nag of a woman whose tongue constantly lashed her husband, Jimmy. One of her lines of attack was the fact that Jimmy was an absolutely no-use, good for nothing wee slob who wasted their money on gambling and drink and cigarettes. Not like nice Mr Reid up the stairs. Mr Reid was a real man. He smoked a pipe instead of dirty wee Woodbines. He didn't drink, he didn't gamble, he was a good husband, he had a good job, he saved his money, he was good to his wife.

Jimmy Patterson was a mild and long-suffering man who never talked back to his wife when he was sober. Indeed he never criticized Mamie Patterson at any time. It was agreed by all of the neighbours that one way and another poor Jimmy didn't have much of a life. Only when he got drunk, which he did every Friday night, did he reveal that he nursed hidden resentments. The anger and resentment strangely enough were never aimed at his wife, but invariably at Mr Reid on the top flat. Despite the fact that Jimmy Patterson was only about five feet two and Mr Reid was about six feet three, Jimmy would stagger up the stairs every Friday night and batter on Mr Reid's door. There could be no ignoring such a racket and eventually John Reid would open the door to be met with Jimmy's usual verbal abuse.

'Think you're perfect, eh? Think you're a saint, eh? Think you're the answer to every woman's prayers, eh?'

Mr Reid, who thought no such thing, just stood sighing and slowly shaking his head.

Eventually Jimmy would shout out, 'Come on then, show us what you're made of. Put up your jukes,' and he would bounce about on the balls of his feet with his fists stuck up as near as he could get to Mr Reid's chin. 'Come on then. Put up you jukes. Show us how clever you really are.'

Mr Reid always tried to reason with him.

'Now come on, Jimmy. You know there's no point in this. We're good friends you and I.'

'You're no friend of mine, you big soft Jessie. I'm going to batter you into the ground. I'm that sick of you I'm going to batter you into the ground till you disappear.'

He would set upon Mr Reid with flaying fists and feet. John Reid would then lift him bodily as if he were no more than a baby and carry him downstairs and into his single end. There, to the background of Mamie's high-pitched, never-ceasing nagging voice he would lay the still struggling man onto the hole-in-the-wall bed and remove Jimmy's trousers so that they could be hidden to prevent him leaving the house again that night. It was a routine, regular as clockwork, and this Friday evening was no exception.

Annalie listened to Mr Reid's feet come plodding back up the stairs and going into his own house across the landing. She went back to the window and gazed out again. In the street below a man and woman were arguing and every now and again the man would slap or punch the woman until they disappeared into one of the closes.

Adam wasn't coming. The sudden realization brought gusty tears. She thumped down on one of the wooden chairs and collapsed arms outstretched over the table to weep noisily and long. Her mind called his name, then it burst into the silent box of a kitchen. She repeated the word broken-heartedly over and over again. 'Adam, Adam.' It was then she realized that she could not go on living like this indefinitely, never knowing if he was coming or not, never knowing when she would have to suffer the pain that she felt now.

She loved him, she wanted him. She wanted him every day, every night, all of the time. She had never been a person for half measures. Every emotion, every part of her body, every instinct told her that she and Adam belonged to each other, were meant to spend their lives together. She hugged herself in the desperation of her need and wept angrily as well as broken-heartedly.

Chapter Forty-two

'What do you think?' Christina posed before Adam in her new furs with an element of defiance as if she actually didn't care what he thought.

Earlier that day she had bought the elegant fur stole and matching muff. Both were composed of Russian stonemartin skins lined throughout with soft satin. She steeled herself for his belittling look or cutting phrase. Much as she tried to hide the fact, he could still upset her. She had no problem whatsoever in dealing with other people, the servants, Beatrice or any of her business associates. With everyone else she had learned to have a proper value of herself and keep others in their place, which was usually at arm's length.

'Furs?' he said. 'Cigarettes, face paint. What next?'

She stared him out. 'Yes, not bad for the minister's daughter.'

It had become fashionable to use make-up, but like smoking cigarettes it was still considered not only daring but shocking in the circles in which her mother and Beatrice moved. The fact that she was only wearing a little very discreetly applied make-up would make no difference to their opinion.

'You look very attractive,' Adam said.

The compliment was so unexpected that for a moment she was completely taken aback. Just for a second or two she was the minister's daughter again, timid, apprehensive, anxious. She quickly struggled to overcome this vulnerability, and succeeded. It was on the tip of her tongue in fact to reply with some sort of biting, sarcastic retort. She thought better of it just in time, however, and instead managed quite a reasonable-sounding 'Thank you'.

From the upstairs drawing room came the scratchy sounds of Beatrice's gramophone playing 'Peg o my Heart'.

'Your mother loves that gramophone,' she said to Adam

with a half smile. 'She tends to be a bit morbid in her taste at times. At least that one's better than 'Memories' that she keeps playing.'

'You should talk,' he said, 'with your piano playing.'

His eyes glimmered with what looked like mischief when he added, 'Why don't you learn some new tunes like "Pretty Baby" or "What Do You Want to Make those Eyes at me For"?'

She flushed, angry at herself for never knowing how to take him, for being so constantly vulnerable and uncertain in his company.

But she managed a short laugh. 'All right. I will.'

His smile reflected in his eyes, but was there mockery in it? She couldn't be sure. Then he lifted his newspaper and it was a grey barrier between them, although she couldn't blame him for his absorption in news at the moment. A new battle was being reported in which everyone was intensely interested. They were calling it the Battle of the Somme and it was described as the largest British land battle since the days of Waterloo. Almost every family in the land knew someone on the Somme, and the Gillespies were no exception because the last they'd heard of Simon, that was where he was.

At first the newspapers had presented the battle as a victory. The big push, they said of the first day of the battle. A great beginning. The army, they said, was fighting with a valour never surpassed and they had excelled everyone's best hopes. Some men were slightly wounded, they said, but losses were by no means excessive. A Punch poem said:

> . . . from mine and desk and mart,
> Springing to face a task undreamed before,
> Our men, inspired to play their 'prentice part,
> Like soldiers lessoned in the school of war,
> True to their breed and name,
> Went flawless through the fierce baptismal flame.

There was a sudden renewal of excitement about the war and when wounded soldiers returned from the battle with the mud of the trenches still clinging to them, they were given a hero's welcome. Crowds gathered along railway lines to wave at the frequent ambulance trains. Others tossed roses into taxis that brought the slightly wounded away. People lined routes to hospitals pressing flowers and sweets on the wounded, or the heroes of the great battle as they were called. Headlines boasted, 'Great offensive continues. Nine thousand five hundred prisoners. British capture Fricourt and make progress east of Village and La Boisselle. A very satisfactory first day. Allied losses slight.'

People knew that because of the war there was press censorship, but they didn't realize the distorted picture they were getting of the Battle of the Somme until letters filtered through from wounded men who mentioned how many had been killed. Nurses passed on news of deaths in hospitals. Army chaplains wrote to relatives of men whom they had buried, and commanding officers sometimes sent a note to the families of victims, but most of all, lists appeared in local papers and in shop windows giving the names of local men killed in action.

Eventually the army would send a telegram confirming what many of the families knew already but hoped had not been true. But it was the horrific growth of lists of the dead that brought the truth home to the civilian population more than anything. Column after column after column – page after page after page of names filled every paper to over-flowing. Then came the realities of those printed pages. The Sixteenth Highland Light Infantry, the Glasgow Boys' Brigade lost half of its strength in the first ten minutes. That first day the British in fact suffered losses of 57,470 men. *The flower of the nation*. In Glasgow whole streets of men were wiped out. Fathers, sons, brothers, husbands all gone. Death had become an epidemic. A shroud was settling over the land.

Christina was becoming more and more worried about Simon. He hadn't written to his mother since he'd last seen her. In a recent letter to Adam, all pretence at cheerfulness had gone. He spoke of coming to the front after the first day and seeing the dead hanging grotesquely on barbed wire like wreckage washed up to a high-water mark. There had been the terrible task of clearing away the decaying, rat-gnawed bodies which fell to pieces when touched. Adam had been angry when he caught her reading Simon's letter. He snatched it from her and, taken aback, she said, 'I'm sorry. I didn't think you'd mind with it's being Simon's letter. I wouldn't of course touch any other letter addressed to you.'

'It's not that,' Adam said. 'I didn't want you distressed by this. Simon's obviously suffering terrible trauma. There's no point in you suffering it as well.'

She had been touched at his concern.

'I'm terribly worried about Simon,' she admitted. 'If only this awful war would finish and he could come back to us for good.'

Adam sighed and shook his head. 'It looks to me as if it's only just started.' Then after a moment he said, 'I feel bloody awful not being out there along with Simon.'

Again she was taken aback. For the first time she had an insight into the man behind the tough and often bitter exterior. She had an almost overwhelming impulse to put her arms around him and comfort him, but at the same time her sense of self-preservation prevented her from doing so. In no way was he ever going to take advantage of her again. Nothing would make her allow him to do so.

'It's not your fault,' she said. 'You tried to join up.'

'I've tried more than once,' he said. 'But it was no use. I suppose doing work for the War Office hasn't helped.

'That's a silly thing to say when you think of it,' Christina pointed out. 'Other building firms have gone bust all around us, but you've survived. It's because you've done the work for the War Office and for the war effort, don't forget. You've built camps and hospitals for the troops, extensions to munitions factories, etcetera, etcetera. The list's endless Adam. You've been working yourself into the ground helping the war effort. You've even taken on jobs that you haven't been paid for yet and don't know whether you will ever be, so no one can accuse you of being a war profiteer. That accusation can perhaps be levelled at me, but never at you.'

She suddenly realized the truth of what she'd just said. He was overworking. He had been travelling about more than ever. Down south, down into southern England as well as up north. He'd had so many extra business worries too – the shortage of tradesmen caused by the call-up. Also those that he was left with were not always willing to travel to the different jobs, especially down to the south of England. She had been so busy with her own concerns and so intent on shutting him out that she had barely noticed his recent pallor, the dark shadows under his eyes and the lines of fatigue in his face.

'You need a holiday,' she said. 'A complete break. We could go away somewhere. We could afford something really luxurious for a treat, and it would do us both good. I'll take time off if you will.'

He gave an incredulous laugh. 'A holiday! Oh, isn't that so typical of you? How you can possibly think of luxury and enjoying yourself in some holiday retreat at a time like this I just do not know.'

She shrugged and turned away from him.

'Please yourself,' she said coldly.

He made no reply but she could feel his eyes boring into her back as she walked from the room.

Chapter Forty-three

Despite remaining outwardly the same Christina had become awakened to a new line of thought. More and more she began to see things from Adam's point of view, particularly where the business was concerned.

Looking back, she began to realize for the first time how fiercely Adam and his father had competed, and how deeply Adam still felt his father's hostile rejection. Scenes, words, came back to her from the past. Moses taunting his son by calling him green and telling him over and over again, 'I've forgotten more about this business than you'll ever know.'

Adam had never had any support from his mother, who was so weak that even Moses recognized there would be no use in leaving her any shares. She'd never taken any interest in the business except to enjoy the fruits of it. His grandmother had been different, too different perhaps, because even now at her advanced age she could interfere and her interference could cause problems.

Then there was the jealously of the other members of the board. With the knowledge of the business that she now had, Christina realized that when Adam had taken it over it had many weaknesses. It was the old man who had been blinkered, not Adam. Adam had been verbally loyal to his father and his father's concept of the business, but all the time he was pushing ahead with new methods and new kinds of contracts. All the time it was obvious that the other people on the board 'knew' that he was not as good as his father. She'd heard them say it a dozen times and more behind Adam's back. He couldn't win in their eyes. Each success he had they countered with 'What did you expect? After all, look what he started with.' Or they'd try to minimize him with 'Of course you know it was really the old man who built this business.'

Then there was the indirect influence of the wives of

the married members of the board. Magnus Doyle's wife, Brendan Doyle's wife, Duncan McCaully's wife, Logie Baxter's wife and Hector McAllister's wife. Their interest in the business was purely a financial one. Unlike Beatrice who just unthinkingly accepted and expected to enjoy the fruits of the business, they continuously indulged in backbiting, nagging and criticism in the wings.

Christina had an almost overpowering urge to help Adam, but did not know how, unless of course to ensure that her side of the business continued to be successful. When the riverside deal had floundered she had been surprised at all the members of the board suddenly attacking Adam instead of her. Now she could see why. They had been ready all along with knives poised, only waiting for an excuse. They could get at Adam through her. That was her only importance as far as they were concerned.

She sympathized acutely with Adam as far as the business situation was concerned. There was still a protective wall around her however, in their personal relations. The few times that she'd allowed herself to peep round the side of the wall and venture a step towards him her foot had always gone wrong and she'd been forced to retreat again quickly. He believed she was cold and unresponsive, and said she was even lacking in normal maternal instincts. Maybe he was right.

She seldom went to the nursery now, but Mitchell brought Jason down in the evening before his bedtime for half an hour or so to be with her. Then she played with the child, a very serious little boy with her grey eyes. He had golden blond hair, however, and neither she nor Adam, as far as she knew, had ever had hair of that colour. However, probably his hair would darken as he grew older.

Usually she took him on her knee and told him a story from one of the books she kept in the morning room at the back of the house. She sat there quite often in the evening because, especially in the beginning, being in the same room as Adam proved too much of a strain. She liked to go to the upstairs drawing room to play the piano, but only if Beatrice wasn't there, and unfortunately that was the place where Beatrice usually sat in the evening and often entertained her own friends.

She knew that Adam visited the nursery on occasions, perhaps more than she knew. Once at least she had come across him there. She made a point of discussing with Mitchell in the morning room the diet that Jason was to have and the general way she wanted him brought up. She didn't want him to be overbabied, for instance, and objected to the coxcomb curl that Mitchell was still training his hair to grow into. She had sent Mitchell upstairs for the brush, and with the child on her knee she had brushed his hair straight over this head, which immediately made him look more boyish.

'That's how I wish his hair to be in future,' she'd said icily to Mitchell.

She had instructed Mitchell too that Jason was to have plenty of fruit and vegetables. No cakes or chocolate biscuits or sweets, except home-made cake for Sunday tea. No fizzy drinks, only pure fruit juice or home-made lemonade. Not long ago she had discovered that in fact Mitchell had been disobeying her, and cakes, biscuits and sweets had all been ordered by her to be sent up from the kitchen every day. Coldly furious, Christina had gone upstairs to the nursery but had been taken aback at first by the sight of Adam kneeling on the floor playing with Jason.

Recovering from her surprise Christina had said, 'Mitchell, I wish to speak to you in the downstairs drawing room in ten minutes.' Then she left without a word either to Adam or Jason.

When Mitchell did come down to stand before her, sourfaced and silent, Christina informed her that orders had been given to the kitchen staff that these foods were not in future to be sent upstairs.

Christina would have dismissed the woman, but she knew how difficult it was these days to get staff. Very few, if any, young women were coming into domestic service, preferring instead the hundred and one other kinds of jobs that were now open to them. It was mostly older women like Mitchell, the cook and the maid in Monkton House and the staff in

273

the manse who had preferred to stay on in the jobs for which they had been trained and had always been used to.

Christina comforted herself with the thought that at least Mitchell was fond of Jason and was, to the best of her ability, conscientious about his welfare. And Jason was fond of Mitchell. Often, after her evening half hour with Jason when Christina had kissed him and said, 'Good night darling. Sleep well. Mummy will see you tomorrow,' she felt a pang when he trotted happily away holding Mitchell's hand. At the same time she had to keep facing the fact that she was not domesticated, and enjoyed the freedom to pursue her business that staff like Mitchell allowed. She could treasure her time of being alone too.

Sometimes she would sit and take notes about some particular negotiation she had in mind, sometimes she would just sit quite contentedly planning some deal or other.

Recently when the weather was good, although July tended to be a wet month in Glasgow, she would walk in the back garden which was long and lush with rhododendron bushes and tall trees. Occasionally she would go out the back garden gate and across to Queen's Park. The park sometimes was busy during the summer months, however, and she shied away from the crowds, not even wishing to meet anyone she knew. She enjoyed the park only when it was empty and she could stroll in silence and in peace.

There were no new deals on at the moment and she had decided to inspect some of her tenemental property. Strictly speaking this was not necessary as Mathieson and the factor saw to this side of the business. Nevertheless, seeing what she had acquired, whether it was land or property, always gave her a deep sense of satisfaction. She only wished she had time to view it more often.

She was an entrepreneurial character and liked to take the long-term view of things, even if it meant taking risks. At the same time she was conscientious and methodical. She liked to have all the facts at her fingertips, no matter who else she had working for her and how diligent and knowledgeable they might be. Sometimes she felt she didn't trust anyone. She tried to tell herself that, as far as Mathieson was concerned, for instance, it was to his advantage that the business should succeed and he should do his utmost to make it do so. Even with him, however, there was an element of caution in her thinking and all her dealings with him.

All her tenemental property was in the Gorbals area, and she took a taxicab there. In the cab she made a resolution that sometime soon she must buy a car of her own and take lessons in driving. It would really be much more convenient than only having the use of the car when Adam didn't need it or even getting a lift with Adam to the office in the morning. She never knew when he would be coming away in the evenings and as often as not she had to phone for a taxi in order to get home. Granted, a car cost a lot of money, but she reckoned it would be a business investment. It was something she really needed now to get around to various business appointments.

She had given the taxicab driver various addresses that she wanted him to slow down or stop at so that she could have a discreet look at them. She became aware that he was indeed slowing down and she leaned forward to look out of the window. She was unprepared for the immediate shock she received. There across the road was Adam's car and Adam himself standing on the pavement just outside one of the closes. Beside him, bold as brass, was Annalie Gordon.

Completely without shame the woman was laughing up at him. There was nothing discreet about her. The street was teeming with people. Groups of men lounged at street corners. Masses of children ran and skipped and played. Women bustled along or hung about at close mouths, arms folded, gossiping. Some stood and stared at the world going by. Some leaned on cushions at open windows and looked down at all the goings-on in the street.

And there they were, in full view of everyone. The well-known, prosperous, middle-class businessman and the slut of a servant girl who had his bastard child. It was disgraceful, absolutely scandalous, Christina felt her cheeks burn and her heart race around her body, completely out of control. She leaned back on the seat and struggled to take long calming breaths.

The cab driver noticed eventually and twisted round.

'Are you all right, ma'am?' he asked.

It was a moment or two before she was able to reply.

'Take me home at once,' she managed eventually.

She could hardly credit it. She kept telling herself that she wouldn't have believed it had she not seen it with her own eyes. Yet of course she might have known nothing had changed. She had thought for a time that he was warming towards her. They had been speaking more often and more naturally. He had on occasions been so nice she had actually dared to think that there might be an element of closeness growing between them.

Bitterly she raged at herself for being such a fool.

Chapter Forty-four

Annalie seldom ventured into the bustling city centre. She determined, however, that her new coat was not going to be bought in a Cumberland Street shop but in one of the more expensive and stylish establishments in town. This was the coat that she would wear when Adam took her out, perhaps to a cinema or a theatre or even for a meal in a posh restaurant. He had not issued such an invitation as yet, but she felt confident that one day soon he would. She was proud to be seen with him and hoped that he would feel the same about her.

She was perfectly well aware that they came from different classes of society, but she was a great believer in the saying that love conquers all. Their love, she felt sure, would overcome all obstacles.

A Wednesday was chosen for her shopping expedition because that was, she knew, a country holiday and the place would be milling with unfashionable country folk, farmers and the like, as well as ordinary Glaswegians. On a Wednesday she would not look so conspicuous in her shabby and unfashionable coat. She was secretly afraid that she would stick out like a sore thumb in Sauchiehall Street and give herself a showing up. Such a situation could be carried off with an impudent swagger and head held high, but being in a mixed crowd would be easier and more enjoyable.

Often chauffeur-driven limousines would draw up in Sauchiehall Street at some of the major stores like Watt Brothers or Henderson's or Copland and Lye and out would step wealthy, furred and bejewelled ladies.

Nevertheless, it was Sauchiehall Street Annalie was determined to visit. Argyle Street had the thronging crowds. You could get bargains in Argyle Street but you wouldn't get style. The well-to-do looking for quality fashions went to Sauchiehall Street.

The street, indeed all the streets in town, were chock-a-block with tramcars, the air alive with the buzz and flicker of electrical discharges as the trams changed tracks. There was horse-driven traffic too plodding through the bustle, sometimes causing havoc as cart wheels were trapped in the tram rail. She was excited to see the odd motor car, and always hoped that it might be Adam's. As she had expected there was quite a mixture of people. Ladies passing in swishing silk, others in more country-looking ginghams. There were shop girls out on errands wearing their long black skirts and long-sleeved high-necked white blouses. There were smart suits with jackets cut like morning coats, hobble skirts, tailor-made costumes, striped suiting and expensive-looking chenille jumper suits. There were velvet hats trimmed with feathers, straw hats trimmed with ribbon and straw hats trimmed with bouquets of flowers.

She ventured into Watt Brothers first and was impressed with the elderly floor walkers in their striped trousers, grey waistcoats and buttonhole flowers. A magnificent Czechoslovakian marble staircase led down to the sunshine arcade which was beautifully lit up. As she walked through she saw all the garments on display plus lovely terrazzo tiles and brass fittings. Taking a good look round everywhere, examining garments and prices, she tried to retain her nonchalant appearance. Nevertheless she was shocked by the cost of the coats in particular. She came out of Watt Brothers saddened by the realization that she definitely could not afford to buy her coat there – although she had seen one or two that she would dearly have loved to have owned. She had imagined herself to be so well off with the few pounds she had in her purse, but they weren't nearly enough to buy the kind of coat she had dreamed about.

Her young face began to darken with anger as she went in and out of all the shops in Sauchiehall Street and still was not able to purchase anything. As she began to work her way down towards Argyle Street she tossed her hair and told herself that she was as beautiful as any woman wearing the kind of coat she'd seen. Her flashing eyes caught glimpses of herself in shop windows as she swaggered defiantly past in her lace-up boots, long skirt, threadbare coat and cheeky straw boater with ribbon flying.

Argyle Street was even busier than Sauchiehall Street. In Sauchiehall Street there was gentility. Argyle Street was more robust. Here even the horse dung smelled stronger, and there was quite a high proportion of shawlies. Some more respectable old ladies were wearing tie-on bonnets with peaks down their foreheads and a pelisse round their shoulders, all in black except perhaps for a wee touch of purple on the bonnet.

Most of the men here wore flat skipped bunnets. Annalie saw only one very stylish man in Argyle Street, in chamois gloves and winged collar, a silver top to his walking cane. He was an elderly man and it could not be said that he was fashionable. There were vast numbers of men in khaki or blue, of course.

Despite her anger at not yet getting a coat to suit her purse, she was really quite enjoying herself. She liked to move about and look around and have plenty to interest her. There was certainly plenty of interest in Argyle Street, including street traders and buskers. One of the buskers there Annalie recognized as a woman who came round the Gorbals on occasions. She was known as Hairy Sairi because winter and summer she wore a coat of what looked like rabbit pelts, and boots with something metal on the soles so that when she tap danced they made quite a racket. As she danced she sang all the old songs.

Annalie soon found herself singing too as she went along. She began to see coats that she could afford, and quite nice ones too. She swithered over smart artificial-silk sports coats. There was one in pink that would have looked very pretty against her dark hair. She realized however, that it wasn't very wise to buy a silk coat for the Scottish climate unless one had plenty of other coats to wear, according to the frequent changes in weather.

Eventually, tired but happy, she emerged from one of the Argyle Street shops with a wide-skirted coat in deep purple with a black velvet shawl collar. It had a high-waisted belt with two large buttons, and had cost literally every penny she had, which meant she would have to walk all the way home. She didn't care, however. She was young and healthy and she looked beautiful in the coat.

Next week, or the next again, or the next after that perhaps, but sometime soon she would buy herself a new skirt and blouse or a pretty new dress. A hat too. She must have the prettiest, cheekiest, darlingest of hats.

She was at the corner with the High Street, a long steep hill rearing up off the Glasgow Cross end of Argyle Street. There giant, shaggy-hoofed Clydesdale horses pulled carts and lorries up to the top, sending sparks flying up from the cobbles. Extra horses with boys in attendance always waited at the foot of the hill to help one-horse carts to pull their load up the steep incline. At the top the extra horses would be unharnessed and the boys would ride them bareback down the hill again. At the end of their working day all the boys raced the horses down the hill and a wonderful sight it was, these noble giants all galloping together with such thunderous noise and sparks flying in all directions.

Annalie started towards home at a brisk pace, but by the time she reached the familiar streets of the Gorbals she was dragging her heels in absolute exhaustion. She was still happy and still clutching her precious parcel under her arm. When her close in Cumberland Street came into view her heart leaped with love and joy. The car sitting there could surely only be Adam's. It was not his usual one, but then he would have bought a new one, for all she knew. It certainly wasn't the doctor's.

Hot and footweary as she was she began to run, one hand holding onto her hat, the other keeping a firm grip of her parcel.

'Adam,' she called.

But it was Christina Monkton, not her husband, who opened the car door and stepped out. Annalie's elation crumpled but she hurriedly composed herself as she approached the car.

'I wish to speak to you in private,' Mrs Monkton said.

Annalie's bearing acquired an impudent swagger.

'My house is on the top flat. Come up there if you like.'

With that she sauntered away into the close and up the stairs leaving Christina to follow as best she could. Annalie was glad that her front room was dusted and smelled sweetly of lavender polish.

'Sit down,' she said. 'The chair won't bite you.'

Christina's eye bored into her with such contempt they almost nailed her to the wall. Annalie felt furious and yet at the same time triumphant. Christina Monkton might now look elegant and sophisticated but Annalie felt sure that underneath she was still the pale-faced, frigid spinster who had lived such a sheltered existence at the manse.

'The kettle's always on the boil,' Annalie said. 'I'm going through to make a cup of tea. I won't be a minute.'

Through in the kitchen she whistled under her breath as she made the tea and set the pot, two cups and milk and sugar on a tray. Although slightly embarrassed and nervous, she didn't feel worried about Christina Monkton's visit, so secure did she feel in Adam's love. Anyway, such was her nature that she always enjoyed a bit of drama and excitement.

Christina accepted the cup of tea in frosty silence. Annalie suspected that she would not have accepted either the seat or the tea had it not been for her unaccustomed climb up the steep stone stairs. They both sipped the hot comforting brew for a minute. It was Annalie who broke the silence.

'You wanted a word in private, you said. Well we're in private now.'

Christina took another few sips of tea before replacing the cup very carefully on the table beside her chair.

'You are encouraging my husband to come here.'

'He doesn't need much encouragement,' Annalie said.

'Have you no shame?'

'None whatsoever,' Annalie said cheerfully.

'I take it there's no point in appealing to your sense of decency. You obviously haven't any of that either.'

'I don't need to sit here and be insulted in my own home by you or anybody else.'

'I didn't come here to insult you. I came here to tell you

281

to leave my husband alone and I'm willing to pay you a substantial amount of money to ensure that you do just that.'

'Do you think you can buy me off?' Annalie said incredulously. 'You obviously think more of money than I do, Mrs Monkton. I love Adam and he loves me.'

'You might love him,' Christina said, 'but he doesn't reciprocate that feeling. Believe me.'

'How would you know?'

Christina gave a short laugh. 'Oh, I know all right. He lusts after you, that's all.'

'No, that's not all,' Annalie said with conviction, yet at the very back of her mind a tiny niggle of worry took root.

'How can it be anything else?' Christina asked. 'He's married to me.'

'He doesn't love you.'

'He hasn't left me.'

'He would if I wanted him to,' Annalie said defiantly.

Christina gave another humourless laugh, 'You must know that's utter nonsense. My husband is a respected businessman. We share a lovely home together. He adores our son. He is part of a whole loving family network. His mother lives with us and his grandmother visits us regularly. There is no place for you in his life unless as a tawdry, backstreet coupling to satisfy his occasional lust.'

Upset now, Annalie jumped to her feet and shouted, 'That's not true. Get out of my house. You don't know what you're talking about. You don't know what it's like between Adam and me.'

Christina rose and flicked at her skirts as if attempting to remove any speck of dirt she might have picked up through contact with the chair.

'He won't tell you that, of course. He wouldn't get his own way with you if he did. Like any other man in that situation, he will lie and lie and lie again. It's a regrettable fact, but a fact nevertheless, that masters of households and their sons regularly seduce young girls like yourself.'

'You're the one who's lying,' Annalie said. 'I know Adam. He loves me. I know it.'

Christina shrugged. 'Why don't you test him, then?'

'What do you mean?'

'Ask him to leave me and come to live here with you.'

Annalie flushed a bright crimson. 'I couldn't ask him to do that. I wouldn't want him to live here. He's not used to this kind of place. But I'm sure if I wanted him to,' she added hastily, 'he would get me a better place for us to share together.'

Christina was carefully smoothing on her long gloves. At the door she smiled pityingly at Annalie. 'He won't, you know. Why don't you find a nice boy of your own class? You would have no trouble there, I'm sure. You're quite pretty in your own way.'

Annalie could have kicked her all the way down the stairs and might have done had the door not closed just in time. Instead she found release in swiping Christina's cup from the table and sending it smashing in a thousand pieces against the wall.

'Bitch!' she shouted. 'Sly, scheming, nasty little bitch.'

Chapter Forty-five

There was no way that Adam could think anything of such a woman, Annalie told herself. She knew that he couldn't be happy living with Christina Monkton because always when he first arrived she could see the tension in him. She would watch him from her window. Sometimes, if there was a horse and cart or a hawker's barrow at her close he would have to park his car further up the road and she could see by his every movement when he emerged from the car that he was under stress. It might have looked perfectly natural to anyone else, but she knew that his aggressiveness, restless, slightly swaggering and arrogant facade was just the wall he constructed to hide the real man underneath. He had found as a young lad on the building sites that such a shield was necessary for his own survival. Not only that, but he'd had to perfect and maintain a tough physical fitness. This had become not only the pattern of his life but an obsession with him. The challenges of older men, individually and in gangs, once a daily threat to him, no longer existed. Only his manner persisted, defiant, always ready to meet challenges head on, but now he created his own challenges. He never took the easy way out and was always on the front line of every job. He costed everything himself, fought for every contract, was a familiar figure on every building site, and never yielded to the temptation of war profiteering as so many businessmen had. He regularly attended a local gymnasium where he subjected himself to a punishing routine, and was also a regular visitor to a local stables, when he could be seen on horseback on his way to the open countryside out by Pollok Estate where he raced the horse through the fields. Sometimes he drove his car suicidally fast too. He said that speed gave him a feeling of freedom and power, but it worried her.

Annalie had once said to him, 'Darling, what are you trying to prove?'

He had shrugged at first. 'I'm not trying to prove anything, just trying to keep fit.'

'But you seem to go at everything so hard. There's bound to be more to it than that.'

Eventually Adam had said, 'I suppose it goes back to the old man and my relationship with him. He never wanted to give up the business, you know, never thought I'd be man enough to run it. Although he never admitted it, I think that he unconsciously felt that to yield up the business would be to lose his masculinity. It was his instrument, you see – his source of social power as well as everything else. He always had great difficulty in delegating authority to anyone, especially to me. He wanted me in the business and yet when I tried to increase my responsibility I was always frustrated by his intrusions, his broken promises of retirement, his self-aggrandizement. I was somehow always a little boy in his eyes, with the accompanying contempt, condescension and lack of confidence. I tried to break away, to leave at one point, get into another business. He did his pathetic old man ploy then – didn't go as far as to admit it, but he got my mother to work on me and say how much he needed me. He'd bribe me then with promises of being a partner – but of course he never followed through. In fact, he paid me such a small salary that he was positively miserly. He always said of course, it was his excuse, that I shouldn't expect more because some day I would inherit the business.' Adam shook his head. 'I can't tell you how many arguments I had with my father. We always seemed to be at each other's throats. He kept accusing me of being ungrateful, but it was just that I resented remaining dependent on him for my living and everything else. On top of that it wasn't easy putting up with his erratic and unpredictable behaviour. I felt constantly hostile towards him, but at the same time, guilty about this hostility.'

After a minute or two's silence he concluded, 'I suppose we were both caught in a father-son rivalry situation.'

'But that's all over now,' she told him. 'You don't need to prove yourself to anybody.'

She wondered for the first time, however, what his business relationship was with his wife. Was the pattern of business tension that he'd suffered with his father now continuing with his wife? He never mentioned Christina to her, never discussed their business or any other relationship. But Christina functioning in any capacity in business could not be a happy situation.

Often she felt that he wanted to talk to her about this most personal aspect of his life. Sometimes she could see the internal struggle he was suffering mirrored in his face, but he always stopped short of even mentioning his wife's name.

Annalie loved to watch his face. It was so alive and expressive, unlike the stiff, cold mask the minister's daughter wore. She'd never thought much about this woman while she'd worked in Monkton House, but looking back she realized now that Christina Gillespie's evasive eyes had been full of secrets.

She was thinking of Adam's last visit. He had brought her a gramophone.

A gramophone! She couldn't believe it. The pleasure she'd already got from it was incalculable. She'd been so happy and excited that she'd clung round his neck and danced with him round the room, squealing with ecstasy and pleasure.

He'd brought her half a dozen records too. 'Romantic ones,' he said. 'Because I know that that's what you like.'

'They'll Never Believe Me', 'Any Time Is Kissing Time', 'Love Will Find a Way', 'You Made Me Love You', 'Will You Remember?' and 'If You Were the Only Girl in the World'.

Already she'd played them all over and over and over again.

Sometimes when he came to see her he would be soothed by dancing cheek to cheek to the music of the gramophone. He would put on a record of something romantic, wind up the gramophone and then take her in his arms, and they would dance slowly round the room, very close together. At other times, if he was particularly tense, she would give him a massage. Often he told her that she was wonderful at massage, sheer magic. Indeed, she felt there was something coming from the core of herself into her hands when she was deftly stroking and kneading his taut muscles. In a way it was like dance, a total involvement with the body.

She would start with his forehead just below the hairline and glide both thumbs at once in either direction to the temples where she would move them in a circle over the sensitive area. This movement was repeated as she moved progressively downwards, towards a strip running just above his eyebrows and always ending with the small circle on the temples.

The next stroke was for the rim of the eye sockets, then the eyes themselves where she would lightly run the balls of her thumbs across his closed eyelids.

Adam loved having his ears massaged and first she would run the tips of her fingers several times up and down the back of his lobes where they connected with his head. Gently and smoothly her fingers would move. Then she would lightly pinch the outer ear and the earlobe between her thumb and forefinger. Next with the tip of her forefinger she would lightly trace the natural hollows inside his ears.

Next both hands, palm up, would slide under his neck then, curving her fingers a little, she would rapidly drum them against his neck as if playing a piano, working up and down his neck and as far onto his back and the immediate area of his spine as she could comfortably reach. Now the scalp, fingers moving the skin itself over the bone.

After the head the main strokes over his naked body began with the chest and stomach, gliding both her hands slowly forward, pressing firmly on the chest an then more lightly on the stomach, keeping her hands together until she reached the lower half of his abdomen, then separating and moving them to his sides. Then there were the gentle pulling strokes on each side of his body, one side at a time, starting at his pelvis just above the thigh and working slowly up to the armpit and then back again.

As Adam relaxed and loosened up he would give appreciative little moans of enjoyment, especially when she concentrated on his abdomen, her palm rotating over it steadily and slowly. Then she moved to his legs and thighs, her hands going slowly down inside each thigh, moving between the natural crease in the skin between trunk and thigh and around his genitals.

She carefully massaged every part of him from head to feet. Sometimes he became so relaxed he slept, and she would cover him up with a blanket and sit beside him watching his face in repose.

Sometimes after the massage he would open his eyes and look at her, all the restlessness, all the arrogance, all the pride, all the bitterness, the wicked look he could sometimes have, gone. His eyes would be soft and vulnerable and from them gazed the man and the boy, the essence of the real person who was Adam Monkton.

And her eyes, with equal honesty, would commune with him on this deeper level, more intimate even than sex.

It was because of these unspoken communions, more than anything else, that Annalie knew they were of one spirit and one flesh. They belonged to each other. Nothing Christina Monkton could say or do could ever change that. The mere fact that his wife had felt it necessary to come and try to stop the relationship between herself and Adam showed that she knew Annalie was his true love, and Christina was going to lose him to her. It was as sure as day followed night and summer followed winter, but she needed it to happen soon. She could no longer be satisfied with only seeing him occasionally. Each meeting was a joyful celebration, each parting a tragic desolation. It was impossible to go on like this. Surely he must feel the same.

Chapter Forty-six

They had been to a concert in the St Andrew's Halls. The Scottish Orchestra had been playing pieces from Beethoven, Mozart, Schumann and Chopin. Monkton had noticed that several men glanced admiringly at his wife and he couldn't help feeling proud of her. She was always elegant, but seemed particularly so this evening in her dramatic outfit of dress and jacket. The dress was of finely pleated black satin and the gold-printed silk velvet jacket swung to reveal a dramatic flash of colour from the flame-coloured lining.

It had been impossible to tell by her quiet, still posture in the hall whether the music had pleased her.

'Did you enjoy it?' he asked.

'Oh yes,' she said. 'The Mozart is my favourite. It's a perfect melody composed with such skill and lovely instrumentation. There's nothing better than the slow movement of his Thirty-ninth Symphony. Although I adored the Beethoven as well – that noble grandeur of the opening movement with its Napoleonic background. That unparalleled poignancy of the funeral march, then the scherzo and that wonderful finale make it in my opinion a truly immortal work.'

It was interesting to see how she seemed to come to life when talking about music. It was the nearest he had ever seen her to looking passionate.

'How about Chopin?' he said. 'His music is supposed to be the music of lovers isn't it? Perhaps that was because of his passion for George Sand.'

Her expression closed up again. She shrugged.

'Perhaps.'

'Too romantic for you, is he?'

He didn't know why he kept niggling her like this. He felt guilty about being unfaithful and kept trying to be nice to her to make up for it. Most of the time, despite his good intentions, he failed miserably and put her down instead.

Impulsively he took her arm and linked it with his as they walked along the street to where he'd parked the car.

'I'm glad you enjoyed it,' he said. 'We must come to concerts more often. It's good to have something we can share.'

'You mean you'd really like to come again?' she asked.

'Of course. I may not be as knowledgeable about music as you are, but I do enjoy it.'

He felt the little quiver of pleasure run through her, but she didn't say any more. They drove home in silence, but it was quite a comfortable silence. There was no animosity in it, only the subtle aura of caution that he so often detected about Christina. In Queen's Drive he assisted her from the car and her small limp hand in his unexpectedly filled him with an almost painful tenderness. There was something about the quiet, elegant figure that felt unusually close to him tonight. He wondered if it had been the music that had matched their moods.

Annalie would have grasped his hand in a firm, warm grip and burst from the car, tossing her head and staring eagerly around. She would have shattered the quiet night with her laughter and excitement. There was no place for Annalie Gordon here in the wide sweep of the driveway. In the white porch with the new Charles Rennie Mackintosh style door, with the elderly maid bobbing a curtsey to them and welcoming them into the richly carpeted hall.

In the bedroom he poured himself a whisky.

'Do you want a nightcap?' he asked.

'Yes thank you.'

They were still standing close together as she took her first sip, then as if it had melted her shell for a few seconds she looked at him with such love in her eyes it made him feel ashamed. The look only lasted a couple of seconds and then disappeared, but it deeply affected him. He supposed it would solve everything if he could love her like that in return. Loving her, he would learn the right way to handle her and bring out the best in her. Maybe that was what she needed to bring her out of her hard shell. After all, if the truth be told, her mother and father had never shown her any real love. Perhaps if he had never known Annalie his feelings for his wife might have deepened in time. But knowing Annalie, knowing her wild, abandoned lovemaking, knowing her uninhibited joy of living, knowing how that abandonment and joy overwhelmed him every time he was with her, meant that his wife paled into insignificance by comparison and thoughts of her disappeared. It was only when he was not with Annalie that the guilt feelings returned and he knew he was not being fair to either woman. He knew the situation could not continue for ever, but he didn't know what to do about it. Every time he thought of the predicament his gut tied in knots of tension. He knocked back his whisky and poured himself another.

'Aren't you drinking rather a lot these days?' Christina said.

He felt irritated.

'What I drink is none of your concern.'

'That's a stupid thing to say.'

His brows drew down.

'Don't call me stupid.'

'You know what I mean.'

'No I don't know what you mean.'

Sometimes he felt an argument with her relieved his tension. At other times the aggravation became more intense until he felt he could strangle her.

'You may forget it from time to time,' she said coolly, 'but I am your wife. That's one reason for concern. The other is, if you become addleheaded with drink you'll begin to make the wrong decisions and the business will be at risk.'

He gave a humourless laugh.

'My God. You're the last person who should talk about putting the business at risk. You've caused nothing but worry in the business ever since the day you tricked me into marrying you.'

'Oh I think you can safely say,' she told him bitterly, 'that

291

you've had your revenge over and over again for my so-called tricking you into marrying me.'

Why the hell did he say that? He silently chastised himself. It had been such a pleasant evening up till now. He'd long since accepted the fact that had he been in her shoes in the manse with tricking someone into marriage as the only option of escape, he would have done exactly the same thing. He not only understood her action, he sympathized with it.

'I'm sorry,' he managed. 'I spoiled a pleasant evening.' He touched her arm. 'Forgive me.'

She nodded putting down her empty glass.

For a moment she looked so pale and fragile and sad that again he felt tenderness towards her. He moved his hand up her arm and gently pulled her towards him. He sensed a very subtle shrinking. Nevertheless she submitted to him.

He enjoyed making love to her but it was a very temporary physical experience. Lovemaking with Christina was like savouring a glass of milk when one was thirsty. Making love to Annalie was like a belt of whisky that intoxicated you and the intoxication kept returning to fever both body and mind.

After making love to Christina he held her in his arms and tried not to think of Annalie.

Chapter Forty-seven

Christina was very satisfied with her meeting with Annalie Gordon. At the time it had been distressing, of course, and it had taken all her self-control to retain an outward appearance of coolness and calm dignity. But she had managed it. Not only that, she had shown how little self-control and dignity Annalie Gordon had. The girl was as common as dirt. Admittedly she had a certain dark, gypsy beauty. Christina could see why Adam lusted after her but for his sake as well as everyone else's it had to be stopped. She had every confidence that it would stop if the plan she had triggered off was carried out to the bitter end by Annalie Gordon. Now that she felt more secure she was a little sorry for the girl. She was obviously in love with Adam and had believed every word he told her. Christina knew only too well herself how persuasive Adam could be, and what a good lover he was too. But he was her husband until death parted them and the quicker Annalie Gordon realized that the better.

She'd told Mathieson she'd been to the Gorbals. Not to see Annalie Gordon of course – only to inspect the tenemental property.

'The whole place was thronged with people,' she told him. 'Surely the houses must be dreadfully overcrowded?'

Mathieson shrugged. 'I suppose that goes back to the influx of Irish and Highlanders. The Irish came over by the boatload after the potato famine. The Highlanders came down after the clearances. All of them were homeless. They were all crowded into the tenements.'

'Right enough,' she agreed. 'There have been plenty of Highlanders in Glasgow and I remember my father telling me that before the railway was built over Argyle Street, Highlanders used to congregate every Sunday evening at the north-west corner of the Broomielaw Bridge. That area was known as the Gaelic Cross. Missionary speakers used to hold services there in Gaelic. They tell me the arcade in Argyle Street under the Central Station railway bridge, is known as the Highlandman's Umbrella because it is where they meet now. And of course, Paddy's Market was where a lot of Irishmen used to meet. Have you heard the story that Irishmen, especially when they got a drink or two, used to drag their coat along the ground behind them in the hope that somebody would trample on it and give them an excuse for a fight. I don't know if that's true or not.'

'Oh I quite believe it,' Mathieson said. 'It's probably this mix of Lowland Scot – they have a radical history – that's given Glasgow its volatile and revolutionary type of reputation.'

'The Red Clyde,' Christina said. 'I've lived in Glasgow all my life and I've never seen any revolutionary types or trouble of any sort.'

Mathieson laughed. 'No, my dear. You wouldn't.'

'Why do you say that?' she asked.

'It's pretty obvious, I would have thought. You've had a very sheltered upbringing.'

'I suppose I have,' she said thoughtfully. 'I certainly got a bit of an eye-opener at the Gorbals.'

'I don't suppose you saw half of it.' Mathieson said. 'Some of them live like pigs, you know. Absolutely filthy. You should hear some of the stories that the factor tells.'

Christina was about to say that the house she had seen inside was absolutely spotlessly clean, but stopped herself just in time.

Only yesterday, after dinner she and Adam had discussed the strategy they had intended to employ at the next board meeting. Adam believed that outside managers should eventually be employed to run all the different areas of the business. Christina agreed with him.

'It's a matter of regeneration,' Adam said. 'No family business that I know of has been capable of sustaining regeneration solely through the medium of its own family members.'

The building side of the business had started with slaters,

bricklayers, plumbers, joiners, plasterers, painters, decorators and various other trades. Recently Adam had bought a quarry to produce his own slates. Christina had helped him in this deal inasmuch as she had been the one to hear that the land was for sale. He had also bought a brick factory so that it was now cheaper to produce his own bricks. But with the business expanding as it was, it was becoming impossible or certainly very difficult for Adam to oversee everything, especially when he had to travel such distances in connection with new War Office contracts. Recently he had even been over to France.

He felt, and again she agreed with him, that it was time to appoint at least one manager.

'One day I'll have to have a property director on the board,' Christina said. 'But the volume of my business doesn't warrant that yet.' Although she couldn't help thinking that on her side of the business she wouldn't have such scope to exercise her imagination and entrepreneurial abilities if there was too much structure.

'You know, of course,' Adam had told her, 'that the other members of the board aren't going to like my idea. They're going to fight it tooth and nail. They don't want any outsiders coming in to run the place.'

'Well you can be sure of my vote,' she told him.

A cautious kind of truce had developed between them in which even some co-operation was developing. He had certainly co-operated in the setting up of the gymnasium in the Gorbals and often dropped in to see how the youngsters were getting on. He'd told her that he could see one or two potentially good boxers developing; he was full of enthusiasm about one in particular and he seemed to enjoy telling her of the lad's progress.

This following evening, while finishing the day's work, Christina was thinking that Adam probably hadn't been with Annalie Gordon for some time. Perhaps her strategy had already worked.

Just then Adam passed her open office door and she called to him, 'Are you going straight home now?'

He stopped for a moment to say, 'No, I've a call to make first. I'll see you later.' Then he was gone.

Her mouth tightened and her fingers nearly broke the pencil she was holding. She had come to recognize that slightly evasive tone, that deceptively smooth casualness. He was off to see his gypsy paramour. Well, he was in for more than he bargained for. She could hardly finish her paperwork for thinking about what would be happening at Annalie Gordon's place.

She was surprised. When she arrived home he was already in the drawing room. If he had gone to Annalie Gordon's he must have been there for only a short time before dashing home, and in a rage by the look of him.

The moment she put her foot in the room he said to her, 'How dare you go to Cumberland Street?'

She gave a sarcastic laugh. 'How dare I go to Cumberland Street? That's a good one, Adam. Shouldn't it be me who's saying that to you?'

She felt annoyed that her plan had gone slightly wrong. Only in a temporary sense, of course. Obviously this evening Adam had not given Annalie Gordon enough time for her to force him to make any choices. As soon as he'd learnt that his wife had visited his mistress he had immediately returned home to confront her.

'How dare you,' he repeated, his voice icy with anger.

'I dared because I thought I was doing the right thing,' she told him. 'I was trying to save our marriage.'

'What marriage?' he sneered.

'Oh, I think we have a worthwhile and growing relationship.'

'A business relationship, yes,' Adam said. 'But there's more to a marriage than that.'

'I know,' she said. 'And you've done nothing to help the personal side of it.'

His reply was halted by the maid entering the drawing room.

'That was Gladys, Ma'am. She says your mother's very upset and could you go round at once. Gladys thinks it

296

might be better if both you and the master went round. The minister's out and won't know what happened.'

Christina felt alarmed. 'What has happened?'

'That's all right, thank you,' Adam said, dismissing the maid. 'We'll go right away.'

Christina had turned deathly white. They went in silence to the little cloakroom off the hall and Adam helped her on with her coat. Habit made her lift a hat from the shelf and adjust it carefully over her hair.

Walking stiff faced round to the manse she kept thinking: 'Please God may it not be a telegram about Simon.' To her surprise Ada Gillespie and not Gladys opened the door. She was obviously in a state of extreme agitation.

'It's Simon,' she whispered.

Adam had started to say that he was sorry but Mrs Gillespie interrupted him. 'He's in the drawing room.'

'Thank God!' Christina said. 'We both thought when you sent for us that you must have received a telegram.'

'He's been invalided out,' Ada whispered. 'He didn't even write and tell me he'd been ill. He couldn't, he said. Oh, my poor Simon, I don't know what to do.'

'We'd better go through, Mrs Gillespie. He'll be wondering why we're taking so long.'

Adam went first and the drawing room door opened rather noisily, making Simon jump from his chair with a cry of distress. Christina was shocked at the sight of him. Painfully thin, bent and hollow, he trembled violently from head to toe. Adam strode quickly across the room and embraced Simon in a bear hug which had the effect of making Simon burst into uncontrollable, convulsive sobbing.

'You're all right now,' Adam said. 'You're safe now. You're at home with your family.'

Christina was too shocked for words. She had the terrible feeling that this was not Simon at all. This was a poor wreck of humanity, a peace of war flotsam that had somehow been washed ashore. Here was a pathetic stranger who bore no resemblance to her dashing, dare-devil brother either in behaviour or in looks.

'I'm sorry,' he was sobbing. 'God, I'm sorry, Adam. What must you think of me?'

'I think of you as my lifelong best friend,' Adam said. 'You're obviously suffering from shell shock and it's not surprising after all that you've been through. Have you any medication?'

'I've got it here,' Ada said. 'There's medicine for during the day and something here to help him sleep.'

'Well,' Adam said. 'You're no doubt exhausted after travelling. I think you should go upstairs to bed, take one of your tablets and have a good night's sleep. Tomorrow when you feel a bit refreshed we'll have a good long talk, you and I.'

Ada said, 'I'll come upstairs with you, dear.'

'No,' Adam told her. 'I'll see him all right. I'll be back down in a few minutes.'

All the time Christina had been standing very still, hands knotted in front of her waist. Ada fluttered helplessly about after Adam and Simon had left the room.

'Oh my poor Simon, my poor boy,' she kept repeating.

Eventually Christina said, I'll ring for tea, Mother. Don't worry. We'll help and in time I'm sure Simon will recover.'

Adam joined her when he returned downstairs.

'How is he?' she asked.

'He's going to need a lot of care. And rest and quiet.'

Christina said, 'I'll help financially, Mother, if you need to employ any extra staff.' She turned to Adam. 'Do you think he needs a nurse or someone to give him special care?'

'I hinted at that but he wouldn't stomach it. He's too desperate to be independent, to behave normally. We'll just have to help your mother and father as best we can.'

'Shell shock, do you think?'

'There are hundreds, if not thousands of cases like Simon. I was reading an article about it just the other day.'

Mrs Gillespie said in a shaken voice, 'He's so completely different. I got such a shock when I saw him. I don't think I'll ever get over it. I dread your father seeing him like that, Chrissie. The shock will be enough to kill him. Certainly it'll break his heart.' Suddenly she dissolved into tears and Adam had to carry her over to the sofa.

They left when the Reverend Gillespie returned and after Adam had explained to him about Simon's condition. The older man's bewhiskered face had gone a sickly grey but he listened in dignified silence.

Christina walked to Monkton House with Adam. Like her father, she also retained a stiff silence. She couldn't trust herself to speak, she was so worried and upset. The sound of Simon's anguished sobbing still echoed in her ears, distressing beyond words.

Upstairs in the bedroom, white-faced and still silent, she undressed for bed.

'Christina,' Adam said eventually. 'It's not good for you to suppress your feelings so much. If you want to grieve for your brother – grieve for him.'

'It was so dreadful, wasn't it?' she managed. 'Knowing Simon, knowing what he was like before.'

Her voice broke and she immediately covered her mouth with stiff palms. He came over and, putting an arm around her shoulders said, 'It's all right to weep.'

Suddenly her need for comfort overcame everything else and she clung to him.

'You'd better get into bed,' he told her, at the same time gently attempting to disentangle himself from her. But she clung desperately round his neck, her eyes wide and distraught. Even once she was in bed she still clung to him, her distress for her brother now confused by the anguish of her feelings for her husband.

Eventually Adam got into bed beside her. He held her in his arms and kissed her tearless eyes until, eventually, his mouth was covering hers and passion was blotting out other more painful emotions.

Afterwards, she realized that even at the height of her distress and passion the thought had entered her head that this time she could and would become pregnant. He would not leave her if she were pregnant. That, she decided, was the best way to keep him.

Chapter Forty-eight

Two distractions happened in the street. No, three as it turned out. Bobby Blair got his call-up papers. His girl-friend Minnie told him she was pregnant. As a result a hasty wedding was arranged before Bobby was due to leave for France.

Flo and Erchie were worried about Bobby's imminent departure, as indeed Bobby was. The creation of a wedding party at such short notice, however, posed not the slightest problem. Flo and Erchie could organize a party, any kind of party, at the drop of a hat. They weren't a bit offended, quite the reverse in fact, when Minnie's father and mother, big Aggy and Michael Hennessy, said that Flo and Erchie should have the party as they were used to that sort of thing.

The actual wedding ceremony was a quiet affair at the Registry Office in town, but the party afterwards in Flo and Erchie's room and kitchen was anything but quiet. All the neighbours were invited. Everyone brought a bottle and no questions were asked how they came by it.

Flo made one of her clooty dumplings and big Aggy made a cake. It wasn't a fancy, wedding type of cake with sugar rose-buds and lovers' knots. There wasn't enough sugar for that sort of nonsense. Anyway, big Aggy hadn't that much of a confectioner's expertise. The cake was big, heavy and plain like Aggy herself. Aggy's cakes always tasted good however, and everybody knew to be prepared with indiges-tion tablets so there was no harm done.

It was one of life's mysteries what big Aggy's husband Michael had ever seen in her. Michael Hennessy was one of the most handsome men anyone had ever clapped eyes on: tall, with smooth tanned skin, black curly hair and laughing eyes that even quickened the hearts of girls as young as his daughter. He was a miner, and had so far been exempted from military service.

Admittedly he had his faults. He was a hard drinker and every Friday and Saturday got literally fighting drunk. He'd fight anybody for any reason or no reason at all. Men had been known to hide up closes and dodge into shops to avoid him if they spied him staggering menacingly along the road. Stone cold sober, however, he was one of the nicest, good-natured of men and he adored big Aggy. Nobody could understand it.

Fortunately for Minnie, she had taken after her father in looks. She had his dark curls and his bright sparkling eyes and everyone thought she'd make Bobby a lovely wee wife. The separation money from the army, they agreed, would be better than nothing.

Minnie, Bobby and Annalie were all near enough the same age and had gone to the same school together. Annalie was happy for Minnie and Bobby's sake that they were getting married. They were obviously in love with each other, but at the same time the prospect of the wedding party made her feel sad. It reminded her that nearly all her contemporaries were either married, or about to be.

So much talk about marriage seemed to accentuate her single and lonely state. She partly blamed her feelings on Christina Monkton, whose visit had deeply upset her. Christina Monkton had seemed so certain of Adam's loyalty, so positive that he would never leave her, and this intensified Annalie's worries about her future. Now, more and more, she was thinking about the disadvantages to herself of her relationship with Adam – the years ahead that would contain so many lonely months, the fact that she would never be able to wear a wedding ring and proudly claim to have a husband.

She would rather have no husband at all, of course, if she couldn't have Adam. More and more she began to dream of being his wife. She began to conjure up little scenarios. She would see herself as the grand lady presiding at the breakfast table in Monkton House. There would be that closeness in the air between her and Adam, the aftermath of the passionate intimacies they would enjoy in the big, soft bed in the master bedroom upstairs. That aura of intimacy would shut everyone else out, would make her feel secure in his presence and give her the self-confidence to deal with anyone or any situation.

She would tell Doris where to get off, for a start. She would stand no nonsense from her, having stood so much from her in the past. As for Beatrice Monkton – oh, how she would enjoy putting her in her place. Every time she thought of this scenario she mentally rubbed her hands in gleeful excitement at the prospect of acting the grand lady over Beatrice Monkton. Revenge would be sweet indeed.

Exactly what would happen to Christina never featured in any detail in these daydreams. If Annalie did think of her, it was with some vague idea of Adam having divorced her and sent her packing back to the manse where she belonged. Annalie Monkton. She savoured the name. Mrs Monkton. Mrs Adam Monkton – of Monkton House, Queen's Drive, Queen's park. She would be a lady then, all right, and everybody would know it. The thought gave her palpitations in her stomach and made her nearly swoon with pleasurable excitement.

At other times, however, loneliness, her single state and life in the Gorbals stretched before her with frightening inevitability. Bobby and Minnie's wedding intensified all these thoughts and jumbled them together with a painful vulnerability. At the same time it was a good party and she enjoyed it, at least at first. Minnie looked very pretty in a cream hobble skirt and long cut-away jacket to match. A wide-brimmed hat with a feather in it was cheekily tilted to one side over her curls. Everyone enjoyed a good feed of Scotch pie, peas and mashed potato, with Flo's clooty dumpling and big Aggy's cake to follow.

Mr Baxter gave a tune on the fiddle that had everyone's feet tapping. Flo and Erchie did their wee number, 'John Anderson My Jo' followed by 'A Fond Kiss.' Flo's father recited a poem by McGonagall, Mrs Mitchell, Flo's house-proud neighbour from across the other side of the landing, sang with closed eyes, clasped hands and great concentration, 'Come Into the Garden Maud'. Wee Cathy, Flo's youngest sang her usual 'Jesus Wants Me for a Sunbeam'.

Teeny Docherty began to sing 'I'll be your Sweetheart' but kept forgetting the words and had to be helped by everybody else joining in. All the time glasses were being filled and refilled and everyone was getting very merry.

Everyone had been so worried about Michael Hennessy becoming drunk, they'd all forgotten about Jimmy Patterson and the Friday chip on his shoulder against John Reid. This careless lapse was the downfall of the wedding party.

It had to be admitted that Jimmy Patterson was not the only one who was inebriated at the time, but he definitely was the one who started the violence. He inadvertently knocked over Teeny Docherty in his rush to get his hands on John Reid. Spud Docherty, Teeny's man, who regularly battered her about, took umbrage at someone else laying a finger on her and with a howl of indignation grabbed Jimmy and smashed a fist into his face. Mamie Patterson, with equal perverseness, took great exception to this treatment of her husband. She grabbed the first thing that came to hand, which happened to be a poker, and began belabouring Spud Docherty with it. Andy Baxter, in the belief that music could calm the most savage breast, launched into a tune on the fiddle. For some unknown reason this had the exact opposite effect. The music galvanized everybody into immediate action. Voices were raised to shout above it. Both Michael Hennessy and Erchie Blair waded in to try to sort out the melee that was already in full swing. Erchie jerked Mamie Patterson off Spud Docherty only to have her turn the poker on him with such vehemence that he was felled by the first blow.

Fearing that murder was going to be committed Annalie ran out to fetch the police. She returned with Big Donald who climbed the stairs with his usual heavy and leisurely tread despite the crescendo of noise racketing down to meet him.

Once inside Flo's house he called out soothingly, 'Now, now,' but before he could say any more someone knocked his helmet off. This was a mark of disrespect that could not be tolerated. Big Donald jerked out his truncheon and laid about everybody left and right. In the end, what with one thing and another, everybody had either to be marched off or carried off to the casualty department of the Royal Infirmary.

There they sat within its grim carbolic-smelling walls alongside a battered and bloody army of other Glaswegians, a motley crew of miserable faces, of bloodstained clothes, of broken limbs and angry-looking bruisings and swellings.

Annalie tried to comfort Minnie who had somehow acquired a black eye. The woman on the other side of Annalie was sitting with her head wrapped in a large towel through which blood could be seen steadily seeping.

Suddenly Spud Docherty not only burst into song but staggered to his feet with his arms outstretched and, swinging about, interspersed lines of 'I Belong to Glasgow' with urgings to the rest of the casualty department to join him in what he referred to as 'a wee sing song.'

Isn't this terrible,' Minnie said. 'What a showing up. And my poor man knocked unconscious trying to save me.'

'Well, at least he *is* your man now,' Annalie comforted. 'I mean you *are* married. Just try and remember the good bits. It was a lovely tea and a great party until that stupid wee Jimmy Patterson tried to go for Mr Reid. He's always the same. He does that every week and Mr Reid's such a nice man and has never said a wrong word to him.'

Minnie sighed. 'Oh well, as you say, the main thing is I'm married.'

Annalie sighed too. 'Yes. You're lucky. I would have been the happiest girl in the world if I'd been marrying my man today.'

'Never mind,' Minnie comforted. 'Your turn'll come.'

'I hope so. Oh I hope so, Minnie,' Annalie said.

Chapter Forty-nine

'You'd surely no need to dash off like that,' Annalie said. 'You'd hardly been in the house five minutes and I hadn't seen you for ages previous to that. I haven't seen you for ages since, either. I was nearly on the point of phoning you or coming up to the office.'

Adam said, 'Don't ever do that. Not unless it's a real emergency.'

'Why not?' She tossed her dark head. 'Are you ashamed of me or something?'

She was wearing her new dress, a wide-skirted, loose-belted tunic in a pretty shade of lavender that brought out flecks of the same colour in her eyes. The posh shop assistant had assured her she looked stunning in it.

'I want to keep my life with you separate with no connection between Queen's Park and here except myself.'

'Oh, very, convenient,' she said.

He spread out his hands.

'What do you expect me to do? I thought I was doing everything I possibly could for you. By the way, you know I passed the word to all the foremen in the different sites around the county about your mother. She's one of the Lee family, isn't she? Saviana Lee?'

It was a distraction that Annalie didn't want at that particular moment. At the same time she was anxious to know about her baby.

'Yes.' she said.

'Well, just yesterday I had word from one of them that there's a Lee family camping outside of Drymen.'

'Drymen!' Annalie cried. 'That would have taken you little more than a hour to go in your car. What stopped you? You know how important it is to me and it might be too late now. They might have moved on last night.'

'I had a particularly busy day yesterday, Annalie.'

'What about the evening?'

'Something turned up in the evening,' he said.

'Oh yes.' Her voice had turned sarcastic. 'And you say you love me.'

'I do.'

'Prove it then.'

'I'll go there now if you like.' He glanced at his watch. 'It means I won't have any time with you this evening, but if that's what you want, I'll go.'

She moved seductively close to him.

'What I want is to be with you all the time, for always. Not here. I know you wouldn't want to stay here, but wherever would suit you. I would go anywhere that you wanted me to as long as it meant being with you.'

'Darling,' he sighed. 'That's impossible and you know it.'

'No I don't know it!' she cried out. 'Why is it impossible if we love each other?'

'I'm married.'

'You don't love her. Leave her. Leave her now.'

His face hardened and he turned away from her. Lighting up a cigarette, he said, 'I can't do that.'

'Why can't you? Why can't you?' she cried out like a child.

'Her brother, my friend, has been invalided out of the army. He's severely shell shocked – in a dreadful state, poor chap. My wife's very distressed and I don't blame her. We're all having to rally round and help Simon. It's the least we can do.'

Suddenly Annalie burst into tears. Adam gathered her into his arms.

'I'm sorry, darling. Now do you want me to stay or do you want me to go and find out if that gypsy camp is still there?'

She clung tightly to him.

'Go tomorrow. I couldn't bear it if you left me now.'

She felt desolate when eventually he did leave. Her body was still hot and throbbing from his lovemaking, but she felt empty and abandoned all the same. She lay in bed after he left her, naked and vulnerable and not knowing how she

306

could survive the long night. She began to drown in guilt and misery as she thought about her baby – another night alone with neither lover nor child.

There were still a few hours of evening left. She could hear children singing outside:

> 'In and out the windows,
> In and out the windows,
> In and out the windows,
> As you have done before.'

A sneery voice was chanting,

> 'Tell tale tit,
> Your granny cannae knit.'

There were shouts and laughter and the leisurely rise and fall of women's voices enjoying a blether at the close mouth. Downstairs, Mamie Patterson was screeching abuse at husband Jimmy. Downstairs too there was much thumping and bumping and clattering and the occasional scream which meant that Spud Docherty was beating his wife Teeny.

Unable to settle, Annalie got up, put her clothes on and left the house to go downstairs to visit old Mrs Sweeny. Old Mrs Sweeny had lost her only son in the war and before that her husband had been killed in an accident in the building trade. She had confessed to being often lonely and was glad of a visit at any time from anybody.

Old Mrs Sweeny wasn't really that old, but hard work and sadness had aged her beyond her years. She still trudged three mornings a week to different houses in Pollokshields and Queen's Park early in the morning to do a clothes wash and have the washing dried and ironed before she left to return home at the end of the day. She was tiny and very bent, with soft wrinkled skin, sad defeated eyes behind small, steel-rimmed spectacles and hair pinned back in a bun. She wasn't at all self-pitying however, and as often as not was bright and cheery in company and could join in a laugh as quick as anyone else.

'Oh there you are, hen,' she greeted Annalie. 'Come away in. It's nice to see you.'

'Sorry I'm a bit late coming to your door.' Annalie apologized.

'No, no. It's never too late for a friend, hen. And I've not got to work tomorrow, so I'm fine. I don't need to go to bed early tonight.'

'Does it not make you angry at times?' Annalie said, settling herself down in a chair beside the fire. 'When you see the way these people live compared with us?'

Mrs Sweeny busied herself making a pot of tea.

'No. I can't say it does, hen. How? Did you get angry when you worked in Queen's Park?'

'I didn't half.' Annalie said with feeling. 'It's funny, I've always wanted to be like them in a way. I mean to be a lady, but at the same time I can't stand any of these stuck-up bitches.'

'Och, don't be angry, hen. It's just the way of the world. They don't know any better.'

'I'm as good as them.'

'Of course you are, hen. Do you take milk and sugar?'

'Just milk, thanks. I've always tried my best to better myself,' Annalie said. 'I keep myself clean and decent. I wear nice clothes. I talk proper. I read the newspapers and I'm always along at the library getting out books.'

'I know, hen. You're a great wee reader.'

'He's no need to be ashamed of me. And what's more I've a lot more life and love in me than that cold stick he has for a wife.'

Old Mrs Sweeny's face creased with worry.

'But she is his wife, hen, and it says in the good book, "What God has joined together let no man put asunder."'

'I don't think it says that in the Bible,' Annalie said.

'Is that not in the prayer book or whatever it is they use for weddings?'

For a few seconds they stared uncertainly at each other.

'I've always thought it was in the Bible, hen,' Mrs Sweeny said eventually.

'Anyway,' Annalie said, 'I love him and he loves me. That's all that matters.'

'Well . . .' Mrs Sweeny said, still very uncertain.

'It says in the Bible to love each other,' Annalie said.

'I don't think God was meaning that kind of love, hen.'

'I love him with every kind of love. I really do, Mrs Sweeny. I couldn't live without him.'

'Now, now. Drink up your tea, hen. There's no use getting yourself upset.'

After a minute or two while they both enjoyed the comfort of their tea, Mrs Sweeny said, 'Life's hard, hen. And sometimes you've just got to live without somebody you love. You haven't any choice, you see.'

'You've had it terrible hard right enough,' Annalie sympathized. 'Life's not fair. That's what I say.'

'Och well. There's always somebody worse than yourself.' Mrs Sweeny reminded her. 'Look at poor Mrs Alison.'

'Her whose son was a conscientious objector?'

'Aye.' Mrs Sweeny shook her head. 'I remember him well. Nice wee laddy. Always was. Many a time he used to run a message for me. He grew up to be a real good Christian, that boy. He believed in the Bible, hen, word for word. He didn't think it was what Jesus wanted him to do, to go to kill his fellow man. But his fellow man here treated him awful bad. Killed him eventually. A lot of them conscientious objectors have died in jail. About seventy already, I've heard. And nearly as many have gone mad.'

'What happened?' Annalie asked.

'Well he never said in any of his letters to his mother, but some of the other lads have managed to get word to her. He was bullied and tormented something awful. One time he had to stand for days in a water-logged pit in the ground. It doesn't bear thinking about what that poor lad suffered. And no one, even around here, ever had a good word for him after he refused to join up. They called him all sorts of awful names, and often when poor Mrs Alison was there to hear them. As if she hadn't enough to worry her, poor thing. Well he's away now to meet his maker and what God thinks about him is all that matters.'

'It says a lot for you,' Annalie told her, 'that you have no bitterness in your heart when your son was killed fighting in the Somme.'

'Och, my laddie and him used to play together when they were wee. What would I be bitter about? Bitterness just hurts you all the more.'

'I'm bitter,' Annalie said. 'I'm bitter against her. She tricked him into marriage you know. I can count. I know when her baby was born and when they got married.'

'It doesn't do any good being bitter, hen. As I say, you just hurt yourself all the more. It'll change you and twist you.'

'I can't help it.' Annalie said. She felt herself get all worked up. Her dark eyes stretched wide, her voice loudened. 'I hate her. I hate her.'

'Now, now,' Mrs Sweeny soothed. 'Drink up you tea.'

'I wish she would die.'

Mrs Sweeny was shocked.

'Oh, you mustn't say things like that, hen.'

'But it's true. She's the only thing that stands between me and Adam.'

Mrs Sweeny looked worried and uncertain.

'I don't know, hen. I mean, you've both been brought up different, right from when you were wee. You once told me he went to a posh private school in Edinburgh, didn't you? That's a wee bit different from going to school in the Gorbals for a start, hen.'

'But he served his time as a joiner as well.'

'Fancy being able to do that after having such a posh background.'

'He's really a wonderful man, Mrs Sweeny. He's so kind as well, yet strong, you know. Oh, I do love him.'

'Oh deary, dear,' Mrs Sweeny sighed and shook her head helplessly.

'And I can't bear this kind of life,' Annalie went on. 'Just seeing occasionally, loving him and then being left without him. I want him. I want him to be with me all the time. I want to belong to him all the time. Oh, I just want him, Mrs Sweeny.'

'But hen, you can't have everything you want in this life. That's a hard lesson you've obviously still to learn.'

In a sudden gesture of exasperation, Annalie smacked

310

her hand up to her head and rubbed them recklessly through her hair, making it tumble down around her shoulders and face. With her flashing dark eyes it gave her a wild look.

'I don't care about lessons,' she cried out. 'I don't care about life, I don't care about anything except him. And I'm not going to allow that cold fish of a wife of his to come between us. I'll kill her first. So help me God, I'll kill her!'

Chapter Fifty

'I'm pregnant,' Christina said suddenly.

Adam lowered his newspaper and looked across at her.

'You sound as if you don't mind.'

'I don't.'

'Why the sudden change of heart?'

'I was thinking, it doesn't necessarily mean that I give up my business. In fact, it doesn't mean that at all. I won't begin to show for months, for a start. And then, even later, I'll still be able to get around. Or even if I didn't feel as able to get around as much as usual, I could use the telephone. Even now I do most of my business over the phone.'

Adam closed his paper, folded it and put it aside. She was glad to note that he looked pleased. No, more than pleased. He looked happy.

'What are you hoping for?' he asked. 'A boy or a girl this time?'

'I don't mind, really, she said. As long as it's all right.' She smiled. 'All its fingers and toes, you know. Would you like another son?'

'I don't really mind either,' he said. 'Although the more sons the better, I suppose, to carry on the business.'

She laughed then.

'How many were you reckoning to have?'

He gazed over at her quizzically for a moment or two.

'You know, Christina, I didn't altogether understand you when I married you, and I sometimes feel I understand you even less now.'

'Does that matter?' she said.

After another short silence he said, 'In the kind of marriage we have, perhaps not.'

'We've been married nearly two years now, Adam. Will you ever forgive me?'

'Why do you ask?' he said cautiously.

She sighed. 'Was it so terrible? I only loved you, that was all.'

'No. That was not all, Christina.' His face and eyes were hardening. She was losing him and she could have bitten her tongue out for raising the subject.

'You wouldn't do anything for love alone,' he continued.

'That's not fair,' she said stiffly, not moving a muscle yet drawing further and further away from him.

'Isn't it?' he said. 'I must say it's been my experience of you so far that you've done little unless for what seemed to you a very good reason. That usually means some sort of an advantage to you, either financially or otherwise.'

She lit a cigarette and said, 'You don't need to say any more. You've convinced me yet again that you don't love me.'

'You asked the question,' he said. 'You brought up the subject. I was only answering you and telling you the truth as I see it.'

She coolly blew out a slow stream of cigarette smoke.

'So now I know how you see it,' she said. 'Did you see Simon today?'

He nodded. 'I called in on the way to the office this morning.'

'I plan to go round in a few minutes,' she said. 'As soon as I finish this cigarette.'

'I'll come with you.'

'How was he?' she asked.

'He was in a bit of a state because it was raining. Remember there was that heavy shower this morning. It reminded him of how it was in the Somme before he left. Apparently torrential rain turned the ground over there into a complete swamp. He said he would never forget seeing one of his drivers return from a trip to collect rations. Apparently only the man's face was visible. The rest was mud. Fresh, moist mud atop mud that was lighter in colour and dry. The man's horse had sunk so deeply into the mud that it had to be hauled out by a chain attached to a truck. The rain, he said, always reminded him how absolutely ghastly life was over there, how it was a region of absolute horror and despair, how morale was becoming so low that the men had to be driven into some of the attacks at gunpoint. He kept repeating over and over again how it was a muddy grave and how the life blood of the British army as well as the German army was seeping into the ground.'

'I dread going round,' she said.

'You'll have to go.'

'I told you I would. It's just so awful seeing him like that.'

'I noticed you managed to avoid going yesterday.'

She stubbed out her cigarette. 'Simon doesn't expect me every day. Damn!' she said, noticing a flurry of sleet outside the drawing room window. 'That's it started again.'

She put on a white glazed waterproof with a high stand-up collar, adding one of the latest fashions in small hats and matching gloves. Adam was going without a coat.

'Adam, you'll get soaked,' she protested. 'Put on a coat. There's one hanging there.'

'For goodness' sake, Christina,' he said. 'We're only going a few yards along the road.'

'Well, take your umbrella then. That'll cover us both.'

A strong wind was throwing hailstones against them as hard as it could when they got outside. They had to bend forward, heads down in an effort to protect themselves from the worst of the blast. Christina gave little gasps of distress and annoyance and was forced to quicken her steps almost to a run to keep up with Adam's long fast strides. She was just about to tell him to slow down when she heard the unholy racket coming from the manse.

Adam was running ahead of her now. As soon as he reached the door he jangled the doorbell and almost immediately it was opened by a hysterical Gladys. Adam pushed past her and Christina hurriedly followed him. To her horror she found her mother lying moaning on the drawing room floor. Her father, putty faced with distress, was breathlessly struggling with a maniacal-looking Simon. Adam jerked them apart, and keeping a firm grip on Simon he told the Reverend Gillespie. 'Go and tell the maid to phone for the doctor. Give her a good slap on the face first. That ought to calm her down.'

Simon was struggling like a madman with Adam now and one blow to the face knocked Adam reeling backwards to crash onto the floor. Christina went running over to him but he pushed her aside.

'Get out of my way.'

He was back up in a moment and struggling with Simon again.

'Simon, what happened, what's wrong? I'm here to help you, man'

'What do they know?' Simon cried out. 'What do they know with their stupid cant and sentimental nonsense? Men are dying in that mud. They're falling into it, being sucked underneath it, suffocating in it and these idiots are talking about how God knows best! He sends it to give the flowers a drink. God sends it to help the poor farmers, God works in strange and mysterious ways. Strange bloody ways, all right. Well, shit on their God! That's what I say. Shit on him.'

'All right, all right,' Adam said. 'Now calm down. Christina, don't just stand there. Pour your father and mother a stiff drink.'

'But they don't . . .' Christina began.

'Just do as I tell you.'

'There isn't any strong drink in this house,' Christina said.

'Well for God's sake use some initiative. Send the maid round to our house for some. They need a glass of brandy to steady their nerves. Can't you see that?'

Christina rang the bell beside the fireplace to summon the maid but Adam said, 'Don't bring the maid in here, go out to the hall and speak to her. If she comes in here she's liable to take another bout of hysterics.'

Stiff faced, Christina went out to the hall where she caught Gladys just in time.

'Gladys, go round to Monkton House and ask Doris to give you a bottle of brandy and some brandy glasses. Run quickly, now. I'll wait here for you.'

In a few minutes the maid returned panting and out of breath, making Christina realize that Gladys, like Doris,

315

was no longer young. She took the tray from her and laid it on the hall table.

'Just a moment, Gladys.'

She poured some brandy into one of the glasses. 'You take this. Take it through to the kitchen and sit down and swallow it over. You'll feel the better of it. I'll take the tray into the drawing room.'

Her mother and father were huddled together on the sofa when she entered the room. Simon sat in one of the chairs over by the fire, twitching and jerking violently. Adam was standing beside him with a restraining hand on his shoulder. Christina poured a glass of brandy and went towards Simon with it, but Adam said, 'Not Simon. See to your mother and father.'

'Surely it would help calm Simon too.'

'I think it would be best to check with the doctor about that. Just see to your mother and father,' he repeated. 'I'll get Simon up to bed now. The doctor should be here any minute.'

After the door closed behind Simon and Adam, Christina poured brandy for her parents and took one for herself. The brandy made her parents cough, but they managed to finish it nevertheless.

'Little did I ever think, little did I ever think,' her father said, 'that one day strong liquor would pass my lips.'

'It was only very little, Father,' Christina said. 'And purely for medicinal purposes.'

'That's true, William. You needed something. We both did. I thought you were going to take a heart attack or something dreadful. We had such a shock, Christina. I mean it was so unexpected. We were only trying to help and comfort Simon and suddenly he just went completely berserk and attacked us both.'

'He's not himself, Mother,' Christina said.

'Oh I know that, dear, I know that. My Simon would never have behaved in that dreadful manner to his parents or to anyone else. I know he's ill, but oh my dear, it's so difficult to deal with. I want to help him, but everything I

316

say or do seems to be the wrong thing, seems just to make him worse.'

'I have tried too,' the Reverend Gillespie said. 'As God is my witness I have sincerely tried, but all to no avail. We go down on our knees every night, Ada and I, and pray for guidance, we pray for God to tell us how we can best help our poor son.'

They heard the doorbell and Gladys crossing the hall and then the doctor's voice as she led him upstairs to Simon's bedroom. Eventually he came into the room accompanied by Adam.

'I've given him a sedative,' he told them. 'He'll sleep peacefully now until morning. I think perhaps the pair of you need something to settle you to sleep well.'

Ada shook her head.

'No thank you, doctor. I'll be all right now that I know Simon is calmed.'

'A terrible tragedy,' the doctor said. 'I remember him as a boy. A right daredevil he was. Nerves of steel, I remember thinking. Well, I'd better be on my way. I'll pop in tomorrow and see how he is.'

Adam saw him to the door and by the time he had returned Christina had poured him a glass of brandy.

'If I were you,' Adam said to the Gillespies, 'I'd get an early night, have a good rest. I'll call in the morning on my way to work.'

'Thank you, Adam,' Mrs Gillespie said. 'You've been most kind.'

'God bless you, my boy,' the Reverend said. 'God bless you.'

Christina and Adam returned to Monkton House in silence. Once there, Adam poured another couple of brandies and lit a cigar for himself. Christina settled down by the fire opposite him, and after taking a couple of sips of brandy she lit a cigarette.

Eventually she said, 'Do you think he would be better in a hospital or someplace?'

'No I do not,' Adam said icily. 'How typical of you to

suggest such a thing. I can guess what the 'someplace' is you're suggesting, of course. The local asylum.'

'I was only thinking of my mother and father. Since Simon's returned they've become old and frail. He's liable to be the death of them and Simon would be the last one to wish that.'

'Oh, it's for your mother and father's sake, is it?'

'Yes it is.'

'He's your brother. Your only brother, for God's sake. How can you, for any reason, want to lock him away in an asylum?'

'I never said anything about locking my brother away in an asylum. I was only asking your advice about what the best thing would be to do in the circumstances.'

This in fact had been the truth. She was reminded of what her mother had said about trying to help Simon. Everything she'd said or done only made things worse. It was exactly the same with her and Adam.

'Well, here's my advice. We go in every day and help your mother and father cope with Simon. If that fails then we have Simon in here and we see that he's properly looked after here all day and every day, and your parents can just visit him until he's properly recovered.'

Only a person who was not in love with his wife could suggest such a thing, she thought bitterly. He'd completely forgotten that she was pregnant. Or, if he had not forgotten, he disregarded what effect having Simon in Monkton House would have on her condition.

'Just you remember,' she said. 'When you're laying down the law, that half of this house belongs to me.'

'My God,' he said, then he shook out his newspaper and held it up in front of him, creating between them the barrier that had become so familiar to her.

She sat staring at it and smoking her cigarette and dying a little with each leisurely, nonchalant inhalation.

318

Chapter Fifty-one

'Come on, woman. What is it you want?' Mr McClusky said irritably. 'Do you think I've nothing else to do but stand here all day?'

For some reason Sid McClusky couldn't fathom, this caused howls of laughter to reverberate round the shop. Mrs Campbell was staring up at the enamel advertisements.

'Oh aye. That's it. Veno's Cough Cure. I'll take a bottle of that. My man's got such a bad cough. It was the gas, you see. These wicked Huns gassed him, so they did. His chest's something terrible now. Such a big strong man he was too, before . . .'

'Anything else?' Mr McClusky interrupted.

'Oh aye. Kitchen Magic pan shine, McDougal's Poppy pipe clay and Reckitt's bag blue.'

Mrs McClusky said, 'You're going to be busy then, hen.'

'Between you and me, Mrs McClusky, that house of mine has never been so clean. My poor man's trying to make himself useful. He's not fit to work, you see, so he tries to help me in the house. He wouldn't like anybody to know about it all the same, so never let on. Did you know I was going out doing stairs now to make a few extra bob? If you need your close done, Mrs McClusky, you know where to find me.'

'Aye. Right, hen.'

Both Annalie and Mrs McClusky had been serving other customers but soon the little rush was over and the shop was empty and quiet again. To pass the time Annalie began dusting and tidying the shelves.

She was thinking about Adam. He was coming tonight to take her to the camp where he thought her mother and baby Elizabeth were. The camp had moved on, but he knew where they'd moved to. She was so excited she didn't know

319

whether to laugh or cry, in fact she'd done both since she'd come to work today.

Mrs McClusky had said, 'You'd better not get too excited, hen. It might not be her. I mean it might be the wrong camp or something for all you know.'

'Adam thought so too,' Annalie told her. 'But he was telling me about what the men had reported back to him. They'd been at the fair in Drymen and saw a woman and child who looked like my mother and Elizabeth, only the woman called the child Darklas so it couldn't have been the right one, they said. But it is, Mrs McClusky.' Annalie had wept with excitement and happiness. 'I know it is because my mother always called my wee girl Darklas.'

Mrs McClusky picked thoughtfully at her false teeth.

'Well I hope for your sake you're right, hen. Have you thought about how you'll manage with a wean, though – I mean, and get out to your work?'

'Och, all the neighbours are very good. They'll help me. There'll be no problem I'm sure.'

'Well, you can always bring her in here if you're stuck,' Mrs McClusky said. 'Never having had any weans myself I'm right fond of them.'

'What!' Mr McClusky howled. 'Bring a wean in here? How do you think we'd get any work done? It's bad enough as it is trying to get things done with you two lazing about under my feet. You'll do no such thing, Annalie. Do you here me? I don't care if you suddenly acquire half a dozen weans, they're not coming in here.'

Mrs McClusky nudged Annalie and, with the little grey whiskers on her face quivering confidentially, she whispered, 'It's his stomach.'

After Adam had arranged to come back and take her to find Elizabeth, Annalie had suddenly remembered the rough-looking men at the camp, and especially the one she had seen looking at her mother in that special kind of way. He had been a lean, fit-looking man in corduroy trousers cut close to the knee for riding horseback. She remembered how tanned his skin was against his yellow-patterned silk neckerchief, and his dark angry eyes and dark hair under a black velour trilby worn without the dent.

'What if they don't let us take Elizabeth?' she'd said to Adam.

'We just take her whether they like it or not,' he said. 'You're the mother and I'm the father.'

'They won't see it like that,' she said. 'The more I think of it Adam, the more I feel sure there's going to be trouble. And there's such awful, rough-looking men there. You might get hurt.'

'Don't worry about me,' Adam said. 'I can look after myself.'

'Yes, with one or two,' she said. 'But with a crowd like that you'd have no chance.'

'All right, all right. If it makes you feel any better,' he said, 'I'll get some of the brickies to stand by just in case.'

'Promise?' she said.

'Promise,' he agreed.

She'd been deliriously happy after that and now Mrs McClusky had promised to let her away early so that she could get changed and be ready for Adam coming to collect her.

Soon she was skipping along Cumberland Street in her impatience to reach home. She passed food queues and was glad she'd got Eck Rafferty to do her messages early that morning. All sugar, chocolate, cocoa, most cheese, wheat, fruit and butter came by ship from overseas. Forty per cent of Britain's meat and even thirty-six per cent of her vegetables also had to be imported. The Germans knew this, of course, and their U-boats were sinking the British merchant ships and making food very scarce. The shortage of grain meant that there was a new bread in the shops made from real flour but mixed with powdered potatoes or beans. This was called standard bread and it was an unpleasant grey colour. Margarine had become a substitute for butter and slogans like 'Save the wheat and help the fleet' and 'Eat less bread' appeared on posters all over the place, urging people not to waste food.

Hillsides and public parks had been ploughed up and

bits of wasteland around the town were being rented out in small sections to tenement dwellers as allotments – on condition that they grew food, usually vegetables, until the war ended.

She'd told Eck just to go into the house and leave her groceries and her change on the kitchen table. She often thought that it was a miracle that any of the Rafferty children could turn out decent, but Eck for one was a hardworking, very obliging lad and as honest as the day was long.

As soon as she arrived home she put the groceries tidily away in her cupboard, put her change in her purse and then began preparing for her bath. She laid out her clean clothes and good shoes, then filled up the bath. She could never quite get used to the incredible luxury of hot running water and being able to step into a bath and stretch out in such luxury. All her life the best she'd had was a cramped zinc bath in front of a kitchen fire. Now everything was sheer ecstasy and perfection. She thanked God and Adam every day for such a blessing.

At times like this, lying back soaping herself and singing lustily in the bath she felt supremely happy and contented, the luckiest girl in the world, in fact. It was only lying in the kitchen bed alone at night that she wept and grieved and tossed restlessly about in a fever of frustration and need.

She was dressed and sweet smelling of cleanliness and baby powder, when Adam arrived.

This time he brought her a bottle of champagne and two real crystal glasses. She knew crystal when she saw it after having worked in Monkton House.

'This,' he said, 'is to celebrate if all goes well this evening and you get your baby back.'

'Champagne!' she clapped her hands, her eyes wide and shining with happiness. 'I've never tasted champagne in my whole life.'

'Well with any luck you'll taste it tonight,' Adam said, and kissed her.

She clung tightly round his neck and pressed her body

against his, but at last he reluctantly pulled away from her, laughing. 'Do you want to go to that camp tonight or not? Any more of this and you won't get the chance. You'll be flung into that bed and that'll be you for the rest of tonight.'

She laughed too. 'No. We'll leave that for later. After we drink our champagne.'

She felt as proud as punch walking from the close with him and then sitting beside him in his car. It was a blustery winter's evening, but the gas lamps were lit and quite a few people were going in and out of the shops in Cumberland Street. Women wrapped cosily in shawls gave her a nod of recognition. Men with jacket collars turned up and white mufflers crossed over their thin chests stared admiringly at the car from underneath their large flat caps. Children danced, mischievously, excitedly around the car and Adam had to sound his horn to chase them away. Then they were off. Bowling down between the black walls of tenements.

She began to sing one of the popular songs of the day, 'Pack up your Troubles in your Old Kit Bag'. He laughed and sang along with her, then they tried 'Here We Are, Here We Are, Here We Are Again' and 'Take Me Back to Dear Old Blighty'.

Soon they had left the tenements behind and were on a dark country road with skeletons of trees etched against a moonlit sky. Annalie was spellbound. She'd never been in the country before. As a child her playground had been the streets of the Gorbals. She'd never even seen the centre of the city until fairly recently and when she did venture into the busy Glasgow streets it was a great adventure which she always savoured with much interest and enjoyment.

The road was snaking towards the hills, the *drom*, as her mother would call it, the line of life. She could see the lights of a village ahead and the twinkling coloured lights of the fairground. As they approached she could see the crowds milling about and hear the music carried by the wind, ragged and intermittent. Now there was the *achin tan* with its bender tents and covered wagons.

Suddenly, Annalie's happy enchantment evaporated. In

its place a premonition, an apprehension of danger was growing.

Chapter Fifty-two

Adam hadn't been home all night, and Christina was tense with worry. Normally if work, or the distance of the work from Glasgow, prevented him from returning home he phoned to tell her so that she could let Cook know how many there would be for dinner. By midnight she was nursing her wrath and certain that he must be with the gypsy girl in the Gorbals.

When she drove to the Gorbals to confirm her suspicions there was no sign of Adam's car in Cumberland Street. She returned to Queens's Park, hardly knowing how she'd got there, she was so distracted. Afraid to undress and go to bed in case there would be a phone call telling her that Adam had been involved in an accident somewhere, she sat stiffly in the shadowy drawing room under a feeble pool of gas light smoking one cigarette after the other. She was tempted to phone the police or the hospitals, but hesitated from doing so in case Adam had just not had an opportunity to phone or had forgotten and would be furious with her for making an unnecessary fuss. Or it could be that he was with Annalie Gordon but had parked his car in another street, in which case he would be even more furious at her for bringing the police into an already volatile situation.

Either way, whether he had forgotten to let her know what had happened or if he had purposely not contacted her because he was with the other woman, she would never forgive him for putting her through this agony of suspense.

Utter exhaustion forced her to go to bed eventually, where she drifted into a restless dreamed-filled sleep. In the morning the first thing she saw was his empty bed. Anger spiced with fear immediately returned, then both were stiffened away by an icy blanket that was akin to shock. She had always been the same for as far back as she could remember. The worse she felt the less she seemed able

325

either to make an outward show of her feelings or to act on them in any way. She ate breakfast in the silent dining room, drank coffee and smoked a cigarette exactly as usual. It was as if this day were no different from any other day.

But within a few minutes she found the telephone directory and jotted down a list of phone numbers of all the major hospitals in Central Glasgow. Then she phoned each one, asking if an Adam Monkton had been admitted. None of them had any record of the name.

Where the hell was he? He couldn't be away on a job, not on a Sunday. He'd never done this before. He'd always found a phone no matter how isolated a building site had been. He had *always* phoned her before, always. And if he couldn't come back the next day he phoned his secretary. It was unforgivable of him to behave in this selfish and thoughtless manner.

Even in the business sense she deserved more consideration than this. She was building up a base of property assets, which was ever increasing her rental income. The tenemental investment was increasing in value as well. In effect she was building up within the family business a financial capital asset base. Apart from that, she was creating business for the maintenance and building side from the repairs and minor work needed for the property that she owned. This was all being done in house, which created a volume of business that the building side didn't need to go out to find. It was more or less guaranteed.

She considered his needs in a business sense as well as every other. Why shouldn't he do the same for her? There were several points she'd wanted to bring up with him today regarding repairs and maintenance on a property she was negotiating at the moment. According to Mathieson it was in a particularly run-down condition and she'd wanted Adam to give her some sort of estimate for the most urgent work before she made a decision, or at least to do some provisional costing. He knew he was supposed to be doing this today. He was holding her up.

Every deal she made was like a juggling exercise with at least six negotiations going on at the same time, and she had to match them all together at the right time one in front of the other. That was the essence of it. It was always very stressful. It had been said that one of the most stressful periods in anyone's life was moving house because it meant putting in an offer for another property while trying to sell the one you had. That was what she did every day. She had nothing against the building side as long as it was efficient. Let Adam get on with it. She didn't need his technical knowledge. She didn't need him. She had the power base of her shares, she had a friendly banker, a knowledgeable agent and a good property factor out there – between them they could guide her through most technicalities. She didn't need to take her jacket off and roll up her sleeves, she was an ideas person. That meant, as far as property was concerned, an ability to look at a site or a building and say, I could do something better with that. What are the market conditions out there? Who might need a building or a piece of land like this? She didn't need Adam. Yet now, without him, she felt paralysed.

She felt suffocated and depressed. She had to get away, but didn't know where to go. She didn't feel able to cope with the questions Beatrice might ask about Adam's where-abouts, nor could she face coping with Simon or her mother and father in the manse. Deep inside her was an icy rage at Adam.

He was with Annalie Gordon. She knew it. He wouldn't get away with this. She would see to it. She would see to it that he would never do this to her again.

She needed air, so she'd go for a drive. She put on her hat and coat – a black cashmere with a high fur collar and cuffs to match – and smoothed on her gloves.

It wasn't the best of days for driving, with fog drifting in from the river and mixing with the soot from tenement chimneys. She could hear ship's foghorns booming and echoing with the kettle-drumming of the riveters in the yards. She felt suddenly painfully lonely as the fog drew her into the dark tunnel of the Glasgow streets.

Chapter Fifty-three

Closer to the fairground now, the music was a noisy jangle. Coloured lights sparkled everywhere, and raucous fairground voices could be heard above the general babble. Crowds of merrymakers milled about, some eating sweets, some enjoying ice cream cones; some with heads thrown back were tipping beer straight from the bottle into their mouths.

Just beyond the fairground and over to one side of it was the *achin' tan*, the gypsy camp. A woman leaning back against one of the covered wagons was wearing a tartan dress and a beaver hat with a large ostrich plume dyed crimson to match the dress. Sitting on a stool nearby was an older woman dressed in black and with soap-stiffened locks sticking forward.

'This is private,' the younger woman said. 'Fairground's over there.'

'My mother's Saviana Lee,' Annalie said. 'Which wagon does she use?'

The woman in black and the younger woman exchanged glances.

'She's doing the *dukkerin* over at the fair.'

Adam said, 'Where's the baby?'

The younger woman shrugged. 'With her, I expect.'

'Don't lie to me,' Adam said. 'She wouldn't take the child into a fortune-telling tent. Not at this time of the night.'

'No harm in it,' the woman said.

'Listen to me,' Adam told her. 'You're probably perfectly well aware of it already, but just in case you're not, that baby is this woman's daughter and we've come to take her home to where she rightfully belongs.'

'There's only gypsy children here,' the old woman said. 'And all sound asleep in bed.'

'Where's my mother's wagon?' Annalie repeated. 'I know my baby's there.'

Now that she had come this far and seeing Elizabeth again was a reality, she couldn't wait to hold her in her arms. The time that she'd been without her suddenly became unbearable. She couldn't suffer another minute of it.

'None of my business,' said the woman. 'You'd better go and see Saviana.'

Adam said, 'We don't need to see anybody and we don't need to waste any time standing here talking to you.' He turned to Annalie then. 'We'll just look inside all the wagons until we find her.'

'Adam.' Annalie caught at his arm.

A little dark-skinned man rose smoothly to his feet like a well-oiled machine.

'Move aside please,' Adam said, moving confidently towards the wagon. The man didn't move. His weight was evenly balanced on the balls of his feet like a dancer. His smouldering dark eyes gave Adam a silent warning.

'Out of my way!' Adam commanded and made to push him aside.

The gypsy's shoulder gave with the push and he pirou-etted smoothly round and to the side as if allowing Adam his way. As he moved however, his right hand shot out with the speed of a striking cobra. Annalie screamed as she saw the glint of firelight glance off the tiny blade. It drove twice up under Adam's armpit.

Grunting in surprise, Adam managed to grab his opponent by the arm and neck and drag him crashing to the ground. Another Rom, grotesquely backlit by the flames of the fire, leapt over the wagon traces and hooked Adam on the side of the head. After the blows to his head Adam lay very still. Pushing an hysterical Annalie roughly aside the two Roms dragged the unconscious form off down the road into the darkness. They took him through the trees and left him on the side of the roadway, then without a word disappeared again, leaving Annalie sobbing by Adam's side.

Despite trembling violently she managed to rip off part

of her white petticoat and stuff it against his body wound in an attempt to stem the flow of blood. It wept like black ink into the white cotton. Distracted, she ran into the road looking one way and the other, praying for some sort of help to come along.

At first she could see nothing and there was no sound. After a few minutes, however, her prayers were answered. She could see in the distance the dark shadowy form of a horse and cart ambling towards them in the slight glow of the carter's pipe. Caught up in an anguish of sobbing she wrung her hands with impatience, willing it to hurry. When it did come nearer she ran towards it.

'There's a man here who has been injured. Oh please help us. Is there a hospital near?'

'There's the cottage hospital,' the man said. 'A couple of miles down the road.'

'Oh could you take us there, please? Oh please.'

'Don't worry, lass. I'll help you.' He climbed down from the cart and came over to where Adam lay. Adam was a big, heftily built man and it was no easy task to lift him onto the cart, but between them they managed it. Annalie then climbed up and sat with Adam's head cradled on her lap. The carter cracked the reins and encouraged the horse into a cumbersome gallop. Annalie and Adam were jerked and jostled about with the movement of the cart as it battered over the poorly surfaced road.

She tried to hold his head steady, kissing his brow and face, smoothing back his hair and whispering to him over and over again, 'You're going to be all right, darling. You're going to be all right.'

The road seemed endless and the rattling and creaking and jarring of the cart created a continuous agony for her. She bent over Adam, trying to hold his shoulders and keep his body still, but it was impossible. She wept at the thought of his life's blood ebbing away.

The hospital was a small, picturesque building set back behind tall trees. The man managed to get the horse and cart right up to the door and in no time white-coated staff were helping him take Adam inside and lift him onto a stretcher trolley before wheeling him away.

The carter had waited to see what was going to happen.

'Anything else I can do for, you?' he asked Annalie as she sat white-faced in the corridor where the nurse had told her to wait.

'Yes,' she said. 'Do you know the building site near here? There'll be a Monkton Builders' sign up.'

'Yes,' he said. 'I pass it often. Many's the time I have a blether with the lads there.'

'Well could you please tell them that Mr Monkton's in this hospital and I'd like to speak to them first thing tomorrow morning. That's if it's not too far out of your way,' she added worriedly.

'No bother,' the man said. 'Don't you worry, lass. I'll tell them all right.' Then suddenly he stopped in his tracks and turned back to her. 'There'll be nobody on the site at this time of night, lass. And tomorrow's Sunday. It might be Monday morning before I find any of them.'

'I was forgetting. Yes. All right. That'll have to do.'

Despite her acute anxiety about Adam, she dozed off occasionally, waking with a start each time and looking around surprised, for a brief moment, to find where she was, then remembering and being overcome with horror and apprehension again. She kept praying for Adam's safe recovery, pleading with God to make him all right again.

At long last, early on Sunday morning, a doctor and a nurse came along the corridor. The doctor told her that they'd treated the stab wounds which luckily had only punctured, the muscle. He explained that Adam's muscularity had in fact saved him from a more serious injury. However he was in a comatose condition due to the severe contusions to the temple. The patient was still in a dangerous condition, he said. It would be a few hours yet before they could give her any definite news. The nurse showed her to a small canteen where she was told she could have breakfast, but she couldn't eat anything. She sat drinking tea for a time and then returned to where she had been sitting. It was the longest day of her life. Night enclosed the place again. She dozed again, until she was awakened by the doctor who this time told her that Adam was going to be all right. He advised her to go home and get some proper rest but before she went she should give the nurse some more particulars.

The doctor went away about his business and the nurse spread some papers out in front of her and said, 'You've given us the patient's name and address. But I don't believe we have a phone number.'

'Adam Monkton,' Annalie repeated. 'Monkton House, Queen's Drive, Queen's Park, Glasgow.' For a minute she hesitated, forgetting the phone number. But then she remembered she had it scribbled on a piece of paper in her purse and she was able to tell it to the nurse.

'Thank you, Mrs Monkton . . .'

'I'm not Mrs Monkton,' Annalie corrected. 'I'm just a friend.'

'Oh, I see.'

The nurse looked taken aback.

'And I'd rather wait here for a little longer if I may. There's someone coming for me first thing in the morning.'

She hoped there was. She hoped too that she could persuade them to return with her to the gypsy camp and help her to get Elizabeth. It was surely the least they could do after letting Adam down on Saturday evening. They were supposed to help him, but more than likely they were at the fair getting drunk.

Her relief that Adam was going to be all right nearly reduced her to tears again. The cup of tea that the nurse brought helped to soothe her, however, and put new strength into her. She had come this far and Adam had risked his life to get her baby. She wasn't going back to Glasgow now without Elizabeth.

Eventually the nurse left her and she fell asleep again, this time deeply. She awoke with a start to see Christina Monkton standing over at the nurse's table, poised and elegant in fur hat and muff. She looked cool and unconcerned. There was no sign whatsoever of any agitation or distress.

She was saying in a calm voice, 'I drove here as soon as

I had your telephone call. Where is my husband? I'd like to see him now.'

'He's still asleep,' the nurse said. 'We'd rather not waken him just yet. It's very early, but Doctor will be making his rounds soon and you'll be able to see him after that. If you just take a seat over there I'll bring you a cup of tea.'

Christina gave Annalie a cold stare.

'I might have known.' she said, 'that you would be at the root of all this trouble, as usual. I warned you before and I'll warn you again. Keep away from my husband.'

Annalie opened her mouth to explain and to defend herself, but changed her mind and said instead, 'Don't worry. I'm just leaving.'

With as much dignity as she could muster she walked past Christina Monkton and outside. In the open, rustic porch there was only one feeble gas lamp. There were no lights in the driveway nor the road beyond. It snaked across the countryside towards the Campsie Hills in one direction and Glasgow, nestling down in the valley, in the other. It was bitterly cold and Annalie began to shiver. Soon, however, she heard noises and saw shadowy figures approaching along the driveway. She couldn't make out how many men there were, even when they crowded around the porch, but there was a considerable number. They were a tough-looking bunch. Some of the Irish navvies reminded her of Patrick Rafferty.

'What happened?' one of them asked in a broad Glasgow accent. 'Where's Mr Monkton?'

'Where were you lot on Saturday night is more to the point.' Annalie said. 'You were supposed to help him, but he went into the camp alone and he was attacked there, stabbed. He's also got a serious head injury. Fortunately it looks as if he's going to recover. I don't know if you lot realize it but he's a brave man, and a kind one as well. He went in there alone to try and get my baby back for me. She was kidnapped and I asked if he could help. He promised he would and he kept his promise, at least by trying his best, which is more than you lot did for him.'

The man looked shamefaced. 'We're sorry about that, Missus. It was just a wee misunderstanding about the place.'

'Oh yes,' Annalie said sarcastically. 'Got lost did you?'

'Look, we'll make up for it now. Those gypsy bastards are not going to get away with this. And we'll get your wean back for you as well.'

'You don't know Elizabeth,' Annalie said. 'So I'll have to come along with you.'

And so they set off with Annalie striding out at the front and the men marching behind her, impatient for retribution and revenge.

Chapter Fifty-four

A watery daylight had spread over the land by the time they neared the gypsy camp. Fire smoke spiralled up, dark grey against pale.

Word of their approach had obviously reached the camp because men were emerging from bender tents and jumping down from wagons. As they drew near Annalie caught a glimpse of her mother disappearing into the back of one of the wagons.

'You see to the Romes,' she shouted. 'I'm going to fetch my baby.'

Hitching up her skirt she ran full pelt towards the wagon and leapt up onto it.

'How could you put me through such agony?' she cried out to her mother as she made to run towards the sleeping child in the corner. Saviana barred her way, arms akimbo.

Seeing her again, Annalie was reminded what a handsome woman she was – and one who possessed the strength of three women, by the looks of her. Nevertheless, Annalie wasn't deterred. From outside the wagon came shouts and scuffling and thumps and grunts of men fighting, nearly drowning Annalie's words.

'You're not going to stop me. I'm taking her home.'

'She belongs here,' Saviana said. 'Among her own people. She doesn't belong with *gaujos*.'

'Don't be silly. She's my child and she belongs with me. Now get out of my way. I'm taking her with me.'

Annalie strode forward but was stopped in her tracks by a blow to her face which made her gasp for breath.

'You get out of my wagon,' Saviana said. 'Get out of this camp and never come back.'

'Not without Elizabeth,' Annalie managed, catching hold of her mother's arm and trying to jerk her aside, only to be

335

felled to the floor this time. The second blow hurt even more than the first and set fire to Annalie's temper.

'You rotten, heartless bitch!' she screamed. 'You've never cared about me. Right from the start.' She struggled to her feet, lashing out at Saviana.

At the same time the child awoke and screamed in fright.

'It's all right, darling,' Annalie cried out, half sobbing despite her anger. 'It's only Mummy. It's Mummy, darling. Don't cry, please don't cry.'

Saviana had Annalie's arm in a vicelike grip now and was hauling her backwards. Realizing that she was on the point of being thrown out of the wagon, Annalie dug her nails into her mother's arm and hung on, making them both tumble from the wagon together. They rolled on the earth, hair and fists, skirts and feet flying.

The gypsy men were spread out in front of the wagons brandishing an assortment of weapons from small sparkling stilettos to heavy kitchen knives. Undeterred, the brickies fanned out, the sharp crunching of beer bottles being broken punctuating the silence. Armed now with a mixture of bottles, heavy brass-buckled belts, pickaxe handles and the occasional knuckleduster, they launched themselves at the gypsy men.

Then all was chaos, roaring, screaming, the meaty thwack of wood on bone. Men lashed out, shadowy forms in the pale dawn light. Others rolled together grappling and panting through the smoking embers of the fires. Horses stamped and snorted in fear at the commotion.

Saviana was beaten. Annalie's temper had not spared her. She had youth on her side. While her mother lay on the ground gasping for breath, Annalie jumped up onto the wagon again and gathered Elizabeth into her arms.

As she ran across to rejoin the building workers who were warily withdrawing from the fray, Saviana screamed after her, '*Gaujo!* You're no daughter of mine. I disown you from this moment on. You've seen the last of Saviana Lee.'

Ignoring her, Annalie said to one of the men as they left the camp, 'How do I get back to Glasgow, I wonder?'

336

'You'll get a bus at the road end. We'll wait with you until it comes.'

'Thanks for your help,' she said. 'You're bonny fighters.'

The man laughed. 'You're a bonny fighter yourself, hen.'

She had baby Elizabeth wrapped in her coat and when the bus eventually arrived she sat all the way to Glasgow cradling her on her knee, patting her, soothing her, singing a lullaby under her breath to her, until the little girl fell asleep again. Annalie had to get another bus from the centre of town out to the Gorbals and by the time she reached home she was utterly exhausted.

Her happiness over getting Elizabeth back was only marred by the thought of Adam's injuries and the knowledge that Christina would be at his side throughout his fight for complete recovery.

The last time Adam had visited her he had brought her toys for the baby in readiness for her return and so, when Elizabeth wakened, Annalie was able to comfort and intrigue her with a beautiful doll and a teddy bear. She cuddled the child and teddy together and played with her, sang and danced for her and made her laugh. Soon it was as if they had never been separated.

Not wanting to be parted from her ever again even for a day or an hour, Annalie took Elizabeth with her to the shop next day. Mrs McClusky was enchanted. '

What a beautiful wee girl.'

Elizabeth favoured her with an enchanting smile.

'Oh my,' Mrs McClusky said, 'I've never seen such a lovely wee girl – what beautiful black curls and lovely big dark eyes. And that lovely smile. She's your double, Annalie.'

Annalie laughed. She was so happy she could have danced all round the shop. Indeed, she did break into a little dance.

Mr McClusky said, 'Has this place turned into a madhouse? Have you come here to work or have you just dropped in to give us a show?'

Mrs McClusky's bewhiskered face creased apologetically

and she silently mouthed, 'It's his stomach.' To Elizabeth she said, 'Would you like a wee biscuit, hen?'

'I don't think she knows what a biscuit is,' Annalie laughed. 'As far as I know she's never had one.'

'Well you're going to have one now, hen. I'll find a really nice one for you.'

'That's right.' Mr McClusky said, 'give the stock away, ruin me as well.'

Annalie laughed again and began helping him with the papers.

Elizabeth proved to be no trouble at all and before the day was out Mrs McClusky was absolutely besotted with her. Annalie noticed that even Mr McClusky had given her a surreptitious pat on the head as he passed on more than one occasion. So at the end of the day she said to them both, 'Would you mind very much if, for a week or two at least, I kept bringing Elizabeth in? Just till she gets properly settled with me.'

'Of course, hen,' Mrs McClusky said. 'The wee soul was absolutely no bother, was she?' she appealed to Mr McClusky for confirmation. The corners of his sour mouth drooped lower, but at least he made no objection as he fussed about serving a customer.

Teeny Docherty was a particular torment to him.

'There was something else, I'm sure,' Teeny said worriedly.

'Will you hurry up for goodness' sake, woman' he said irritably.

'Oh aye. I think it was A1 Soap Powder. Or . . . wait a minute. Was it a bottle of Parazone? I think maybe it was Parazone, Mr McClusky. But if it wasn't can I bring it back?'

'No you cannot bring it back. Here you are, one bottle of Parazone. Now is that all?'

'Eh er . . . Hang on a wee tick, will you?' Teeny looked anxiously all round the shop. 'I've a feeling there was something else, Mr McClusky. If you just give me a minute or two.

'I've given you at least half an hour already.'

'I think it was something for weans. It could have been sweeties. Or could it be ginger, do you think? They like their drink of ginger.'

'Aye,' Mrs McClusky interrupted. 'It'll be ginger, hen. They like the Irn Bru.'

'Oh so they do, Mrs McClusky.' Teeny looked relieved. 'Right oh. I'll have a bottle of Irn Bru, Mr McClusky. And I think that'll do me.'

'Well thank God for that,' he said after Teeny left the shop. 'I'm not surprised her man batters her. I often feel like battering her myself.'

'He doesn't mean it,' Mrs McClusky explained to Annalie. 'He wouldn't hurt a fly.'

Annalie laughed. Spontaneous, joyous laughter was always bubbling to the surface now. She was so happy to have her baby back. They were never apart now, night or day. At night she would cuddle into the child in the kitchen bed after singing her lullabies, and even when Elizabeth was sleeping Annalie would lovingly shower kisses onto her dark curls and soft face. The only thing that would have made her happiness complete was if Adam had been with her.

She longed for him, not only for herself but for Elizabeth's sake. She wanted him to see the child and to love her and be as proud of her as she was. She was worried about him too and she had phoned the hospital several times. Eventually she had been told that he had made a good recovery and had gone home to convalesce. She had longed to phone Monkton House and see how he was progressing, but thought better of it. She knew it would anger him if she intruded into his other life.

It still frustrated as well as saddened her to think of this attitude of his. She knew at the same time that she was being unreasonable to expect anything else. She didn't see why it was, however, that if they loved each other they shouldn't be together for always. He would have to make a choice sooner or later, and the sooner the better as far as she was concerned.

She still dreamed dreams of being a fine lady and living in a mansion and having her children go to posh, private schools and enjoy all the good things of life.

Elizabeth must never have to endure the deprivations that her mother had to cope with in the Gorbals. Elizabeth must get her chance in life. She must not be trapped in poverty, ill health and ignorance as so many good, kind people were in the Gorbals and other poor districts of Glasgow. Few, if any, ever had the chance of breaking out of this trap. Elizabeth's only chance was through Adam. Surely when he came next time and saw the child he would love her. The very next time she would force the issue to a head once and for all.

'It's the minister's daughter or me,' she would say.

Chapter Fifty-five

Christina enjoyed the challenge of taking over the building side for the couple of weeks Adam was off work. She studied tenders and estimates for jobs and had several meetings with the manager. As a result she obtained a wider understanding of the building side.

The kind of contracts they did now, thanks to Adam, were much bigger than those the firm had tackled in prewar days. They still did the basic types of work they had done for many years and on which the company had been built – every kind of maintenance and alteration, carpentry, plumbing, electrical work and roofing. They also repainted rooms and on several occasions had built on small additions.

'It seems to me you've solved the immediate problem,' Christina said at one meeting with the manager. 'What I think you want in the long run, is more foremen. If you had a really good foreman all the time on these two jobs that we've been discussing, then surely you wouldn't have to spend so much time dashing about. You could concentrate more on the planning side.'

'It's not like it was in the old days,' McAndrews said. 'I don't know where all the decent people in the building trade have gone.'

'Of course you do,' Christina said. 'It's obvious, isn't it?'

McAndrews sighed. 'The war's changed everything. All right. I'll advertise and see what happens. I wouldn't pin any hopes on the results.'

'I'd be much keener to promote some of our existing people,' Christina said. 'You've told me you've got some good, sensible craftsmen.'

'That's true,' McAndrews replied. 'But none of them look like foremen.'

'I wouldn't have thought,' Christina said, 'that they would

until they *were* foremen. It's your job to convince them that they can, and indeed will become, foremen.'

McAndrews opened his mouth to say something, then stopped as if thinking better of it. After a few moments he said, 'All right, I'll give it a try. There are a couple of quite conscientious types that might fit the bill in time if I persevere with them.'

She suspected that he had been about to say something like 'What do you know about it? – a mere woman.' But either he'd lost his nerve or he had heard something of her reputation and felt she might know more than he gave her credit for. One way or another, she had acquired a knack of gaining respect in business circles.

She hadn't met with much resistance from the other board members when she announced that she was taking over. They knew, of course, that she had Adam's proxy vote to back her up and he, being the next biggest shareholder, would have carried the proposal. Apart from that, however, it was as Adam had always said. The other members were quite content for the most part to collect their directors' salaries and the interest on their shares without doing very much to earn either. What they could get out of the business in terms of financial gain was really all that interested them.

It meant more than that to her, and Adam knew it.

She had managed to refrain from mentioning the gypsy girl to him and from questioning him about the circumstances in which he had acquired his injuries. When she felt he had fully recovered she would speak to him, meantime she could wait. The incident would give her a very good lever with which to force him to stop his illicit relationship with the girl. By the looks of things he was the only one who could stop it as the girl had obviously no intention of doing so. It had to come to an end. There was no doubt about that.

Adam was normally a down to earth, sensible kind of man and if Christina had been a superstitious woman she would have believed that Annalie Gordon had cast some sort of spell on him to make him behave as he had.

Sometimes, sitting at her desk, fingering her pencil or

eraser, she would wish that she could write Annalie Gordon off or rub her out completely – anything to make her disappear from their lives. She and Adam would get on all right if it wasn't for her. They were building quite a good relationship together now. They talked together. Admittedly their talk was mostly about business, but in that area he was acquiring a growing respect for her. He was very fond of Jason and now that there was another child on the way, if the new baby was another son it would strengthen the ties she had with Adam. He wanted sons to carry on the business. It was a good business, well worth carrying on from generation to generation.

She was somewhat disturbed to discover, however, that Adam was allowing bricklayers to work on the Sabbath. She tackled him about it in the evening and he'd explained that Iron Masters needed the brick walls of their furnaces repaired and Sunday was the only day of the week the fires were allowed to burn low. The intense heat and the danger involved in working in the furnaces meant it was an unpopular job, but somebody had to do it. Christina saw his point, but she was still unhappy about it.

'Well,' she told him, 'all I can say is, I hope my father never finds out. He has enough to worry him just now with Simon without him fearing that you and I are destined for perdition because we allow people to work on the Sabbath.'

Her respect and admiration for Adam grew when she examined all the contracts for which he had been responsible. He had built five different camps for the War Office. There was the pier for the Fisheries Board and the Board of Agriculture for Scotland. There was the work in France. There was the National Filling Factory for the Ministry of Munitions. There was the Shore Depot for the Admiralty. There was a canteen. There was a chemical works, to mention but a few in these past years, and all this, she realized, in an industry that was in general very backward in technology. All concrete was mixed by hand, all materials were hoisted on a jenny-wheel hand-operated crane or carried by hod. All bricks were carted by horse and cart, and bricklayers' mortar was made in a roller pan, generally at a depot, and carted by horse and cart to the various sites. Monkton's had only recently acquired a concrete mixer and a steam-operated crane, one of the first in Scotland to do so. Before he had adopted the new machinery, however, he had made sure it justified itself financially. He had also worked out the effect of mechanization on employment.

As she studied the books and papers she became more and more impressed by the tendering and costing system he had developed. It was backed by a first-class control of labour productivity and the use of materials. He had started a new system of costing while buildings were in the course of erection. The process of traditional house building, for instance, was split up into a series of separate operations and the expenditure in man hours, materials and money was measured continuously. One of his tenders, she discovered, had been so competitive with other contractors and the government department was so surprised by it, that he was warned by them that he would certainly lose money. He was even given the opportunity to withdraw. He had confidently refused, however, and carried out the work at a profit. Now she realized why he had to travel about so much and work such long hours. He did all the costing himself. She made a mental note to talk to him about this and suggest that he start to train at least one tenderer. Tough and energetic as he was, if he went on like this and the firm continued with its present growth rate, he would work himself into the ground.

Even in the short time that she had taken to go round the different sites it was obvious that working conditions in the industry in general were atrocious and the Monkton firm was no exception. Nothing was done to alleviate harsh conditions when the weather was bad, and feeding facilities on the sites were confined to the brazier. There were no paid holidays and employment could be terminated at one hour's notice for a labourer and two for a tradesman. If time was lost because of rain or frost, pay was lost as well. It was a hire and fire industry of ruthless competition where the weakest went to the wall. The work was tough, the men

344

were tough and she could see now why Adam had to be tough.

Chief sport of the navvies at weekends was fist fights, after the drink had worn off. Men like that would have had no respect for a leader who was a weakling. As it turned out it was Adam's natural and cultivated physical fitness that had saved his life. The doctor at the hospital had said the injuries he'd received both to his head and internally, and the bleeding that had been caused by the stabbing, would have killed most men. He was only allowed out of hospital on the promise that he would recuperate in bed at home for at least a couple of weeks. Already, however, he was getting up and prowling restlessly about the house, much to Christina's anxiety and annoyance. Indeed, he would have been back at work had it not been for the express orders to the contrary of the doctor and the desperate pleadings of Beatrice and herself. She had assured him that he had no need to worry. Everything was under control. She wasn't putting a foot wrong.

A humorous quirk had twitched at the corner of his mouth when he'd said, 'You'd better not. To err is human, to forgive is not company policy.'

She loved his occasional flashes of humour. She loved his toughness and capacity for hard work. She loved his tenderness with their son. She loved his sharp business acumen. She loved his sense of justice and fair play. More and more she loved and admired everything about him.

She toyed with the idea of going to see Annalie Gordon again. No doubt the girl did not know that she was pregnant. The loose-fitting, loosely belted tube dresses that were so fashionable just now were useful for hiding the condition. The coat she had been wearing when Annalie Gordon had last seen her had been a loose-fitting, wide-skirted garment which was also efficient in disguising the pregnant state. She mentally stiffened away from the idea of another visit. She could not bear it to appear as if she were coming to plead with the girl or to seek pity. There had to be another way.

Christina spent a long time sitting at her desk, twisting at her pencil, staring into space and trying to think of one.

Chapter Fifty-six

Adam had only been back at work for a few days when it was decided that his mother had to go to hospital for a minor surgical investigation. As far as they knew she had suffered no pain, but, as she'd confided in Ada, there had been a little bleeding and the doctor had suggested they try to find the root of the problem. To Adam and Christina she'd only mentioned that she had developed a little internal problem that would soon be put right in the local hospital for women. Adam had booked her into a private room and made sure she had the best attention that money could buy. He was very shocked when she died under the anaesthetic. They all were. Even Mitchell was visibly shaken. Ada was quite devastated.

Beatrice's body had been brought home and her coffin lay in the bedroom she'd once shared with Moses Monkton. Curtains were drawn across the windows, enclosing the house in muffled silence. A steady stream of people came to pay their last respects and spoke in subdued tones about what a beautiful and elegant woman she'd always been – except old Martha Monkton, who informed everyone in a loud voice that it looked as if she was going to outlive them all.

The Reverend Gillespie had conducted the funeral service and afterwards a funeral tea was served in Monkton House for all the family and a few close friends. Simon was there, a frail trembling figure like a bent old man. Both Ada and the Reverend Gillespie kept eyeing him anxiously, apprehensively, unable to be sure at any time how he might behave.

Christina felt worried about both her parents, but especially her mother. Ada seemed to have shrunk, and her eyes – usually filled with a compassionate, sympathetic expression – where dark with suffering. In common with most people now, her enthusiasm for the war had gone. Apart from her experience within her own family she had visited too many grieving women, mothers who had lost their sons at the Somme and other battles.

She told Christina, 'I kept imagining them in their loneliness, grieving and remembering the prattle of their little children long ago. Boys who are now lying in graves in France and Flanders. These mothers that I see, Chrissie, are not only grieving and miserable, they're rebellious in spirit. I see their mood in the strained expression in their eyes, in their unshed tears. There's such a rage in their hearts at what they regard as the purposeless sacrifice of their sons, lost, wasted.'

The waste didn't look to be anywhere near ending, either. The whole country, the whole world it seemed, was deep in a terrible nightmare from which where was no awakening.

Christmas 1916 and New Year 1917 had been a miserable time for all of them although Christina and Adam tried to make something of Christmas for Jason's sake. They put up a tree and exchanged presents and had Jason with them for Christmas lunch. Now one and a half years old, he was a bright and active little boy, very excited to be allowed in the drawing room and the dining room for the unusually long time. He made Christina and Adam laugh by dancing around the tree, wide-eyed and flushed with delight. They laughed too at his squeals of childish pleasure as each parcel was opened and the way he rushed at them both in turn to hang round their necks and kiss them as they both sat on the floor surrounded by a sea of coloured paper and presents.

It was with relief and thankfulness that Christina decided that Adam was no longer seeing Annalie Gordon. He had been away from home as usual on different jobs and so he could have had ample opportunity to visit the girl. However she had made a few discreet inquiries from time to time, helped by a private detective. He had reported that Adam had been exactly where he was supposed to be.

'You're perfectly certain?' she'd asked the detective, 'that he made no visits to the Gorbals when he was supposed to be away on one of these jobs?'

'Yes,' the detective assured her. 'On each occasion he went to the site and did his day's work. Then he went to his local digs and didn't reappear till early morning when he started work again.'

Grateful for this change in his behaviour she had responded by being as sympathetic and supportive as she could at the time of his mother's death and since. She felt sorry for him because she could see in the darkening of his eyes and the tightness of his mouth that he was suffering. His way of coping was to fling himself all the more energetically into his work.

In that area of their lives they had now reached the stage where there were able to talk quite freely. They listened to each other with interest. They didn't always agree with what the other said, but they discussed each proposal or idea and gave it serious consideration. He had taken up her idea of training someone in the tendering and costing, and had now engaged a young man and had started training him. There was no danger of losing the man to military service because Richardson had been exempted from military service on medical grounds. She had not asked what the medical grounds were. He looked healthy enough.

On Christina's side of the business, she had been investing in more land. She had bought up some farms on the outskirts of Glasgow, though one of them was quite far away from the city. Mathieson had become increasingly worried about this.

'You're collecting white elephants here. What building could there ever be so far out of town? All you'll be able to do is to try to sell to another farmer and I can't see you doing that. Obviously the original farms have failed.'

'I'm following my instincts more than anything here,' Christina had told him.

Mathieson groaned. 'Oh no. Don't tell me you're going all feminine on me and starting to work on the basis of female intuition? Believe me, you'll get nowhere in business that way.'

'At the same time,' she said, 'there's some method in my madness. The way I see it, towns expand. They grow bigger. They don't shrink and become smaller, do they?'

Mathieson still looked uncertain and worried, and Christina went on. 'And if the population of Glasgow does grow and the town does expand new houses will be needed and new land on which to build them. I've seen how desperately overcrowded the centre of Glasgow and the poorer suburbs are. At some point somebody will have to do something about that problem.'

Mathieson said, 'The poor are there because of lack of moral fibre. The root of the overcrowding and the conditions of housing of the poor is thriftlessness and intemperance and want of self-respect by most of them.'

'Maybe so,' Christina said. 'Although,' she added dryly, 'I can't help thinking it must be rather difficult to have high moral standards when you're living practically on top of each other like that.'

'I still think,' Mathieson repeated, 'that you're making a mistake in laying out so much capital in acquiring these run-down farm properties.'

'I thought I made it only too plain,' Christina said. 'It's not the properties I'm interested in, in these particular deals. It's the land. One day someone's going to want that land and want it badly.'

'Your intuition again, I suppose?' Mathieson said.

'Call it what you like. It's probably I've just got used to taking a long-term view.'

'Well,' Mathieson said, 'I hope you can hang on long enough. You've laid out a lot of money without any immediate prospect of an income from it.'

'I realize that,' Christina said. 'My other holdings will just have to cover it.'

She knew she was taking a big risk. As far as she was concerned, however, risk-taking was what the property business was all about. That, plus imagination and cool nerves.

Towards the latter part of her pregnancy she was doing most of her business by phone at home in Monkton House. The house depressed her. It was still too much in Beatrice's taste. Only the morning room had been redecorated and furnished to her own taste. She vowed that once her pregnancy was over she would start having alterations done to the decor of every other part of the house. She also planned structural alterations – a conservatory added to the back, for instance.

Little day-to-day domestic concerns and also the problems of the manse encroached more on her time while she was working from home. She became more aware of newspaper headlines too and the general news of the war. The Germans had recommenced their unrestricted submarine warfare, and food had become scarce. Washington had severed diplomatic relations with Berlin. There was the fall of Baghdad and the beginning of the February revolution in Russia. There was the first battle of Gaza when America entered the war. Shortly after that the Arras offensive began and Vimy Ridge was stormed. The Nivelle offensive also began and all the time men continued to be slaughtered. A whole generation of men was disappearing.

She went into labour very unexpectedly and had to depend on Mitchell to help her upstairs to bed and phone for the doctor. Before Adam had returned from work that evening she had been delivered of twins, both boys. Adam was pleased and proud, she hadn't seen him look so happy for so many months.

'We'll have to get a nursery maid to help Mitchell,' she told him.

He readily agreed, although he said, 'Why do you keep calling her Mitchell? She's Nanny to Jason and Nanny Monkton to everyone else. You know perfectly well that's her proper title.'

She knew he was right, but she shrank from any closeness with the woman and 'Mitchell' seemed to keep her more at arm's length. She had to admit to herself that Mitchell had been very supportive during her pregnancy. She was efficient and dependable and had relieved her of quite a few of the responsibilities of running the household.

'I'll try,' she told Adam. 'It's just that I've got so used to the name Mitchell.'

After that, every time she said the word 'Mitchell' Adam corrected her until she capitulated and became used to the more usual term.

They called the boys Daniel after Adam's grandfather and William after her father.

She felt proud of her sons herself and when the midwife brought them both to her, one cradled in each arm, she smiled with satisfaction at them. She and Adam and their three sons. They were a solid family group now. They were unassailable. Her place as wife and mother was secure. For the first time she completely trusted Adam and felt safe.

Chapter Fifty-seven

Over and over again Monkton kept telling himself that he couldn't go on endlessly having his cake and eating it. The fact that he had a wife and three children now to think about made his self-indulgence with Annalie seem all the more reprehensible. He still loved Annalie. There was no getting away from the fact, but such was his desperation at times, he almost wished she could find someone else. At the same time he felt an agony of jealousy at the thought. He knew perfectly well it wasn't fair to her to keep her dangling on like this with no hope of any further development to their relationship yet there was no way that he was going to consider affecting the security and happy future of his children. For that reason alone he had no intention of leaving Christina. But Elizabeth was his child too and he loved her just as much as his sons.

He was furious when he discovered that Christina was having him followed by a local detective. The last time he'd set out for the Gorbals he noticed the man. As a result instead of visiting Annalie as he'd intended he made a detour to one of his nearby building sites. On arrival at the site the man was obviously still hovering in the background. Hardly up to the best Hollywood standards, Monkton thought with grim humour.

His feelings of being trapped intensified as did his resentment against Christina. Yet at the same time he knew he no longer had any right to feel such indignation against her. He struggled to contain his rage and instead of tackling her about the detective he enjoyed a perverted satisfaction in defeating her objective in this. He stopped going to the Gorbals for a time. Instead he sent Annalie a ticket to Oban where he would be working on a job for a week. He booked her in at the same small boarding house where he would be staying and saw even more of her and Elizabeth. It was wonderful coming home to her every evening, helping her to bathe Elizabeth, then playing with the child afterwards, telling her a story and putting her to bed.

'Story Dada,' was the nightly cry. 'Story Dada.'

Then there were the long nights with Annalie in the double bed, where their lovemaking alternated between feverishly passionate and joyously playful. Her cries and squeals either of passion or of laughter shattered the silent darkness of the house. He joined in her noisy exuberance, not caring who heard them, trying to hush her only when he feared they would waken Elizabeth in the next room.

Having Annalie with him became like an addictive drug. That first time at Oban much to his irritation he had noticed the detective again. He took some satisfaction in the fact that the man had to hang about outside while he for most of the time was comfortable and warm in the site office.

After Oban there had been no sign of the detective and Monkton was able to relax with Annalie more often, although always, at the back of his mind, was the remorse, the guilt, the confusion of continuing such duplicity. More and more it was a relief to escape from both women and spend time in the gym purging his pent-up emotions either by doing some bagwork or sparring with one of the men. Quite often he dropped in to the boy's gym in the Gorbals, although somehow that made him feel worse. It reminded him how decent Christina could be and increased his shame. Recently she'd acquired another empty shop as part of her tenement property and she'd made this available as premises for a girls' club.

He hadn't been too happy going to his local gym either, recently. He'd been looking forward with great confidence to big Geordie's bout with a Jap fighter known as the Yellow Peril. He'd backed Geordie with quite a large sum of money and believed he was at least competent enough to give a good show of himself with the Jap. It turned out that Geordie's strength did him no good. The Jap played with him like a cat with a mouse, doing just what he liked. The more Geordie exerted himself the more he fell down, first one way then the other. Monkton soon lost count of the falls and all hopes of Geordie gaining a single one. The Jap won easily, and Geordie put up with some severe punishment before he collapsed.

Sometimes Monkton found release in driving his car as fast as it was capable of going. At other times he galloped his horse furiously along country roads and across fields. That was what helped him most. He loved the feeling of freedom and control that speed gave him. He flung himself into his work too, concentrating all his attention on it – at least he tried to, but didn't always succeed. Sometimes his personal frustrations and anger would boil over, putting him on a short fuse with the men. The truth was, no matter what he did or where he was, his mind, his heart, his life – everything – was in constant turmoil.

To add to his confusions he had come to realize that, in a way, he loved Christina too. He supposed, looking back, he had always had a certain brotherly fondness for her. Since their marriage, despite their differences they'd shared more than just memories of youthful affection. They shared a home and a lot of time together. They shared business interests. They had their children in common. Despite his recurring anger against her the bonds between them had strengthened over the years. There were occasions now when he even became short-tempered and aggressive with Annalie, but his temper only sparked off her temper. They fought tooth and nail only to end up in each other's arms again, their making-up more passionate, more intimate than ever.

Sometimes she gave him a massage. They massaged each other – ordinary massage and erotic massage. There was the feather-light stroking, moving their hands so that their fingertips were barely brushing against each other's skin, working up and down the entire length of each body sometimes slowly, sometimes a little faster, sometimes in straight lines, sometimes in waves, circles or spirals. Feet were massaged by running one finger slowly all the way in and out between each pair of toes. Next the fingers smoothed up the legs until one hand was working in tiny circles around the tip of the tail bone, before working lightly down to the genitals and back firmly around the tail bone again.

He massaged her vagina by pressing lightly with both thumb tips together straight upwards to the top of the vaginal inner lip. Then he separated his thumbs, one going to the right, one to the left. He brought them down between the inner and outer lips all the way to the perineum. With her forefingers, one to the right and one to the left she followed the edges of the scrotum to the base of the penis, continued on to the penis until she brought the tips of each forefinger together again at the base of the underside. Then she moved both forefingers together straight up the length of the penis and down to the opposite side of the head. She separated her fingers again and followed the ridge round to the underside of the penis again. With her fingertips once more together she went back down the penis, around the scrotum all the way back to the perineum over and over again, without stopping.

Yet something had to stop.

Chapter Fifty-eight

There was a fight going on about whose turn it was to do the stairs. It was the factor's orders that the stairs and the close had to be washed once every week and each tenant had to take a turn. The trouble lay as usual in the middle flat. Teeny Docherty was a right slitter. Every stair had one. Not only was her house a mess, but when it came to her turn of the stairs, if she remembered to do it, she made a right mess of that as well.

'All she does,' Mamie Patterson accused, 'is slosh water about. She never even wrings her cloth out properly. Never once have I seen her pipeclaying the sides. But, as if that wasn't bad enough, half the time she never takes her turn. It's her turn today and she's just trying to wriggle out of it.'

'No I'm not,' Teeny Docherty said. 'I honestly think that I did it last week, hen.'

'Well you're thinking wrong, I'm telling you. I did it last week. And the week before for old Mrs Sweeney. That stair's always perfect. There's not a spot on it when I'm finished with it. And you're the one on the stair that has all the weans as well.' This was an accusation that Teeny couldn't deny.

'Aye,' Mamie's husband Jimmy said as he returned up the stairs from the back yard where he had been emptying the bucket for his wife. 'I'll say that for you, hen, you're the best one at washing the stairs and cleaning the house. She's never done cleaning,' he said, turning to Teeny and Annalie. 'Dirt's her enemy, but she'll never conquer it.'

'Och, get in the house you silly wee nyaff,' his wife told him, 'and don't talk with that cigarette in your mouth. It's always wobbling about your face and dropping ash all over the place. You wouldn't get John Reid doing that. He smokes a pipe like a man and never once have I seen him drop a bit of tobacco or ash any place at any time.'

Annalie with Elizabeth in her arms had earlier been making some attempt to referee the argument, but now she said, 'Well I'll have to leave you to it. It's time I was up the stairs getting ready for my work.'

'I'm surprised you need to work,' Mamie said. 'You with your well-off fancy man.'

'Jealous are you, Mamie?' Annalie said.

Teeny gave a big toothless grin. 'Wish I had a well-off fancy man.'

'I would have thought you'd have enough with the man you've got,' Mamie said. 'What would you be wanting another man for?'

'I suppose it's not so much the man,' Teeny confessed. 'It's more just being well-off. That's what I'd like to be. I'd maybe put up with a well-off old man with a bad cough.' She favoured them with an even wider gumsy grin.

'You're not well-off,' Mamie said. 'And until you are and you can pay somebody to wash your stairs for you, you'll have to do it and you'd better start doing it right now.'

'But are you sure I didn't do them last week, Mamie? I thought . . .'

Annalie went upstairs and into her own house, laughing to herself. She was feeling very happy. She'd had a nice dinner round at Aunty Murn's. Nobody could beat Aunty Murn at making soup. Elizabeth had enjoyed it too.

Annalie put the child down on the floor and gave her her teddy and one of the dolls that Adam had brought her. Then she set about preparing vegetables and a milk pudding for their evening meal. She was usually too tired to be bothered when she came home at night. She was working from one o'clock till nine. She also laid out clean clothes for the morning and Elizabeth's night clothes. Then she banked up the fire, swept the floor and did a bit of dusting before giving herself a wash. After brushing and arranging her hair she donned her long-sleeved white blouse and long black skirt, which she felt was a smart outfit for serving in the shop. She had been working about the house in her bare feet. Now she put on her boots and laced them up, singing happily to herself as she did so.

Things were working out much better between her and Adam. They were not yet as she wanted them to be – but they were going in the right direction. He not only managed to see her fairly regularly when he was in Glasgow, but when he was away on a job he now took her with him.

He had warned her that he would not be able to travel with her nor probably go out with her. 'I'll be working most of the time, he said. 'From early morning till probably quite late at night. But at least I'll see you at night and we'll sleep together and I'll feel happier that you and Elizabeth will get a break away from here. Fresh country air or the seaside will do you both good. While I'm at work you can take Elizabeth for a walk out into the country. Or if it's the seaside we're at take her along the shore. Enjoy yourself. As long as you won't mind being by yourself during the day.'

She had been ecstatically happy and showered him with kisses and danced round the kitchen with him. She enjoyed being away and seeing different places. But more than anything else, what made her happy was that he actually wanted her to be with him. She had never felt more close to him, never more like his wife in everything but name. And he'd really taken to Elizabeth.

'I've never seen such a beautiful child,' he said. 'And she's so good-natured.'

Another time she'd caught him looking in a very serious way at the child and she had asked why he looked so worried.

'I was just thinking,' he said, 'that a beautiful child like her shouldn't have to be brought up in the Gorbals.'

'I couldn't agree more,' Annalie had told him.

He'd said no more then, but she believed he had continued thinking along these lines. It made her so happy that she could have sung out loud. Often she did and danced around with sheer exuberance and joy. One day, she felt sure, he was going to make a choice without her needing to press him, and he was going to choose to be with her and Elizabeth – to share his life with them, not just occasionally but all the time.

Soon! Soon! she kept singing to herself. Often she said it out loud and Elizabeth began repeating the word too. Then they would both laugh together. It was so wonderful having her baby back with her again. She was never lonely now.

'Come on, darling,' she said to Elizabeth. 'Time to go and see Mr and Mrs McClusky now. You like them, don't you? Oh dear,' she said as the child yawned, 'you're a sleepy wee girl, aren't you? Never mind, you'll have your afternoon nap in Mrs McClusky's back shop. Mummy'll take her shawl with her and that'll do to wrap you in and keep you nice and cosy.'

All was quiet as they went downstairs, or as quiet as a tenement stair ever could be. There was the tinkling and clattering of dishes and cutlery as Mrs Reid set the table for her man's dinner – which today was sausage, cabbage and potato, by the smell of it. Andy Baxter was playing 'Roses of Picardy' on his piano accordion. Teeny and Mamie had disappeared inside their respective homes. Teeny, no doubt, had capitulated and promised to do the stairs but had forgotten about it the moment she had gone inside to the rabble that her children were making. Annalie could hear Mamie nagging at Jimmy behind her closed door and downstairs again Shug McKerrigan was mournfully practising on his bagpipes.

Quite a few people greeted her as she swung cheerfully along Cumberland Street. – 'Hello, Annalie' or 'Hello, hen'. Most of them made some remark about Elizabeth – 'Oh, isn't she a lovely wee soul. You must be awful proud of her, hen' or 'She'll be good company for you now' or 'Oh my, you're as alike as two peas in a pod, so you are'.

As usual Mrs McClusky was delighted to see the child.

'Where's my wee pet then?' she greeted her with outstretched arms.

'Here we go again,' Mr McClusky growled. 'Am I supposed to serve all these customers myself?'

'I'll just put my jacket through the back,' Annalie said. 'And then I'll get cracking.'

'About time,' Mr McClusky said.

In the back shop she sang 'Roses of Picardy' at the top of her voice until Mr McClusky bawled through at her, 'Will you be quiet? I can't hear myself think in here,' and turning to his wife he added, 'and will you put that wean down and get on with your work.'

Neither of the two women paid much attention to Mr McClusky. Annalie came through when she was ready and Mrs McClusky put Elizabeth down, and Annalie said it was time for her wee nap. It wasn't as if the customers were all agitating to be served, in fact they were enjoying a gossip among themselves and were in no hurry to have this pleasure interrupted.

After settling Elizabeth down for her nap, Annalie set to work with great gusto. It was only much later when she began to tire that her thoughts turned to Aunty Murn. She had to admit to herself that her aunt had never been quite the same since Eddie and Davie had been killed. Her hair which had been grey before was now pure white, and often Annalie noticed a dull, empty look in her eyes. Once when Annalie came in unexpectedly to the kitchen, Aunty Murn had been sleeping on the rocking chair. She'd awakened with a start and said, 'Oh, trust you to come in at the wrong time. I was just enjoying a wee while with the laddies.'

Annalie was taken aback.' You were dreaming about them, you mean?'

Aunty Murn sighed. 'I suppose you could say that. But they were so real,' she added wistfully.

Most of the time she was just the same as she'd always been, the rock in Annalie's background, the strength that bound the family together, but these occasional lapses into weakness worried Annalie. She was beginning to see Aunty Murn had been much more deeply affected by Eddie's and Davie's deaths than she had at first realized.

Annalie was worried about Mrs Rafferty too – more than worried, deeply saddened. The last time she'd seen her was when she'd been cutting through Commercial Road to catch a tram to town from Rutherglen Road. Mrs Rafferty had been coming out of the close from the dunny and Annalie knew that she had seen her, but Mrs Rafferty immediately dodged back again into the close. Wondering what was wrong, Annalie made a point of stopping.

'Is that you Mrs Rafferty?' she called into the shadows.

Mrs Rafferty emerged again, eyes blinking and furtive, her body visibly shrinking inside the shawl she shared with her baby.

'Were you hiding from me?' Annalie said, half laughing.

'Oh, I'm awful sorry, hen,' Mrs Rafferty said. 'It's not that I didn't want to say hello, but you see, a nice wee lassie like you shouldn't be seen with the likes of me.'

Mrs Rafferty had certainly gone down hill, as Aunty Murn would have said. Her shawl was matted and dirty. Dirt was ingrained in the puffy ankles showing under her skirts. On her feet were only frayed felt slippers. Her hair was greasy and tangled, her face puffy and unhealthy looking. She smelled of stale sweat and sex.

'Don't be daft,' Annalie said, but she felt deeply concerned about the state of her friend.

'Better go, hen,' Mrs Rafferty said. 'What'll folk think?'

'I don't care what folk think,' Annalie said. 'I don't forget how good you were to me when I needed a friend.'

'And we had some good times, sure we had?' Mrs Rafferty said. 'I'll never forget them either, hen.'

Annalie wouldn't have described her stay down in the dunny as being a good time, nevertheless she knew what Mrs Rafferty meant.

She hadn't been able to get the picture of the woman out of her head since the meeting, and wondered what would become of her and the baby, not to mention the other children. If the baby survived being eaten alive by rats the chances were it would die of one of the diseases that children so easily fell prey to. No doubt one of these days it would be taken away in the fever van and perhaps that would be a mercy.

She went through to the back shop and looked down at her own baby. How lucky they both were with a man like Adam to love, help and protect them.

'Soon,' she whispered down to Elizabeth. 'Soon, soon.'

362

Chapter Fifty-nine

'The war seems to be going a bit better for us now,' Christina remarked to Simon. 'Don't you think so? I was just reading about the victory of Passchendaele Ridge.'

Simon looked at her with shadowed eyes and bitter mouth. 'I think and feel with the poet Charles Sorley,' he said.

> 'When you see millions of the mouthless dead
> across your dreams in pale battalions go,
> say not soft things as other men have said . . .'

'I just thought,' she began.

'I know what you thought,' Simon interrupted. 'You thought like Mother and Father. You thought like everyone else who's never been near a trench nor knows anything about the realities of conflict that Rupert Brooke's picture of war as a brave adventure for young heroes is the true one. Well, let me tell you, Rupert Brooke never served in the trenches. He was a sub-lieutenant in the Royal Naval Division and he died from illness on the way to Gallipoli. Wilfred Owen is the one who knows what he's talking about:

> 'What passing bells for those who died as cattle?
> Only the monstrous anger of the guns,
> Only the stuttering rifles rapid rattle
> Can patter out their hasty orisens.'

She wished she'd never mentioned the war. It was a bad mistake. She realized that now.

'Surely the politicians will get together and stop it soon?' she said. 'It was the politicians who started it, wasn't it, and it'll be them, I suppose, that'll finish it?'

'True,' he said. 'True. I remember a song that the men used to sing. A bitter song it was, expressing contempt for politicians. They certainly believed that the politicians were responsible for the miseries of the war and especially for the fighting in the trenches.' He suddenly burst into a verse of the song,

> 'Oh see him in the House of Commons,
> Passing laws to put down crime,
> While the victims of his passions
> Trudge on in the mud and slime.'

It was always an ordeal to visit the manse nowadays. Simon was still in a very bad state and his behaviour was seriously affecting her parents. Her poor father was the butt of most of Simon's bitter abuse. He had become an aetheist and never seemed to tire of telling his father why. The Reverend Gillespie had changed from a big, supremely confident, self-righteous kind of man to someone who was at times uncertain and at other times pathetically blustering. He always tried valiantly to cling to his faith, his belief in the righteousness of the Bible and its teachings.

Simon's condition at least had brought the Reverend Gillespie and his wife closer together. Indeed, they clung to each other in mutual self-defence, yet their love for Simon had not diminished. On the contrary. They were drowning with desperate pity and concern for their son.

She was glad at last to escape from the intense emotional atmosphere of the house to the frosty winter air. There was a thin layer of snow on the ground and the trees fronting all the gardens in Queen's Drive, thickly leafy in summer, were now white skeletons, revealing all the handsome semi villas and villas lying behind them. No one was in sight. It was a quiet, private kind of street. Christina seldom saw any of her neighbours. Indeed, most of them she would not even recognize if she saw them. Here, people kept themselves to themselves. Here children were not allowed to play outside. Instead they took walks with their nanny to Queen's Park. There they played sedately under the watchful eye of the nanny, who made sure that they were not contaminated by any specks of dirt or contact with the wrong kind of people. In a way Christina was dreading Christmas, which was only a few days away. She had been round to invite her mother and father and Simon to Christmas dinner. Adam had suggested lunch, with the children sharing the meal.

'You know how fond your mother and father are of the children,' he reminded her. 'And Jason would love it. The twins could be propped up in their high chairs just for a short time.'

'I wouldn't hesitate to invite them,' she told Adam. 'But it's Simon. You know what he's like. He might be all right. On the other hand, he might have one of his outbursts and frighten the children. I don't want to risk that.'

Adam had reluctantly agreed that dinner would be the best idea in the circumstances.

'It's a pity, though,' he said. 'Simon's fond of the children too.'

'I can have Nanny and Etta bring them down for their usual half hour, or perhaps a little less that evening. Anyway, Mother and Father and Simon can see them then.'

It certainly wouldn't be so bad with Adam there. His strength seemed to strengthen Simon, his calmness calmed her brother.

Often her mother told her, 'I don't know what we'd have done without Adam. Both your father and I misjudged him when you first married him. We realize that now, and many a time we've asked God's forgiveness.'

The dinner didn't promise to be a very easy meal. They were fortunate in a way. The food shortages didn't affect them too much, even though rationing had now begun. There had been no problem in getting a turkey. Monktons often did work for Jacksons the butchers, making structural alterations. Also several recent burst pipes had been promptly attended to and at a ridiculously low price. Much the same could be said for the grocer's, the dairy, the fishmonger's and the baker's. All the shop assistants knew they could depend on very generous tips at Christmas and New Year. Christina saw to it that the house staff were well paid too in comparison with other similar establishments. The reasons for her generosity were not altogether altruistic, of course. Staff were not only difficult to get, but hard to keep these days. There had to be very good inducements in order to tempt people.

They were having old Mrs Monkton to lunch instead of dinner, knowing that her loud voice might spark Simon off into some sort of trauma. He had a hypersensitivity to any kind of stimulation such as noises, sudden movement or flashing lights. The anxiety about him was so constant and pervasive that they even worried in case the crunching of the gravel underfoot might trigger off some kind of reaction in him when he visited them on Christmas day.

'Little did I ever dream,' she'd confessed to Adam recently, 'that I would come to believe that my once good-natured brother might be capable of murder.'

'Oh, it's not as bad as all that,' Adam said. But they both knew that Simon was capable of great violence at the slightest provocation.

On Christmas day however, Simon remained under control. There always was some degree of underlying sadness about being with Simon because of the pathetic wreck of a man that he had become. However, at least the meal passed in a relative calmness and comparatively pleasant family atmosphere. The children's visit to the drawing room had been a success too and her mother and father had looked almost relaxed as they listened to Jason's childish and happy talk about all that Santa Claus had brought him.

In the evening, after the visitors had all gone, Adam poured two brandies and settled down opposite Christina by the fire. He raised his glass.

'Cheers.'

'Here's to us,' she said. 'Here's to the success of your new contract.'

'I'll drink to that,' he said, downing some of his brandy.

The fire sent a warm glow around the room. Christina reminded herself that come the spring she would have the whole place decorated to her own taste.

'What are you thinking?' Adam's voice broke into her reverie.

'This room needs redecorating. I was thinking of having it done in the spring.'

'My goodness.' his eyes twinkled with amusement. 'You! Thinking of domestic matters?'

'It's our home,' she said, and the sound of the word 'our' gave her a deep sense of gladness.

'Yes, and you run it very efficiently. I was only joking.'

'I try to be a good wife,' she said.

He stared across at her, his eyes serious now.

'Yes,' he said eventually. 'I believe you do, Christina.'

The brandy warmed her inside and gave her the courage and the degree of recklessness necessary to say, 'Can't you try too, Adam – to make our marriage a success?'

His eyes narrowed a little.

'You're thinking of the physical side, I suppose.'

She felt her face and neck suffuse with heat and she was unable to meet his stern stare.

'We get on so well together in every other way now,' she said. 'I don't see why we shouldn't . . .'

'Yes you do, Christina,' he interrupted, but in quite a gentle tone.

'I'm offering myself to you,' she said. 'Are you refusing me?'

'How could I refuse you?' he said, 'You're a very attractive woman, but I've always been honest with you, Christina.'

'I know, I know,' she said. She didn't want him to say anything more. She didn't want to face the fact that he didn't love her. Not now. Not tonight. She believed that if physical closeness were added to the increased trust between them, love would surely grow.

They made love on the thick, soft rug in front of the warm fire. He undressed her and encouraged her to reciprocate by undressing him. Their lovemaking was in fact an encouraging and teaching process by him for her, and under his tuition she relaxed and opened out and accepted him into the deepest parts of herself. He was part of her and she was part of him. No matter what might happen in the future, this was her certainty now.

Chapter Sixty

Teeny Docherty was always very excited if she got a piece of news or gossip to pass on. It gave her some importance, some standing in the community. The trouble was, often when she got to the most thrilling part, she would forget the rest of the story, much to everyone's intense frustration and irritation. Much time and effort would be spent in trying to jog Teeny's memory, usually without success. It had become a common occurrence to see Teeny hugging her shawl around her thin body, eyes huge as she imparted a vital titbit at a close mouth or in a shop.

On this occasion she was in the shop and it was to Annalie she was eager to impart her news.

'Do you know a Mrs Wilson down the other end of Rutherglen Road?' she asked Annalie.

'No,' said Annalie.

'Well I was talking to her this morning in the steamy. I don't usually go to that steamy but the one up at Commercial Road end was all booked up so I had to go down there because I had that much washing for my man to do and he's that fussy about his shirts. Anyway, I got talking to this woman in the steamy. I didn't know her either, but you know how you get talking to folk. Well, she started talking to me actually. She was that proud of her lassie who's just got a good job in a big house. It's just as a kitchen maid, but Mrs Wilson feels she could gradually work her way up. She's just a young lassie, you know, but Mrs Wilson had great hopes for her that she'll get on in life.

An instinctive wariness began to grow in Annalie.

'What big house is this then?' she asked.

'Eh . . .' Teeny's excitement froze in mid air. 'Eh . . .'

'For goodness' sake, Teeny,' one of the other customers groaned, 'I wish you wouldn't start things you couldn't finish.'

'I can, I can,' Teeny said. 'It'll come to me in a minute. Just give me a minute.'

'Here we go again,' Mr McClusky said. 'I don't run this place just for you crowd to have a good gossip. Did you not come in for any messages?' he demanded of Teeny.

'Eh . . .' Teeny was still clutching desperately in mid air. 'Eh . . . Monkton House. Monkton House!' she repeated in triumph and gave a delighted flash of gums all round. 'Monkton House! That was it. Monkton's the name of the folk that live there. I thought right away, that's the name of Annalie's fancy man. Wait till you hear this . . .'

Everyone leaned expectantly towards her only to be met with a sudden blankness of the quivering face and wide-stretched eyes. After a moment's awful silence, one of the customers said, 'See you, Teeny Docherty. One of these days one of us is going to murder you.'

'If you just give me a minute,' Teeny managed. 'It'll come back to me. You know what I'm like.'

'We know what you're like all right,' Mr McClusky groaned. 'Now have you come in here for any messages or have you not?'

Her few moments of glory gone, a miserable Teeny said, 'Aye, I'll take a packet of my man's fags. What's the kind he likes again?'

'Woodbine,' Mr McClusky said.

'I can't mind if it's ten he usually gets or twenty. Can you, Mr McClusky?'

'Twenty,' Mr McClusky said, and banged them down onto the counter. 'Anything else?'

'Aye. Eh . . . Err . . . I'm sure there was something else. If you just give me a minute, Mr McClusky. Eh . . . Eh . . .'

Suddenly she howled at the top of her voice, making Mr McClusky jump and shout at her angrily. 'What's up with you now, you silly idiot? Howling like a hyena like that. You nearly frightened me out of my socks there.'

'A devoted couple,' Teeny gasped breathlessly to Annalie. 'Mrs Wilson's wee lassie said the cook told her that Mr and Mrs Monkton were a devoted couple and they'd three beautiful children to prove it.'

'Three children?' Annalie echoed in disbelief.

'I know, hen,' Teeny said. 'You thought there was just one, and you thought he was unhappy with his wife too, didn't you, hen? I knew that.'

'Oh that's terrible, so it is,' another customer said and there was a general murmur of agreement.

Mrs McClusky's bewildered face quivered in indignation.

'He's been leading you up the garden path, hen.'

A fat beshawled customer nodded sagely.

'Aye. Men are like that. They'd tell you any fairy tale just to get their own wicked way with you.'

Somebody else joined in with 'Still, I wish I was half as well off as you, Annalie. I mean he's good to you, hen, isn't he? A woman's got to watch what side her bread's buttered on.'

Another, seeing Annalie's stricken face, tried to give a word of comfort.

'Och, I wouldn't worry too much, hen. As Aggie says, he's been good to you and that's the main thing. Men are just randier than us. That's all. They can't help it. It's their nature. His wife'll not be giving him enough of that, you see, and you're a fine-looking lusty lassie.'

Annalie felt so devastated she had to go into the back shop and sit down, leaving the customers to discuss the whole question of men and their wicked ways. Mr McClusky made a valiant attempt to regain some sort of order. Annalie could hear him shouting at the top of his voice, 'Will you stop you blethering and get your messages? Do you hear me?'

Mrs McClusky had come through to the back shop with her. 'He'll be wakening the wean if he keeps on like that. I'll speak to him when I go back through, hen. You sit there until you come to yourself. You've had a terrible shock, I know. I mind my sister Jessy had something like that done to her, only her man kidded on that he wasn't married and she found out he was. By this time she had a wean to him too. Poor Jessy was terrible cut up, specially when he went back to his wife.' She thought for a minute, remembering. 'Of course, Jessy's man wasn't well off like yours. I suppose when you're well off you can have your cake and eat it. Just sit there until you feel better, hen. I'll manage fine by myself.'

It seemed to Annalie for a minute or two that the whole world had turned upside down and inside out. She didn't know where she was or what to think. She felt as if she'd had a body blow and she was suffering from shock as well as pain.

Had it never been anything more then than a common seduction? A bit on the side? Had he just been lying to her, cheating her, deceiving her, making a fool of her while all the time he had been having normal, loving, sexual, married relations with his wife? The pain was so bad her face twisted with it. She bent forward with it, hugging herself in an effort to find comfort. She would have sat like that for ever had it not been that Elizabeth woke up and came toddling towards her.

'Mama.' The childish voice held a note of apprehension and fear.

'It's all right, darling,' Annalie said, quickly putting her arms out for her. 'It's all right. Mummy's all right.'

She lifted the little girl onto her knee and nursed her backwards and forwards, backwards and forwards while Elizabeth sucked her thumb and leaned her warm body against her.

'Biccy,' Elizabeth said eventually.

'Yes, all right pet. We'll go through to the front shop and Mrs McClusky'll give you one.'

Annalie silently thanked God that the shop was empty when she went through.

'How are you feeling, hen?' Mrs McClusky asked sympathetically.

'Awful,' Annalie said. 'But I'll survive, I suppose. The trouble is, Mrs McClusky, nothing stops me loving him. I'd love him no matter what he did to me.'

'Och, you poor wee soul.'

'At the same time,' Annalie continued, 'I do have my pride.'

'Of course you have, hen.'

'What should I do, do you think?'

Mr McClusky unexpectedly intervened at this point.

'Think about your wean. She hasn't done anybody any harm. She should have a decent chance in life.'

'Oh you've never said a truer word, Sid,' Mrs McClusky heartily agreed, then turned back to Annalie. 'Look what's happening to the Raffertys and Teeny Docherty's crowd and a lot more besides. The chances are the boys'll end up in the jail. Half them are wee hard men already. The lassies will either end up on the streets or they'll get married and be old and worn out before they're thirty. Look at Teeny. She can't be that old. A walking wreck she is, that woman.'

This prospect of what life might hold for Elizabeth made Annalie feel even more shocked and devastated than before. Mr McClusky was right. She must put Elizabeth first. Elizabeth must get a decent chance in life. Most of the women in the Gorbals didn't know any better, hadn't seen any better. They were just surviving everything that life threw at them from day to day the best way they could. Mostly they survived by helping each other. They did this not only for purely practical reasons. In their innocence they possessed a wisdom far deeper than the greatest leaders of men. They knew they were of one flesh with the rest of humanity. They knew they were not like marbles, separate and only bumping against each other occasionally. They were part of the one body and so they cared about each other and had this deep knowledge without being consciously aware of it.

Somehow, Annalie managed to finish her day's work. Although she could have put on her nice warm coat, she had brought her shawl instead because it was warmer for Elizabeth to be wrapped in. She was glad of it as she was buffeted by an icy wind on her way along Cumberland Street. The shawl kept her warm too, and she needed the warmth for comfort.

With a supreme effort of will, she continued the evening with the usual routine. She prepared supper and fed Elizabeth, gave the child her bath and even played with her and sang Elizabeth's favourite songs. Eventually, tucked into the hole-in-the-wall bed, the child fell asleep. Annalie sat down by the fire and wept. If Adam didn't love her as she'd always believed he did and she challenged him now, could it be that he would leave her and Elizabeth, desert them completely? How could she pay the rent for this big house if that happened? A rent for room and kitchen and bathroom was far beyond what she could normally afford. It was true what the other women said. She was indeed well off compared to most others. There had been growing unrest again about the rents and the time it was taking to do necessary repairs.

The main problem in the winter was water coming in through the roofs. People were constantly complaining about this and as a result the slater had become known as the reporter, because he was always saying, 'Aye, I'll report it to the factor, Missus. Don't worry, I'll report it.'

Patched-up jobs were always done and were never successful for very long. This had happened only once to Annalie. When the water had come in a second time she had told Adam and the repair had been done promptly and properly.

She'd felt guilty about this. She knew of so many other people who were still suffering from leaking roofs and the wet rot caused by constant dampness. The ill-health and misery resulting from these conditions were legend. Sharpened by the pain of her suffering, her neglect of the plight of her friends and neighbours came into urgent focus. She became one with them. Pain ripped the veil of love from her eyes. She knew with absolute clarity that the people in the Gorbals were her people. She belonged with them. Their roots were her roots; their suffering her suffering.

She saw Christina and Adam Monkton with their luxurious life in Queen's Park as alien beings, a different breed, people from across a divide so vast it was completely impassable.

She knew where her loyalties lay. And the knowledge frightened her.

Memories of her own desperate situation came flooding back. As she wept noisily by the fire, even memories of her stay at Mrs Rafferty's returned to frighten her. She crouched for a long time under the puttering gas light before creeping exhausted into bed beside Elizabeth and cuddling close against the child for warmth and comfort.

Chapter Sixty-one

The next time Adam came to see her she made love with him deeply, sweetly, passionately with all her heart and soul, all the love that was in her. Afterwards Adam rolled onto his back, one arm flung above his head and gasped, 'Oh Annalie!'

She got up and put on her clothes. He watched her, his eyes still dark with passion. 'You're so very beautiful.'

They were in the front room and as usual she had used some of her precious coal to light the fire. She had cleaned and polished the room very thoroughly before he arrived and had made up the bed with her special crisp, white linen sheets. The room had always been her pride and joy, her bower of love, her sanctum. She sat down beside the fire and gazed across at him.

'I love you,' she said.

'And I love you, darling.'

She shook her head.

'Please don't lie to me any more, Adam.'

'Lie to you?' He got up immediately and began pulling on his clothes. 'Annalie, what's wrong? Why are you talking like this?'

'I'm frightened,' she said.

'Darling.'

He came across and gathered her into his arms. 'What's happened? Why are you frightened? What are you frightened of?'

She looked straight into his eyes.

'Adam,' she said, 'do you love me enough to leave your wife and live permanently with me?'

He let go of her and stood up. He lit a cigar, then said, 'That's unfair.'

A wave of anger brought the blood pounding to her head. She wanted to scream at him. She wanted to thump her fists against him. She wanted to scream: I'm unfair? What do you think you've been? But she was so very frightened.

'Why is it unfair?' she asked.

'I've got a wife and family.'

'Yes,' she said. 'Three children.'

'You don't understand.'

'That's true, Adam. I don't.'

'Look, Annalie, what's come over you? We've been perfectly happy.'

'I've been happy because I believed that one day we would live together as man and wife.'

'You knew that was impossible.'

'No I didn't know.'

'Well it is,' he said. 'Look, I'm sorry, Annalie, but really, I can't do that. But it doesn't mean I don't love you.'

'Just that you love your wife more.'

'I didn't say that. I admire and respect my wife, but it's you I love. I've loved you from the beginning and I'll love you till the end.'

'But not enough to give up your wife and live with me instead.'

'It's not as simple as that. Life never is.'

Once again she saw the position with terrible, painful clarity. She saw the successful business man with the perfect partner in the woman who shared his business interests. A woman of his own level of intelligence, of his own area of experience, of his own class. A woman who could effortlessly grace his home and entertain his business and social acquaintances. A woman who could be an advantage to him in every way. A gypsy girl from the Gorbals had no place in that world. He knew it and now she knew it.

She gazed up at his tall, barrel-chested figure, his black hair, his dark eyes. She tried to impress them on her mind for ever like a film she could play back on her lonely days.

'You know that I love you, Annalie,' he said.

'Yes.'

What else could she say? What else could he say?

'Surely that's all that really matters?'

376

Maybe it was. But she'd had a dream. It had become part of her. How could she live without it?

He glanced at his watch.

'I'll have to go now. Will you be all right?'

'Of course,' she said, managing a proud toss of her head. 'Nothing's changed, has it?'

'No,' he said. 'Nothing's changed.'

As usual, before leaving he went through to the kitchen to kiss Elizabeth goodbye. She was sound asleep and looking as beautiful as ever.

Annalie watched him bend over her and kiss her tenderly on the cheek. It was then, seeing the love in his eyes as he looked down at his daughter, she realized what she could do for her. If only she had the courage.

'Goodnight, darling.'

His attention had turned to her again, but she was so terrified by a tornado of thoughts she was no longer aware of him. Until his hands gripped her shoulders.

'Annalie, are you sure you're all right?'

'Yes,' she managed. 'I'm overtired, that's all.'

It didn't sound like her voice. She had never been so afraid. Never needed him so much.

She accompanied him to the front door and just before leaving he blew her a kiss. Then he was gone.

After shutting the door she leaned her brow against it. She stood like that, unable to move, for a few minutes. Eventually she went through to the front room and stood staring out of the window, down at the gaslit Cumberland Street below.

Chapter Sixty-two

Annalie needed to blot out her thoughts, needed release for the great tide of emotion building up inside and threatening to overcome her. She turned her attention to the plight of her friends and neighbours again, as much for her own sake as for theirs. Because of the continuing rise in the cost of living everyone was finding it more and more of a struggle to make ends meet. People were getting into arrears. Evictions had started again. One family, all that they possessed having been taken away on the horse and cart by the bailiffs, was now in the Poor House. Another family had already spent two nights in the freezing cold sleeping in the open on Glasgow Green. Annalie's anger clung to the plight of these people and to her other friends and neighbours like a lifeline. Unable to cope with her own traumas and problems she turned all her emotions and energies to helping others. She roused the women of the district to march behind her to the factor's office to make a noisy protest. The houses weren't worth any rent, she told the factor, until they were made habitable. The factor gave the usual argument about the cost of repairs, maintenance and management of tenement property and how it had increased by one hundred per cent since 1914.

Annalie, backed by the other women, countered. There had been no proper repairs or maintenance done since 1914 and most of the tenement properties were slums. They weren't going to pay any rents unless the proper repairs were done and the houses made habitable for decent human beings.

Some of the women, incensed by the conditions in which they were being forced to live, started shouting abuse at the factor and milling about his office in such a threatening manner that he shouted to one of his clerks to phone for the police. On being told at the police office that such a large and menacing crowd had gathered, reinforcements were sent and several of the women were arrested. These included big Mrs McAllister who had caught the factor by the lapels and literally lifted him off his feet in one angry confrontation. Another normally very respectable woman had laid about both Mr Fintry and one of his clerks in sudden indignation at the conditions she'd had to suffer living up a cesspool of a close in Florence Street.

Annalie, smaller and younger, had been swept back by the tide of violence of the older women and in this way had at least escaped arrest.

'Is this not terrible?' Aunty Murn said. 'Decent folk being flung into jail. And you'll be next, I'm warning you,' she told Annalie.

But Aunty Murn's distress only added to her own and flung her with even more recklessness into the whirlpool of anger and desperation that was filling the streets. The number of meetings at street corners and in back courts increased. A variety of proposals were made and voted on. Bells were once more procured to warn in advance when eviction was taking place. Every woman in the district would rush to the scene, some carrying toddlers, some with children trotting beside them, some with babies bound to them with their shawls. Somebody always brought a stool or something to stand on and one or more of the women, often including Annalie, would stand up and denounce those who were responsible for the eviction. Then when the sheriff's officers came along in their big, horse-drawn lorry to throw the family out and take all their belongings away, all the women would cram the house, the landing, the close, the street, and prevent the officers from carrying out the eviction. Afterwards the doors and windows of the house would be barricaded up to protect it from the sheriff's officers.

Often meetings were held in the shop while Annalie was supposed to be working. Mr McClusky's voice was continuously raised in protest against the invasion of his premises. As Mrs McClusky pointed out however, they needed a lot of repairs done to their house.

'I'm sick and tired of badgering the factor – as you well know, Sid,' she reminded her husband. 'And you've said yourself that the close is a disgrace, not to mention the back court.'

It had been during one of these shop meetings that Adam had turned up unexpectedly. Annalie was perched up on the counter addressing the women when the shop door crashed open and Monkton's tall, burly figure was framed in the doorway. His eyes, hard and angry, took in the scene – the rabble of beshawled women, Annalie shouting to make herself heard above the others. Elizabeth was sitting on the floor, temporarily forgotten by everyone, her face and pinny smeared with chocolate from the biscuit she had been eating.

A silence fell over the women. It was laced with embarrassment, shyness and guilt. Respectfully they moved back to allow him to enter. Instead he called over to Annalie, 'I want to talk to you. Come outside and bring the child with you.'

Once outside he said, 'What the hell do you think you're doing? Get up to the house at once.'

Annalie tossed her head.

'You can't talk to me like that.'

'I'll do more than talk to you in a minute if you don't get a move on,' Monkton said, this time getting a hold of her arm and dragging her bodily along the street. She was carrying Elizabeth in her other arm and was forced to make a jerky and ungainly progress to her close and from there up to the top landing.

With each step her protests became louder until, by the time he was putting the key in the door of the flat she was shouting furiously at him and Elizabeth was crying in fear and distress. Inside the flat he kicked the door shut behind him.

'Take Elizabeth through to the kitchen' he said. 'Get her properly cleaned up and give her some toys to comfort her. Then come through to the front room. I want to talk to you.'

For the child's sake Annalie struggled to control her rage.

She took Elizabeth into the kitchen and washed her and spoke soothingly to her until she was quiet and comforted, then she sat her down on the rag rug in front of the fire with some of her toys.

'Be a good girl now, darling. Just you wait there till Mummy goes through to the room for a few minutes.'

She had to stand for a moment in the hall however, to try to gather her wits together. She was still shaking with anger at Monkton's rough treatment of her. Yet at the same time her love and passion for him raged inside her with a force that far exceeded her anger. After a few deep breaths she went into the front room.

'How dare you manhandle me like that?' she said.

He was waiting for her, standing legs apart, thumbs hooked in waistcoat pockets.

'I'll do more than man-handle you if I ever catch you neglecting that child again.'

'Neglecting Elizabeth! When have I ever neglected Elizabeth? I don't know what you're talking about.'

'I know what you've been up to,' Monkton said. 'Where has Elizabeth been when you've been rabble-rousing? That's what I want to know. Who's been looking after her? Nobody, by the looks of things today.'

'Any time I haven't been here I've seen that she's been with a neighbour or my aunty.'

'So she's passed around between God knows all who, and ill-treated for all you know.'

'Ill-treated!' Annalie scoffed. 'What nonsense! Of course she's not been ill-treated.'

'Your place is here looking after your child.'

'And your child,' Annalie reminded him.

'Yes, my child. And I won't have her neglected.'

'I've never neglected Elizabeth,' Annalie protested.

'You *are* neglecting her. You shouldn't even be working in that shop. If it's money you need I'll give you more.'

A rush of tears filled her chest. It wasn't money she needed, it was him.

'Keep your money,' she said. 'I don't need it. I don't need anything from you.'

'Don't talk nonsense. You need money to look after Elizabeth properly. You need money to live. You need money to run this house, but by the look of that kitchen through there you haven't been spending much time running it recently.'

'Normally that kitchen's perfectly tidy, but I was so tired last night when I got in I just didn't have time to do anything.'

'I'm not surprised,' he said. 'You've time enough to go badgering the factor though, speaking at street corners, having meetings in that shop shouting at the pitch of your voice. No, wonder you're tired.'

Everything was going wrong but she couldn't see what to do to put anything right between them again.

'Oh, it doesn't surprise you, eh?' she flung at him sarcastically. 'You drop in here whenever it takes your fancy. You come from a luxurious big house and a woman who has servants to pander to her every whim. She never needs to lift a finger in her house. It would be surprising if *she* got tired right enough.'

His dark brows lowered, his scar twisting at one side and giving him a menacing look.

'That's enough. Leave my wife out of this.'

Annalie tossed the tumbling, tangled hair that had long since shed its restraining pins.

'Why should I?'

'Because I say so.'

'That's not good enough. I notice though that you don't tell me that she's nothing to do with me, because of course she has. She has everything to do with me, hasn't she? She's the reason for us being like this.'

'If you mean by "being like this" the fact that we're quarrelling just now, that's got nothing to do with my wife. That has to do with Elizabeth and you not paying enough attention to her, not spending enough time with her to look after her properly. That's what this is all about.'

No it isn't, no it isn't, her heart screamed silently at him.

'You're not married to me,' she said, pushing past him. 'So I needn't allow you to have anything to do with Elizabeth. Just get away from here and leave both of us alone.'

He caught her and whirled her roughly around to face him again.

'I'm not finished with you yet.'

'Well I'm finished with you. Finished with you for good.'

The words were out before she could stop them. Terrible, cruel, lying words. There was silence for a minute. His hands still gripped her shoulders, holding her quite close to him.

Eventually he said, 'Annalie, look me straight in the eyes and tell me that again.'

At first she remained rigid, refusing to raise her face to his. He gave her a little shake.

'Do you hear me?'

She looked up at him and was lost in one of those deep, intimate gazes that they had shared so often in the loving past. Then their mouths and bodies were merging in sweet and loving union. But still her heart wept.

Chapter Sixty-three

'When they come up in court I hope they get long sentences. They deserve to go to jail for a good long spell to teach them a lesson and to be an example for the others.'

Fintry the factor's thin face was flushed with anger and he kept fiddling with his steel-rimmed spectacles and glancing over at Christina.

'Why on earth are they going to such lengths as this, though?' Christina wanted to know. 'Surely their conditions can't be as bad as all that? I've done most of the repairs you've reported to me. As many as I could afford.'

'Oh I know, Mrs Monkton,' Mr Fintry assured her. 'And haven't I been trying to tell them? But no, they wouldn't listen. They'd rather listen to that trouble-maker Annalie Gordon. The quicker the police catch her and put her behind bars the better, as far as I'm concerned.'

'I understand the houses are shockingly overcrowded.' Christina said. 'But that's not my fault.'

'Of course it isn't, Mrs Monkton. Of course it isn't. It's their own stupid fault. They'll neither work nor want. They behave like animals and they live like animals. That's just how they are – always have been and always will be.'

Christina inhaled deeply at her cigarette.

'They surely can't expect me to re-roof all the houses, re-plaster the walls, rebuild stairs, renew all plumbing and sewage systems.'

'Of course not,' Fintry cried out indignantly. 'Why should you?'

'It's uneconomical,' Christina said. 'If I went bankrupt, what good would that do any of them?'

'Exactly,' Fintry agreed.

'Still, I suppose I'd better go and have another look around the place. I'll go incognito and on foot this time. Perhaps that'll give me a better idea.'

Mr Fintry's mouth quivered and almost smiled.

'Incognito, Mrs Monkton? I hardly think so. An elegant woman like you is bound to stick out like a sore thumb in a place like the Gorbals.'

Christina sighed. 'No. It'll be easy enough. There's so much black, so much mourning on the streets now, all I need to do is wear a black coat and a black hat and veil my face.'

She knew the very coat, a long, black, old-fashioned thing at the back of her wardrobe that she had worn for funerals when she lived at the manse. She had been meaning to throw it out or put it in one of her mother's jumble sales along with some other clothes that she no longer wore. She had been so busy, however, she had never got round to it.

She tried it on as soon as she got home and was amazed at the different image it gave her. It reminded her, with unexpected pain, of how she used to be. She quickly took the coat off and flung it aside, and only donned it again the next day with extreme reluctance. She felt it was her duty, however, to go and have a closer look at her property in the Gorbals.

A rummage through hat boxes the previous evening had produced a black hat with a veil that came from the brim, securely looped under the chin and swept up to the back of the head. The dowdy black ghost in the mirror would be unrecognizable, she felt sure, even to her husband. Satisfied in that respect, but uneasy and unhappy in every other, Christina left the house and got into her car. In a very short time she'd reached the end of Pollokshaws Road from which she could cut down Cumberland Street and into the Gorbals on foot.

It was like entering another world. Soon she was sucked into the caverns of high black tenements. A cold wind and a continuous smir of rain added to her discomfort. Despite the weather, children who looked no older than Jason played about the gutters with dirt-smeared faces and ragged clothes. Occasionally she plucked up courage to plunge into the darkness of one of the closes and penetrate through to the back yard.

Some of the closes she entered were tiled and appeared reasonably clean and respectable. Others appalled and depressed her. She shied away in distaste from the smell of urine and cats that seemed to pervade so many of the buildings in the meaner streets.

Mixed with her depression and dismay was a niggle of resentment as if the people there were to blame for her feelings. Surely, she thought, they at least could keep the place clean. Soap and water were cheap enough and readily available. Surely no one could have any excuse for not keeping themselves and their dwellings clean.

After wandering down several side streets she came to the part of Cumberland Road where a narrow, roughly cobbled street cut off it. Christina hesitated. The city was in that hazy state between light and darkness, and she suddenly realized she had been walking for a long time. A grey mist had descended over the streets, penetrating every alleyway and close. Horses and carts plodding heavily along Cumberland Street disappeared like wraiths. The cacophony of sound in the streets became strangely muffled and distant.

She decided it was time to make for home. There was nothing much to see here that she hadn't seen already. Anyway, the side street at which she was standing looked as if it was only used for commercial purposes, probably storage. There certainly seemed no sign of any human habitation. Then she thought she saw something moving further along the road. By the size of it, the figure could only be a child. Curiosity made her start walking towards the shadowy figure. She nearly twisted her ankle a couple of times on the rough, uneven cobbles and found she had to pick her way along with great care and attention. As she came near the figure she saw it was a small boy standing just outside a dark close mouth. He was painfully skinny, white-faced and shivering in a thin shirt and ragged trousers. He could have been anything between nine and twelve.

'Why are you standing outside in the cold like that?' Christina asked him. 'You'll get pneumonia.'

'I just came up for a minute, Missus. Just to get a breath of fresh air.'

'Do you live up this close?'

'There's no upstairs here, Missus. I live down the dunny.'

'Well go back downstairs and get a heat at your fire. You can always open the window for a little fresh air.'

'We haven't got any windows in our house.'

'No windows?' Christina echoed incredulously. 'But you must have at least one window.'

'No we haven't.'

There was a hint of accusation in Christina's stare.

'I find that very hard to believe.'

'I'll show you if you like,' the boy said. 'I'll take you down to our house.'

He turned into the darkness and after a moment's hesitation Christina followed him. After only a few steps complete blackness swallowed her up and made her heart quicken with apprehension. Her gloved hands feeling along the wall for guidance soon became wet and clammy with the dampness from the rough stone.

'Mind your feet. There's stairs just here,' the boy said and he began stamping and shuffling his feet in a most peculiar manner.

The stench as she began to descend the stairs was so nauseating she had to struggle with herself violently not to be sick. The tension of the struggle was giving her a headache.

'Why are you stamping your feet like that and making such a racket?' she asked the boy.

'It's to stop the rats running over us, Missus.'

Horror and terror absorbed her completely now. With a scream she managed to stumble back and retrace her steps until she was out on the cobbled street again. Choking for breath and fighting to contain her sickness and hysteria she leaned back against the wall of the building, her palms stiffly covering her mouth.

'Are you all right, Missus?' she heard the voice of the boy at her elbow. It took her a minute or two before she could even nod a reply. Then hastily she fumbled in her purse, found a pound note and pushed it towards the boy.

'Take this. Buy yourself something warm to wear.'

Then, without waiting to hear his thanks she stumbled away. When she found herself back in Cumberland Street the lamplighter was coming along with his long pole, stabbing the lamp posts into puffs of yellow.

She felt suffocated, depressed by the smells, the sounds, the gathering darkness, the black jungle of tenements. Horror was at her heels, pressing all around her. She began to run and didn't stop until she reached her car and shut herself inside it. It took a few minutes before she could gather her breath back and calm herself enough to be able to drive away. She made straight for the factor's office and marched into Mr Fintry's private room without stopping to knock.

One of the clerks rushed after her and into the room crying out, 'She just went right through before I had time to stop her, Mr Fintry.'

'How dare you . . .' Mr Fintry began, and then when Christina lifted her veil he hastily rose and in some agitation came round to the front of his desk to greet her.

'Mrs Monkton. I didn't realize it was you. Is there something wrong?'

'Have you any brandy?' Christina asked, lowering herself shakily onto the nearest chair.

'Brandy?' Mr Fintry echoed in astonishment. 'Well, em . . .' He gazed helplessly at the clerk who was still hovering in the background.

'I think we've a little in the first-aid cabinet, Sir,' the clerk said. 'Shall I fetch it?'

'Yes, and quickly.' Then turning to Christina, 'Are you ill, Mrs Monkton?'

'You could say I feel sick,' Christina said, closing her eyes and putting a stop to any further conversation until the clerk came hurrying back with the brandy.

'Thank you.'

She accepted the glass tumbler from him and gulped its contents. Afterwards she took a deep, shuddering breath.

Mr Fintry said, 'Mrs Monkton, are you all right? Is there anything else I can do for you?'

'Yes.' Christina managed. 'You can answer a few questions.'

'Certainly, Mrs Monkton. Certainly.' He fussed over to his desk and sat down behind it. 'I'll be only too happy to oblige.'

'Did you know,' she said, 'that there's a family living down a dunny in a room that has no windows in it? I think it must be a single end.'

'Oh yes,' Fintry said. 'There's more than one. Was there any particular one you were thinking about, Mrs Monkton?'

'More than one?' she echoed. 'How many?'

'I believe we have five on our books. And yes, you're right. They're all single ends.'

'And you collect the rents? You knew about this?'

'Is there something wrong, Mrs Monkton? I know some of these people have been very difficult tenants and have got into arrears from time to time, but I've always done my best to see that they pay up.'

Christina closed her eyes for a moment or two while she said, 'Mr Fintry, no human being should be expected to live without light and air. It is unthinkable.'

Opening her eyes she stared steadily across at the man behind the desk.

'I want these people out of there immediately. Immediately, do you hear?'

'Evicted, you mean? Well that might take a few days to . . .'

'No I do not mean evicted. We've always got a few empty properties on our books, haven't we?'

'Well yes, but . . .'

'No buts about it, Mr Fintry. I want these people moved from where they are into one of our empty properties. I want every one of these windowless rooms shut up, and never to be used again for human habitation. See if you can rent them out for storage purposes.'

'But, Mrs Monkton, a couple of our empty properties are

rooms and kitchens. One of them is a two room and kitchen, I believe.'

'I don't care,' Christina said. 'Get them out of there. If you've to put them into a bigger flat charge them for a single end until you get them organized and another single end becomes vacant. But just get them out of there. And when I say immediately I mean right now.'

Mr Fintry looked absolutely flabbergasted.

'But Mrs Monkton!'

'Right now,' she repeated, rising. 'Give them the keys. Tell them they've to be out of there by tomorrow lunch time at the latest.'

'Well I . . .' He rose too.

'And in future,' Christina said, 'I want detailed information about the type of accommodation we're letting to each and every tenant.'

She had never been so glad to reach home and the safety, the comfort, the warmth of Monkton House. The first thing she did was rid herself of the black coat, hat and shoes. Then she stripped off every garment she was wearing before donning her dressing gown and hurrying along to the bathroom for a hot bath.

In the bath she scrubbed herself meticulously from head to toe, even washed her hair so that every vestige of the foul-smelling dunny in the Gorbals would be banished from her. Afterwards she applied a little fresh make-up and donned a fashionable beige-coloured dress that fastened high on one shoulder. By the time Adam arrived home she was looking her most coolly elegant, completely self-possessed.

Their evening meal, however, was unusually silent. Normally to some degree or other they exchanged news and views about the day's business. Monkton did not ask her if there was anything wrong although occasionally she caught him staring thoughtfully over at her. She waited until they were in the drawing room and he had lit a cigar before she spoke.

'Do you remember I told you I had bought two or three farms?'

"Yes. I wondered why at the time, but I guessed you'd some scheme afoot.'

'I was wondering if I could do something about one of the farmhouses.'

'What do you mean, do something?'

She hesitated, then shrugged.

'I thought I could perhaps have it converted into a kind of holiday house for some of the Gorbals children. I was thinking, probably a lot of them have never even seen the countryside or known what real fresh air is like.'

There was silence for a long minute.

'Are you serious?' Monkton said eventually.

'I've never been more serious about anything before in my life. Would you go out with me and have a look at the farmhouses and advise how best to tackle this project and give me an estimate on the work needed?'

There was another minute's silence.

'I don't want to put a damper on what sounds like a worthwhile project, but have you thought about how you're going to fund this?'

She nodded. 'I'll try registering it as a charity. I could also put out a few feelers for voluntary subscriptions. I have a lot of contacts. We both have. Can I depend on your full cooperation in this?'

'We'll go out and look at the properties tomorrow.'

'The other members of the board are not going to like it,' she said.

'I'm aware of that. I hope you know that Scott Mathieson isn't going to like it either. Or your bank manager.'

'I'll deal with them.'

'All right,' he said. 'I'll deal with the other members of the board. I never imagined this was what you had in mind when you bought those farm properties. I must admit there are times when I admire your nerve, and this is one of them. You seem to thrive on taking risks and yet, to look at you . . . ' Shaking his head he gave half a laugh. 'And knowing your background . . . '

'It could be I was always waiting for the chance to react against the dull, safe background of the manse.'

'I'm afraid it's neither dull nor safe now,' he said.

She nodded, tight-lipped. She was thinking that even the horrors of her brother's condition would not compare with those of the boy she had seen earlier in the day. His life, his health, his future did not bear thinking about. By the looks of him he would never reach Simon's age. At least, up to the point of his illness Simon had had a happy life. He had been loved and cared for in a home with adequate material comforts. The compassion she felt for her brother did not diminish. It was only that on this day her feeling for a stranger was even more harrowing and intense.

'Give this job priority,' she said suddenly. 'Arrange for the planners to go with us tomorrow, get everything organized as soon as possible and the minute I get the go-ahead I want the work started. I want every needy child in the Gorbals to get out of there and onto that farm without a minute being wasted.'

Monkton was staring curiously at her.

'All right, all right,' he said soothingly. 'You have my word on it. It's as good as done.'

She lit a cigarette and stared across at him through a grey haze of smoke. She was still badly shaken by the days events, and behind her cool facade her emotions were in turmoil, her nerve ends exposed.

He looked so strong, so aggressively in charge of himself. She longed to tune into that strength, to be possessed by it, to be overwhelmed by it. Never before had she felt such an aching need for him in both body and soul. Her need mixed with desire and the desire became a physical agony. For a moment, drawing deeply on her cigarette, she closed her eyes.

'Adam' she said.

He raised a brow.

'What?'

She wanted to tell him about the desire throbbing and expanding inside her. Staring across at him she met the full impact of his dark eyes. She blew out a steady stream of cigarette smoke. She heard her cool voice, she felt herself shrug.

'Nothing. It doesn't matter.'

Chapter Sixty-four

Christina felt on edge. Annalie Gordon was watching her. Twice she'd seen her out of the corner of her eye – once when Christina was coming from the office. Her car had gone into the garage for servicing and Adam was giving her a lift home. They were walking from the yard round onto Pollokshaws Road when she'd noticed the girl in one of the closes. She had immediately slipped her arm through Adam's and smiled up at him. There had been a flicker of surprise in his eyes. He knew she was not a touching kind of person. She liked her own space, but he returned her smile and they walked towards the car. He opened the door for her and assisted her inside.

The other occasion was when they went with Nanny, the nursery maid and the children for a walk in the park. She had taken Adam's arm then too, and did not mention that she'd seen Annalie Gordon watching them. She decided it was more prudent to keep silent and try to work out what the girl was up to.

She was having problems too in getting new staff, and had not yet been able to engage a suitable housekeeper. This meant that she had to start work later every morning. First she had to see Cook and arrange the food for the day's menu for the children and themselves and discuss other household matters. She also had a daily word with Nanny to make sure that all was running smoothly in the nursery. At least she was relieved that Etta, the nursery maid, seemed to be settling in happily. She seemed a warm, affectionate girl and no doubt would balance up Nanny's stiff efficient manner.

'Household problems,' she told Mathieson. 'I've been trying without success to find a housekeeper. I must admit Nanny has been a rock but I can't expect her to keep supervising the staff and general household matters. She's got enough to cope with in the nursery.'

'This damned war,' Mathieson said. 'When will it ever end? How is your brother, by the way?'

'I believe there's been a slight improvement. He seems a bit calmer, but then one can never be sure what might trigger him off again. Adam's very good with him.'

'Monkton's doing well too. Another job down south, I hear.'

'Yes. He left earlier today. He'll be staying down there until Friday.'

Annalie Gordon was waiting by the front door when she arrived home that evening. Christina was startled at first because it was dark and the girl had been standing in the shadows. Quickly recovering her composure she said, 'What are you doing here? What do you want?'

'I need to talk to you,' the girl said.

Christina hesitated, but only for a moment, before saying, 'Very well.'

Once inside, she led her into the morning room, her private sanctum. It was here she felt most at ease. She indicated a seat.

'Thank you,' Annalie Gordon said politely and perched on the edge of a chair by the fire.

She was wearing a cheap-looking coat and a straw boater with ribbons hanging down the back. A ridiculous outfit for a winter's evening. Christina could see by the morning-room window that it had begun to snow. White flakes were swirling wildly about in a mad dance against the blackness, but there was luxurious warmth and comfort inside. The gas lamp bathed the room in amber light and the fire burning brightly helped to chase away the shadows.

The room was elegantly furnished in quiet good taste. The curtains, not yet drawn, were in soft blue velvet. The carpet was of the same shade and the sofa and easy chairs were covered with a delicate floral chintz picking out the same subdued shade of blue. There was a white bust of Mozart, but no other ornamentation. The room had a calm, uncluttered look.

Christina said, 'You wanted to talk to me.'

The girl took a deep breath.

'Firstly I wanted to make sure of something. Would you, for any reason, be willing to give Adam up?'

'No, never,' Christina said without hesitation. 'Nothing in the world would persuade me to do that.'

'That's what I thought you'd say.'

Christina raised an eyebrow. 'Well?'

Annalie took another deep breath.

'We can't go on like this,' she said. 'I've thought it all out. What would be for the best – the best for Elizabeth. I've been hearing some good things that you've been doing recently. Things you're doing for children.'

'Elizabeth?' Christina echoed.

'My baby. Adam's daughter. I don't want her brought up in the Gorbals. I don't think Adam wants that to happen either.'

'I see,' Christina said, and indeed she did. She'd had much practice in sizing up situations to her potential advantage with much more astute and sophisticated adversaries than Annalie Gordon. The girl wanted her to rescue her baby from its present environment. There were two options, as Christina saw it. One, she arranged for both mother and child to go to the farm. Or two, she could give the child a more permanent chance by offering her a home at Monkton House. Her natural instincts shrank form the latter course. What would people think? It would throw light on a scandal best kept in the dark, would put her in a humiliating situation. Yet the advantage of keeping Adam that this option offered was indisputable. Christina lit a cigarette and inhaled deeply before breaking the silence.

'You want to do a deal with me?' Christina said.

'I suppose you could put it that way.'

The girl's voice was uncertain and unhappy.

'All right. Here's a deal for you to consider. If you gave me your solemn word that you would never have anything more to do with my husband. I would give you my solemn word that I would bring up Elizabeth as if she were my own child. She would have every possible advantage in life.'

The girl looked so obviously distressed that Christina suddenly felt sorry for her. She was only a servant girl after all. She couldn't have been expected to resist Adam's amorous advances and she obviously loved the child.

'You do believe me?' Christina said.

Annalie nodded.

'Is that what you want then?' Christina asked. 'Is it a deal?'

'Do you promise to be good to her?'

'I've told you,' Christina said. 'I've given you my word. She will be one of the family, treated exactly the same as my other children. And she will have Adam, don't forget.'

The girl was obviously struggling against tears.

'She calls him Dada.'

Christina stiffened away from any sign of sentimentality.

'Have we a deal? she repeated.

There was silence for a long minute in which every drop of colour drained from the younger woman's face.

Eventually she said, 'Yes, on condition that you explain to Adam that I'm not doing this because my feelings have changed for him in any way. On the contrary. Tell him I'll always feel the same for him. It's just I couldn't go on the way we were, but at the same time I couldn't make Elizabeth suffer for anything I could or couldn't do. I've always wanted her to have a good life.'

'And she will,' Christina said.

'And you promise you'll explain to Adam?'

'Of course,' Christina said.

Annalie nodded. 'I'll bring Elizabeth to you tomorrow.'

'No,' Christina said right away. 'Go and fetch her now.'

She had always known a good deal when she saw one and had never allowed it to slip through her fingers.

'Now?' Annalie's voice trembled. Her eyes widened.

'It will be better for you if you get it over quickly.'

'I suppose you're right,' Annalie said. 'And she'll be asleep by now and not know anything about it.'

Her eyes acquired a stricken look. 'But when she wakes up and finds herself in a strange place she'll be frightened.'

'I'll see that she's comforted. Don't worry, and the other

children will be there as a distraction and there are lots of beautiful toys. She'll settle in in no time, I'm sure.' She picked up the phone. 'I'll get you a taxi.'

As soon as the girl left, Christina went upstairs to the nursery to speak to Nanny. Despite her cool exterior she felt deeply shaken. The girl's distress had been so acute it had affected her more than she'd realized at first. The fact that she'd just taken on the responsibility of another woman's child also became an urgent reality.

'There will be another child arriving tonight,' she told Nanny. 'A little girl called Elizabeth. From tonight onwards she is one of the family and I want her to be treated as such. There has to be no difference between her and my other children. You understand?'

'Don't worry, Madam,' Nanny said coolly. 'I'll see that she's properly cared for.'

'I'm sure you will. Now send Etta to me. I want a word with her as well.'

To the nursery maid she said. 'There's a little girl called Elizabeth coming to stay with us this evening. She'll be asleep when she arrives. When she wakes up she'll feel frightened and not know where she is. I'm depending on you to comfort her, Etta. Will you give me your word on that?'

'Oh yes, Ma'am,' Etta said. 'I'll cuddle her all night if needs be.'

'Thank you, Etta. I'll ring the bell later when she arrives. I want you to come down and collect her.'

'I'll be ready and waiting, Ma'am.'

'Thank you. That will be all just now.'

Christina returned downstairs to watch discreetly from the drawing room window. As soon as she saw the taxi come up the drive she rang the bell for the nursery maid, then went out to the hall and opened the front door.

Annalie Gordon looked so wretched and uncertain as she entered with the baby that Christina knew she was right in thinking that speed was of the essence. Etta, plump, rosy-cheeked and kindly-looking, was now in the hall beside them.

Christina said, 'Etta, this is Elizabeth. Take her up to the nursery, please, and remember, be good to her.'

'Yes, Ma'am. Indeed I will, Ma'am.'

Etta put out her arms for the sleeping child.

Panic widened Annalie's eyes.

'It's better this way,' Christina said firmly. 'I'm keeping my side of the bargain. I expect you to keep yours.'

As if in a daze Annalie allowed Etta to take Elizabeth away. Instinctively, Christina knew that something was needed to clinch the deal, to make sure that the girl would not suddenly change her mind and, with one of the inspired guesses she often found so useful in dealing with business adversaries she said, 'Elizabeth will be a lady.'

The words seemed to give the girl immediate strength. Her lips firmed, her chin raised, her shoulders straightened.

'Good,' she said.

Christina leaned against the door for a moment or two after Annalie had gone. Despite her deep layer of distress and sympathy for the girl she felt the same thrill, the same excitement, the same suspense, the same triumph that she had felt so often in the past when she was dealing in property within the building business. But there was still another challenge, another manoeuvre to make before this triumph could be complete. She had still to deal with Adam. He could ruin everything if she weren't very careful. Every loose end must be safely tied up.

She was waiting for him the next day in the drawing room when he returned and wasted no time in opening the subject.

'Annalie Gordon was here,' she said.

'What!' He looked up in surprise from lighting a cigar. 'Why?'

'I felt sorry for the girl.'

'What happened? Why did she come here?'

'She brought me her baby.'

'Elizabeth? She's here?'

'Yes.'

'Why?' Adam said. 'I don't understand.'

'Oh?' Christina raised her brow. 'I thought you would.

She thought you would. She's young, she said. She still had a chance to meet somebody else, get married, have a family, have a husband beside her all the time. She said if you loved her you would give her that chance.' Christina lit up a cigarette. 'I think she's got her eye on someone else already, if you ask me. Anyway, she said you'd want Elizabeth and in exchange for her freedom and new chance in life she was giving up all rights to the child. It would be easier, she said, and I agreed with her, if she never saw either you or Elizabeth again.'

She had never seen Adam so shaken. There was no hiding the pain in his eyes. He said nothing and she blew a leisurely stream of cigarette smoke into the still air.

Eventually she said, 'I gave my word that the child would be treated as one of the family and I've already spoken to Nanny and Etta to that effect – Elizabeth has to be treated in exactly the same way as our other children. 'I take it,' she said coolly, 'that it meets with your approval?'

He still did not speak. They remained sitting in silence, one on each side of the fire. Eventually, he heaved himself from his chair.

'I'd better go up to the nursery and see her,' he said.

'Yes,' Christina agreed. 'She'd like that.'

After he left the room, she too rose. She stood gazing at her reflection in the mirror above the mantelshelf. She looked pale and discreetly elegant, quietly self-contained. There was not a sign of her secret jubilation, her soaring triumph, her secret tears of thankfulness and relief.

Oh, congratulations, she was saying to herself. 'You'll never make a better deal than this. Never if you work for a hundred years in the property and building business. This is your deal of deals. Oh, congratulations, Christina Monkton. You've won the master builder!

Also by Margaret Thomson Davis in Arrow

RAG WOMAN, RICH WOMAN

The 1920s – and in Glasgow slums a girl is growing up with a passionate desire to better herself ...

Rory McElpy lives with her wastrel father, rag-woman mother and ten brothers and sisters in a Glasgow slum. It is the 1920s and the depression is taking its bitter toll. Rory is determined to better herself – and her fierce desire to be as genteel as her friend Victoria receives a boost when she meets intense, politically minded Matthew Drummond at a dance ...

But Matthew's ambition exceed Rory's – and she is left behind with nothing except her punctured dreams. A survivor, Rory conceives her own idea for a business and pursues it with a ruthless, single-minded drive ...

'*Stirring sagas of family life, generously spiced with sex, tragedy, humour ... and excitement*' – Evening Times

DAUGHTERS AND MOTHERS

'*The stylish work of a born storyteller*' – Glasgow Evening Times

Glasgow in 1945 is a gaunt, war-weary city of queues and coupons – yet it offers a new world of opportunity to the indomitable Rory Donovan. By turning her abundant energy and shrewd business skills to the flourishing black market, Rory can give her twins all the social advantages she so envied in her childhood friend Victoria. But Helena and Douglas soon pose the sort of problems money can't solve.

For Victoria, the war's end heralds her husband Matthew's move to London as an MP, while her daughter Amelia's self-destructive search for love has produced a child conceived at a drunken VJ Day celebration.

Then the past catches up with Rory and Victoria and shakes them to the core. The tragedy proves to be a turning point with far-reaching consequences for those they love and cherish . . .

Daughters and Mothers continues the sparkling saga of ambition and conflict that began in *Rag Woman, Rich Woman*.

'*Marvellously rich and evocative novel of life in post-war Scotland*' – Western Mail, Cardiff

'*The flesh-and-blood characters in this page-turner seem as real as the folk in your own family*' – Sunday Post

WOUNDS OF WAR

Glasgow in the sixties – where the legacy of war still lingers . . .

The war changed Joe Thornton so violently that Jenny is now afraid of her husband . . . Widowed by it, vain, silly, Hazel is adrift in the world, her props alcohol and her strong-minded daughter, Rowan . . . And Amelia's private war with her mother-in-law is still going on . . .

Their children have their own battles to fight: the civil rights movement for Rowan; Ban the Bomb for Harry Donovan and the Thorntons. And for all of them, there is the family battlefield.

But with the help of charismatic Rebecca, the three women find their painful way through friendship and new loves to their own kind of peace.

More bestselling fiction available in Arrow

KING HEREAFTER

Dorothy Dunnett

From the creator of the Lymond series and a superb story-teller, with a fanatical worldwide readership, comes this enthralling novel about Macbeth of Scotland.

It is the eleventh century, and Europe is full of young kings – some dreaming of a new civilisation, some content to live as their forefathers have done, and all ceaselessly fighting, befriending or betraying each other.

Such is the world of the real Macbeth, part Christian, part Viking, who has the imagination and determination to move himself and his people out of a barbarian past and into flowering nationhood. In this brilliant re-creation of his life we see him as a man of extraordinary courage, wit and skill . . . utterly self-reliant yet profoundly in love with the woman he marries . . . a pirate of the sea yet a prince with the foresight and passion to set him apart from other men.

'The novel that Mrs Dunnett's readers have been hoping for . . . a brilliant pageant' – The Times

'An extraordinary feat of creative imagination' – Scotsman

THE HILLS IS LONELY

Lillian Beckwith

'*A bouquet for Miss Beckwith*' – ERIC LINKLATER

When Lillian Beckwith advertised for a quiet secluded place in the country, she received the following unorthodox description of the attractions of life in an isolated Hebridean croft:

Surely it's that quiet here even the sheeps themselves on the hills is lonely and as to the sea its that near I use it myself every day for the refusals . . .

Intrigued by her would-be landlady's letter and spurred on by the scepticism of her friends, Lillian Beckwith replied in the affirmative.

The Hills Is Lonely is the hilarious and enchanting story of the extremely unusual rest cure that followed.